FLESH
WOUNDS

Also by Christopher Brookmyre

CHRIS BROOKMYRE

FLESH WOUNDS

Little, Brown

LITTLE, BROWN

First published in Great Britain in 2013 by Little, Brown

A CIP catalogue record for this book is
available from the British Library.

ISBN HB 978-1-4087-0408-0
ISBN CF 978-1-4087-0409-7

Typeset in Caslon by Palimpsest Book Production Limited, Falkirk, Stirlingshire
Printed and bound in Great Britain by Clays Ltd, St Ives plc

Papers used by Little, Brown are from well-managed forests
and other responsible sources.

MIX
Paper from
responsible sources
FSC
www.fsc.org   FSC® C104740

Little, Brown
An imprint of
Little, Brown Book Group
100 Victoria Embankment
London EC4Y 0DY

An Hachette UK Company
www.hachette.co.uk

www.littlebrown.co.uk

For Grace and Jack

Mortal Thoughts

'I'd best be getting a shift on,' Stevie announced, for perhaps the third time. 'There's none of us getting any younger.'

He glanced at the clock behind the gantry. The first time he'd said it had been around half ten. Now it was just after eleven, and he was half an hour older but no nearer the door. He'd have to watch that: he could be sitting here all day if he didn't get his arse in gear.

Sheila wouldn't allow that, though. She was opening for business in an hour. It was just that the seat felt that bit more comfy on this particular morning, the craic that bit more engaging. When he got to his feet the spell would be broken and he'd be impatient to get on with his day, but for now it was tempting to stay in the moment just a wee bit longer.

It looked like a lock-in, and it wasn't even noon. Nobody was drinking anything stronger than espresso, and they did this five or six days a week. It started off all business, Stevie's way of making sure he was up to speed on everybody's operations, but once the important stuff was out the way it could degenerate into blethers, everybody too comfy to get up, too full of breakfast to want to leave their seats. Some days the patter was better in the morning over teas and coffees than on late nights when everybody was half pished. At such times he was inclined to tarry, just sit in his favourite seat and take in what was around him rather than holding court; or maybe that truly *was* him holding court: everything playing out for his benefit and no pressing need to remind everybody who was in charge.

He had turned forty-nine that day. He didn't doubt Sheila had something planned for later, but this morning nobody had brought it up, and that suited him fine. Folk talked about taking stock on birthdays, but Stevie had seldom done so. In his experience, there were other watershed events in life that more naturally precipitated moments of reflection, though truth be told he was usually too busy living it to stop for photos. It was a sign of getting older that he occasionally found himself wishing he had taken a step back here and there in order to appreciate what he had. You always heard the older football players saying that: the young guys in the team don't appreciate what it is to be playing in a cup final, because they think it's always going to be cup finals.

He was sitting at his usual seat, his usual booth, up at the back wall of the Old Croft Brasserie, as it was known these days. It wasn't his name on the licence, and since POCA he had made damn sure there was no documentation identifying it as his property, but it was *his* place, and had been indisputably his place in many other ways long before he'd had the money to own it.

It was all about the food now. Even the cocktail bar where the snug used to be had fallen victim to the last re-fit, as it let them seat up to a dozen more covers. It was simple economics: they did okay with the scran, but the mark-up on the wine list made it look like the cocktail bar had been giving drink away. However, as Stevie surveyed the Old Croft from his favoured perspective, he could picture everything as it was when the place was still the Bleachers Vaults, and the only wines behind the gantry were Buckfast, El-D and Lanliq. In his mind he could still see the yellow walls, stained by decades of nicotine, the faded photos and press clippings in their cheap frames, the narrow range of generic spirits upside down above their optics, the peeling Formica and chipped wood panelling that coated the bar, and the frosted lavvy-window glass that let in the only natural light during the day but principally served to let passers-by know they should keep on passing by, whether they fancied a drink or not.

No matter how many changes it went through, there was nonetheless a permanence about being in this place, a way in which it could put him back in touch with how he'd felt at different stages in his life. He could still see the wee shaver he once was, fronting up at sixteen and hoping to get served; still see the cracked plaster on the ceiling as he lay bleeding on the lino, waiting for an ambulance the first time he got stabbed; still see the faces at the bar of boys long since dead: including some by his own hand or, more latterly, by his word. Times like this, he found himself missing even some of those guys, or at least missing the guys they once were, before they made themselves his enemies.

Stevie was one of Scotland's top gangsters. Had to be true: he'd read it in the *Daily Record*. Like there was a league table or something, or a chart. Up two places this week, it's Steeeeevie Fullerton! As for 'gangster', what kind of patter was that? The only folk who still used the term in this country were the sweetie wives in the press and wee daft boys kidding on they were darkies. Nobody who could reasonably be considered fitting of the term would dream of applying it to themselves.

Stevie knew a lot of criminals but precisely no gangsters. There were boys you worked with, boys you did business with and, very rarely, boys you trusted, but none of them had been in a gang since they were about fifteen: daft wee shavers out looking for mayhem, easy scores and, if they were really ambitious, their hole. Maybe the papers should name 'Scotland's top daft wee shaver', perhaps as part of a 'ones to watch' list of future gangster contenders.

He looked at the raggle-taggle assembly before him in the Old Croft Brasserie: Doke, Gerry, Haffa and himself. Stevie thought of the strange loyalties and improbable allegiances that had brought them all under one roof. To call this a gang would be to ignore greater levels of complexity than they had to cope with on an average shift at the UN.

Sheila gave his cheek a rub as she walked past, picking up his empty cup and saucer. It was part gesture of affection and part reminder that he hadn't shaved yet. He was planning to wait until he came back from the gym so he'd be smooth this afternoon and into the evening. It was growing back so fast lately that his five o'clock shadow tended to turn up at lunchtime. Used to be he liked having the old designer stubble; used to suit him, make him look just the distinguished side of rugged. These days, although he could dye the grey out of his hair he couldn't hide the salt-and-pepper when it came through on his jaw, which meant that if he missed a couple of shaves he just looked like a jakey. So did wearing the sports gear he used to favour. He kept himself in good shape, was never out the gym and arguably as fit now as when he'd been in his twenties, but the gear didn't work on him any more. Past forty, the only folk you saw wearing tracky bottoms outside the gym were bin-rakers and big fat heifers. As a result, it was suits all the way for him now. Bespoke ones, naturally, always the best, but though they made him look smart they couldn't make him look younger.

Why did it bother him so much, he wondered? It didn't seem to trouble Sheila that he was looking older, although maybe she just loved him too much to say. He knew for sure it didn't bother him that Sheila was getting older. Though he could see the changes in her from when they first got together, it always felt like the latest version was an improvement. He'd always liked the fact that she looked older than him: it was one of the things that attracted him in the first place. She had seemed like a woman who had seen plenty of the world and knew what she wanted as a result. That was why he must have been one of the few men of his means ever to leave a wife near-on a decade his junior for one three years older than him.

He gazed at her, heading for the kitchen to discuss tonight's menu with Angus, the chef. The place belonged to Stevie, and it was Angus's talents that had all the trendy types venturing out to the wilds of Croftbank, but Sheila ran the show, like she always had.

She was working behind the bar here when they first met, another reason this old place felt like a portal to the many ages of his life. His eye drifted to the store room next to the toilets, just past where the swing doors now granted access to the kitchen. That was where they used to sneak off to on her breaks, sometimes with her first husband Donny working through in the snug. He could picture it, feel it, smell the mixture of perfume, cigarettes and drink. Her on her knees, giving him a gobble like nobody ever had before. Christ, he was getting hard thinking about it. He could fair go shagging her right now, in the store, up against the shelves like old times.

Better than old times. He fancied her more now than he ever had. The years were not diminishing Sheila, they were improving her; improving him too in so many ways, in the life he led, the things that were within his grasp, the freedoms that were now open to him. And yet, and yet . . .

Look at this place. Haffa was in raconteur mode, recalling the time a team of Gallowhaugh boys had organised an ambush inside Stevie's first nightclub, Nokturn, and they turned the place into something out of a John Wayne movie, utterly wrecking the joint. 'Wild West George Street,' Haffa described it, eliciting a laugh all round as it did every time he used the phrase, which he did every bloody time he told the story.

The downside of that anecdote, always unspoken, was that it was also the night Jazz got slashed, which set in motion the chain of events leading to his death.

Before that, they'd been sharing bittersweet reminiscences about Glen Fallan, the old stories given a sharper edge these past couple of years since it emerged that big Single wasn't quite as unthreateningly dead as everybody had previously believed.

Stevie thought Gerry was havering when he said it had been more than twenty years ago, but when he did the sums it was right enough. No' real. It still felt like something that had happened recently: since the millennium, at least. Some folk cast a long shadow, and the period after they had departed always seemed shorter than the time you knew them, even if you had only known them for a fraction of the years they'd been gone. Glen Fallan: aye, there was a face Stevie missed, in spite of everything, though not from hanging round the Vaults. Not his style. Ever the lone gunman; often literally.

Stevie's cousin Doke then told the story about the Egan brothers going on the lam because they knew the polis were after them, and hiding out at their mammy's house two doors down. Aye, polis were never going to think of that. Fucking geniuses.

Doke was standing there in a two-grand suit, keys to an Aston Martin in one pocket, keys to a house in Thornton Bridge in the other, but like Gerry, like Haffa, like Stevie himself, it seemed all he wanted to talk about was old days, old faces, old streets.

Stevie had a Bentley Continental GT outside. He loved that machine like it was part of him: loved the growl of its engine, the gleam of its lines; loved what it said about him. It boasted more than six hundred brake horsepower, did nought to sixty in four seconds and its low-slung suspension was so smooth it handled like one of those lightcycles from *Tron*. But driving it had never given him a fraction of the excitement he had experienced behind the wheel of a stolen Escort XR3i when he was sixteen, his brother Nico riding shotgun, their cousins Doke and Jazz in the back, Stevie throwing the car around like it was the dodgems.

That thought was what finally gave him the nudge to get moving. It was one thing to miss your youth, but nostalgia could seduce you into thinking that the best of you lay in the past. To wallow in it was the same as staying here in this seat instead of going out to meet the day.

Fuck. That.

He climbed to his feet, giving Doke a phone gesture and receiving a subtle nod in response. He would be expecting him to call around teatime, and not to wish him happy birthday.

Stevie squinted against the late-morning sun as he opened the outside door. It was a cool and crisp November morning. Perfect for driving. He loved to see the metal glimmer of the Bentley's flanks in the sunlight, the solidity of the alloys picked out in a sharp contrast to the black rubber of the tyres. This was nicer than summer: the windscreen would stay clear without a thousand beasties kamikaze-diving it between the car wash and the health club.

He put the Bentley into drive and glided out towards the main road.

Stevie was aware that the older he got, the more he was vulnerable to thinking he had peaked and plateaued; that it was too late in the game for anything much to change, least of all the way he played it. There was a seductive instinct to stick instead of twist, to protect what he already held, and implicit within that was an acceptance that this was as good as he could expect it to get, as high as he could reasonably aspire to climb.

It was the death of Flash Frankie Callahan that had most fuelled this insecurity. A powerful adversary suddenly taken out of the picture, a supply line cut off, a very big slice of the market up for grabs: it should have been the start of a new era. Instead, Stevie had been squeezed in the aftermath, losing market share and watching, helpless, as someone else took over Frankie's operations.

The part of him that was still young and hungry was able to read a lesson in it, though. That it was Tony McGill who had been the phoenix from Frankie's ashes should have been a lesson to everybody.

Tony had a criminal career going all the way back to the fifties, running rackets and smuggling operations before anybody in Glasgow had ever had their first jag of brown or their first sniff of cocaine. Tony had watched as the logistics, the economics, the very nature of the game altered. He was a T-Rex caught in the teeth of a snowstorm at the onset of the Ice Age, an apex predator rendered suddenly vulnerable by a changing world. Different breeds had evolved to overtake him: breeds such as Stevie, once upon a time, and inevitably the once-mighty T-Rex was felled.

Tony was past sixty when he got out of prison a few years back, and after serving as long as he did, he must have stepped through the gates into a world he barely recognised. Nonetheless, Tony hadn't considered himself too long in the tooth to get back in the game, or thought that his most prosperous years were behind him. He had still run a decent-sized show from inside, despite the limitations of that chubby wee fanny Tony Junior.

Stevie had often heard boys described as 'working for Tony McGill' when they had never come within fifty miles of where the man was securely locked up, and none of them meant that they were working for Teej, as his arsehole son was known.

They said beware the vengeance of a patient man. They also said the best revenge was living well. Tony could thus consider himself thoroughly avenged. After Flash Frankie went up in flames, it was Tony who took possession of a massive misplaced shipment of brown, before stepping in to replace Frankie and his crew as the Scottish outlet for a seriously major supply line. Not bad for a

7

guy who used to bask in the acclaim of being 'the man who kept the drugs out of Gallowhaugh'.

It was an astonishing turnaround in fortunes, only a few years after his release from jail. Stevie wasn't sure how becoming Glasgow's primary heroin conduit sat with his parole conditions, but didn't imagine Tony lost any sleep over it.

Tony had learned from past mistakes. He had adapted, proven an old dog could learn some new tricks. Nonetheless, when you analysed his success, you could see he was like one of those veteran football managers who replicated their success at each club by signing the same type of player and playing the same system. There were adaptations, sure, but at a fundamental level they always went with what they knew.

In Tony's case, the linchpins of his strategy were bent polis. They had made him bombproof once upon a time, and they had played their part in putting him back on the map in jig time once his stretch was done.

However, those veteran managers could eventually get found out. They became too reliant on the tried-and-tested formula, and their recipe for success became their weakness. Something that predictable would eventually expose a vulnerability if you watched and waited long enough, though only if you had the means to exploit it.

Stevie hadn't, until now.

He might have turned forty-nine today, but his birthday present had come early. Out of nowhere he'd been offered precisely what he needed to change the game in this city. And like all the best deals, the vendor didn't have a clue as to the true value of what he was selling.

Unlike the others, Stevie wasn't going to let his zest for the present become sapped by the soporific temptations of nostalgia. The future was opening up before him, and it was going to make his past look like a pre-match warm-up.

He drove the Bentley into the car wash, waved to a space between islands that once housed petrol pumps by a teenager in grey overalls and a Metallica T-shirt. He didn't know the kid's name but the kid knew his. He signalled to his mate and they jumped to it, leaving the woman in the Ford Focus at the next wash station wondering what was the script.

Funny he should be thinking about Tony as he drove to use this place: in a way it was the first sign, way back when, that Stevie was outgrowing him, and that the rules were changing in ways Tony couldn't grasp. The older man didn't understand why Stevie was putting money into running a car wash, even after he had explained that it wasn't just cars that were going in dirty and coming out clean.

There was some heavy metal rubbish playing from a pair of puny speakers perched on the water heater that fed the cleaning lances. Stevie cranked up the Bentley's stereo and let the sub-woofer take care of the noise pollution. Bit of Simple Minds: *Sparkle in the Rain.* That didn't count as nostalgia; just a basic matter of it being better than any of the shite that was out nowadays.

The kid in the Metallica T-shirt knelt down and began squirting some stuff on his alloys, while a biker-looking bloke in what most closely resembled fishing waders hefted the lance. He gave the car a once-over with some hot water to start with, then began coating it in foam.

The windscreen got it first, then the entire vehicle was insulated in a layer of white bubbles. As always, this part made Stevie feel a little uncomfortable, blind and isolated in what suddenly seemed a cramped wee capsule. There was only a thin film between him and the outside world, but he felt suddenly very detached. It was easy to imagine what it would be like to be inside a car buried in an avalanche. He recalled a dream he'd had, two or three times in fact, about being engulfed in a different kind of snow. It piled up around him, higher and higher until he couldn't escape. That was before he quit sampling his own merchandise.

This bit never lasted long, however. They'd start with the brushes any second, though they seemed to be taking their time this morning. He considered rolling down the window a little to ask what was keeping them, but thought better of it, as chances were a brush would come right along it at just that second.

Instead he relaxed, deciding to enjoy the isolation, alone with his thoughts and his music.

A hole suddenly appeared in both the foam and indeed the windscreen itself, a spiderweb of crazing extending like ripples from its centre. The bullet that shattered the glass carried on through Stevie's chest, bouncing off a rib and spinning end on end through his heart. It was liquidised midway through its final beat, but his brain had still enough oxygen for him to look through the dissolving suds and glimpse a tall figure levelling a silenced handgun and pulling its trigger three more times.

He had a skull for a face: death incarnate.

It was the last thing Stevie saw.

Waves

Jasmine slipped her phone back into her pocket and climbed out of the Civic. People had been streaming out of the car park as she drove in, making her worry whether she would find a space so close to the theatre, but there were plenty in sight once she crested the hill.

She had just read a text from her friend Monica, apologising that she wasn't going to make it. The message had arrived while Jasmine was driving along the M8 half an hour back, but she hadn't heard the alert over the sound of the Honda's stereo, nor felt a vibration as her leather jacket had been draped over the passenger seat. Monica's own car had broken down somewhere around Cramond, and with the AA bloke telling her the alternator was gone, it wasn't going to be a quick fix.

This meant Jasmine was going to be on her own, which made her stop for a moment and consider her options. She felt perfectly comfortable going to the cinema by herself, or even, at a push, seeing a play, but this was a gig. Nobody went to a gig alone, did they? This was daft, though. There was no explicit social convention that she was about to violate; just the threat of her own self-consciousness, which in this case would be a mixture of insecurity and delusion. Why should she be conspicuous? Nobody was going there to look at her.

Besides, she had paid for the tickets and been looking forward to it: posted as much on Twitter and Facebook like an excitable wee lassie and had luxuriated in the prospect of *being* an excitable wee lassie for a couple of hours. So despite the doubting voice that was whispering how sad she would look to be sitting there like Nelly No-Mates at a rock concert, she decided it was profoundly sadder still to even contemplate driving home again.

I'm not sad, she thought to herself. I'm okay.

She walked down the slope towards the Alhambra, the road in front of which was teeming with excited people. That was when she deduced that she shouldn't have been surprised to find a parking space, due to the demographic. Only a very small proportion of this crowd would have turned up in a car as they were predominantly too young to be in the position to own one, or even to learn to drive. The fact that it struck her as unusual to be surrounded by so many people her own age or younger – and a clear majority of them girls – warned her she was becoming too accustomed to spending her time around middle-aged men.

She needed to get out more, even if it was on her own.

The support act was already on stage when she made her way into the stalls. She guessed they were local, or had a lot of pals who had made the trip, as they were being cheered with conspicuous enthusiasm by a portion of the crowd close to the front. The band were lively and enthusiastic, loving their time on a stage that was itself probably bigger than any of the dives they had played before.

Jasmine glanced around the place, taking in the venue. She had never been inside the Dunfermline Alhambra, and had assumed it would be a nightclub. Instead it turned out to be a grand old 1920s theatre-cum-cinema, a doughty survivor of the great bingo-hall attrition.

Whilst taking in her surroundings, her professional abilities also noted that somebody nearby was taking an interest in *her*, and thus she was reminded of another reason why she had her reservations about going to a gig alone. There was a guy leaning against a pillar about ten feet away, and she clocked him staring at her on two separate passes. Suffice to say, she was the better skilled at keeping her scrutiny undetected.

He looked like he might more usually be occupied outside the venue at this point, breaking into vehicles in the car park, but even if he'd looked like Sam McTrusty, she wasn't interested tonight. Okay, maybe if he actually *was* Sam McTrusty, but this chancer looked more like Ned Untrusty. It provided the impetus to swap the standing-only stalls for a seat upstairs, and the chance to enjoy her favoured perspective of any proscenium-arch space.

Her ticket was for down below, she and Monica having been planning to get sweaty in the mosh-pit, but the bouncers weren't fussed. The circle wasn't full, and venues were always more wary of letting you into the standing area if you were supposed to be upstairs.

Jasmine loved just sitting inside these grand old auditoria. In her head she could hear Dot Prowis, her old lecturer at the Scottish Academy of Theatre and Dance, expounding with typical gusto on how 'any space can be a theatre, and a theatre can be any space', but Jasmine's idea of what a theatre should look like had been hardwired in toddlerhood, and this was it. It wasn't just the pros-arch (thrust optional) that defined a proper theatre, but the presence of at least one circle, and the more the better.

The Alhambra's stretched back from the balcony in row upon curving row of tip-up cushioned seats, saggy in the stuffing and infused with the fags and farts of close to a hundred years. Jasmine was in the fifth row, the steep rake affording almost as good a view over the rail as the first. She took in the painted plasterwork, the angels flanking the wings, and a part of her was transported to the place all such theatres took her: her mother's side.

It would have been her mum's birthday tomorrow. This was another reason she felt apprehensive about being out here alone, exposed, and yet also a reason she knew she ought not to go home either, stuck in the flat with nothing to distract her.

Someone had once told her that the pain and the sadness would come in waves. In the early stages, those waves would engulf her, crash against her so relentlessly that she might feel she could not possibly survive. However, as time went on the intervals would become longer, the waves a little smaller. Gradually it would get easier, but the waves would never stop coming.

This had proven true, but there were no guarantees, no absolutes. Now and again one of those waves would be higher than her head, though she was getting better at anticipating when. The anniversary, Christmas and birthdays – her mum's and her own – were always going to be difficult, but sometimes it was the unexpected trigger that was the worst: the element that came at her sideways when her gaze was fixed ahead. The lead-up to these painful dates had proven harder than the days themselves, but so far on this occasion she was holding it together; feeling quite robust, in fact.

I'm okay, she told herself.

A girl of about fourteen shuffled along the row in front, accompanied by a bearded bloke in a Big Country T-shirt, presumably her dad playing chaperone. Jasmine resisted a twinge of self-consciousness as she looked around, feeling conspicuously the only person sitting unaccompanied. For all anyone knew, her friend was away at the toilet, or getting drinks.

More pertinently, nobody would be looking at her anyway, she reminded herself. It was an unfortunate side-effect of spying on people for a living that she could occasionally fall prey to an irrational paranoia about what unseen eyes might be trained upon her. Shaking this off, for a wee change she asked herself what anyone might see if they did happen to look at her right then, and decided to her surprise that she liked the answer.

She recalled a line in *Shirley Valentine*, one of her mum's favourite movies, which they used to watch together when the weather got them down, because it was like going on a ninety-minute holiday.

'I think I'm all right,' Shirley said. 'I think if I saw myself, I'd say: "That woman's okay."'

I'm okay, Jasmine told herself.

She'd had a good day at work.

She'd had a lot of good days at work, in fact. Over the past year or so she had become a great deal more accepting that this was what she did now; this was who she was. It was changing her. She had stopped thinking of herself as tragic, afflicted by circumstance and buffeted by the fates. She was good at what she did, and consequently Sharp Investigations was doing quite well, thank you. Certainly any evening spent in the company of her college friends still trying to eke out careers in the arts these days afforded her a different perspective from the previous one of having her nose pressed against the sweet-shop window.

It wasn't just the fact that they were permanently skint; the things that seemed so shatteringly important to them were beginning to strike her as petty and insubstantial, and she was becoming decreasingly shy of saying as much. She recalled with mischievous pride an exchange she had over dinner at her friend Michelle's place, where Michelle's flatmate and fellow dancer Gareth was unloading at quite unnecessary length about a review of a show he'd performed in at the Fringe.

'You're exposed up there: you lay yourself completely bare, utterly vulnerable. So when you read something like this you feel violated. These people know what they're doing: they aim to wound you. They want to see you bleed.'

'Oh for fuck's sake,' Jasmine had said, perhaps one glass too many of vino bringing forth veritas. 'Man up, it's only a review.'

'Of course it's only a review *to you*,' Gareth retorted. 'You've never had one, so you wouldn't know. You'd need to have been up there on a stage to understand what I'm talking about.'

There had been a time when this might have crushed Jasmine, to have her former aspirations thrown back in her face. That time was over.

'Well, Gareth, you've got me there. But look at it from my point of view: once you've been shot at a couple of times, by somebody who is not aiming to wound, it kind of makes it hard to see what's so violating about some wee wank at the *Scotsman* only giving you two stars.'

She was developing – some might say cultivating – a reputation for being spiky and a little unsympathetic, and she had stopped worrying about whether this meant she was wounded and embittered. Instead she had decided to wear bitch and see how it fitted. It wasn't an everyday garment, but like the leather jacket she had on for the gig it felt just right now and again, when the context called for it.

She was okay. She was definitely okay.

Then she saw a ghost.

The support had finished and the seats began to fill up more while the road crew got busy dismantling their kit. People returned from the bar bearing pints in plastic tumblers, while others, arriving in time for the headliners, scanned the rows for a free spot, the seating being unreserved. Jasmine felt a growing buzz as the roadies made the final preparations: taping set-lists, draping towels, checking pedals.

She watched a guy and a girl make their way along the row two in front, apologising cheerfully to the people having to stand up to let them past. They were around her age, both wearing T-shirts bearing the band's name, though not identical garments. They didn't look up as they progressed, only at the people they were shifting and occasionally at the stage, so they didn't see Jasmine, meaning she had no way of knowing whether the guy recognised her, but she definitely knew him. Having realised he was familiar, it took her a few moments of mentally thumbing through images until she could find a background against which he fitted, but when she got there it froze her.

His name was Scott, or possibly Sam. She didn't quite remember that part, but she remembered that he had still been in fifth year at school, although looked older. She could remember which school (Glasgow Academy); she could remember the drainpipe jeans and Diesel-logo belt he'd been wearing; and she remembered how he kissed. It had been soft and slow, each kiss all there was and all he wanted: no wandering hands, no impatiently thrusting tongue.

The reason the context took a while to come up was because it was so close to her current one. She had danced and chatted and eventually snogged with him the last time she'd seen Twin Atlantic play.

It had been just before her mum got the diagnosis.

They'd traded numbers and he'd phoned, leaving messages. She never called back.

The lights went down and the Queen track playing on the PA was silenced, replaced by a sudden upsurge of excited screams. The band took the stage rather modestly, walking to their instruments with quiet purpose, almost as though conscious they hadn't earned these cheers yet.

An electric guitar picked out its first notes with delicate

precision, rousing more screams of recognition, then Sam McTrusty raised his head to the mike and began to sing.

'*Yes, I was drunk . . .*'

It was her favourite song, one that always moved her, and the one she had most been hoping they'd play. Right then, though, it was more than moving her. She felt it wash over her. Felt a wave wash over her. Felt herself go under.

There was something intangible about watching a band play live, some quality that could not be recreated on any format, so that the most perfect recording, reproduced on the most sophisticated equipment, would never be more than a shadow on the cave wall. Despite having listened to both albums hundreds of times, it was as though she hadn't truly heard Twin Atlantic since that other gig, and it connected her to that time in a way she just wasn't ready for.

The ghost was herself, the person she had been that night.

And as the music played, the ghost possessed her. Suddenly she could see through that girl's eyes again, see everything she had back then, everything she imagined was still before her.

Everything she was about to lose.

This wave was swamping her, rushing in over her head. She was drowning.

She couldn't be here. She had to get out.

Jasmine shuffled along the row, her petite frame allowing her to squeeze past without asking people to stand up. She kept her head down, face angled towards the stage so that no one could see it.

We never want strangers to see we are crying. Why is that? She didn't know. All she did know was that she was so very, very much alone.

Her mother was gone. She had no father, no boyfriend, and tonight, no friends at all.

She was not okay.

She managed to hide her tears until she reached the stairs, where she failed to stem the outpouring of huge, blubbing, abject, snottery and undignified sobs. She grabbed a banister for support, fearing she would collapse if she didn't have something to hang on to.

'You all right there wee yin?' said a voice.

17

She couldn't see properly for tears. It took a moment to focus once she had wiped her eyes.

It was Ned Untrusty. Christ, had he followed her up to the circle?

She wanted to tell him to go away, but she could hardly answer 'Yes, I'm fine.'

A dozen sarcastic replies failed to reach her tongue. She felt so weak and insubstantial that he could have mopped her up and wrung her out into a bucket.

She could hear other voices now, and became aware that house staff were gathering to enquire and assist.

'She just needs some air, I think,' said Ned. ''Mon outside for a second.'

He put a hand on her shoulder and she let him lead her because she knew that it would make the staff back off, and avoid turning this into a circus.

He had a Glasgow accent, which surprised her, as she had assumed he would be a local.

She felt humiliated by having to accept his help, but she couldn't say why. Was it because she'd caught him staring and subconsciously rejected him? Or would she have felt humiliated at this point, having to accept the assistance of any stranger? Her desire to settle for him over a clucking assembly of staff indicated the latter.

He held the door for her and escorted her out onto the pavement. The air did help. As soon as she stepped outside she felt an outrush of pressure, a dissipation of everything that had besieged her.

'Let me get you a wee drink,' he said.

'No, I'm okay.'

'Just some water,' he insisted. 'And maybe a hanky, eh?'

Close up she realised he was younger than she had assumed: maybe eighteen or nineteen. The age was right, but little else about him seemed to fit a Twin Atlantic concert. It was easier to picture him stopped at the lights in a souped-up Peugeot, moronic dance beats thumping through the rolled-down windows.

She didn't want to be fussed over, didn't want to be in any way indebted to this chancer, but at least it would get her a moment alone while he went. She sniffed and nodded.

He returned after a few minutes bearing a bottle of still water and some napkins.

'There you go.'

She accepted the water numbly with one hand and took the proffered napkins in the other.

As she mumbled her thanks she felt gratitude tinged with surprise at his solicitude. Disloyal as it felt to admit it, it was her mum's fault. She had always been wary of guys who looked like they might be fly men or hardcases, especially if they had Glasgow accents. Growing up in Edinburgh, Jasmine had come to imagine the city along the motorway as being like some lawless frontier outpost, an impression her mother did little to dispel by never, ever going there.

She dabbed at her face, grateful she had decided against mascara. The tears had stopped, the sense of being engulfed lifted, like she had come up for air.

She took a few gulps of water, feeling a light breeze on her face and a pulse of bass in her body as the music throbbed from inside the theatre.

'That better?' her unlikely Samaritan asked. 'You okay?'

He hadn't said anything, hadn't asked her what was wrong, for which she was grateful. He seemed a little distracted now though, perhaps impatient to get back to the show.

'I'll be fine now, thanks,' she told him, but he made no move to return inside.

'I think I'll go to the Ladies, give my face a splash,' she said.

It was somewhere he couldn't follow her, a good way of breaking the connection. She just hoped he wouldn't be hovering outside the loos, waiting for her when she came out. 'Thanks,' she added, by way of hinting that he was dismissed.

'Nae bother. Look after yourself,' he replied, remaining where he was.

'You not coming in?' she asked, trying to keep the relief from her voice.

'Gaunny spark up, seeing I'm out here anyway. You want one?'

She declined and went back inside.

After her visit to the loo she returned to the circle and took a seat near the end of a row, where she didn't need to disturb anyone to get past. Down and to her left she could see the guy she'd snogged, nodding to the beat. She didn't experience anything weird this time, from seeing him or the band. The spell was broken. She could just enjoy the music.

Sam McTrusty was singing how it was 'the end of our sweet universe' but she wasn't feeling anything cataclysmic any more. She'd been there and come out the other side. Besides, it was a song about getting stronger.

She was okay.

Dead Calm

'Bloody typical,' said Beano, braking sharp but smoothly. 'The sun comes out and everybody wants their car washed at the same time.'

Detective Superintendent Catherine McLeod looked up from her phone and took in the dual carriageway ahead. Both lanes were choked with cars, while on the other side of the central reservation the traffic was at a steady flow, albeit in far greater volume than would be normal for the time of day.

'Too congested to be rubber-neckers,' Beano added. 'They must have closed the lane nearest the entrance.'

'More likely both lanes,' Catherine suggested to the young Detective Constable. 'They'll be diverting everybody back before they reach the car wash.'

'Got you. Hence how busy it is on the other side. This must be the queue to do a U-turn. Will I blue-light us through?'

'I'm sure he'll still be dead when we get there,' Catherine replied, yawning and stretching in the passenger seat. 'But yeah. Quicker we get there, the less time uniform have to trample all over our crime scene.'

Beano switched on the blue light and gave the siren a blast that was brief to the point of polite. In front of them, cars began to edge left and right, slowly clearing a narrow channel between them.

Catherine went back to her phone, thumbing through emails and mentally triaging them. There was nothing urgent, but maybe that was just her current perspective: nothing felt very urgent today. That was the upside of fielding a case like this; she knew she could comfortably forget about all the tuppence-ha'penny stuff for a while. This would be priority number one for everybody, including the brass, until they were all satisfied that it was the end of something rather than the beginning.

'You're exuding a Zen calm this morning, boss,' Beano observed.
'Am I?'

'Sure. Something like this comes in, I'd half expect you to be
ordering me to drive along the pavement right now, lights and
sirens, with pedestrians diving left and right like it's *Carmageddon*.'

Catherine didn't reply as this wasn't really a conversation. Beano
was talking too much, and she knew why. He was nervous about
where they were going, because he knew the body would still be
there.

Beano didn't like murder scenes. Once the body was bagged, no
probs: it just became his place of work, and young DC Thompson
loved to work. But today, he was aware that the victim had not
been moved, and despite the blue light and his remarks about
driving along the pavement, Catherine knew he was in no hurry
to reach that car wash.

He hated seeing corpses; in fact, you could extend that to say
that he didn't like seeing the aftermath of violence full stop. Nobody did; or at least Catherine hoped not *many* did, but it was an
unavoidable reality of the job. Some people hid their revulsion
behind bravado, immersing themselves in gallows humour because
turning it into a joke gave them an emotional distance. Others
simply became desensitised over time, though even the most hard-
bitten could be blindsided now and again. Nobody's defences were
impermeable, and none of them could predict what might cause
the human truth of it to leak through.

Beano didn't seem to have any such mechanisms for self-deception,
or any great talent for masking his feelings. He was visibly horri-
fied whenever he was forced to clap eyes on a murder victim, and
was highly squeamish when confronted with the sight of any kind
of physical injury. The irony of how this sat with his appetite for
horror movies and ultra-violent video games was the subject of
both puzzlement and scorn, depending upon the observer's own
moral hang-ups.

He was the youngest member of the team, and Catherine owed
it to him as a professional courtesy to rein in her maternal instincts
when they tempted her to view him as some innocent wee boy, but

sometimes when she looked at him that was exactly what she saw. It was what she liked about him too.

A history graduate, he had been fast-tracked via the Accelerated Careers Development Programme and seemed acutely sensitive to the possibility of resentment at not having come up through the streets. The upside of this for Catherine was that he was determined nobody could ever accuse him of needing to be carried, to which end he endeavoured to work harder than anybody else. Catherine had never known a grafter like him. Shortly after joining her department he had broken his leg, falling off a garage roof in pursuit of a suspect. He had allowed himself precisely one afternoon by way of convalescence, then hobbled in on crutches with his leg in plaster from thigh to foot, insisting he be given every piece of desk-bound scut-work that anybody needed doing.

It was inevitable that he'd end up under her charge. Her husband Drew had recently remarked that 'everybody on your team is a little bit broken'. It wasn't a criticism. They were discussing qualities in her staff that she described as valuable fragilities.

Beano's was that he couldn't stand to see anybody getting hurt. Some people would regard that as a handicap for working in the often brutal sphere of law enforcement, but Catherine's view was precisely the opposite. Anthony Thompson wanted to protect people from harm, and his very squeamishness served as a reminder that such was the very purpose of their profession.

In that respect, his job was already done for the day, as the harm-reduction dividend of Stevie Fullerton fielding a few bullets was incalculable. Unfortunately, this morning's anonymous benefactor was unlikely to be much of a humanitarian either, and it was Catherine's job to identify him.

The car continued its tentative progress between the two rows of largely stationary vehicles, Beano giving the siren a brief burst every so often, whenever it appeared a driver had failed to spot them in his or her mirror. Catherine could see the car wash up ahead, the canopy of what had once been a petrol station visible over the tops of the queuing cars. She was sure her dad had

23

stopped here once, when she was a little girl, filling up that beloved Wolseley whose wood and leather interior she could still smell.

Their progress ground to a complete stand-still half a dozen car-lengths short of the roadblock. There were several vehicles slewed across their path, angled in tight parallels that made it impossible for them to veer left towards the pavement. They were trying to nudge their way into the right-hand lane, where drivers were impatiently queuing to execute a U-turn through a break in the central reservation whenever gaps in the oncoming traffic allowed.

'Could do with having a uniform or somebody from Traffic out there regulating the flow from the opposite direction,' Beano suggested.

'They're probably all too busy contaminating my crime scene,' Catherine replied, more breezily than she had expected.

Held up en route to something this big, ordinarily Catherine would have been fidgeting with frustration by this point, but amid his nervous chattering Beano had been right about one thing: she did feel very calm today. She felt coy acknowledging this even to herself, but she had to admit she knew the reason why.

Drew had an earlier start than her, as he was heading through to Edinburgh for a meeting. He had left her to doze while he showered, dressed and fixed the boys' breakfasts, then brought her coffee and a croissant in bed. This was fairly normal. As he had placed the mug and the plate down on her bedside table, carefully picking out a spot amid the books, papers, phones and jewellery, she could hear the strains of the Mario Kart theme hailing from the living room, the boys getting in a fix before school. This was also fairly normal, at least since Drew reinstated their privileges on condition that they play only on the same team or in cooperative games. Prior to that they had been serving a ban on early-morning video games due to the sessions regularly ending in a barney, the invariably defeated Fraser reacting to each reverse at the hands of his older brother by descending into tearfully raging accusations of cheating. Duncan, for his part, would react with exasperated outrage,

24

or sometimes just laugh, both responses equally effective in sending Fraser into the red zone.

Drew had sat on the edge of the bed and brushed the hair from her face, laughing a little at her apparent difficulty in keeping her eyes open. He leaned over and kissed her neck. He smelled lovely, a bouquet of shower gel, aftershave and fabric conditioner. All of this was normal too; standard procedure, even.

He kissed her a little lower, delicately tugging at the strap of her nightie until her right breast was exposed, whereupon he softly kissed her nipple as she lay there in her dopey haze. This, while not an everyday occurrence, was far from out of the ordinary either. They even had a name for it: a rude awakening.

What happened next was a long way from normal, and she still wasn't sure where it came from. She took his left hand and gently placed it on top of her panties.

Drew stopped for a moment, looked up into her eyes as if to say 'For real?' She bent his head back towards her breast by way of answer.

She knew the boys were occupied downstairs, and equally she knew Drew was showered and dressed and about to leave, so maybe she thought she had the safety net that it couldn't really go anywhere. But it did.

She had to twist around and put her face into the pillow to stifle the screams she wanted to unleash, her orgasm degenerating into flushed and slightly embarrassed laughter. This was followed by a belated concern that she might have mangled his wrist somewhere amid the process, and finally an apology that the circumstances precluded reciprocation.

Drew said she didn't owe him anything. 'The thought of what just happened is going to keep me high all day.'

'High?' she asked. 'Or hard?'

'Bit of both.'

There was no denying the pleasure of it, or that it was responsible for the enduring calmness of mind she was still enjoying, but this was partially offset by a lingering unease over just where this impulse of abandon had come from. That part scared her just a little, as it had been as though somebody else was driving for a while. God knows she had more reason than most to fear what lurked unseen beneath the skin.

Beano sounded the siren again and finally squeezed through the gap. An officer in uniform stepped forward upon spotting them, lifting cones to clear a way through the roadblock.

'Is it true Traffic were first to the scene?' Beano asked, teeing her up.

'Yeah. Hope Fullerton's tax disc was up to date and his tyre treads were deep enough. Probably wrote him up for loitering before they noticed the bullet holes.'

Beano drove the car up on to the broad pavement and parked it parallel to the dwarf wall that bordered the forecourt. Three further police vehicles were already lined up in front, two of them blocking the entrance and exit.

They both climbed out of the car and walked around the rear of the strategically parked ambulance that was hiding Fullerton's vehicle from the gaze of curious drivers on the far side of the dual carriageway. It was a sky blue Bentley Continental GT. But of course. It was the epitome of automotive ostentatiousness, a 'sports' car nearly five metres long and weighing more than two thousand kilograms, propelled by an absurdly large engine that was nonetheless unnecessarily powerful even for the task of pushing this enormous lump of metal around. People talked of certain cars being a dick substitute, but the Continental was more than just a penis with wheels, it was a pound sign with power steering. There was no car on the road that said 'wanker with money' quite like it, which was why it was so popular with guys like Fullerton.

It sat between two disused petrol plinths, its paintwork strangely blotchy where foam had evaporated without being rinsed. Suds were still slowly dripping from its flanks and collapsing as the tiny bubbles continued to burst, creating a sad little corona, like a meringue mix someone forgot to put in the oven.

Catherine first saw Fullerton in profile through the smeared window on the driver's side. From that distance he looked like he could be asleep at the wheel, his head slumped forward onto his chest. Only the hint of a dark stain just inside his jacket collar betrayed that he wouldn't be waking up. She saw little that ought to trouble Beano, and nothing at all that troubled her.

She should feel something, she told herself. He was a human being, somebody's husband, somebody's son. All the clichés, all the stuff she usually drew upon whenever her conscience needed a jump-start in order to give a fuck.

Nothing. Empathy failed her. She knew too much about him, knew that a quick death with no warning, no time to know fear, was a kinder fate than Stevie Fullerton had doled out to his victims.

As she proceeded through the forecourt she observed that there was one other car on the premises, a silver Ford Focus. Catherine guessed its driver was the woman she didn't recognise, standing next to DC Zoe Vernon and two paramedics inside the kiosk that served as both office and supply room. The front was glass from floor to ceiling, affording an unobstructed view of the Spartan arrangements inside. A cash register and a desk were all that survived from the premises' previous incarnation. Instead of newspaper racks and rows of confectionary, there were barrels of cleaning products and a small fridge on top of which was perched a filthy and aged kettle. DI Laura Geddes was talking to two guys who looked like car-wash staff: a lank-haired and ashen-looking teen and a burly older bloke sporting a lot of tattoos.

Glancing up, Laura gave Catherine a nod of acknowledgement but then went back to her conversation, taking notes. One of the two males she took to be Traffic also clocked the new arrivals and strode across the forecourt to greet them, checking his stride at one point, as though avoiding an invisible pillar.

A breath of wind blew through the place, suddenly filling Catherine's nose with sharp chemical scents. There was something nastier in there too.

'Kevin McCallister,' the uniform introduced himself. 'I was first on scene.'

He was straight-backed, with a determined seriousness in his expression that nonetheless betrayed unease. He looked like he was worried he was about to be told he'd screwed up, but was coaching himself to remain stoic in the face of it. Catherine felt for him. Her jokes with Beano had just been banter, but there was a certain truth in this being out of the guy's comfort zone.

It wasn't the body that would have unsettled him. The gory sights McCallister must have seen would doubtless top anything Catherine had ever confronted, and probably have Beano in therapy. But finding himself Johnny-on-the-spot when one of the city's most notorious crime figures had just been gunned down was not covered in the Traffic Division's playbook.

Catherine recalled a story Cal O'Shea told, about a crash team finishing up following a prolonged resuscitation and wondering what had happened to the (very) junior doctor who had been carrying the cardiac arrest bleep. As they were leaving the ward they saw him climbing out of a cleaning cupboard. Poor bugger had been walking right past when the thing went off and knew he would be the first on the scene.

'Detective Superintendent McLeod. And this is DC Thompson. When did you get here?'

'Eleven fifty-two. Got the call at eleven forty-nine. We were running a speed trap down the Gallowhaugh end of the dual carriageway. Victim was already dead when I got here. I know how to feel a pulse,' he added, the grim certainty of his tone heading off any question over this.

Catherine nodded. She had little doubt that Constable McCallister had often been there to witness the moment when somebody died, rather than merely surveying the aftermath like she was used to. Nonetheless, he'd only been three minutes away. It wasn't like the body had had time to go cold.

'He can't have been dead long,' she suggested.

'There was a delay in us getting the call,' he replied, a look of irritation on his face, and not at her. 'The woman in the Focus, a Mrs Chalmers, said the older of the car-wash workers went inside to the office and got on the phone, so she assumed he was calling emergency services. After about ten minutes had gone by and there were no sirens she made her own call, just in case, and that turned out to be the first.'

'Mr Hairy Biker knew it was an emergency but the number he dialled wasn't nine-nine-nine?'

'Stevie Fullerton owns this car wash,' McCallister replied. 'His name isn't on the paperwork – since the Proceeds of Crime Act he probably doesn't officially own his own underpants – but everybody knows it's his.'

'At least when we notify the relatives it won't be a shock.'

'Why wouldn't they phone an ambulance, though?' Beano asked.

'Four shots to the chest,' McCallister said. '*They* didn't need to take a pulse to know he was dead. Whoever they phoned must have told them to sit tight and say nothing.'

'When did the ambulance get here?' Catherine asked.

'A good ten minutes after me. So when it turned up I kept the paramedics back from the body, made sure they never touched anything. Told them to deal with the witnesses instead.'

'Well done,' Catherine told him, privately taking back everything she'd said in the car. He had thought on his feet and acted to preserve the crime scene, ensuring the body was left in place.

She glanced towards the Bentley, looking now almost head-on through the kaleidoscope of the shattered windscreen. She couldn't see Fullerton's face as his head sat too far forward, just a mop of artificially black hair, the dye job betrayed by a ring of grey roots at the crown.

She caught another tang of something rank.

'What's that smell?' she asked. 'It's a bit early for him to stink, rotten as he was.'

'It's vomit,' said McCallister. 'Mrs Chalmers threw up just outside her car there. She's okay now. She's had a cup of tea and been checked out by the paramedics. Marginally more use than the other pair. They're both pretty shaken up, but on top of that they're bricking it in case they say anything they're not supposed to.'

'Was it you who IDed the victim?'

McCallister nodded.

'I checked with DVLA that that's his reg, but I was only getting official confirmation. I recognised the motor – as somebody who sees him driving that thing about here all the time I knew it was him right away. Never seen him looking better, to be honest.'

Catherine watched Laura make her way out of the kiosk, picking her steps carefully and similarly slaloming around what she now assumed to be Mrs Chalmers's pile of puke. At least she'd held it in until she made it outside of her car, otherwise it would have been a hell of a valet job for some poor bastard.

'Afternoon, boss.'

'DI Geddes. An auspicious day, wouldn't you say?'

Laura glanced towards the Bentley.

'Not for the late Mr Fullerton.'

'You'd be surprised. It's actually a very special day for him. His birthday, no less.'

'Serious?' Laura asked.

'No kidding. It'll save the widow a few bob on engraver's fees for the headstone. She can just get ditto marks under the day and month.'

'Well, somebody really pushed the boat out to give him a birthday surprise. I'll never complain again about just receiving M&S vouchers.'

'What are you getting in there?' Catherine asked, indicating the kiosk. 'Give me the Twitter-feed version.'

'It's mostly the woman's Twitter feed so far. Metallica boy and Leatherface – that's Andrew Gerrity and James McShane respectively – aren't being entirely forthcoming, because—'

'Yeah, we heard,' Catherine interrupted.

'Concerned about upsetting the master of puppets, as it were,' suggested Beano.

'More like pastor of muppets,' Laura replied. 'To be honest, you haven't missed anything. You'd be as well stepping in.'

Catherine didn't like to conspicuously micromanage her detectives, or make them feel like teacher was looking over their shoulders, but today was different. Teacher would be looking over *her* shoulder on this one, so her instinct was to be more hands-on, which was why she had come down to the scene in person. She would do this and

30

then back off. Paradoxically, the bigger and more important the case, the more she was forced to delegate. It was a delicate balance: it was crucial that she didn't give them any reason to doubt that she trusted their abilities, but sometimes just letting them know she was taking a closer interest was enough to make them all up their game.

They walked over to the kiosk. It looked small from the outside, but denuded of racks and gondolas there was a lot of floor space. Mrs Chalmers was dressed in a navy blue skirt and matching jacket. A laminated lapel badge identified her as working for a bank. Catherine gauged a mumsy late thirties, pictured her hugging the kids that bit tighter when she picked them up from school or nursery later that day.

The witnesses were standing with their backs to the window so they didn't have to look at the guest of honour out there amid his crown of suds; metaphorical scum surrounded by the literal.

Mrs Chalmers looked up anxiously as Catherine and Beano entered, visibly intimidated by the arrival of authority but instinctively eager to assist. By direct contrast the other two made their own subconscious acknowledgment of rank, stiffening a little against the glass. McCallister was right: they were scared; not of the gunman, and certainly not of her. She doubted two car-wash workers would have any higher involvement in Stevie Fullerton's operations than the knowledge that he was the unnamed proprietor, but being ringside when he got executed had dumped them at the eye of a storm. All they would feel secure in doing, in compliance with the only instruction they would have been given, was 'tell the polis nothing'.

Catherine introduced herself and made a general request for a quick recap, addressing it to no one in particular. She knew who would respond and who wouldn't, and she wanted them to relax, thinking Mrs Chalmers was doing all the driving for them.

'These aren't formal statements,' she added. 'We'll get those later. Right now we just need information we can work with.'

Mrs Chalmers nodded, responding like she'd be partly to blame if the perp wasn't apprehended.

'I was about halfway through getting my car washed when the

31

Bentley pulled in,' she said. 'At that point Mr McShane here dropped the brush he was using and just walked away.'

She looked a little flushed as she said this, self-conscious about grassing the guy up but incapable of lying to the polis. God, Catherine loved the Mrs Chalmerses of this world.

'VIP customer?' Catherine asked, to no response.

'They both started working on the Bentley, and they had just covered it in foam when another vehicle drove into the forecourt. It went right around the side and parked in front of the kiosk just there, facing the exit, engine running, like he was nipping in for a newspaper.

'I got out my phone to text a friend about something because I thought I'd be sitting there a wee while, so I wasn't looking at the man as he got out of the car. But then I noticed Mr Gerrity getting down and lying on the wet ground. I thought he was looking under my car, but then I noticed that Mr McShane was doing the same, and that's when I saw the man with the skull mask.'

'Did he order you to lie down?' Catherine asked them. 'What did he say?'

Gerrity looked to McShane, Catherine unable to quite read the dynamic. He was either deferring to the older guy for an official response or asking whether he had permission to answer.

'"Lie down,"' said McShane. 'That's all. Two words. It was enough, with the gun and the mask. I just assumed we were getting knocked over.'

'And no doubt wondering who might be desperate, crazy or just ignorant enough to rob a business belonging to Stevie Fullerton?' Catherine suggested. She allowed a twinkle of humour to come into her eye, inviting him to betray his agreement with a smile. None came, which told her plenty. He was acting out of fear rather than loyalty. That would make him an easier nut to crack. She just had to make herself a scarier prospect than his employers.

'What else was he wearing?'

'Combat gear,' Mrs Chalmers replied. 'You know, that camouflage material. Dark green, with a hooded top under the jacket. He had the hood up, which is why I didn't notice the skull mask when he drove in.'

'Was it like a corner-shop Hallowe'en mask? Or a more expensive latex affair?'

'Neither,' said Mrs Chalmers. 'It looked solid, sturdy, with mesh instead of holes.'

'Like a protective mask for paintball or airsoft?' Beano asked.

'I wouldn't know. I thought it was a robbery, though I didn't see the gun at first. But when he stepped forward, right to the end of the bonnet, I certainly saw it then. It was like slow motion and yet over in a flash. He fired four times into the Bentley. I was just frozen because I couldn't believe what I was seeing.'

'Anybody get much of a look at the gun?'

Mrs Chalmers looked like she didn't understand the question, which was okay as it wasn't really aimed at her. McShane stared blankly, giving a tiny shake of the head, but she caught a keenness flash across Gerrity's eyes before he censored himself. He was like a kid in class who knows the answer but doesn't want called a sook by his pals. Gamer, she thought. He knows exactly what it was, because he recognised it from some FPS on his Xbox.

'I'm not asking for its serial number, just, you know, was it a revolver, an automatic?'

'Automatic,' Gerrity answered. 'With a silencer.'

'Glock? Beretta? Deagle?'

He shrugged. He wasn't sure or he wasn't biting.

'What about the car, then?'

'It was a green jeep,' asserted Mrs Chalmers.

'Jeep with a capital J?' asked Laura, not letting the certainty of Mrs Chalmers's tone trump her perception that the woman didn't exactly come across as a petrolhead.

'Oh, is there a . . . I'm not sure. I just meant, you know, one of those big rugged things, like something out of the army.'

So that was a small j, then.

'What about you guys?' Catherine asked.

They both shuffled and shrugged, Gerrity's furtive glance once more betraying that he was censoring himself; not that she needed any more tells. This was the one area they were most likely to have been given specific instruction on, and she knew why.

'Did you see what way he went? When he drove out?'

They both shook their heads.

'Me neither,' Mrs Chalmers said apologetically. 'I had ducked down behind the dashboard. I was afraid he was going to come after me because I was a witness. I did hear something, though. A crunch, like his car hit something on the way out.'

Catherine nodded and turned to Beano.

'DC Thompson, could you take Mrs Chalmers outside and have her describe where this crunch sound might have come from?'

'Yes, boss.'

Catherine then addressed the paramedics.

'Perhaps you could make sure Mrs Chalmers doesn't have a relapse of her nausea or comes over faint if she catches another glimpse of His Holeyness out there.'

It took them half a second, but they sussed the message, and she had little doubt that Gerrity and McShane were way ahead of them. Zoe held the door open for the paramedics, then Catherine rounded on See No Evil and Hear No Evil.

'Neither of you is much of a liar,' she said.

They both stiffened, mustering what defences they had.

'Don't worry, that's a good thing. It tells me you're generally honest. It indicates you're neither accomplished nor experienced at lying, especially to the polis. And the reason I know this is that the experienced liar knows when *not* to lie. The experienced liar understands something called "plausible deniability".'

McShane met her gaze, trying to maintain his game face. Gerrity just stared at the floor and looked worried.

'You didn't see which way he went? It's a fucking dual carriageway. There's only one way he *could* have gone. See? Lying when you don't need to: very big giveaway. I ask what kind of car the guy drove and you claim you didn't notice. That sound like plausible deniability to you? You work in a fucking car wash, you look at cars all day. You're expecting me to believe you can't ID a make and model in about a tenth of a second? I'm guessing you could tell me how many inches the *alloys* are on any particular motor the instant it drives on to that forecourt. So not only am I damn sure you know what kind of vehicle he drove, but given you were lying down eye-level with the plate, I reckon you know the registration too.'

Neither of them said anything, but McShane's face was getting flushed. Not only was he an inexperienced liar, but he was embarrassed at how obvious it was. Nonetheless, he could clearly still think of worse things he might have to endure than embarrassment. She was going to toss him another.

'Mrs Chalmers saw you make a phone call, and we know you didn't dial nine-nine-nine. I don't know who you called but it won't take me long to find out, and I'm guessing whoever you spoke to told you to keep your mouths shut and tell the polis nothing. The reason being they'll be wanting to track down the shooter themselves, conduct their own wee interrogation and exact their own revenge. That is not going to happen, and you should be grateful that it's not going to happen, because in the extremely unlikely event that it *did*, the first step in our subsequent investigation would be to arrest you two for giving them the information that facilitated it. So either you can tell us here and now as witnesses or you can tell us later when you're being sweated on charges of obstructing a police investigation, conspiracy to pervert the course of justice and conspiracy towards whatever mayhem is unleashed by the bampot who was on the other end of that phone.'

Their powers of recall improved quite exponentially after that.

They both identified the shooter's vehicle as a Land Rover Defender, 2004 vintage according to the plates, though they had slightly divergent recollections of the full registration. It would be enough. McCallister would get on to DVLA and discover which green Land Rover Defender bore the closest approximation to that plate. Chances were he would also discover that it had recently been reported stolen, but maybe they'd get lucky: sometimes these gangland headcases forgot to worry about such discretionary measures.

The Only Way is Apple

Jasmine put her foot down gently on the accelerator and squeezed the push-to-talk button on the gearstick with her left hand. It was such a natural action these days that she found herself doing it in her Civic when she was talking hands-free on the phone, even though there was no button to push.

'Subject proceeding left left left on to Lancefield Quay, two cars cover,' she reported. 'Do you have eyeball?'

'Echo Two. Yes yes,' replied Martin Grady. 'Could probably see subject's vehicle from orbit. Wish all our marks were such attention-seeking fannies. Easy money today.'

'Foxtrot Five. Speak for yourself,' Jasmine replied. 'You're not the one who has to catch *his* eye.'

'Delta Four,' broke in Andy Smith. 'In that case I hope Foxtrot Five isn't wearing jogging breeks and an Aran sweater.'

'Foxtrot Five. Fuck you, Delta Four.'

'Delta Four. Roger.'

Jasmine wasn't supposed to be working today, but she was grateful to be busy. She had allocated herself a day off for her mum's birthday, planning to do some shopping, take in a movie, maybe hit the range later. All of these were intended to keep her occupied and distracted in what she hoped would be a pleasant way, and thus act as a bulwark against what else the occasion might precipitate.

Work, as it turned out, was going to produce the same effect, but it was never guaranteed. She knew that there had been every possibility she would spend the day in a stationary surveillance vehicle in what she had termed 'condition Godot'. Sitting there waiting for something to happen, with nothing to occupy her thoughts, was precisely when she'd be most vulnerable to the demons of her grief. To that end she had left her work schedule blank, but Harry Deacon had called her before she set off for Dunfermline the previous night and practically begged her to come onboard. Her reluctance was therefore both genuine and deep-seated, manifesting itself in a contemplative pause so long that Harry was offering triple time by the end of it.

It was a job that had fallen into Galt Linklater's lap at the last minute, and that Harry was prepared to make it worth so much to her indicated how much it was worth to them. As sub-contracts from the big firm made up a substantial part of Jasmine's business, there was more than one reason this was an offer she couldn't refuse.

The subject vehicle veered right to get out of the upcoming filter lane, a manoeuvre Jasmine guessed had been suggested by its sat-nav. The subject wasn't from around here, which pretty much went without saying given that he was driving a bright yellow Maserati. In Glasgow, even the drug dealers drew the line at that kind of ostentation. There was bling and then there was painting a target on yourself.

'Foxtrot Five. Lights through to green no deviation Broomielaw. Still two cars cover, but I think I can hear his stereo.'

'Echo Two. Can confirm audio. Subject's windows are down and his music is shite. Repeat: subject's music is shite.'

Foxtrot Five was her call-sign. Harry Deacon had initially assigned her Juliet Six for Galt Linklater work, but she requested the change in honour of her late uncle Jim. Foxtrot Five had been the call-sign Jim gave her when she first went to work for him, and she still recalled with embarrassment how long it took her to get the hang of the radio protocols, starting with the basic one of saying your own call-sign first to identify yourself as the next speaker.

Strictly speaking, Jim wasn't her uncle. He was her mum's cousin, but after she died, in that time when everybody told her 'if there's anything I can do, just ask', he was the one person who actually *did* something. Jasmine had been forced to drop out of drama school, and he gave her a job, albeit not one she had wanted or considered herself remotely cut out for at the time. She had assumed he was doing it purely out of his natural generosity and a sense of familial obligation, but it turned out that there was a less altruistic reason for her recruitment: the same reason Galt Linklater kept her on a retainer and why Harry Deacon had been pleading down the phone yesterday.

Jim had been an ex-cop. Harry Deacon was an ex-cop. Just about everybody at Galt Linklater, in fact, was an ex-cop, and the problem with ex-cops, when it came to surveillance work, was that they looked like ex-cops. Not only did Jasmine look nothing like an ex-cop, the host of people she *could* plausibly look like made her very effective at this game. She was the one they never saw coming, the one the guys at Galt Linklater referred to as their ninja.

They also referred to her as Crash, ever since she had engaged in an uncharacteristically extreme gambit in order to serve papers on a particularly elusive subject. It was a nickname she had encouraged because it helped supersede the use of 'Jazz'. This had been a predictable informal handle throughout her school and college years, and one towards which she had been entirely ambivalent until a couple of years back. Following one of the most difficult conversations of her life, she couldn't hear the word without thinking of what it represented, and none of that was good.

Andy Smith's voice broke over the airwaves.

'Just got a shout from HQ,' he reported. 'Wee traffic bulletin: stay clear of Shawburn Boulevard. It's a car park right now. Major incident. Polis everywhere. Just so you know.'

'Thanks for that,' said Martin. 'Won't affect us, though. A tenner says subject is heading for the Apple shop.'

'No bet,' said Jasmine. 'On this guy's list of places worth visiting in Glasgow, that will be number one. There will not be a number two.'

'He's an artist, though,' Martin replied. 'Apple tech is for creative types, remember. It's his creativity that draws him towards it. As opposed to, say, the fact that he'd be baffled by a mouse with more than one button on it.'

The mark was known, these days at least, by the name D-Blazer, a boyband refugee who had successfully reinvented himself as a rap star and was playing two nights at the SECC. In his lip-synch and choreography days he had been plain old Darren Blake, trading on an Essex wideboy image to distinguish himself from his more clean-cut fellow recruits with whom he had been packaged together by a record label to form the wet and insipid Desire.

However, even plain old Darren Blake had been a calculated construct. D-Blazer's real name was Darrien Hopscombe-Blanchard, and while it was true that he was an Essex boy, it was fair to say he was trading on certain misperceptions about what was, after all, one of the most prosperous areas of the UK. We weren't talking Dagenham or Romford here. He had indeed grown up in the county of the three swords, but as his family had owned a substantial swathe of it for several centuries, this was hardly surprising. Martin had suggested that the Blazer in his rapper name referred to his father's golf-club attire.

Jasmine followed his Maserati through the city, dropping back now and again to let someone else take point. If Darrien had punched the Apple shop's address into his sat-nav he'd be in for a disappointment, as it was on a wholly pedestrianised thoroughfare.

His journey was taking him further north, past all the obvious routes towards Buchanan Street, before heading east.

They had picked him up at his hotel, the Crowne Plaza, which was just next to the exhibition centre. There was a tour bus parked at the venue, but that was only for the dancers, backing singers and those loser types who actually played musical instruments. D-Blazer preferred to take his own wheels on tour, partly because he liked the chance to drive his toyz around, and partly because he liked to be seen. This made him, as Martin had implied, a private investigator's dream.

'Subject proceeding right right right on to Renfrew Street,' Andy relayed. 'I should maybe have taken that bet.'

'You'd be ten pounds down,' Jasmine told him. 'Concierge at the hotel will have told him to park at the Buchanan Galleries.'

The reason for Harry's largesse and for Galt Linklater's urgency was that D-Blazer was currently the subject of a paternity claim. A nineteen-year-old student from Chelmsford by the name of Nikki Ainsworth maintained that he had fathered her baby girl, Danielle, during a six-month affair that the twenty-seven-year-old rapper terminated once he discovered she was up the jaggy. D-Blazer, for his part, claimed that she had 'flung herself at me but I hardly never went near her', and that she was now 'just vibing negs into my aura', by which Jasmine interpreted him to mean that her claims were merely a nuisance act motivated by spite.

Nonetheless, for all he was trying to appear nonchalant in his dismissal, Mr Hopscombe-Blanchard was refusing to submit any DNA for a paternity test. In light of this, the word 'hardly' took on a quite pivotal significance within his previous utterance.

'Foxtrot Five. Subject is a stop stop stop and park at Buchanan Galleries car park level five. I have eyeball and am proceeding on foot.'

Jasmine switched to her earpiece and climbed out of the van as Andy and Martin confirmed their own positions. They would be parked in a matter of seconds, then they would enter the mall at different levels, catching up to inconspicuously commence a three-way foot follow.

Jasmine was soon able to assure them there was no rush. D-Blazer was setting a very easy pace in order to maximise his chances of being recognised.

'Subject is proceeding south south south and moving as though he is the Pink Panther bursting for a shite,' she informed them, describing the ludicrous gangsta gait he was rocking.

He was affecting an air of being lost in the music playing through his absurdly encumbering gold Beats headphones, trying to look like he was in one of his own videos.

Jasmine privately suspected he had the music way down just in case somebody called his name and he didn't hear it, but as she monitored his progress through the mall, she observed that he wasn't short of attention, and came to understand the real purpose of the headphones. They were a prop so that he could select whose solicitations he had or hadn't noticed. His hearing was pretty sharp if you were young, female and pretty, though apparently he would settle for big tits as a substitute for this last criterion. The first two were non-negotiable.

Jasmine stopped and had a glance at her reflection in a shop window. She wasn't wearing jogging bottoms and an Aran sweater, but nor was she looking ready to hit a club right then.

Harry had only secured her services last night: he hadn't divulged the details until she showed up at Galt Linklater's offices this morning. She was wearing a reliably flexible (i.e. very lived-in) pair of jeans and a rather shapeless long-sleeved top, chosen both for comfort in the event of sitting for hours in a van, and to prevent anyone being able to peek through gaps in her blouse in the event that she was sharing said van with certain GL personnel.

She got out her phone and called Harry. He took a while to answer, and sounded a little distracted when he finally did.

'Hello?'

'Harry. It's me.'

'Who's me?'

'Jasmine,' she told him, trying not to sound irritated. Time could be an issue.

'Jasmine. Christ, sorry. Have you got a new phone? If you have, you should really update us on your—'

'I don't have a new phone.'

'Shite. That means I must have deleted you as a contact on mine.'

'I hope that's not a roundabout way of letting me go.'

'As if. No, just me being a techno-numpty as usual. What can I do for you?'

'I need budget approval on a couple of emergency items.'

'Like what?'

She told him.

'Just as long as you keep receipts for your purchases. And you wear them to the Christmas night out.'

'Sure, Harry. That's totally going to happen.'

She hung up then told Martin to make ground and take point.

'I'll intercept him on his way back to his car,' she explained.

'Why, where are you going just now?'

'Where do you think? I'm in the Buchanan Galleries and I have no Y chromosome. I'm going shopping.'

'Delta Four,' broke in Andy. 'Where do they sell those?'

She assumed he was joking.

Jasmine engaged in an unaccustomed bout of speed-shopping, quickly scouring the stores for the most pneumatic push-up bra she could find, then hunting for a top that would best showcase the resulting cleavage.

She knew she had to pitch it just right. It wasn't a question of grabbing something low-cut or popping open a few buttons on a tight blouse. The look was not supposed to suggest she was about to start her pole-dancing shift. She needed to carry off an image that seemed plausible for cutting about the shops at this time of day, but that in D-Blazer's eyes would be interpreted as 'I don't mind showing my tits off at half eleven in the morning, so just imagine what else I must be up for'.

Once she had bought what she needed, she headed back to the changing room she had most recently visited, showing the woman on duty the carrier bags and receipts. Her name-badge said Collette.

'I need to wear these now,' she explained.

'Prêt-à-porter right enough,' Collette replied, with a precisely pitched combination of dryness and warmth that Jasmine reckoned Glaswegians must learn as a rite of passage.

As Jasmine changed she heard the ongoing commentary from Martin and Andy in her earpiece. The subject was doing his best to hold court in the Apple store and was starting to annoy the management, who were used to all customer adulation being focused exclusively upon their products.

Jasmine was relieved, though not surprised. If it turned out D-Blazer had blanked the Apple store and headed down to the Gallery of Modern Art to look at the latest installations, it would have ramifications for her chances of carrying this off. He was one of those London-centric wankers who thought modern everyday reality stopped at the M25, and with it his cares and woes. Galt Linklater had been given this job because it was assumed that, outside the capital, D-Blazer would be off his guard. This hypothesis would be supported by his gravitating towards regional satellites of his normal frame of reference: the Apple store, certain clothing chains, Nando's. A trip to GoMA, for instance, might have indicated that he was engaged with his surroundings and more switched on than they were giving him credit for. It would also have made Jasmine pass out on the spot with sheer astonishment.

She exited the changing rooms with her old clothes in the new bags, estimating from the reports that she would have time to hit the John Lewis make-up counters and let the demo girls do their worst.

Collette gave her a brief assessment as she left, succinctly passing her judgment in merely two words: 'Hello boys.'

Jasmine just about managed to keep a smile off her face. Part of her was delighted, while another part told her she was going to hell for this.

Hidden Content

Catherine saw Forensics finally pull up at the rear of the forecourt. She guessed they had been held up in the tailback, without the blue light to clear a path. She went outside to meet them, leaving Laura and Zoe to work on Rose Royce.

Beano was standing out on the pavement close to the exit. Catherine assumed he had walked Mrs Chalmers over there so that the ambulance would spare her – and him – a view inside the Bentley, but he was beckoning Catherine with a wave.

'We might have caught a wee break,' he said as she approached. 'Mrs Chalmers was right about what she heard. Look.'

He squatted down at the end of the dwarf wall, where it resumed on the left-hand side of the exit towards the dual carriageway. It comprised red brickwork beneath a series of light grey slabs, the nearest of which was unique in having been painted white. Presumably this was to denote the inside border of the exit, or perhaps someone had intended to paint the lot and then decided he couldn't be arsed.

'The paint's quite fresh, and it's had a bash,' Beano said, picking at it with his fingers to illustrate where it was already coming away. 'So there will be a scrape and a transfer of paint on the left-hand flank of the shooter's vehicle. Match the samples and we can place it here for sure.'

'Well spotted,' she told him. 'And here's just the people to tell.'

Beano glanced across to where the pathologist Cal O'Shea and his assistant Aileen Bruce were pulling on plastic overalls.

'Yeah, I'll direct them to the paint and you direct them to the birthday boy.'

Poor Beano. As murder scenes went, this was hardly the set of a Rob Zombie movie, but he was suffering all the same. To be fair,

44

it wasn't as though he had the screaming heebie-jeebies; he'd just be a lot happier once the body was covered by a sheet.

'Officer Thompson, why don't you take Mrs Chalmers down the road to a coffee shop and wait there until she can get someone to drive her home and sit with her?'

'Oh, no,' Mrs Chalmers insisted, as Catherine anticipated she would. The straight-arrow types never wanted to make a fuss, even when they were suffering from borderline post-traumatic stress disorder. 'I can drive myself. I'm fine.'

'I'm sure you are,' Catherine told her. 'After witnessing something like this, people are sometimes so fine that they drive through a red at the first set of lights and head straight into the oncoming traffic. Go with Officer Thompson. Call someone who can come and get you.'

Mrs Chalmers rather feebly nodded her assent. The scenario Catherine had just painted must have struck her as all too plausible and she suddenly didn't feel quite so sure of herself.

Beano gave Catherine an appreciative look.

'When does this stuff stop freaking you out?' he asked quietly, out of the witness's earshot.

'You're doing fine, Beano,' she assured him with a pat on the arm.

He didn't point out that she hadn't answered his question.

That was because she didn't like what the answer said about her. She didn't know when the sight of a murder victim had stopped bothering her, and hadn't even been conscious at the time of passing through such a watershed, but she knew it had been a very long time ago. Of course, every so often one could get under her skin, but she couldn't have said when that had last happened.

The sight of Stevie Fullerton buckled up and buckled over in his Bentley certainly wasn't going to do it. Her great fear, of course, was that now nothing could.

She was always more vulnerable to these thoughts when Cal O'Shea was present. The pathologist liked to joke about how sanguine she was around murder scenes, which was generally interpreted as a humorous play on the gags and remarks he had to endure about spending his days cutting up dead bodies. He liked to make out that he found her intimidating and 'spooky'. This could also be interpreted as deflection, but Catherine was never sure to what extent he was actually joking. Cal had this penetrating and inscrutable gaze, the kind that felt like he could see beneath the skin of the living as analytically as his scalpel let him reveal the secrets of the dead. It piqued a paranoia that he could see inside her, and she was afraid of what he might have found.

She thought Aileen was moving a little deliberately and wondered if she'd done her back, then she turned just enough for Catherine to notice the protuberance that was nudging her overalls. Of course: she remembered hearing that Aileen was pregnant, but it had been a couple of months since she'd seen her.

It briefly struck Catherine as quite jarring to see a bright young woman, blossoming with child, spending her day focused upon a murdered corpse. Maybe that meant she wasn't totally numbed to the horrors after all.

It seemed incongruous but, on reflection, imminent new birth around recent death was pure cycle-of-life stuff. The wean was in the womb, for God's sake. It wasn't like Aileen had taken along a five-year-old on Bring Your Daughter To Work Day.

She spent a few minutes catching up, asking how Aileen was getting on, trading a few stories about the debilitating effects of having placenta-brain. Cal left them to it, heading off to get started.

When Catherine broke off from chatting, Cal seemed to have disappeared. She walked carefully around the forecourt, tracing an imaginary perimeter surrounding the victim, and found him crouched down at the open door of the Bentley.

'Are you going to introduce us?' he asked without glancing back. 'He's rather shy. Perhaps if you broke the ice . . .'

'My apologies. Stevie Fullerton, this is Cal O'Shea. Cal O'Shea, this is Stevie Fullerton. You might want to wish him many happy returns.'

'Oh, it's his birthday?'

'His forty-ninth and last.'

'Some way to give a guy his bumps,' Cal observed. He was

leaning carefully into the car without touching anything, looking up at Fullerton's bowed head.

'Aye. Four bullets to the chest at close range.'

'And, it would appear, one to the middle of the fore . . . Oh no, I'm mistaken. Goodness gracious.'

Cal had this idiom of exaggerated politeness that he sometimes engaged as a means of undercutting the crudeness of the language whenever a group of cops were in conversation, but it also tended to kick in when he was genuinely surprised.

'What is it?' Catherine asked.

'Come closer and you'll see.'

Catherine approached gingerly, stepping through the puddle of evaporating suds and leaning over Cal's back.

He cupped Fullerton's head with one gloved hand, then took a pencil and delicately used it to brush away a lock of hair that had been overhanging the victim's brow.

'I thought it was another gunshot wound, but rather the gunman appears to have drawn some kind of symbol on Mr Fullerton's forehead using his blood. No idea what it signifies, but happily it's not my job to find out.'

Catherine looked at the symbol, crudely smeared in dark, dried blood, and suddenly felt as though the disused petrol station was on board an oil tanker pitching in stormy seas. Something inside her lurched and she felt for a horrible moment like she was going to faint. She stumbled forward a little, her hand reaching out to rest upon Cal's back for balance.

Now she knew what it felt like to be Beano. If he had still been here she could have told him that, regardless how many murder scenes she had attended, this one had rendered her officially spooked. She just couldn't tell him why.

'Are you okay?' Cal asked, turning around.

Catherine stood up slowly, wary of exacerbating her light-headedness.

'Just got a wee bit of a fright there. Wasn't expecting to see something like that, that's all.'

'Changes the picture somewhat, albeit only a little. What we

47

have now is a gangland execution latte given extra flavour by a little squirt from the ritual-killing syrup dispenser.'

Catherine exhaled in a long controlled breath, composing herself as she heard the clack and splash of Laura Geddes hurrying towards her. Laura looked fit to burst as she approached, but her news was jolted into a holding pattern by whatever she saw in Catherine's face.

'You okay, boss? You look like you've seen a ghost.'

'I'm fine,' she said. Like Mrs Chalmers was fine. 'Cal here just showed me a wee macabre flourish to the killer's handiwork. I'll tell you in a minute. Have you got something for me?'

Laura's expression said *Do I ever*, but Catherine couldn't read whether this was a breakthrough or a complication.

'DVLA came back on the plates. One of them is the registration of a green Land Rover Defender, and it's not been reported stolen.'

This was good news, but it didn't account for Laura's expression. There was something more.

'Whose is it?'

'The owner is listed as a Mr Tron Ingrams. Better known to you and me as Glen Fallan.'

The Sacrifice

Sparks danced in the cool morning air, golden flecks turning silver as she held the steel to the turning stone. She worked the pedal with her left foot, angling the blade first towards then away from herself until the cutting edge gleamed for a deadly few millimetres either side of the tip. It had to kill with one blow, and she knew that every turn of the wheel would later concentrate a little more lethal pressure at the end of the arc when she swung from her shoulder and brought the blade to bear. Every flex of her calf muscle in driving the pedal down was thus a kindness, a courtesy.

The sun was low and bright, prompting her to shield her eyes until she reached the relief of the shadow cast by the coop. It was noticeably colder there too, the finest of hoar still dusting the moss-choked grass where the shade had preserved it. It was like two states of being, two realms, existing side by side, utterly different and yet separated by nothing, borders denoted only by their distinction. The bright realm was dazzling, vibrant in its colours, welcoming in its greater warmth. The shadow realm was cold and muted, yet it protected the fragile, gossamer adornment that coated each blade of grass and contoured each barren rut like a sculpture.

She cast a glance across to the house, then walked back into the sunlight from where she lifted the chopping block and the bucket, carrying them back with her into the shadow. She placed the block amid the whitest patch of hoar, at the dead centre of the shade, and rested the cleaver against it, handle up.

Bracing herself for the smell, she opened the coop and stepped inside. It was one mercy of the colder weather: the reek was always that bit less volatile, fewer molecules excited by heat and borne into the air by convection currents. The place seemed quiet, just the sounds of pecking and scratching from its occupants, as though they were all too wrapped up in their own concerns of a Saturday morning to be bothered with squawking to their neighbours.

'Maybe have a blether later, once I've got all this pecking and scratching out of the way,' they were perhaps thinking. That's what she was like, anyway. That's why she was tending to this before going over to see to the horses. She always preferred to get chores out of the way before turning to pleasures; even with a list of duties, she would tend to them in ascending order of palatability. Her sister was the exact opposite, an arch-procrastinator who seemed unburdened no matter what was piling up on her plate. She wished she was the same, more able to live in the moment, but she knew herself well enough to understand that this was just how she was made. She couldn't relax and enjoy anything while there were responsibilities still waiting to be met. In the short term, that meant killing a chicken for Mum before going to the stables, and in the long term it meant that for weeks, even months she had been unable to see past sitting her exams. So much so, in fact, that it was at her parents' insistence that she was going out tonight when her instincts and conscience were angrily dictating that she could not afford to let up on her studies even for one evening.

She found the hood hanging by its strap on the hook where it was supposed to be. That was because it was her who did this last time; Lisa seldom took her turn, and when she didn't manage to wriggle out of it she usually found some way of making everybody think it would be simpler in future just to do it themselves. 'Losing' the hood had been a case in point.

She chose a candidate with little deliberation and popped the hood over the hen's head. It was a small thing, but it made the whole undertaking so much easier, a fact presumably not lost on Lisa when she failed to return the hood to its rightful place. It made the birds more placid, sometimes rooted them to the spot, sparing the time-consuming and temper-shredding (not to mention dignity-rending) farce of chasing the chookie around like Benny Hill. But perhaps more importantly, it spared her from looking it in the eye between that moment of choosing and the bird's imminent end on the block.

50

That was why they hooded prisoners before the gallows, blind-folded men in front of the firing squad. People thought it was a courtesy to the condemned, so that they wouldn't have to literally face their death, but it was actually for the benefit of the executioners. How could you shoot somebody while you looked into their eyes? How could you watch a person be hanged if you could see the agonies racking their face?

They should bring it back, people kept saying. People who had never killed anything, not even a chicken.

She took the bird outside briskly, entering an almost automatic process from the moment the hood was in place and her grip firm on the hen's neck. There would be no dallying, no ponderance, only the swiftest of action. She was at the block in moments, where she held the bird by its legs and tail in her left hand, its neck straining back against its body as soon as it touched the wood. With her right hand she reached for the handle of the cleaver, always keeping her eyes on the bird, and in a practised movement drew it up and decisively down, severing the head completely. A streak of red violated the purity of the frost, and she let a little more spill in a deliberate arc before bringing the twitching bird into place above the bucket. She stared at the spray and the arc, like some runic symbol whose meaning she could not read, all the while continuing to hold the bleeding carcass over the bucket. She admired the rune's grace and simplicity, imagining herself the keeper of something truly ancient that was sacred to this spot and this act, unchanging over centuries.

She could feel the bird buck and spasm, the muscle reflexes pulsing against her grip, and as she looked at the crimson pattern stark against the whiteness, she felt a small burning echo of shame. She recalled with guilt the time something truly was imparted to her from a previous generation, when her father taught her and Lisa how to do this.

Lisa had been eight and a half, she seven. There was never any question of her waiting until she was Lisa's age for her chance to be taught or even permitted to do anything: she always had to have a go at the same time, compelled from as young as she could

51

remember to prove she was as big, as fast, as strong, as clever as her older sister.

Dad hadn't expected either of them to manage it by themselves, but he knew it was important to make them part of this, so that they would be prepared when that time did come. What he clearly didn't expect was their reaction. She had insisted on going first, as usual, and had been accommodated, as usual, by a father happy to follow the path of least resistance and an older sister who was in no rush to be at the front of this particular queue. Dad made her grip the bird in both hands, showing her how to hold it against the block and very carefully ensuring both bird and daughter were steady before bringing down the blade.

She recalled a pulse of tense anticipation as he swung, her hands squeezing reflexively tighter, and of jolting fright as the impact seemed to pass through her, from the ground at her feet and the warm body in her grip, then a relieved kind of elation mixed with a brief feeling of achievement. She remembered giggling a little, nervously, in the stillness of the moment. Then the bird jerked back to life in her hands and she lost her hold in her startlement, allowing it to drop to the ground, where it proceeded to hare off in the direction of the stables.

Dad was trying to inoculate them against the horror and instil a solemn sense of purpose to the act. However, he was a bit late: they must have seen their mum do it a hundred times, initially paying fascinated attention as they stopped to stare, later merely aware it was going on in the background of whatever game they were playing.

She remembered that the first time she saw a chicken's head severed and roll off the block, she had felt much as she did when she was shown a magic trick: a mixture of surprised delight and confusion as she tried to reconstruct the action and the outcome. But once you've seen it, you've seen it. They were already inured to the blood, albeit there remained something incredible about the speed of the transformation from living state to dead, side by side, bright realm, shadow realm.

Dead chickens running around with their heads off was altogether new, and, for a while at least, hilariously so. She and Lisa went charging delightedly after it, shrieking with laughter and excitement as it veered erratically across the grass. Between them they signally failed to corner the fugitive, which only came to a stop when it ran full-tilt into the side of the stables, a conclusion to the chase that precipitated further hysterics from its two pursuers.

The laughter stopped abruptly when they turned around and saw the thunderous glower across their father's face. He didn't need to say anything: in that moment, they understood immediately that what they were doing was wrong, and on an instinctive, fundamental level *why* it was wrong. No, he didn't need to say anything, but he said plenty nonetheless. If he wanted to ensure that she never forgot his words, then he did his job well. She could recall them still, almost a decade later. His voice was calm, measured, a man who knew the need to scold had been obviated by a mere look, and who wanted his girls to listen, not cower.

'We're taking this creature's life to preserve our own. Killing something is a sacrifice – it's always a sacrifice, and a sacrifice should be solemn. We'll live off this creature today and tomorrow too. We owe it our gratitude and we owe it our respect, our courtesy . . . and our kindness.'

She remembered looking down at the headless body, now lifeless on the ground, and weeping. She didn't feel bad that they had killed it, but for the indignity of the chase.

That was why she had glanced towards the house before moving the block and the bucket, and felt an echo of that shame as she contemplated the rune. She wanted to see what the blood looked like against the frost, but she didn't want anyone to notice that this was what she was doing. It was merely an echo of shame though, not shame itself, because this wasn't to disrespect the act of sacrifice. She was making it feel like a ritual, because ritual served to remind her of the significance of actions that had become almost automatic.

She would remember the rune always, she decided: this cold morning, this sunshine, this symbol in blood newly imbued with meaning. And she was right, but not for the reasons she envisaged in that moment.

Suspect Motives

Glen looked in the rear-view mirror again. The BMW was still two cars back behind his Defender. He had suspected it was following him for the past five miles, and now that he had come off the motorway onto an A road, there was little question.

He changed gear and accelerated. As he returned his right hand to the wheel, he realised he was trembling: physically trembling. He felt shock, fear and anger: anger at himself first and foremost, because he had fucked up and was now paying the price.

When had he last felt like this, felt so afraid? Not since child-hood, when he had known enough fear to last two lifetimes.

Since then, he had made a friend of fear: he had learned to listen to it, to draw power from it and to retain control when it was threatening to flood his senses. This was not the fear of which he had made himself a pupil, however. This was something different, something paralysing and debilitating, shot through with helpless-ness and doubt.

Nothing was under control, and he was just plain scared.

He felt the impulse to reach for the phone, an impulse he had felt twenty times in half as many minutes. On each occasion it was stayed by the knowledge that it was futile, and yet that knowledge wasn't enough to stop his instincts from suggesting it again.

He kept his foot steady on the pedal, accelerating gradually, trying to be inconspicuous, trying to look normal. But nothing was normal any more. He knew this road so well, must have driven it a hundred times, but it looked different today. Everything looked different.

Arable fields lay either side of the tarmac, bordered by hedge-rows. A river snaked in s-bends down the slope to his left. A couple of miles ahead he could see woodland, human-planted evergreens in their regimented rows hugging the hillside, punctuated by firebreaks and pylons. He knew there were Forestry Commission tracks snaking through there. He could take the Defender offroad, lose the BMW on the axle-breaking trails hidden beneath the canopy of pines. It would buy him time, but time to do what?

He had no game plan here. He was lost and blind. This was what happened when you broke your own rules.

He had been stupid, let impulse seize the reins and ride off at a reckless pace, leaving judgment trampled in its wake. He had been listening to fear, as he always did, but his emotions had caused him to misinterpret what it was telling him.

Up ahead he saw a helicopter rise above the trees, banking as it crested the hillside. Then he caught a flash of blue light in his rear-view mirror and saw the BMW pull out to overtake the Skoda that was sitting between them.

There was no question now. The blue light had been placed on the dashboard and the police car was closing on the Defender. Behind the Skoda he could see three more vehicles similarly identifying themselves and joining the chase. Instinct had told him what that BMW was, way back on the motorway, just as instinct had told him he was making a mistake a few hours before that. In both cases it was now far too late to do anything about it.

Christ.

He remembered about the gun, still secured in its hiding place under the chassis. There was no way of getting rid of it now.

Another glimpse in the mirror showed the BMW gaining. Something inside urged his right foot down, though it was laughable to think of trying to outrun the thing in this battered Land Rover; not on the open road anyway. The BMW had plenty more in reserve; it wasn't readying itself to overtake or cut him off, just closing in and watching to see what he would do. Behind it, two of the other cop cars were slewing across the tarmac to form a roadblock, stopping any following traffic from passing that point. Something was about to happen, and soon.

He stared forward again as the Defender approached a bend, the road curving steeply to the right, mirroring the course of the nearby river. The woodland was still a long way off.

He tried to recall whether there was a break in the hedgerow coming up, a route over fields that would take him into the forest. The BMW was close enough that if its driver read his intentions, he might well be able to floor the accelerator and cut the Defender off. Glen would need to be absolutely committed to it, prepared to risk flipping the vehicle by making the turn at the latest possible moment and the highest possible speed, and that's why it wasn't going to happen. He didn't see what hiding could achieve now, didn't really understand why he was still driving. Flight was an instinct, not a plan.

It was over, then, even before he rounded the bend and saw the two police cars nose to nose, a van tucked sideways behind them, blocking the road less than two hundred yards ahead. Not just cars, either: it was an Armed Response Unit, two men in position on either side of the roadblock.

Glen knew there were four Heckler & Koch G36 assault rifles pointed at his vehicle, capable of firing at a rate of seven hundred and fifty rounds a minute. Even if he slammed on the anchors for an emergency stop, the Defender would come to a standstill at a distance of roughly an eighth of the carbines' effective range.

He braked steadily and deliberately, the BMW and the Vectra behind it decelerating in response, maintaining the same distance.

The Defender came to rest roughly fifty yards from the roadblock, at which moment two more armed officers leapt from the Vauxhall, each packing HKs. There were now one hundred and eighty rounds primed to come at him at nine hundred metres per second. The response team from the roadblock began to move forward in formation, keeping him covered at all times, while the two behind took up kneeling positions on the ground.

Glen thought once more of the pistol stashed under the chassis, momentarily entertaining a grimly fatalistic thought. That would be giving them what they wanted, wouldn't it? That would end all of this: cut off the tentacles reaching out from his decades-old misdeeds to the people he loved. But would it protect them? Would it keep them safer than he could if he were still alive?

No.

Glen put his hands in the air, high and wide and highly visible. He heard a voice scream at him to get out of the vehicle and lie down on the ground. He climbed out of the Defender, felt hands upon him before he could even drop to his knees. His face rattled the tarmac, forced against it by a boot on the back of his neck while someone else wrenched his arms up his spine and slapped the cuffs on him.

'I am arresting you on suspicion of the murder of Stephen Fullerton. You do not have to say anything . . .'

He watched the erstwhile roadblock part slowly as the two police cars reversed away from each other in order to let the custody van drive through. Glen's head swam as they picked him up and dragged him towards it.

You do not have to say anything.

What was there to say? He was at their mercy now, and he wasn't expecting much of that.

There was only one way left for him to play this, a way he had learned a long and very dark time ago. He would not resist. He would let them have their way, let them dole out the damage until they themselves were tired from the blows. Then, once they were satisfied that he couldn't take any more, he would strike.

Elementary, My Dear (Crick and) Watson

Jasmine chose her spot carefully, making her approach as the subject was about to pay at the ticket machine in the lobby just off the parking bays on the fourth floor. It was risky to pick a location so close to the point when he would no longer be on foot, but she knew there would be fewer distractions in this enclosed space: for a couple of minutes she would be the only game in town.

She watched him from the corner of her eye as she approached, so that she could pretend to suddenly notice him, but she needn't have bothered concealing her gaze. His own was locked on to her tension-sprung tits.

'Oh my God. Oh my God. It's really you, isn't it? You're D-Blazer. I'm coming to see you tonight.'

'Seery 4 really it me, chicka.'

Jasmine could hear that number. She had also earned a 'chicka', D-Blazer's second-person coinage for female specimens of which he approved.

'Oh my God. How was the show last night? I bet it was *blazin'* hot. I tried to get tickets for both nights but the first one sold out *sooo* fast. God, listen to me wittering, I just can't believe I've actually *met* you.'

'Believe it, chicka. Iss realla dan real.'

'Blazin' real.'

'Madass real.'

She giggled and, she would have to admit, jiggled. The effect was like a hypnotist's pendulum. Christ, were men really like this?

She simpered and talked up his unlistenably dull 'music' in a bubbly and effusive way, sounding star-struck but flirty. If somebody had filmed it, she would not have recognised herself. It was sometimes disturbing to consider the ease with which she could inhabit a completely alien persona and yet remain outside it, observing the performance, with particular regard to the audience's response.

'I can't believe I'm asking this, but I'd totally leather myself later if I didn't while I've got the chance. It's . . . we're having this charity auction at college. I just had this pure mental idea. Can I have a couple of your hairs? I could auction an autograph but that would be so old, pure geriatric. Something that actually used to be *part* of D-Blazer would be totally for real.'

'Pure mental?' he asked. 'I love that. Is that proper Scottish?'

She could not and did not believe that he had never heard the phrase 'pure mental' before, and inferred from his pretence that she was doing well and he was looking for ways to please her.

'Totally. So can I really do it?'

'Do it, yeah. Do it pure mental.'

Jasmine whipped a pair of tweezers out of her bag and yanked a small cluster of hairs from his head before he could change his mind.

'Oh man, these are going to be worth so much,' she told him.

'I'm rockin' like the Midas boy, chicka. Even my hair turn to gold, you *know* it.'

'Mad-ass real. Oh, but hang on. Nobody's going to believe that this was 4 real yours. Tragedy. Tell you what, can you scribble something to verify it?'

'Yeah. D-Blazer hair come wif like a fishal certificate of offenticity.'

Jasmine produced a sheet of wrapping paper and tore off a scrap, then she attached the hairs to it using a piece of Sellotape. She already had a roll she'd picked up at Galt Linklater that morning, but she had bought another one in John Lewis, along with the wrapping paper, so it looked plausible for her to just happen to have this on her.

D-Blazer obligingly scribbled on the blank side of the wrapping paper: 'This is to certify that this is a sample of genuine D-Blazer barnet, seary 4 really.' He added a signature below.

'That's *undeniably* real,' she said approvingly.

'Realla dan,' he agreed.

'Thanks so much. I'll let you get on now. I must be costing you more parking time.'

'No, chill a mo, chicka. Tell me some totally Scottish stuff I can use tonight. What make the crowd mental here?'

Jasmine gave it some thought.

'Tell them they're bowfin',' she replied.

'Bowfin'?'

'Yeah. It means they're really cooking. They'll love it. Tell them they're absolutely bowfin'.'

Once D-Blazer was safely out of sight Martin followed Jasmine to her van and filmed her removing the hairs from the 'authentication certificate' before placing them in a clear plastic tube.

'One DNA sample, verified by the subject with his signature,' she said, dropping the tube and the signed scrap of wrapping paper into a padded envelope.

That was all it took: some live cells from the hair follicles would be enough to establish whether Darrien Hopscombe-Blanchard had 'never went near' Nikki Ainsworth, or whether he had '*hardly* never went near her'.

If the test was positive, little Danielle would still most likely grow up without her father, but at least she would be afforded some certainty as to who he was.

Jasmine had enjoyed no such privilege. Her mum, her relatives and her mum's friends had maintained a conspiracy of silence throughout her upbringing, leaving her only with indistinct impressions, like blurred shadows or the ragged outline where a figure had been crudely cut from a photograph.

Despite her efforts over the years, she had established very little for certain. She knew that he was dead, and that this fact was not mourned. She knew that he was a brutal individual and a remorselessly violent criminal. For a while she thought he might be a man called Glen Fallan, for he met all of those criteria, including the widespread belief that he was long deceased.

Fallan had put her straight with the bluntest and most painful of confessions: he was not her father, but rather the man who had killed him.

Despite her pleading and despite his avowed debt to her, Fallan would only tell her two more things: the first was that her father's first name was James; and the second was that he was more familiarly referred to as Jazz.

Maps and Legends

Dougie Abercorn was hovering outside Catherine's office like an anxious relative waiting to speak to the surgeon. His demeanour sported little of his accustomed calm or the unctuous self-assurance that frequently strayed the wrong side of oily.

She had been planning to give him a call at some point, preferably before interviewing the suspect, so this didn't just save her a job. It told her as much as she had expected to glean from what she had anticipated would be a typically guarded conversation. The main thing she had sought to establish was readable simply by him being here with questions for her, and by the look on his face.

He hadn't seen any straws in the wind. This was not in the script.

Abercorn was in charge of LOCUST, a unit set up specifically to investigate the activities of criminals such as Stevie Fullerton. The name derived from Organised Crime Unit Special Task Force, losing an acronym-inconvenient F and gaining an L to help it trip off the tongue. Unfortunately it tended to trip off the tongue amid outpourings of scorn and bile reflecting the speaker's distaste for its perceived ineffectualness and the underhand way it conducted its business. As well as ascribing a symbolic significance to the absence of Force, the abbreviation was widely referred to as standing for Letting Off Criminals Under Secret Trades. The term was supposed to conjure an unpleasant image that would reflect its implied target, but as an entity that gobbled up resources and seemed to contribute nothing but grief, it had proven an inadvertently apposite self-description.

It had often been said that LOCUST had a name longer than its list of convictions. Since certain events two summers ago this was no longer quite so true, but the fact that it had convicted almost as many cops as it had gangsters meant that Abercorn's team hadn't won themselves any more friends on the force.

Catherine negotiated her own uneasy and complex working relationship with him, rendered all the more delicate initially in having to overcome the awkward fact that she had been overlooked for Abercorn's job. To say it had stung was a colossal understatement, but while the injury to her professional pride remained, in the years that followed she had increasingly come to think that she had dodged a bullet.

'What's for you will no' go by you,' the redoubtable Moira Clark had counselled, when offering herself as a sounding board for Catherine's rage. The one-time Detective Chief Superintendent had been Catherine's boss and mentor in the early days of her CID career. She was still the person Catherine sought out when she needed reliable judgment, although getting a bit of face-time was harder now than before Moira hit her thirty, as she was on so many panels, committees and advisory bodies that it was laughable to talk about her having retired from the force.

Back then her words had sounded trite, real granny's-knee philosophy on a par with telling the newly jilted that there were plenty more fish in the sea. In time, however, Catherine had come to understand the truth of it, particularly in accepting that the post really wasn't for her. She had wanted it so badly, but the reason she wanted it was also the reason she didn't get it, and the reason she wasn't cut out for it.

'You hate these people, Cath,' Moira had told her. 'The Stevie Fullertons of this world, the Frankie Callahans, the Paddy Steels. Don't pretend otherwise, and don't kid yourself that it doesn't go unnoticed.'

She wouldn't deny it, and nor was she under any illusions about how obvious it was. Quite the opposite, in fact: the brass knew she had a strong record for bringing in bodies, and they were aware of her driving passion for the task. Perhaps naively, she had thought that this same passion would make her the ideal person to head LOCUST, but after Abercorn was promoted over her head, she came to appreciate that it would have been a match made in hell.

Abercorn was a political creature. When people said that, it was often a euphemism for somebody who was good at playing the system, impressing the right people and hell-bent on climbing the greasy pole. In his case, applied to organised crime in Glasgow, Catherine understood that it referred to qualities she simply did not possess. He could play a long and patient game, one riven with unpalatable compromises and least-worst solutions. He cultivated relationships in the underworld, knew that you sometimes had to let them get on with their business so that you could *understand* their business, map their infrastructure so that you could recognise it when it manifested itself elsewhere, on a larger scale. Abercorn could play one operator off against another, or keep the law off a particular dealer's back because his activities might lead to someone bigger further up the chain.

Catherine would have found it hard to let any of them get away with so much as a parking ticket. She didn't want to map their infrastructure; she only wanted to take a hammer to it.

It was an open secret that Abercorn had done deals with Stevie Fullerton. She knew this for a fact because she had been party to one of them. It had been a pragmatic necessity, a means to an end and she had found it utterly galling while Abercorn just viewed it as the price of doing business, merely another day at the office.

Abercorn was fly. He understood that Stevie thought this meant he had 'a polis in his pocket', and that his vanity prevented him from auditing what was going the other way. To Abercorn he had been part source and part useful idiot, but useful he had undeniably been.

Which was why Abercorn was now hopping around like a wean needing the toilet. He liked to give the impression that nothing that happened in the Glasgow underworld ever came as a huge surprise to those inside his unit – usually before explaining how they hadn't shared any of this intelligence in advance because it would have infringed upon aspects of another investigation. This, however, had blindsided LOCUST almost as much as it had blindsided Stevie.

'I was giving a talk at Tulliallan,' he said. 'I just got back. I came as soon as I heard.'

'You must be devastated. You were practically family.'

There was a time when Abercorn would have interpreted this as a dig rather than mere banter – mainly because it would have been intended as such – but their relationship had matured to one of mutual, if mutually cautious, respect.

'I won't be sending a wreath,' he replied, 'but I won't pretend this doesn't lob a very big rock into my millpond.'

Catherine opened the door to her office and beckoned him inside. It was looking unusually neat following a ruthless clear-out, and she felt oddly self-conscious about the impression this might give. She recalled her assumptions that Abercorn's office would be an antiseptic exemplar of anal neatness, and how they were subsequently blown away by seeing a chaotic firetrap that unambiguously conveyed how hard the guy must be working.

'Do you know what this might be about?' She wasn't expecting much of an answer. Abercorn was always so guarded with his information that sheer habit must occasionally prompt him to reply 'I'm not in a position to disclose that' when somebody asked him the time. Even if he knew, he wouldn't say, but sometimes the way he didn't say it could give her a few clues; not least as to whether there *was* something he was holding back. If he talked about not wishing to speculate, that meant he had a theory he wasn't prepared to share. If he gave her something that sounded solid, then the real story lay somewhere else and he wanted to keep her attention away from it.

'I don't have a fucking scoob,' he said, which was a new response and one she was inclined to take at face value, particularly in light of the fact that said face was looking unaccustomedly glaiket.

'Seriously,' he went on, 'our pants are round our ankles here. We picked up no chatter, no rumblings. Something this big, ordinarily you'd detect seismic activity in advance: a rise in tension, a sense on the street that something was brewing. So I have absolutely no idea who might have done this.'

Catherine had to pause for a beat as she considered whether this last remark had been in reference to who might be ultimately behind the shooting, but then she realised Abercorn was speaking literally when he said he had come as soon as he heard. Clearly he hadn't heard the half of it.

'We know whodunit,' she told him. 'We've got Glen Fallan in custody down in the cells.'

'Glen Fallan? As in . . .?'

'We've got three witnesses describing the shooter as driving a green Land Rover Defender. Between them, they gave us a plate that matched Fallan's vehicle. A couple of hours after the shooting a motorist down near the Borders phoned in a report of a green Defender driving erratically, almost running them off the road. We scrambled an ARU and intercepted Fallan near Hawick. The vehicle clipped a wall on the way out of the car wash, and I observed the damage myself at the scene. I'm informed there is a bash on the left-hand side of the Land Rover and white flecks of paint consistent with possible transference. We'll need to wait for Forensics to test the samples, but I'd put the house on them matching up.'

'Jesus,' Abercorn said, eyes wide.

'But better still, we've got tape. Traffic cameras filmed the Defender on Gallowhaugh Road just before the shooting, and on Shawburn Boulevard just after it. We can put him at the scene, time-stamped, unless he's got a great explanation for how come someone else was driving his motor at that point yet he was back behind the wheel by the time it reached the Borders. Believe me, the "who" is well covered. I was hoping you could help with the why.'

Abercorn puffed his cheeks, slightly over-selling the look of somebody who had been put on the spot. He was still reeling from her revelation, and looked like he was trying to buy himself time while he decided what it was politic to reveal.

'Glen Fallan? That's before my time. I know he and Fullerton had history, but I would have categorised it as *ancient* history.'

'History?' she scoffed. 'The rumour I heard was that Fullerton tried to kill him, and up until two years ago it was widely believed that he'd been successful. I also heard that this was in retaliation for Fallan disappearing Stevie's cousin. I don't think that kind of thing is ever ancient enough to be considered water under the bridge.'

'I'm just saying, it was more than twenty years ago, a wee bit before my shift started. I'm not sure I know much more than you do about that stuff, and when I say "know", I'm just talking about rumours I heard, same as you. Gangland mythology: a mixture of sensationalist gossip, wishful thinking, calculated misinformation, Chinese whispers and revisionist bravado. Twist that kaleidoscope for two decades and you're not going to see anything you can put much faith in.'

Catherine had to concede the point.

'I've got officers talking to Fullerton's people but I'm not expecting them to give us anything. I'm sure they'll all be baffled as to how anybody could possibly wish the slightest harm upon such a gentle spirit and widely respected pillar of the community.'

'All the while quietly making their own inquiries as to who might be behind the hit. That's assuming they don't know you've arrested Fallan, but even then, they'll be working on their conspiracy theories.'

'Fallan did used to work for Tony McGill,' she suggested.

'And so did Stevie Fullerton,' Abercorn replied. 'That's Glasgow bam politics for you: it can be labyrinthine in its complexity and yet staringly obvious at the same time. The further back you go, the murkier it gets, and this particular love triangle goes all the way back to the late eighties.'

As he spoke Catherine thought of the one element of this that definitely had its roots in a time two decades past, and revisited her unease at how it had resurfaced.

'There was a symbol daubed on Fullerton's forehead,' she told Abercorn. 'We'll be keeping it out of general circulation because – among other reasons – we don't know what the hell it means.'

She drew a version of it on a notepad, her hand trembling a little as she gripped the pen.

'You ever seen this before?'

67

Abercorn stared at it for a moment then shook his head, but he tore the page from the notepad and took it with him when he left. So that wasn't necessarily a no.

Born in a Stable

The hen had bled its last. She placed its body delicately on the block and took the bucket over to the drain at the foot of the thickest roan pipe, a few feet to the left of the kitchen windows. The grate was discoloured, stained by thousands of such outpourings as she was depositing now, going back at least a hundred years. She would rinse out the bucket and fill it with water, as hot as the kitchen tap could produce, then immerse the chicken for a couple of minutes for ease of plucking. No great sense of timeless ritual about that, though it had been going on for precisely as long. Just mess and tedium.

She hated the plucking far more than gutting the bird, had done ever since the yuck factor had abated through familiarity and repetition. There was a precision to removing the hen's insides contrasting unfavourably with the sense of chaos she felt tugging the clutches of feathers from its skin. The gutting process she regarded as good practice for when she would be a vet: the controlled incision, the separation of the organs, the delicate touch required in excising the liver and bile duct, the rupture of which could turn the bird an extremely unappetising shade of green.

No, she felt no more squeamish about the prospect of eviscerating a dead chicken than she had about killing it, though it brought a flush to her cheeks to remember the embarrassment it had caused her at school a few weeks back when she made the mistake of mentioning this domestic duty among a group of her classmates. Her words had barely left her lips when she realised they constituted another gift to the cliques who already viewed her with gleeful disdain: an awkward oddity, precipitated upon the perfection of their posh little circles from some stinky rural backwater. A farmer's daughter, would you believe, a filthy-fingered throwback to a primitive age, presumably existing without running water, television and hairspray.

As she saw the looks, first of revulsion and then of smirking delight, she understood sharply how what she considered mundane to the point of being a mere chore was so removed from the normal lives of her peers as to seem horrific to them, and she some kind of freak or monster. She got the very strong impression that they thought this was something she ought to feel ashamed about, in some cases because it was barbaric and in others because it marked her out as of a very low caste. They might *eat* chickens, but didn't generally mix with the kind of people who were paid to kill and prepare them. However, she didn't feel ashamed and she didn't feel monstrous. Instead she saw the rest of them as all the more cosseted, all the more bloody useless.

She had moved to the new school start of third year. Coming in two years late it was inevitable that she would find it cliquey, and as a private school it certainly didn't disappoint her expectation that some of her fellow pupils would be demonstrably snobby. However, she had endured cliqueyness and snobbery at her old school too, the difference being that at Laurel Row the criteria for denigration would not include being a virgin or getting straight As in her exams. The teaching was undeniably better than at Calderburn High, assisted in part by the lessons not being constantly interrupted by attention-seeking headbangers, and for that she would endure any amount of immature bitchiness if it served her academic ambitions.

Not that it didn't sting to have silly little girls who had never done a hand's turn think they could look down on her as their socioeconomic inferior because dear daddy was in banking rather than farming. It burned all the more, in fact, given that such snobbery was the very reason she needed to make the switch to Laurel Row if she wanted to get in to vet school.

You needed an A in both Higher physics and Higher biology in order to be accepted for veterinary medicine at Glasgow University, which was an understandable requirement; however, there was a subtle and nasty piece of social filtering at play in the further stipulation that these must be acquired at the same sitting. It looked innocent enough on paper, to anyone who didn't know that time-tabling commitments across Scottish comprehensives dictated that physics and biology be taught during the same periods. Schools didn't have the staff to offer all classes at all times, so there were certain standard conflicts and you had to choose: geography or history, French or art, physics or biology. Nor would the Glasgow Vet School accept an A for one in fifth year and the other in sixth: you had to get both at a single shot, and to do that you had to go private – by which means the Glasgow Vet School could keep out the scruff.

She recalled her parents railing against the inherent snobbery of it – an acridity to her dad's anger fuelled by the money he had paid out to vets over the years – but there was no principled stance from them once they realised how deeply she felt her vocation. The only principle they stood by was of striving to give their daughters the best chance in life that they could afford, and so they dug deep and paid the fees (not to mention bought the books and the jotters and the uniforms and the rail tickets and the bus fares) that allowed her to attend Laurel Row.

So for all their efforts and sacrifices, she was never going to moan about getting sent out to prepare a chicken on a cold Saturday morning while her pampered classmates were no doubt still tucked up in bed, and nor would she nag her sister about shirking her turn, Lisa, who had never made any fuss about the fact that she still went to plain old Calderburn.

She emerged from the kitchen with a bucket of scalding hot water and a thick pair of rubber gloves. It was as she made her way back towards the block, in the centre of her blood-painted rune, that she noticed the bottom half of one of the stable doors to be marginally ajar. It was the leftmost door of the three-stall barn, where her treasured Lysander was stabled. Lisa's horse Demetrius was in the centre, with the third stall empty since their mother, Hippolyta, had died the preceding November.

It was normal for the top section of a door to be left unlatched overnight, but never the bottom half. She strode to the block and immersed the bird, from which closer perspective she was able to observe that the door was in fact not ajar, but only appeared to be so because it was off its higher hinge and consequently hanging askew, the bottom-right corner resting against the ground an inch or so inside.

She felt something course through her, a wave of deepest dread disproportionate to this small jarring note that had precipitated it. Fear that anything should be wrong with Lysander, perhaps, heightened by a guilty anxiety that any such calamity had in some way been provoked by her occult indulgence over the morning's kill.

As she unlatched the top half of the door and pulled it out towards herself, she was further disquieted not to see Lysander's head emerge in typically immediate response. Then she heard a deep, wheezing sound from within, more like a discordant bray than his familiar whinny. She tugged impatiently at the bottom half of the door, feeling its true weight for the first time as it scraped against the ground. The rectangle of solid wood hauled the also-damaged bottom hinge further away from the frame and then collapsed forward, popping a screw and twisting the metalwork like an arm-wrestler in defeat.

The low morning sun penetrated where it could inside the stables. Before she entered, the light picked out debris on the floor: a shattered wooden saddle rack, a bridle hanger mangled like a cheap umbrella in a gale, haynets ripped and scattered, stirrups, bits and girths strewn amid broken fragments of salt lick. And beneath it all a dark glistening, turning from black to the colour of a days-old bruise where the sunlight struck it.

She tried to speak but no words came, only the sound of her heightened, gulping breath.

Lysander's head now responded to his awareness of her arrival, lifting meekly from where he lay on his side. His hindquarters were towards her, so at first she could see only the back of his head, that familiar silhouette of his ears and the poll between. Then as he turned his neck she saw that there was only a bloodied hole where his right eye should be.

Inside her, the desire to run and the desire to be with him fought a mighty duel. The latter prevailed and she swallowed back her horror, scrambling down to the floor alongside him. The straw-strewn stone was sticky with blood, and she felt herself crumble as she saw its many sources. There were gashes all over his body, one as much as a foot long in his girth, another so deep along his barrel that she could see the white of his ribs.

It was only as she asked herself what kind of beast could have got in and done this that it occurred to her to be scared.

The Silent Treatment

'Is his lawyer here?' Catherine asked, catching up to Laura in the corridor outside the interview room. She was impatient to see Fallan braced but was determined there would be absolutely no errors. Experience had warned her that the slam-dunk cases could be the most vulnerable to technical errors; they slipped in due to complacency. Every i would be dotted, every t crossed. She wanted this to be airtight.

'He hasn't asked for one,' Laura replied.

'He's refused?'

'No. He hasn't said anything.'

'At all,' added Beano. 'Not even to confirm his name.'

Catherine's nose picked up that horrible antiseptic smell that came off whatever they mopped the floors with down here. She never got used to it. It made her think of Dettol and sick, the way her bedroom smelled for about a month when she had whooping cough as a kid.

'It's catching,' she told them. 'I just spoke briefly to Zoe Vernon. She's been at the Old Croft Brasserie, talking to the folk Fullerton was with this morning. Emphasis on talking *to*. Very little coming back.'

'The Glasgow omertà,' sighed Laura, by way of acknowledging a complete lack of surprise.

'The silence of the bams,' said Beano. It was a familiar exchange.

'Zoe told me she threw in Fallan's name,' Catherine went on. 'She said there were practically exclamation marks appearing above their heads at that point, but when she asked what they knew about him they were claiming they'd never heard of the guy. Problem is, none of them want to admit to a relationship between themselves and Fallan or between Fallan and Fullerton because

74

of the implications. We're going to get nothing from these people, so let's make this count.'

'Do you want to take the lead, boss?' Laura asked.

'No. I won't be backseat driving either. I'm just going to watch.'

Beano held open the door and they filed in. Fallan glanced up briefly, taking in the personnel, then returned his focus to the Formica. Catherine noticed that she was the only one with whom he made even fleeting eye contact.

Beano and Laura took seats across the table from Fallan, while Catherine stood behind them, leaning against the wall with her arms folded.

In these confined quarters she was acutely conscious of his physical presence. She wondered how much damage he could inflict on the three of them, even with his hands cuffed, before back-up stormed in and wrestled him to the floor. It wasn't merely his size, as he was roughly the same height as Beano, but something deeper that her instincts were responding to. He wore a loose dark green T-shirt, faded and sweat-stained. He was wiry in places, muscular in others, his skin tanned to a dirty, weathered-looking shade. He clearly belonged outdoors in a wide open space, and she realised that this was what was piquing her danger sensors. He was a creature out of his natural environment, the sense of power and threat he gave off inversely proportional to the size of the cage that was constraining him; a cage that she and two colleagues were currently sharing.

She studied his posture as Laura began the interview. Catherine liked to think herself a practised reader of suspects' non-verbal communication, but in this respect Fallan was talking in riddles. There was a vigilance about him and yet a resignation too, like he knew he was in for the long haul but couldn't drop his guard. He seemed sullenly resentful and yet anxious, determined but not defiant.

This was as much as anybody was going to learn, as body language was the only one in which he was prepared to communicate. Laura was firing out the questions, Beano occasionally chipping in with a follow-up, but Fallan's lips remained completely still.

'How long have you known Stevie Fullerton?'

Silence.

'When did you last speak to him?'

Silence.

'The way I heard it, Stevie tried to have you killed way back when. Left you for dead. Revenge is a powerful motive. One that, in my experience, juries don't require a lot of imagination to get their heads around. Why did you decide to kill him after all these years? Could you just not quite let it go? Or did something change recently that made him a threat?'

Silence. Silence. Silence.

His expression remained impassive, never betraying any suggestion that they had laid a glove on him.

'We found a handgun stashed in a specially welded niche underneath your vehicle.'

Nothing.

'We've got three witnesses who saw the gunman drive into the car wash in a green Land Rover Defender, two of them quoting a licence plate registered to your name.'

Nothing.

'Our witnesses also describe the vehicle as scraping a white-painted slab on the edge of a wall while driving away after the shooting. We observed a scrape and evidence of transferred white paint on the side of your vehicle at exactly the level of the slab.'

Nothing.

Fine, Catherine thought. Give us the Sitting Bull routine if you like, but there could only be one reason why none of this was coming as a surprise.

He glanced up every so often, occasionally making eye contact with one of them, but it was random, sporadic, never in direct response to a remark, far less indicating that any particular words had struck home.

The closest they came was when Laura showed him a drawing of the sign daubed on Fullerton's head.

'What does this symbol mean to you?' she asked, turning it around and sliding it across the table towards him.

He stared at it for a moment and then looked up, but not at

76

Laura. His eyes went instead to Catherine. She wasn't sure what she saw in them: curiosity perhaps, and maybe nothing at all, just the projections of her imagination. Admittedly, she wasn't at her most coldly analytical right then. Her heart was thumping and she could hear her own pulse thundering in her ears. If his gaze had been greater than fleeting he would have gleaned more from her in that moment than they had prised from him throughout the entire interview.

The only time Fallan registered a response was when Laura showed him the stills. Time-stamped frames of your own car approaching and leaving a murder scene would be a hand to test anybody's poker face, but Fallan's was as good as she'd seen. There was no dismay, no oh-shit realisation, but there *was* something. It wasn't in his eyes, or even his expression, but in his body language. As he looked at those irrefutable images something resolved, something was implicitly understood.

'So as you can see,' Laura told him, 'given what we're holding, your silence isn't doing you any favours. You're covered from all sides. The sooner you surrender, the easier it will be on you.'

That was when Catherine belatedly deduced what was really going on here: why he was edgy but patient, impassive yet alert. It was like he was cornered, trapped behind enemy lines, but lying low, assessing his situation, getting the lie of the land. She realised that Fallan was the only one garnering any information right now, and that this interview was so far only benefiting him.

She suggested they all take a break. Laura didn't need to be asked twice.

Beano went off to get everybody some tea. Fallan hadn't responded to the offer, but Beano brought him one anyway, dropping a couple of sugar sachets and a swizzle stick next to the plastic cup.

Fallan reached for it as Catherine took a sip of her own, the fumes filling her nostrils as her eyes locked on to his fingers closing around the cup. There were marks on all of his knuckles, an ancient scarring that spoke silently and chillingly of brutality but that disturbed her in a manner far disproportionate even to this gruesomely suggestive spectacle.

It was the smell of the tea, the sense closest to memory working in combination with this sight to dredge up a recollection not merely of scent and vision, but of gut-wrenching feeling. She had experienced this recall two years previously, as he sat in front of her in a hotel dining room, having breakfast with the ingénue private investigator Jasmine Sharp. That had been when she realised who Fallan really was.

She felt her revulsion rising up, threatening to overwhelm her. She had to get out of the room.

'Let's leave our guest to drink his tea in peace,' she said, ordering an adjournment to the hall. 'His throat must be parched from all that talking.'

Catherine stepped out first, even the smell of whatever bogging gunk they used to mop the corridor a welcome breath after what the tea was making her feel inside the interview room.

'So how are you liking the strong silent type now?' she asked Laura. This was a dig at the fact that Laura developed a bit of a fascination with Fallan after they first met, having seen only the side he wanted her to: that of gallant protector of the young and vulnerable Ms Jasmine Sharp.

Laura wouldn't speak openly about it, but Catherine knew she had suffered at the hands of an abusive partner, which was partly why she left Lothian & Borders and transferred to Strathclyde. She hadn't been damaged enough to fall into the familiar trap of deluding herself that her own abuser would change, but Catherine suspected part of Laura desperately needed to believe in some noble masculine ideal, which Fallan had come to represent in her wounded mind.

Catherine surprised herself with the bitterness of her tone. She realised that she couldn't stand the idea that Laura – that anyone – didn't detest Fallan like she did. She wanted Laura to see what she saw when she looked at him and thus to share her hatred, but she couldn't do that without exposing what lay buried at its foundations.

'I don't understand why he's doing this,' Laura confessed in frustration. 'Denying nothing. Refuting nothing. What does it benefit him?'

'He knows he's fucked,' said Beano. 'Nothing he *can* say will help him, so he's happy to let us do all the running.'

'But we're piling the bricks on top of him and it's like he's just lying down to be buried.'

If this was confusing Laura, it was making Catherine wary. She had sussed that Fallan wasn't lying down to be buried. He was lying low, lying in wait, and she couldn't help wondering what for.

'Something about this feels off,' Laura said. 'Why does a guy like Fallan suddenly go rogue and reckless, after going to such efforts to put his past behind him?'

'Maybe it was never behind him,' Catherine suggested. 'Maybe he just got better at covering it up.'

'He was pretty good at covering it up back then,' Laura replied. 'He doesn't have a sheet.'

Beano looked incredulous, then swapped it for mild surprise that Laura could have overlooked the explanation.

'Ingrams or Fallan?' he asked.

'Neither,' Catherine admitted. 'But that says more about his resourcefulness than his morality. His father was the notorious Iain Fallan, a quite legendarily corrupt police officer. Glen Fallan grew up learning everything there is to know about how to stay off our radar.'

'Which is exactly my point,' Laura stressed. 'Why would a guy so accomplished at avoiding detection drive up in his own car and shoot somebody in front of three witnesses?'

'I couldn't say,' Catherine replied. 'But here's what I do know: you can be waiting twenty years for a guy like this to fuck up, so when he finally does you don't look a gift horse in the mouth. You're letting your judgment be skewed by the fact that Fallan helped us out a couple of years back, maybe because he was going through some kind of midlife crisis and decided he needed a bit of redemption. It doesn't work like that though, not for what this bastard's done in his time. If he's looking to pay his dues, there's a publicly funded programme for it: it's called the Scottish fucking Prison Service.'

Loyalties

Jasmine was putting some pasta on the boil when she heard her doorbell ring, jolting her into sudden self-consciousness as she sang along to Chvrches just a little too loud. She looked at the clock and noticed to her surprise that it was after nine, so this set her on guard a little. It hadn't been the light and tentative, sorry-to-disturb-you ring of a neighbour come to ask a favour or hand over a misdelivered letter, but the firm, insistent press of somebody who expected an answer.

Part of her was pleased to see that it was so late. She had been to the range and lost track of the hours, which had largely been the purpose of the exercise. Work had started at just after six, a surveillance with an early start because they had to be outside the subject's house in Pitlochry before the school run. She had clocked off at four and needed to occupy herself for the remainder of the day. A bout of her new favourite pastime had delivered.

She had first tried air-rifle shooting while investigating a missing person case, she and Fallan tracking down a former police marksman to his current job running the field sports centre attached to a big hotel in the Borders. Fallan and the instructor had remarked that she was a natural, and she assumed they were winding her up until she saw the paper targets they had retrieved. She had enjoyed the experience more than she could possibly have anticipated, and often found herself thinking back to it, remembering the feel of the weapon in her hands and the sensation of the kick against her shoulder. She was curious to know whether her results had merely been beginner's luck, so when she overheard one of the Galt Linklater guys talking about a range of which he was a member out near East Kilbride, she had asked if she could come along as a guest.

Now she was a member herself, as well as the slightly

self-conscious and enduringly dubious (as opposed to proud) owner of two different rifles. The gas gun was more accurate because there was no recoil and so she could maintain her stance between shots, but now and again she went back to the spring-powered rifle because it was the type she had first used, and because she enjoyed the rhythm and the ritual: break, prime, load and fire.

Shooting had become an invaluable source of peace, calm and relaxation. When she was on the range she could reduce her world to an impregnable little vortex. There was only the target, the cross-hairs, her finger, her breathing, her pulse. Time became elastic in the moments before she squeezed the trigger; seconds stretched and minutes compressed. Sometimes she could reach for the next pellet and find the tin empty, discovering that two hours had just dissolved.

Jasmine put her front door on the chain, remembering, as she always did, Glen Fallan asking how likely it was that she'd be attacked by an angry Girl Guide: this being in his estimation the upper limit of the potential intruder this security measure was capable of stopping. She opened the door just a little and spied a female figure in trainers, three-quarter-length lycra running trousers and a T-shirt. Her flushed face was familiar but out of place, so it took Jasmine a moment to recognise her. The authoritative doorbell ring should have helped, she realised.

'Hi, Jasmine. Sorry to trouble you so late. I'm Laura Geddes, remember? I work with Catherine McLeod. Do you mind if I come in?'

'No, sure.'

Jasmine undid the chain and led Laura inside to the kitchen, doubly curious as to the nature of this visit given the hour and the dress code.

'Can I get you something to drink?'

'Just some tap water would be great.'

Good answer, Jasmine thought. Apart from milk for tea she was down to one can of Irn-Bru and in pressing need of a trip to the supermarket.

Laura gulped down half a pint and accepted a refill before taking a seat at the kitchen table. She had tiny beads of moisture on her forehead and arms, a fresh smell of the outdoors about her. It reminded Jasmine uncomfortably of how her mum used to smell when she came home on those occasions Jasmine was off school sick and had been indoors, laid up in bed all day.

Laura's hair was different, which was another reason Jasmine had struggled to place her. It was shorter and she had dyed it, resulting in a blonde bob that was at odds with Jasmine's residual mental image of her. It made her seem a little brighter, more open. Laura had often given Jasmine the impression she was hiding behind her hair when it fell across her face. She had seemed skittish rather than shy, and a little mirthless. For all that, she always seemed more approachable than her boss, but this wasn't saying much.

Catherine McLeod was a Detective Superintendent, but in Jasmine's mind her official rank was Queen Crabbit Cow. If Jasmine tried on bitch every so often to see how it felt, then McLeod must have had it spliced into her genes. She didn't know what she had ever done to piss the woman off, but Jasmine always got as much warmth from her as a dying penguin's last fart. It seemed particularly unfair given that Jasmine's contributions had helped her close two major cases; but rather than gratitude, this only seemed to inspire resentment. Admittedly there was the small matter, in one of those cases, of Jasmine seriously perverting the course of justice, but McLeod didn't know about this, so that couldn't be the reason she was so down on her.

It wasn't about Jasmine though, she knew: it was Fallan she hated. Any time Jasmine had been in McLeod's company, the big man had been part of the deal. Jasmine had thus fielded her share of suspicion and disapproval in accordance with McLeod's 'fly with the crows, get shot with the crows' principle.

As Laura sat at Jasmine's table, pasta bubbling on the cooker just behind her, she wasn't radiating hostility or attempting to intimidate; Jasmine got the impression she was here to share, but there still seemed something about her that was closed off, defensive and even afraid. Laura might let you be her ally but she wouldn't let you be her friend.

'I've been trying to get you on your phone, but you weren't answering. I was out for a run and my route took me over this way, so I thought I'd just see if you were home.'

Jasmine didn't remember ignoring any calls or seeing that she had missed any. She wondered whether Laura had the right number for her; she certainly had the right address. She hadn't previously given thought to the fact that McLeod and her people knew where she lived, but they were the polis, after all.

'What can I do for you?'

Laura took another gulp of water and wiped her brow with her forearm. The tiny beads of sweat were starting to pool and run in the warmth of the kitchen.

'There was a murder yesterday. I don't know if you heard about it.'

Jasmine had seen something on the front page of someone else's *Daily Record*, but hadn't paid it much heed other than to connect it to the traffic congestion Andy Smith had warned about.

'Fleetingly. Over in Shawburn?'

'That's right. It was a guy called Stevie Fullerton.'

Laura stared at her a moment. Jasmine felt she was being scrutinised to gauge any possible reaction.

'I've got an alibi.'

'Do you know who he was?'

She vaguely remembered the name. It had been one of many thrown accusatorily at Fallan by McLeod the first time she met her, the policewoman gatecrashing their breakfast when Jasmine was lying low at a city-centre hotel. Whether Fullerton had been a criminal associate of Fallan's or a gangland rival, she couldn't remember. Even from the context it had been clear McLeod was digging up ancient history.

'Gangster,' Jasmine answered. 'Drug dealer. General malefactor. What do I win?'

Laura didn't appear to be in the mood for banter, though to be honest Jasmine couldn't remember there ever being a time when she was.

'He was shot four times in the chest at a car wash. Several

83

witnesses plus CCTV gave us the perpetrator's licence plate and vehicle, which did *not* turn out to be stolen. We apprehended the suspect and have him in custody.'

'Congrats. Sounds like a quick result. What does it have to do with me?'

'The suspect is Glen Fallan.'

Jasmine didn't have a snappy comeback for that.

The mere mention of his name always provoked a confused mix of emotions. This was the man who had confessed to killing the father she'd never met; yet even after that confession she had invited him into her flat again. On more than one occasion he had sat where Laura was now, and while he was at her table Jasmine had felt safer than at any time since the loss of her mother.

Perhaps unable to immediately process the enormity of what she had been told, among her first instinctive responses was a laughably petty disappointment that he had been in town without telling her.

'He hasn't been in touch with me,' she said, growing awkward in the lengthening silence.

'We know. He hasn't been in touch with anybody. Since his arrest he's made no phone calls, refused legal assistance and is answering no questions.'

The same instinct caused Jasmine to wonder why he hadn't got in touch to say he was in trouble. Then she wondered what gave her any reason to think that he would.

'Did you know he kept a gun concealed in his car?'

'I take it we're off the record right now?'

Laura nodded.

'I wouldn't be here talking to you if he didn't keep a gun in his car. He saved my life more than once. I know the guy's got a past, but I thought that's what it was: the past. I can't believe he would just shoot some gangster, though. Not unless it was self-defence.'

'It wasn't. It was execution-style, while the guy's view was blanked out by foam on his windscreen.'

Jasmine had no response to this.

On the hob, the pasta was threatening to boil over. She turned down the gas a notch, unsure if she was even hungry any more.

'Do you know what it was about?' Jasmine asked.

'No. Nobody's talking. Not Fallan and not Fullerton's people. Nobody will tell us anything. That's why I'm here. I was hoping you might be able to help.'

'I don't know anything about Fallan's history. He knew my mum way back when, but neither of them was ever forthcoming about those days.'

'Maybe the time has come for you to do some digging, then. There's questions you can ask that we can't. People who might speak to you who would never talk us.'

'So you're asking me to do your job for you and play my part in helping send Fallan to jail?'

'We can do that easily enough without your help, Jasmine. Catherine McLeod thinks all her Christmases have come at once: she's got Stevie Fullerton on a slab and Glen Fallan on a plate. It's just that, to me, there's something I can't place, something about this that feels a little . . . off.'

'It must feel *very* off for you to be telling tales out of school like this.'

Laura's expression darkened, a hunted look coming over her, as though she may have misjudged her circumstances.

'I came here in the strictest confidence,' she said firmly. 'I hope that's understood. I don't need to tell you how motivated Catherine is about this.'

'Like a dog with two dicks, I'm guessing.'

'Eating Winalot laced with Viagra. But that's why I'm concerned, in case there's an angle we might be missing. Fallan isn't helping himself, and we can only respond to what's in front of us, so if there's more to this than meets the eye you might be the only person in a position to look for it.'

The Penitent

Catherine pulled her car into the driveway and brought it to a stop, then spent a few moments in silence, performing a little ritual that had become her custom before entering her home. She had read about a mental exercise carried out by certain tennis players in order to prevent self-recrimination over a poor last point seeping into their thought processes and undermining their efforts for the next. They would walk away from the baseline and cross an imaginary barrier before turning around. When they re-crossed the barrier, they left behind whatever had gone before and thought only of the point to be played.

Catherine's mental exercise was her way of leaving the job in the car, and not taking it with her into the house. She would allow herself a little while to perform a quick audit in her head, creating a list of the things that needed to be addressed *only when she got back into the car*, as there was nothing constructive she could do in between times. During this brief tally she would also force herself to acknowledge what was going well or had been resolved, rather than merely fretting over her to-do list and picking at the scabs of problems.

Drew always said she should never be afraid to share her worries, to unload on him when she needed a sounding board, but she had become increasingly dubious as to whether this ever achieved any kind of catharsis. She seldom felt any better afterwards, and was conscious of having polluted their home, like she had been ankle deep in blood and shit then come home and tramped it through the carpet.

It was Drew's way of trying to be supportive and understanding, but it was also what he hoped was a bulwark against her periodic descents into a state of emotional isolation – *'this dark place you go'* – that had proven mutually wounding in the past.

'*You're angry on the road to that place and you're unreachable when you get there,*' Drew once put it. '*But what's hardest is you're numb for days afterwards.*'

He thought if she could let out a little at a time it would stop the build-up of pressure, but what he didn't understand was that it wasn't the pressure of the job that led her there. It was the job that helped keep her away from it.

The job wasn't easy, it exposed her to some very horrible things, but she knew she needed it. What she didn't need was its effluent leaking into her family's home, so she had taken steps to prevent that.

Sometimes she was self-conscious about Drew seeing her through the window, just sitting there with the engine running, as she had never told him about this. She had an excuse prepared – she would say she was listening to the end of something on the radio – but either he'd never noticed or simply had never been curious enough to ask.

She gave herself a little longer than usual on this occasion, aware she was particularly tense. Her audit told her this was not warranted. Things had started very nicely for her, and largely gone well. Murder on the streets was nothing to feel happy about, but when it was your job to deal with it you developed your own scale for measuring these things, and Fullerton's death was definitely at the sunnier end of the spectrum. So she had one killer dead and another one dead to rights. By any reasonable reckoning, this had been a good day.

So why did she feel like the ground was about to open up?

She turned off the engine. That was the symbolic moment when her working day ended, her line on the tennis court, but even as she did so, she realised that it was another symbol that was disquieting her thoughts. Why it had reappeared, she didn't know, but what it represented could not be wiped from memory by crossing an imaginary line.

The house sounded unusually quiet as she strode inside and hung up her coat. She could hear the strains of Frightened Rabbit from the kitchen and could smell the curry Drew was cooking, but there was no sound of TV or video games from the living room, nor the attendant shrieks of laughter, excitement or dispute. She wondered if there had been a banning-worthy incident, and if so, knew she would need to hear Drew's account of it so that she was on message with the official coalition policy before Duncan and Fraser started lobbying her.

She went upstairs to the loo, then popped her head around the door of Fraser's bedroom, anxious to make sure everything was okay. He was kneeling on the carpet, poised over the plastic cage and miniature wrestling figures that he'd got for his birthday, staging some elaborate scene and augmenting it with his own sound effects and American-accented commentary. He was so rapt that he failed to notice her, so she withdrew again and had a quick glance inside his big brother's room, which was empty.

She assumed he would be sitting in the kitchen, probably reading, but she found Drew in there alone. She greeted him with a kiss, anticipating that as they were alone this would probably extend to him squeezing her bum as a nod to what happened that morning, with the implication that he was no longer quite so content for it to remain unreciprocated.

There was no grope though, and the kiss was brief. Something was up.

'Everything okay?' she asked. 'Where's Duncan?'

He looked at her with an oddly knowing expression and said, 'In the attic. Reading.'

It took her a moment to catch up to the significance of this, but when she did, Drew's affirmative nod told her he could read her progress.

'Pop-up tent?' she asked.

'Yes.'

When Duncan was four, he had flooded the bathroom while playing with a deep-sea diver doll; or, more accurately, had started the tap running and put in the plug then gone off to get a toy shark and, during his search for this item, found something else to play with and forgotten entirely about the bath. Drew had been downstairs in the kitchen feeding Fraser his lunch, and was only alerted to the situation when water began to drip through the ceiling and onto the cooker. When Catherine came home from work that evening she found Duncan in the spare bedroom in the attic, looking through picture books inside his pop-up tent. He had taken himself away up there as a kind of retreat, a confused four-year-old's act of contrition.

In the years following he had similarly removed himself whenever he knew he had seriously screwed up. It forced Catherine to seek him out and climb inside the little tent in order to speak to him. She came to realise it was his way of saying sorry and acknowledging his fault when he didn't have the words or the strength to articulate his feelings, or even to broach the subject.

It hadn't happened in a couple of years, so she assumed he had grown out of it. These days he was mature enough to make his apologies or, just as often, argue his case. Clearly, this was a biggie.

'What happened?'

'He got into a fight at school.'

Catherine felt something clench inside her, and tried to bring her rational mind to bear upon rampant physiological instinct. Keep it in proportion, she told herself: he was upstairs reading, not in casualty, and Drew looked more worried about her reaction than about Duncan's welfare.

'I got a call just before I went to pick the boys up. Mrs Gardine asking if I could nip into the office for five minutes when I came round to the school. She was very good about it. She was discreet and professional, but in not so many words let me know she didn't believe Duncan was the instigator, and that the other boy has previous. He's a P7 and apparently no stranger to the inside of Mrs Gardine's office.'

'So how come Duncan's upstairs eating crow in his pop-up tent?'

Drew's face bore an awkward mixture of discomfort, regret and incredulity.

'Because the P7 got second prize.'

If there was also any paternal pride in there, he knew to keep it hidden, but Catherine couldn't detect a trace. Mostly there was just concern and confusion, as if Mrs Gardine had told him Duncan had started speaking in tongues.

'Duncan burst his nose. The proverbial blood and snotters

everywhere: mostly blood. He's very freaked out. I can't get him to talk about it. Ate his tea in silence then took off up the stairs.'

'You seem a bit freaked out yourself,' she observed.

'I'm astonished. He never got it from me. I couldn't fight sleep as a wean.'

Catherine made her way up to the attic conversion and found the pop-up tent erected in the same corner as all those times before. Weird how kids' minds worked: two or three years must be an eternity to them, and yet these fine details came back like they'd been placed in secure storage.

He was taking up a lot more of the tent than last time, and there was little chance they would both fit in there now. She managed to draw him out and they sat together on the end of the spare bed. It took him a while to start talking, but she coaxed him along eventually.

'He was trying to get me to fight, saying he was going to batter me worse if I didn't fight him,' Duncan told her. 'At first I was just scared. Then he hit me in the face. He kept slapping me, and he kept saying: "Ye gaunny dae anythin', ye gaunny dae anythin'." I thought I was going to cry. I hoped that would make him leave me alone, and it did, kind of. He started laughing in my face, going: "Ha ha, check him greetin'."

'Then I don't know what happened. It was like a volcano inside me. It was like being sick: it's coming and you can't stop it, it just has to come out. I'm really sorry.'

With that he broke down and buried his face in Catherine's chest, sobbing quietly. It took her a lot of strength not to join him. He was eleven now, and these days she could see in him the rangy teenager he would soon become, but right then she could more clearly see the four-year-old who flooded the bathroom.

This was the hardest stuff, the heart of all maternal fears. You couldn't be there to protect them from all the things that might happen to them, and nor could you protect them from the things they might do.

The things that could not be undone.

The Last Kindness (i)

She stood outside the stables waiting for her dad to come back out, hugging herself, suddenly feeling the morning's cold seep right into her bones. Lysander made that distressed braying noise somewhere within, weaker this time.

Her dad emerged, his face grey, older somehow than when he entered. He seemed reluctant to look directly at her, started to speak, abandoned the attempt, let his mouth emit a sigh instead, carried inside a wispy jet of steam. Then something inside him became taut, and he met her expectant gaze.

'Demetrius is okay,' he said.

She waited for him to continue, then when he did not she made her prompt in desperation. 'Is there anything we can do for Ly?'

He said nothing, but gave a curt nod and proceeded towards the house.

She enjoyed a moment's hope as she assumed that he was going inside to call the vet, but a moment was all it lasted. She wasn't a silly little girl who believed the grown-ups could make anything all better. She had seen her dad's face as he emerged from the stables, and she had seen what lay within.

Her dad strode out of the back door again, this time with a black canvas carrying harness slung over his shoulder. Lisa appeared behind him, a mixture of concern and confusion on her face. He turned around and told her to stay inside, a sternness to his voice that rooted her in the doorway like there was a forcefield in front of it. She would have many questions, but knew that the answers were ones she would not want to hear.

She felt the tears well up in anticipation of the moment he marched past her, which would mark the point at which she had no role but to mourn. Instead, however, he stopped beside her and unwrapped the rifle from its covering.

'You should do this.'

She shook her head.

'It won't just be giving vaccinations and delivering foals,' he said, softly enough for it to sound tender, firmly enough for her to understand that he expected her to comply.

'I can't,' she said. 'Not Ly.'

Her dad took her chin in his right hand, as always a tenderness to his touch despite the rough skin of his calloused farmer's fingers.

'This is the last kindness anyone can give him. That's why you should be the one.'

She looked up into his eyes, saw reflected her pain, her fear, her love, and she understood. She nodded and reached for the rifle.

It was a P14, the one with which her dad had taught her to shoot, and the same one her dad had been taught to shoot with by her grandfather. She had held it a dozen times, but it never felt so heavy, so solid, the rounds so long and formidable. As she slid the bolt and placed one in the breach she eyed the taper of the bullet's point and thought of it as a hypodermic needle.

She took a breath of cold air and stepped inside. Lysander's head did not turn, his mercy to her ahead of her mercy to him. She could not look again into that black, ragged hole, and she wanted even less to look into his remaining scared and helpless eye.

She shouldered the butt, levelled the muzzle around two feet from the back of his head and thumbed off the safety catch, but for a moment it was as though there was a second safety catch preventing the trigger from moving. She could feel the heat of his body, hear his laboured breathing, and could not bring herself to pull back her index finger. Then he made that pitiable braying sound again and she knew what was her duty, what mercy she must dispense: the ministration of this last kindness. She swallowed back a sob and steadied her breathing, removing herself to the routine of how she had been trained to take each shot and, detached in the mechanics of technique, she pulled the trigger.

92

Missed Calls

Jasmine stood at her living room window and watched Laura jog away down the street into the darkness, wondering as she stared at the retreating figure what her visit was really all about. She recalled that Laura had always shown an interest in Fallan, never sharing her boss's conviction that he was only playing nice to further some darker hidden purpose. Nonetheless, Jasmine also knew that she was fiercely loyal to McLeod, so if she was going off the reservation like this it was more likely to be motivated by a desire to prevent her boss from making a mistake. Either way, it suggested there was something about this apparently simple case that was making her wary.

Jasmine sat down to her plate of pasta, forcing herself to eat despite her diminishing appetite. If nothing else, a full stomach might help her sleep, something that threatened to present a struggle now that her brain had all this to process. She had placed her laptop on the table in front of her plate, and as she waited for it to boot up she asked herself what she truly knew about Glen Fallan.

By his own confession he had been a gangland enforcer and hitman. She had heard him described as an ice-cold killer, 'like the ice doesn't feel anything when it freezes you to death'. Jasmine had witnessed first-hand the fear he inspired when he allowed some two-bit chancer to recognise him, in order that the guy would be sufficiently intimidated as to cough up some vital information. There was no question what kind of man Glen Fallan had once been. But having buried that man for two decades and gone to such lengths to become someone different, why would he let himself be drawn back into that world?

After that same gatecrashed breakfast, and on all of the occasions on which their paths had crossed since, he had shown no sign of reciprocating McLeod's hatred. Fallan was instinctively untrusting of cops – sometimes downright hostile – but his conduct towards McLeod in particular was measured and deferential. One might even say contrite.

'She recognised me,' he told Jasmine, though he confessed he couldn't remember from where; that, in fact, reflected the enormity of his guilt. 'I hurt so many people . . . McLeod could have been somebody hiding behind her crying mother while I threatened her father. One of the countless witnesses you don't see because they're never going to tell anybody.'

He had murdered Jasmine's father, and yet even in the final stages of her cancer Jasmine's mum had engaged her cousin Jim to track Fallan down so that she could see him again before the end. Everyone else assumed he was dead, but her mum knew otherwise; Fallan had been sending her money for twenty years. When Jasmine found out and confronted him about it, he had explained that it was part of his penance for what he had done. However, Jasmine couldn't imagine her mum accepting a penny, let alone seeking a deathbed visit, if that was all he was to her.

Fallan would only say that they were 'good friends in very bad times'. This suggested that even back then there must have been a secret side to him that contradicted what everyone else knew.

Either that, or a secret side to her mother.

She keyed in a search on the Fullerton killing and her eye was drawn to a headline two results down, below the BBC report. It took her to the *Daily Record* website.

MANY BLOODY RETURNS

SLAIN gangland supremo Stevie Fullerton was gunned down on his BIRTHDAY, it emerged today. The feared crime boss had turned forty-nine on the very morning he was shot dead at a Shawburn car wash.

A tube of penne tumbled from Jasmine's fork, missed the side of her plate and rolled across the table, leaving a thin trail of sauce.

The man Glen Fallan had shot, a man with whom he had a history going back more than twenty years, had been born on precisely the same day as Jasmine's mother. The significance of this remained uncertain, but she sincerely doubted it could be entirely coincidental.

If there's more to this than meets the eye . . .

As she cleared away her plate and placed Laura's empty glass next to the sink she considered how curious it had felt that the detective should come by in person while out on a run. Then she remembered Laura mentioning having failed to get through to Jasmine's mobile.

Jasmine retrieved the phone from her pocket and verified, as she had thought, that there were no missed calls. In fact, now she came to think of it, she had received no calls whatsoever today or the day before, an extremely unusual state of affairs that prompted her to recall Harry Deacon's confusion over his phone not recognising her number.

As an experiment, she called her landline using the mobile, then dialled 1471 to check the incoming number.

It wasn't hers.

With a horrible surging sensation she thought of the neddy guy at the Twin Atlantic concert, who had been scoping her down in the stalls, then had just happened to appear upstairs as she exited the circle.

She'd been too out of it to notice at the time, but in retrospect certain aspects of his manner didn't add up. He hadn't once asked her what was wrong: the guy had found her crying and played the good Samaritan in escorting her outside, but apart from inquiring very generally whether she was 'okay', he had not once asked who or what had upset her. Then, once he had given her the drink, he had seemed impatient to get away, no longer the concerned passerby. She had assumed it was because he was missing the show, but he had stayed outside when she said she was going back in. He probably took off the moment she was out of sight.

She quickly slid the backing off the phone and removed the battery to get a look at the sim. It wasn't hers. She'd had the same one for years, and her provider's logo had changed recently. This card bore the new design.

Christ. The sleekit, opportunist wee bastard. But why wouldn't he just steal the actual phone? she wondered.

Because it would get reported, as she was about to do now. This way, he had enjoyed a couple of days' grace to do whatever he wanted with her sim: selling it off to hackers to be cloned, running up all kinds of bills; she shuddered to think. The damage could be in the thousands.

She phoned up her network provider, hoping they had a human being manning their emergency line at this time of night, and distantly wondering whether she could remember saying yes to whatever insurance package they had offered to cover against this kind of fraud.

Probably not.

She could picture the digits spinning like a fruit machine on her imaginary bill as she was bounced around the system, held in various queues and asked the same security questions over and over again. She must have explained her predicament four times, which only served to reinforce her fear that it was unprecedented and therefore uniquely disastrous in a way that would void her cover even if it turned out she had opted to take it.

Eventually she was put through to somebody who was able to tell her what usage was showing up on her account.

'Are you sure the card has been stolen?' asked the girl at the other end of the line, which would have invited no end of acidly sarcastic replies had Jasmine not been in abject need of her cooperation. 'It's just that there's been very little outgoing activity. Just one text and one phone call, both to the same number.'

Relief and confused curiosity flooded through Jasmine in equal measure as she wrote down the number and the times of both the text message and the call. The digits meant nothing to her, but the fact that they had been dialled by someone else, on a different handset, gave her a horribly creepy feeling, like knowing a stranger had been inside her flat while she was out, even if it turned out he had only stolen a paper clip.

As a kid she had learned all of her home phone numbers, and those of her best friends, committing them so indelibly to memory that she could still rhyme off some of them, years after she last had reason to dial them. By contrast, these days there were people she phoned several times a week whose actual numbers she had only ever seen as she copied them across from a text message to a contact file.

Hesitantly, she began dialling the number on her mobile, wondering how she would phrase the question if somebody answered. She didn't get that far, however. Before she had entered all of the digits, her phone was suggesting an autocomplete, ready to let her skip the last few keystrokes.

She stared at the device like it was an alien artefact, double-checking against what the girl had just dictated, but there was no mistake. Before and after the shooting of Stevie Fullerton yesterday morning, somebody had been using her phone number to contact Glen Fallan.

Unwarranted Sympathy

Catherine had been inside Fullerton's house once before, in the company of Dougie Abercorn two years back. Just like now, Stevie hadn't been around, though on that occasion he had absented himself voluntarily.

It felt empty, and not just through being bereft of its owner. She had been in attendance plenty of times as officers tramped through a murder victim's property, and developed a poignant sense of who had lived there, of the presence that had been erased. Fullerton's place lacked any kind of personal stamp, its material opulence expressing nothing other than wealth. It was gaudy but soulless, parts of it suggesting an attempt to recreate a Las Vegas hotel suite in the unlikely environment of Uddingston; others like a transplanted section of a furniture showroom. And like a hotel suite or a shop display, it felt transient, a place to be passed through, not lived in.

There was a superabundance of marble and glass brick, galaxies of inset lighting overhead, a dining suite that looked like it had never hosted a meal and a ludicrous bathroom boasting Roman pillars either side of a staircase leading up to a Jacuzzi. All of it was expensive, and it could be described as merely excessive rather than outright tasteless; tasteless would at least have had a little more warmth.

But maybe this was partly an effect of the welcome.

Fullerton's wife, Sheila, was monitoring proceedings with a simmering combination of suspicion and resentment, chaperoned by her late husband's cousin and 'business associate' David Donnelly, known to his pals as Doke.

'You know, Stevie was the victim here, no' the fuckin' accused,' Donnelly had grunted when Catherine showed them the warrant to search the premises.

They would find nothing connected to criminal activity, just the same as if they had searched the place last week. These guys worked hard to put layers of deniability between themselves and their activities. Doke knew Catherine understood this, which was why he was viewing what he anticipated as a futile search as harassment.

It wasn't, though. It was procedure. They were trying to establish a motive for why Fullerton had been killed, which was why there was also a team searching Fallan's place in Northumberland.

Sheila Fullerton was about five-two in heels and looked like she'd weigh six stone soaking wet. She reminded Catherine of a girl at school, of whom she had made the mistake of thinking mousy simply because she was slight. The girl had been all the more ferocious in compensation for her stature, and Catherine bet she was a pushover compared to Sheila here.

She was dressed like she was twenty years younger, in a short black lycra skirt and low-cut black top matching her dyed jet-black hair. Her gaunt face was hard-set, a sharp angularity to it that struck Catherine uncharitably as rat-like, though this impression wasn't helped by the hostility she was giving off like fumes rising from petrol. If she was feeling anything more conventionally associated with the bereaved, such as pain or sadness, then she *wasnae lettin' the fuckin' polis see it.*

She stood in her kitchen, leaning against the sink, arms folded, searing her uninvited guests through eyes narrowed to slits.

'Well seeing you're all sneaking about here now that he's gone,' she said to Catherine, her voice dry and hoarse. 'There's none of you would have had the nerve to look him in the eye. Accused him of all sorts but you never pinned anything on him. Now you can write your own version, make up whatever you like, can't you?'

It sounded like it was intended as a rhetorical question, and Catherine guessed she was expected to tolerate it or to ignore it. Perhaps she should have.

'I'm sorry, I'm not sure I follow. I was confused by the Glasgow gangster double-think: on the one hand you want to make out Stevie never did anything wrong, and yet at the same time you're boasting about how badass he was. Which is it to be?'

Catherine saw a shudder pass through Sheila, an anger seizing her so tightly for a few seconds that her breathing became audible across the kitchen. It looked like a retort was thought better of, and when she did speak again her voice was softer, measured, but close to breaking.

'I know your type, hen,' she said. 'You thought he was shite. You think *I'm* shite. Well, let me put you straight. He might have . . . He was . . .'

Now her voice did fail her, breaking down for a moment, and when it returned it was barely above a whisper.

'He was *my husband*.'

She said it as an appeal to Catherine for compassion, for her to see her as a woman and understand what she had lost.

In that moment Catherine caught a glimpse of herself and didn't like what she saw. She felt shame upon her cheeks and looked at the floor, wondering how this hate could so diminish her humanity.

When she looked up again she offered Sheila a different face.

'I'm sorry.'

Tears came now from those narrow, angry eyes. The façade was cracked. She grudged Catherine seeing it, but she was helpless and she knew it. Catherine offered her a tissue, which she accepted.

'He was my husband. I loved him. And now he's dead.'

Just for a moment they were what they should have been: a widow recently bereaved and a police woman offering consolation and support. But just for a moment was as long as it lasted.

'We want to find out why that happened,' Catherine said softly, but she could see the barricades were already going back up.

'Why don't you ask Glen Fallan?' Sheila replied acidly. 'I hear that's who you've pulled in.'

'We already did. He's not been very talkative.'

'No, he never was.'

'Did your husband mention Fallan recently? Did he have any reason to believe he was under threat?'

Sheila's face was stone-set once more. She was back in character.

'I'm not letting you bastards use this to dig up shite about Stevie.

If you want to know why it happened, then that's for you to ask *other* people.'

'Other people are where we go next, but here's where we have to start. For instance, your husband's mobile phone was missing when we found him. We think the gunman took it, though we haven't found it yet. We need the account details so we can get in touch with his provider and trace who he's been in contact with.'

Catherine knew that they could get this anyway, indeed might already have it, but if she could get Sheila to volunteer something, to cooperate even just symbolically, then it could be the trickle that led to a torrent.

Sheila folded her arms and stared back like a toddler in the huff.

'It's your call, Mrs Fullerton. But sooner or later you're going to have to ask yourself what means more to you: being the keeper of the flame or finding out the truth.'

Catherine was almost at the kitchen door when Sheila spoke.

'There's a concertina file in the walk-in wardrobe, in the bedroom. Stevie keeps all the utility bills and stuff in there.'

'Thank you.'

Sheila swallowed.

'Kept,' she added, closing her eyes.

Catherine relayed the instructions to Beano and sent him upstairs to retrieve the file. She had considered going herself, because part of her was pruriently curious to see the bedroom concerned. However, another part of her knew that the smug amusement factor of tacky opulence was always in competition with a rising anger at where all the money had come from; and still another part felt that she was the tacky one for contemplating this trespass of Sheila's dignity.

Through the huge floor-to-ceiling windows of the front hall Catherine could see Laura outside on the lawn, talking on the phone. When she caught Catherine's eye, she pointed to the device to indicate that she had news.

Catherine waited until Laura's call had finished then strode outside, meeting her on an expanse of monoblock that ought to have its own postcode.

'Forensics,' Laura said. 'Bit of a good news, bad news package.'

'I'll take the bad up front. I always ate my Brussels sprouts first so I could enjoy the turkey.'

'Fallan's gun didn't fire the shots.'

Catherine tutted. This was disappointing, but not a body blow.

'Ballistics did a test-fire already?' she asked. 'Figures: they only make you wait when it's good news.'

'It never got as far as a test-fire,' Laura told her. 'The gun under Fallan's vehicle was a nine-mil Beretta and the shell casings turned out to be twenty-twos. Low-velocity subsonic, ideal for a silencer.'

Catherine wasn't perturbed.

'Doesn't surprise me. The Beretta fires high-velocity stopping rounds: that's the defence weapon he keeps stashed for tight scrapes. He'd ditch the one he used for the hit. What's the good news?'

'The transferred paint is a match.'

'Brilliant.'

'So that puts his vehicle there for sure. Can't claim it was fake plates.'

'Good going,' Catherine told her. 'It's coming together.'

'A motive would be nice.'

Catherine's attention was suddenly drawn to the approach of Beano, who was conspicuously unencumbered by a concertina file.

'Did you not find it?' she asked.

'No, no, it was where she said. The concertina file's at the foot of the stairs. It's just . . .'

Beano had an odd look on his face, one that reminded her of Fraser when he was about to ask something that he already suspected might be really daft.

'What?' asked Laura impatiently.

'Don't laugh, but I think I've found something.'

'You're fair selling it to us with that build-up,' said Catherine. 'What is it?'

He grimaced a little, as though bracing himself for a backlash, then presented a small white plastic rectangle on the palm of his hand.

'This was sitting on the shelf, right next to the concertina file. It's a library card, for the Mitchell.'

Laura failed to honour his request for no laughter.

'And what significance are you ascribing to that?' she asked.

'Are you kidding? Finding a library card in a gangster's house is like finding a crack pipe on the space shuttle.'

'Beano's right,' Catherine said. 'The only books they read are football biographies and true-crime memoirs by other hard men, just to see if they get a mention. And they don't borrow them from the library.'

'The card shows that he only joined up last month,' Beano went on. 'I think Stevie might have been doing some research.'

The 3025 Tour

Glen had never heard a key rattle with such resonance as when it was locking a cell door with him inside it. It clattered and rang, slamming home the bolt with a reverberating finality, and with a clutch of several other keys jangling on the ring the retreating polisman sounded like Marley's ghost. Seemed a miserable bastard as well. They all did, though Glen couldn't see why: the cops were acting frustrated but he knew they had to be happy.

He had killed Stevie Fullerton, and now they had him on toast.

They didn't need him to talk. Everybody knew what had happened between him and Stevie. It was simple.

Except that nobody *truly* knew what had happened between them, and it was never simple.

He thought about the last time he saw Stevie: shocked and fearful, facing his end under Glen's gun. That wasn't how he wanted to remember him.

He preferred to picture the first time.

These were the days – the last days – before drugs became the only game in town. Looking back, it was easy to depict guys like Tony McGill as though they were King Canute, locked in futile efforts to hold back an unstoppable tide, but the picture was different from the beach. Back then, nobody knew the extent to which drugs were going to dominate, not even the people dealing them. Folk went with whatever worked for them at the time, and rode any gravy train as far as it would take them, or until something quicker and easier might come along. Tony was raking in money from a plethora of more conventional scams, rackets and operations, some of which he'd been doing for decades, some of which had been dreamed up in recent months, and certain others of which it could be said went back centuries.

The practice of bootlegging booze connected Tony to a Scottish tradition that probably dated back to the evening that the first excise law was passed. The practice of beating up restaurateurs and publicans if they didn't buy it was a twentieth century refinement, but the basics remained the same, right down to the sea being the preferred conduit. No beacons and signal fires on the Ayrshire coast, however; not with P&O running such a regular service. Among his many nicknames, Tony was sometimes referred to as the Travel Agent, and credited with having sent more folk abroad than Thomson Holidays. By the time Glen started working for him, the running of that particular operation had been entrusted to Tony's eldest son, Tony Junior, but the methods remained the same. Half of Gallowhaugh knew that if you wanted a cheap holiday you could get free ferry tickets plus a bit of spending money from Teej as long as you drove to Hull or Dover in one of his modified vehicles and made a few specified bulk purchases prior to your return. Families were ideal, as nobody suspected their VW camper van had been remodelled to hide crates of spirits or cigarettes under false floors or behind what still looked like cabinets, beds, sinks and stovetops.

This aspect of the operation practically ran itself, which was probably the main reason Tony felt comfortable entrusting it to his son – together with the blindness many parents seemed to have regarding their cherished offspring's limitations. Such nepotism aside, more generally Tony wasn't shy of giving younger guys responsibility, as proven by his early recruitment of Glen. His philosophy seemed to be that if you were good enough, you were old enough. A case in point was a burgeoning young talent from Croftbank who already commanded a great deal of respect from Tony, despite being even younger than Teej.

Stevie was at most only two years older than Glen, and didn't even look that, but he had already served a long apprenticeship of thieving and scamming. He was smart and ambitious, with a sharp eye for the details of how shops and businesses operated their security.

At the age of thirteen, when other kids were sticking cassettes down their jooks in WH Smith or grabbing a handful of pick-and-mix and running out of Woollies, he had perfected a distraction technique that brought in hundreds of pounds at a time from big city-centre stores. It was a three-man gig; or more accurately three-teen. Two of them would start arguing on the shop floor, eventually breaking into a fight. They'd really go at it too, making as much noise as possible, screaming and swearing, bashing into clothes racks and knocking things over. This would unfailingly cause the shop staff to abandon their tills and charge over to intervene, at which point Stevie would slip quietly behind the counter and lift every note they had. Some of the big-name stores had started fitting locks to the tills, so where possible he'd grab a set of keys too. It turned out they were often standardised across the whole chain, so a key lifted from Argyle Street in Glasgow would open a till on Princes Street in Edinburgh, making a day-return on the train well worth the dodged fare.

When Glen first met him, it was to hand over a stack of National Savings books that Tony's bagman, Walter, had mysteriously been accumulating.

Walter was older than Tony – by ten years, Glen would learn – but seemed older still in his manner and appearance. He always tuned the car radio to Radio 2 and knew the words to all these slow songs from before Glen's parents' time. He'd sing along quietly to himself, a habit that for a long time concealed the fact that he and Glen never had a conversation. Everything about him seemed to belong in the past, even his name. Glen had never known anybody called Walter. It seemed a remnant from another generation, long since abandoned by modern fashion, like Mildred or Horace. The only Walter Glen could think of was Walter the Softy from 'Dennis the Menace', which may have contributed to the name being shunned. Glen didn't imagine that anybody ever thought of this Walter as a softy. He was short, skinny and pale, but so was a cut-throat razor when it was folded up. He spoke quietly rather than softly, a gravelly rattle together with his staccato brevity giving a rasping quality to a voice he seldom raised. He smoked constantly and never seemed to eat.

Amid their more substantial collection rounds, they kept stopping off at pubs and houses where people would hand over these wee blue books and Walter would pay them twenty quid. Glen had already learned not to ask Walter any questions not immediately pertinent to their next port of call, because it was as futile as it was frowned upon, so it was only when he was introduced to Stevie that he found out what the deal was.

It was the first time Glen ever had the feeling that somebody was regarding him with more than mere caution. He wouldn't go so far as to describe it as excitement, but Glen got the distinct impression that his reputation had preceded him. There was a palpable sense that Stevie was pleased to be in his company, and keen to impress. Glen had learned fast that people didn't often appreciate unsolicited questions about their activities, so he had no intention of enquiring after the purpose of the savings books, but Stevie enthusiastically volunteered a detailed breakdown of this latest scam he'd dreamed up, which they came to know as the Three-oh-two-five Tour.

'You can just walk into a post office and open up a National Savings account with barely any ID,' Stevie explained, a savings book pinched between his thumb and forefinger. 'Ten quid down, then a week later they send you one of these. We get dozens of folk to apply, then we buy the books off them, like Walter's been doing.'

'But you've got books in their name now,' Glen observed.

'Aye, but they tell the post office their savings book never appeared and the NSB fire off a replacement. The original book is still live, though, and you can make a deposit at any post office in the country. Pop in, hand over your honk and the lassie behind the counter writes your new balance in the book, then slaps the post office stamp on the end to show it's legit. Cheque deposits work the same way, except they write "ch" next to it. But here's the thing . . .'

Stevie opened the book and held up the first right-hand page for Glen's inspection.

'There's only enough space for five deposits or withdrawals per page, see? So what we do is fire in a bent cheque for three K.'

'Why three K?'

'That's the max they'll accept for a single drop. So, the next day, you go in somewhere different and deposit a fiver. Day after that, another post office, another fiver. Same again until day six, when the magic happens. You hand over your fiver, and the lassie behind the desk writes in your new balance and stamps it.'

Glen got it. 'With no "ch" in the margin.'

'Bang on, the big man. Doesnae matter if the stolen chequebook's been reported and cancelled: your balance says three-oh-two-five, and now you're allowed to withdraw fifty pound a day from any post office in the country, then drive to the next post office and lift fifty more. Get a wee team together and a stack of wee blue books, then you go for a drive. Start off Glasgow, through Falkirk, Stirling, Embra, then doon the A1 to Newcastle, work your way across to Carlisle, back up the M74 through Motherwell, Hamilton, Rutherglen.'

As he sat in his cell, Glen allowed himself a sad, regretful smile, still able to see Stevie's boyish grin as he laid it out.

'There's four of us, we're lifting two hunner pound every stop. It adds up . . .'

It sure did. Several thousand a day, and Tony would be getting his slice without lifting a finger: his role in facilitating the collection of NSB books meaning that for all it was Stevie's scam, it was still part of Tony's business.

Money was always being kicked back to Tony from activities that on the surface he had absolutely nothing to do with. Glen and Walter even picked up payments that had accrued from recent armed robberies. Glen garnered that this was often in respect of crucial information that had come Tony's way and that he had chosen to share with select individuals on the understanding that they wouldn't forget who had caused opportunity to knock. Information, in fact, kicked back to him as much as money, but the conduits by which it did so were far more covert and multifarious. Arguably, over the years, Tony's trade in information had been his most valuable sideline, though it wasn't an argument many people would make out loud.

People gave Tony money for all kinds of motivations, disclosed or not, but the principal one was to guarantee their future wellbeing.

Protection. It was the foundation stone of organised crime in Glasgow. It came in a number of different guises, evolving over the years, but fundamentally it boiled down to the modus operandi of the playground bully: *geez that or I'll batter your melt in*.

There was an old tale in Glasgow about the manner in which most practitioners first learned to play this game as kids, namely offering to 'watch your motor, mister?' to guys who had just parked their cars on the way to the football. The story went that a bloke once pointed out the Alsatian dog sitting in the back seat of his vehicle and told the two wee boys who had offered their services, '*He* watches my motor.'

To which one of the kids responded by saying to his mate, 'Check that, Charlie. A dug that can put oot fires.'

For decades, Tony and his predecessors had been 'ensuring' that business premises and their owners didn't come to any harm in a notoriously violent city. Occasionally Tony took it further, by 'doing a Victor' if he considered a business to be a tempting enough prospect.

'I liked it so much, I bought the company.'

Glen didn't know how much Victor Kiam paid for Remington, but he didn't imagine a delegation of his representatives threatened to kneecap the previous owners unless they dropped the price to a nominal fee, nor that the vendors ended up working at what used to be their own business for the pittance Victor deigned to pay them.

Times were changing, though, and what was simple in the sixties wasn't so straightforward in the age of the economic miracle. It was way before anybody had uttered the word 'globalisation', but even back in the mid-eighties, Tony McGill could have told you that the independent business was becoming an endangered species on Britain's high streets. Everything from garages to jewellers to pubs and restaurants was becoming part of a chain. You couldn't go up to Ronald McDonald, hold a knife to his red-pubed bollocks and tell him to pay you a cut if he didn't want his gaff going up in smoke. However, Tony hadn't survived as long as he had without knowing when to move on to pastures new, and in one particularly astute development, this was more than a mere figure of speech.

'You're gaunny need your wellies for this one,' was Walter's overture.

'How? What's the job?'

'Dropping in on Wurzel Gummidge's boss. With the state of the economy now, it's getting that farmers are the only buggers left in Scotland with any money. Tony reckons it's aboot time they shared oot some of those EEC subsidies they get for not growing anything.'

To say they were plundering virgin territory didn't begin to cover it. They were like the first ship-borne cats to rampage through New Zealand, effortlessly preying on flightless birds that didn't even recognise a need to run, far less a predator.

Censored Details

Catherine stood up as Graham Sunderland walked in through the open door of her office. She knew he was coming, even before she saw his approach through the glass partition, because he'd phoned a couple of minutes ago to make sure she was at her desk before 'popping over'. This made her curious, and a little uneasy. The Detective Chief Superintendent didn't 'pop' anywhere. For a man of his status he was far from a self-important individual, but it had been a long time since he'd needed to tread lightly around these parts.

She guessed it was about the Fullerton case, but that was the source of her unease, as she had made sure he was thoroughly up to speed on how it was progressing.

He glanced quizzically down at her desk, his eye drawn immediately to the document that was open in front of her, due no doubt to the thick black bars defacing parts of it.

'Looks pretty hardcore,' he said. 'What is it?'

'It's courtesy of the MoD, concerning a Royal Marines commando by the name of Tron Ingrams.'

Sunderland gazed back blankly.

'Fallan,' she clarified. 'He had his name changed legally, got all his documents in order and then signed up to serve his country.'

'A good way to disappear if you're trying to reinvent yourself.'

'I'm not sure how much reinvention there is when your job is still all about killing people.'

Sunderland looked a little shocked at her tone.

'I know you're a bit of a peacenik Catherine, but I think that's a bit of a harsh generalisation regarding—'

'I wasn't generalising. He was a sniper. It's one of the few details that hasn't been redacted. Look at this: his actual service record looks like a Saudi newspaper, all these black bars.'

'How long did he serve?'

'Just shy of twelve years. Long enough for it to be widely assumed that he was dead, but apparently not long enough to let sleeping dogs lie.'

Sunderland grimaced a little, as though reeling from a regrettable truth. She knew that he had worked under Fallan's father, back when Sunderland first joined CID, and deduced that whatever sympathy he felt was not at the fate of Fullerton.

'I gather he's been charged,' he said.

'Yes, sir. Dom Wilson at the PF's office is handling the case.'

'Too bad Wilson's old man stepped back from the limelight. It would have been amusing to watch father and son cross swords as prosecution and defence.'

'Well, technically . . .' she reminded him.

'I know,' he acknowledged. 'And did I hear right that Fallan still hasn't asked for a lawyer?'

'Strange but true.'

Sunderland took this in while looking away out of the window. Again that regret.

'Were you aware of him?' she asked. 'When he was younger, I mean.'

He nodded gently.

'Only through his father.'

'Is there much that you know about him from back then? We're still struggling to come up with a clear picture for the motive.'

'I know we failed him,' Sunderland said. 'Nothing you've heard about Iain Fallan was exaggerated, and he was no gentler with his family than he was with anybody else. I was young and he was my boss. I tell myself I was powerless, that there was nothing I could do, but there *were* things I could have done . . .'

He looked for a moment like he might be about to elaborate, but no. Whatever he had come close to revealing was hastily covered up again like the black marks on the Ingrams file, as Sunderland's face became all business once again.

'I've got something for you,' he said, producing a USB stick from his jacket pocket.

'What's this?'

'You ran a subscriber check with Vodafone, regarding Fullerton's mobile. Intelligence bureau passed it on to Abercorn by mistake.'

She took it from him, restraining an instinct to snatch. Abercorn's name could do that.

'By *mistake* . . .' she began, but Sunderland held up a hand. Don't go there.

And she wouldn't. Not with Sunderland, at least.

Catherine took a last sip of the coffee she'd been drinking before Sunderland showed. It was tepid and bitter but his visit had left a worse taste, and now she was going to address it. She tossed the cup into her wastebasket and headed for Abercorn's office.

His door was open and he was typing, his attention so fixed upon the keyboard and the screen that he remained oblivious to her standing in his doorway until she deliberately cleared her throat. She held up the flash drive but said nothing, leaving it entirely in his court so that she could analyse his response.

He stared at her hand and then at her, confusion on his face at being yanked from his immersion giving way to annoyance as he deduced the reason for the interruption.

'What?' He sounded genuinely irritated, but it was a good gambit if he didn't want to give anything away.

'*No chatter,*' she quoted. '*No rumblings. Our pants are round our ankles.* So what are you doing intercepting my subscriber check on Fullerton's mobile?'

'I didn't *intercept* it. It got sent to me by mistake.'

'Just at random? What, of all the folk it could have been accidentally sent to, by sheer chance it turned out to be the one person with the biggest interest in Stevie Fullerton's business?'

'No, of course not at random: that's the point. Somebody at Intell must have seen Fullerton's name and assumed the check was for LOCUST. I was going to bring it to you, but I'm up to my eyes here, so when Sunderland came in . . .' He held out his palms and sighed with exasperation. 'Look, Catherine, not everything I do is a fucking conspiracy, okay?'

113

Catherine belatedly saw the logic in this and was bracing herself for a sheepish moment of apology, but it looked like Abercorn was beating her to it. He seemed aware that he had lost the rag and appeared to be climbing down.

'I'm sorry,' he said. 'Just a lot on my plate.'

'It's okay.'

'No, look, I've got something for you here.'

He sounded more conciliatory than Catherine could ever remember, and began rummaging in the chaos of his desk.

'I asked around about your symbol: you know, the thing on Fullerton's head. A couple of older guys recognised it. Goes back to the late eighties, they said: perhaps significantly, the time when Fullerton and Fallan were partners in crime. It was, among Glasgow bampots, what might these days be called a meme.'

'A meme?'

'You know, an idea that replicates like a virus. It was associated with a brief spate of tit-for-tat gangland murders, and from there it kind of bled into the wider bam consciousness. Started off getting daubed on dead guys as a way of saying: "This is payback for the pal of ours that *you* killed and daubed this symbol on." Before long it's appearing as graffiti, daft wee neds putting it on folk's walls as a way of saying: "You're getting it." They were copying it because they thought it carried some kind of heavy hard-man kudos.'

'Tit-for-tat?' she asked apprehensively. 'So do they know where it started?'

'Yes and no. And by that I mean they know whose was the first body it appeared on, but nobody has a clue what it signified, or whether it already had a precedent we don't know about.'

'Who was the first body?'

'Low-level headcase named Paul Sweeney. He had links to Tony McGill.'

Abercorn handed her a brown paper wallet, inside which was a ten-by-eight crime-scene photo. She felt something inside her lurch in anticipation of what she might be about to see.

'But more significantly,' Abercorn went on, 'the fourth and final one in the to-me, to-you cycle was Nico Fullerton, Stevie's brother.'

Catherine opened the envelope and felt a modest flush of relief. The shot was taken from down low, probably a crouching position, looking up at the symbol spray-painted on a wall. She could make out the bare feet of Nico Fullerton's corpse in the bottom right of the frame, but was spared any more gruesome details by the angle of the shot.

'How did you dig this up?' she asked. 'Who were the officers you spoke to?'

'I didn't say they were officers,' Abercorn replied, which was when she knew that was all she was getting.

Protection From Harm

They heard the sound of a car driving into the courtyard in front of the house, the engine amplified as it bounced off the stone walls of the dairy shed. It seemed insensitively noisy given the way it broke across the silence around the kitchen table. They had been sitting like that for so long, waiting for Dad to say something that would make sense of what had happened, or at least indicate which way was forward from here, but he said nothing, lost in thoughts that he did not wish to share. She looked to her mum for comfort, but Mum's expression betrayed the gravest concern at what she read in her husband's face.

The front doorbell rang: loud and long and brash. It was the spur that finally prompted her dad to speak, but only to order: 'Ignore it. We're not at home.'

It rang again following a pause hardly brief enough for anyone to have answered the door under ordinary circumstances.

'What if it's . . .' Mum suggested, 'I don't know, the police, maybe?'

The insistence of a third ring cemented this idea in her mind, but it made no odds to Dad.

'There's no emergency here. Whoever it is can call back.'

There was not a fourth ring.

'Shouldn't we *call* the police though?' Mum asked, once the growing silence from the front door had extended enough to suggest that whoever it was had given up. 'I mean . . .'

'Aye,' Dad responded. 'I will. I just need a wee while. I'm in no state to talk to anybody. None of us is.'

As another hush fell she listened out for an engine starting again, followed by the usual sharp cut-off as the vehicle cleared the dairy shed and its wall ceased to echo back the sound. It never came.

Instead there was a sharp three-beat rap at the back door, which was then opened unbidden from outside with the brisk familiarity of a relative or family friend.

They all looked up to see a cadaverous little man stride into their kitchen. He was bird-like in his build, but there was a harshness to his face and an assured coldness about him that warned he could look after himself. He wore a funereal charcoal suit and a plain white shirt with no tie. The shirt looked crisply white, but maybe this was just against the greyness of his complexion.

Behind him stood a younger man dressed in a jeans and a black polo-neck. He was tall, rangy and impassive. Her eyes were drawn to his: analytical, penetrating, examining her for weaknesses.

The older man smiled confidently, like a favourite uncle expecting to be welcomed into the hearth, but as he opened his mouth to speak Dad beat him to it.

'We're not at home to visitors,' he stated, standing up from his chair.

'This won't take long,' the man said, placing his hands on the back of an unoccupied chair. He spoke like a skeleton, a rattling voice devoid of warmth.

'I said . . .'

'Apologies, ladies, but I need to ask you to leave us,' the intruder went on, as though Dad hadn't spoken. 'There's something your father has to discuss with me.'

'We're not going anywhere,' she told him. 'Who the hell do you think you are, walking into our house?'

He fixed her with a brief but bitter stare then turned to her dad, speaking in clipped tones intended barely to conceal anger.

'I said I want to talk to you alone. Tell your wife and daughters to leave, and if you've the sense, warn the lippy one to keep a civil tongue in her heid.'

Dad looked at the intruder, then at his accomplice, who was leaning against the sink, his hand close to the knife block.

'Girls, Jean, do as he says.'

'Actually, tell you what,' said Cadaver, glancing towards her.

'Why doesn't the lippy yin make herself useful? Fix us both a cuppa tea, hen. There's a good girl.'

She looked to her father, who couldn't meet her eye.

Mum said she would get the tea, but Cadaver insisted it be her.

She served it from the pot to the two of them, Cadaver giving her an exaggerated smile in response, a sneering skull. The rangy one took his without looking at her, like she wasn't there any more. It was as though he had assessed the things he needed to concern himself with in his immediate environment and was satisfied that she wasn't one of them.

Her gaze lingered upon his hands as he lifted the cup. There was an angry scarring across his knuckles, like they'd been in a fire or something.

Once the tea was served, Cadaver told her to leave. Mum ushered her through to the sitting room at the front of the house; Lisa was there already, tearful and trembling.

They could hear only the sound and tone of voices, but could make out no words. It was only Cadaver who was speaking: polo-neck said nothing; Dad little more.

'Who are they?' Lisa asked. 'What do they want?'

'I don't know,' Mum said, but there was a dread stillness about her that suggested otherwise.

Nobody mentioned Lysander. Nobody had to.

Outside the window, she could see the car: it was a nice one, a BMW. It looked new, gleaming and powerful alongside Dad's Chrysler with its mismatched paint patches and rusted skirts.

After only a few minutes they heard the kitchen door open and footsteps on the tiles. Mum opened the sitting-room door anxiously, in time to see Cadaver stride down the hall. He didn't even cast them a glance as polo-neck opened the front door and they let themselves out.

Behind them was Dad, a morass of conflicting emotions upon his face, none of them good. He was about to slam the door when Cadaver turned and placed a restraining hand on its outside edge.

'Just so's we're clear,' he said to Dad, casting a quick glance at the three women looking on. 'You talk to the polis, and it'll no' be your daughters' *horses* that get cut up. You get me?'

And with that, he lifted his hand from the door and walked away, sauntering with demonstrable absence of haste towards the BMW, where polo-neck was starting the engine.

Dad stared at the intruder's retreat through the open door for a few moments, then a shudder ran through him and he turned, stomping back towards the kitchen. He returned a few seconds later clutching his rifle, striding along the hall with a look that chilled her more than what she had discovered in the stables.

As one, she, Lisa and Mum converged to block him, all of them in that moment envisaging the same course of events that ended with their father in prison. Mum gripped the barrel of the weapon and forced it upwards towards the ceiling, while she and Lisa barged him against the wall, restraining him with hugs and pleas.

As the engine started up and the BMW pulled out she watched the fury and defiance in her father's face subside into anguish and defeat. They could all feel his straining recede, and when they stepped away he sank to the floor and broke down, shaking in his tears.

What's in a Name

It was difficult to imagine a starker contrast between the places Anthony Thompson could be despatched to in doing the same job, even working the same case. From a crumbling former petrol station awash with soap suds and vomit, host of the bullet-riddled corpse of a dead drug dealer, to the wood-panelled halls and green-domed majesty of the Mitchell Library, Glasgow's cathedral of the written word.

He loved driving past this place at night, the stone walls reflecting its light so that it gave the impression that the building itself was refulgent, a beacon at the heart of the city. And he loved the Glaswegian quintessence of the fact that this beacon was cheek-by-jowl with pubs and curry houses, and thus never seemed an aloof ivory tower isolated from its environment. Working with other squads, it would have been easy to interpret his being the one sent to the library as a joke, a reference to his being a fast-tracked graduate. And by joke, of course, he meant a means of undermining him by once again emphasising the perception that his career path meant he had more experience among the books than on the beat.

Under Detective Superintendent McLeod, he didn't have to worry about making such an inference. Not only had she never made any digs about the Accelerated Careers Development Programme, but she had little tolerance for the subtle denigrations and territorial pissing that often masqueraded as 'banter'. Before working with her he had heard her described variously as 'schoolmarmish', 'a snobby cow' and 'an uptight bitch'. These descriptions, it hardly needed to be said, had come exclusively from male officers of the sort most inclined to engage in the 'banter' she proscribed. The same male officers who joked that he was 'just one of the girls' now he was part of her team. This was in reference to the supposed gender balance under McLeod's command. It was intended as an insult, but if he was just one of the girls then that suited him fine, because he was rubbish at being just one of the guys.

This didn't mean he spent his evenings reading poetry before weeping openly over the TV news; more likely, playing *Team Fortress 2* or *Starfire IV* before settling down to a late-night slasher movie. Some people couldn't equate his enthusiasms with his attitude, but really it was simple. He liked a lot of blokey things. He just didn't like blokishness.

He could be confident that the boss hadn't meant anything by despatching him to the Mitchell, but it was nonetheless still a possibility that he had been nominated for a fool's errand. She had agreed that he wasn't totally havering when he decided that a library ticket was an unusual – and therefore suspicious – item to have found in the possession of the late Stevie Fullerton, but it wasn't exactly a severed head in the fridge. He couldn't help but think nothing was expected to come of it. In essence, he had unearthed a lead commensurate with his own stature, by which he meant that if it had been that good an idea she wouldn't have entrusted the follow-up to him.

That said, the other thing this assignment reflected was that they were still striking out with regard to establishing a motive. While it didn't indicate that they had reached the desperate stage, they were definitely moving towards 'anything is worth a punt' territory.

Preliminary discussions with the Procurator Fiscal's office indicated they were confident that they already had enough to convict Fallan, but McLeod wasn't going to relax until she knew what the murder had been about. She was determined that there be nothing about this investigation that could trip them later, no overlooked element that might jeopardise what was otherwise shaping up to be a straightforward prosecution. They had Fallan nailed to the scene with a gun in his vehicle and a history of enmity with the victim. They had the who, the where and the how, but the absence of *why* yawned like a pit just waiting for them to tumble into.

It was a huge case in terms of the victim's profile and the resultant

121

media interest, so he knew there must be major pressure on McLeod, particularly as it looked like an open goal. The boss was determined she wasn't going to be responsible for a van Vossen.

There was something else going on too, something deeper and more personal. The very calm he had remarked upon earlier had dissipated as soon as Fallan entered the equation.

Even before that, there was something unsettling about the boss's coolness at the scene, her lack of any compassion for the deceased. Fair enough, nobody was going to be erecting a statue to this guy, but she seemed – if not overtly happy – certainly satisfied that he was dead; and if she had any regrets over Fullerton's demise they were probably regarding how quick and sudden it must have been.

It was jarring. He liked working for McLeod because she *was* compassionate. There was an atmosphere under her command that he could relate to, that made him want to deliver for her. It was hard to define precisely what it was; easier to pin down what it was not. It wasn't about putting on the mask of don't-give-a-fuck, and 'fighting the battle of who could care less', as Ben Folds put it.

Obviously, on the downside he had to endure being called Beano, which he hated, but it was a small price to pay, and he never doubted there wasn't a certain affection in it.

It was always awkward when somebody new used it though, as there was a presumption there if they hadn't earned their Beano privileges. Other guys seemed to wear their nickname like a badge of pride, craving the group acceptance it conferred. He was not immune to this aspect of being Beano, and down the years there had been nicknames he accepted and enjoyed. As a kid he'd been Ants, and when older, Tico, a handle that endured on the football pitch even now.

Anthony was what his mum always called him. It was what Jennifer had called him, and she used to say it like she loved the feel of it on her tongue. He thought of himself as Anthony, and that was what he wanted McLeod to call him too. However, in a way he felt he hadn't earned his Anthony privileges from her; he'd be Beano until he gave her reason to see him otherwise.

He made his way through the building to the reception desk

opposite the café, where he gave his name and waited for the woman he had spoken to on the phone.

'Have you got the card?' she asked.

He dug it out of his pocket and she scanned it by sliding it along a reader connected to her computer.

'As I explained over the phone, there's more than one person of that name on the system, so I couldn't just tell you what books this Mr Fullerton had been reading.'

'I think with this guy it was probably more like colouring in, but I remain open to surprise.'

She grinned at the remark without taking her eyes from the screen.

'Well, he'd have had a tough time colouring these in,' she reported. 'He's been looking up newspapers using the microfiche archives. Old *Daily Record*s.'

'When?'

'Twenty-five years ago.'

'No, I mean when was he in here?'

'Four weeks back. Same day the card was issued.'

'Can I see the editions he was looking up?'

'Sure. Come on and I'll set you up. You might want to grab a coffee though. You could be sitting there a while. I can't tell you precisely which editions he was looking at, only the dates covered by each spool.'

She escorted him upstairs to a row of microfiche readers, stopping off to retrieve the appropriate spools en route. She showed him how to load the microfiche then gave him a quick tutorial on navigating and zooming in and out of the pages. Once she was satisfied that he had it sussed, she wished him good luck and left him to it. Fullerton had selected spools from two periods roughly six months apart, but as each spool covered one month, there was no deductive reasoning to be brought to bear in order to narrow the search. It was going to be a BFI job: brute force and ignorance.

He scanned the first few editions quite methodically, taking in the changes in design and typography, the graininess of the photographs and the absence of web and email addresses in the adverts.

He tarried a little over the sports pages, the near-hysterical tone of the sensationalised coverage all the more ridiculous viewed through the prism of time.

He began scanning the news pages, parsing the headlines and trusting his judgment that the most plausible candidates would be recognisable at a glance. He reasoned that if he got through the month without any ideas, he'd go back again and focus on the obits and intimations.

There were a few possibilities on the first spool, but nothing leapt out at him. A bank robbery in Braeside; a drugs seizure in Balornock; the murder of a young woman in Capletmuir; the killing of a passer-by who had intervened in a street fight one fateful Saturday night.

These could be the news pages of today's edition, Anthony reckoned. Same crimes, same places, and quite possibly some of the same polis, but he needed a tangible link to the here and now, to what the paper would call 'a gangland slaying' in Shawburn.

He could probably rule out the murdered woman. He had taken note of it because it was one of the biggest crime stories in that spool, but really it had only got so much play because it had started off as a mystery, the quintessential nightmare for every woman, every daughter's parents. She didn't come home one Saturday night, then was found strangled in woodland the next day, on a pathway close to the railway station where she had got off the train. Julie Muir, she had been called. Twenty-one years old.

Though he knew it wasn't germane, he dwelt a moment upon her name because somehow it seemed wrong to gloss over it. It felt like a kind of prayer, a gesture of thought for someone who once had a life and a world, but who was now forgotten by history, erased by one man's violence. By that token he did the same for thirty-four-year-old father of two Andrew Leiper, who had tried to save some young bloke from a kicking on Sauchiehall Street and been stabbed to death for his trouble.

A few editions on, the strangling story was updated and effectively ended with the arrest of a convicted sex offender. Poor girl had been in the wrong place at the wrong time.

Julie Muir. Anthony couldn't help but think what age she would have been now, the life she should have led.

The street-fight story reached its conclusion even sooner, Andrew Leiper's teenage killer found and named within forty-eight hours. Billy Fergus. Anthony wrote it down, intending to see where else the name might pop up, and whether he or even Leiper had any connections to Fullerton or Fallan.

Then he moved on to the second spool, which was when he hit the jackpot.

WILD WEST GEORGE STREET
Bloodbath as gang battle rages through city nightclub

REVELLERS fled in horror as carnage erupted inside trendy city nightspot Nokturn last night. Terrified witnesses spoke of SLASHINGS, glass attacks and flying chairs amid pools of BLOOD as a fight at the bar escalated into a mass brawl.

'It was like a scene from a WILD WEST movie,' said one witness, who did not wish to be named. 'One minute everybody's dancing, and the next there's about thirty people BATTLING it out, joining in from all sides. The violence was indiscriminate. I saw bystanders getting BOTTLED. These guys were just lashing out at anybody. Girls were in tears and SCREAMING. There were guys in there absolutely SOAKED in blood.'

Details were sketchy in this wild-eyed initial report. Given the time of night when it was likely to have kicked off, the story would have broken pretty close to deadline, real hold-the-front-page stuff. A reporter must have made it there in jig time, or maybe been lucky and been in a pub nearby. Anthony guessed the 'witness who did not wish to be named' didn't actually exist; this would simply have been a front for whatever reports the hack had been able to cobble together on the pavement outside before phoning it in.

The next day's coverage had more meat on it, and more personnel. As well as carrying genuine quotes from named witnesses, it also indicated that a reporter had been despatched to the Royal Infirmary to get verifiable detail on the injuries. These seemed to be listed in descending order according to the number of stitches, with top billing going to one James Donnelly, who received forty-eight after having his face opened from his temple to his chin.

The witness accounts were chaotic and contradictory: people reconstructing snapshots taken when their judgment was at its least reliable, reassembling fractured memories in the wrong order. It was something he was all too familiar with. Refracted through the lens of tabloid hysteria, it was even worse. Some things were gradually coming into focus, however.

NIGHTCLUB BOSS WEIGHED INTO HORROR BATTLE

THE MANAGER of a city nightspot that was turned into a blood-bath two nights ago threw himself into the fray, according to eye-witness reports. Nokturn impresario Stephen Fullerton (24) was seen trading blows as chairs, bottles and glasses flew during the carnage that left more than twenty injured, but DENIES it had anything to do with a feud between rival gangs.

Fullerton, who describes himself as a legitimate businessman, admits that he became involved in the fighting but INSISTS he has no idea what provoked the mass brawl.

'I have no clue who these people were, but they were HELL-BENT on making trouble. My cousin was SLASHED while just standing at the bar. There was no warning, no provocation. When it all kicked off I had to run down there to pull him clear so that we could get him medical attention.'

Twenty-four and he already ran a nightclub, Anthony thought. Bet he never got any shit about accelerated career development.

A couple of days further on, the story flashed up again, with an informed and sober perspective on the matter garnered by the paper's chief crime reporter. This time, the 'source who did not wish to be named' was more plausibly anonymous, clearly somebody who had the inside gen, and perhaps his own agenda for leaking it.

'It was Thomas Beattie who slashed James Donnelly,' our source told the *Record*. 'There were about thirty witnesses within ten feet

126

but I doubt it will ever reach court. None of them will be daft enough to come forward.

'There was already bad blood between Beattie and Donnelly, going back years, but the slashing was a pre-arranged signal for a major rammy to kick off, launched by crews from Gallowhaugh and Croftbank. They were teaming up to wreck Nokturn in order to take Fullerton down a peg or two, but the truth is, this kind of mayhem was all they had left. Stevie's operating on a different level to these guys now, and they know it.'

Anthony noted the starchy, forced formality of the namings. Thomas Beattie was not referred to as Tommy or Tam; James Donnelly given not so much as a Jimmy. It was always possible that they were known as Thomas and James, but he doubted it. There was a detectable primness to the paper's tone, as though by acknowledging their street names it would be condoning crime culture, yet all the while it was peddling vicarious thrills to a curtain-twitcher readership.

The paper squeezed every last drop out of the story, reheating it when they got any tangential new angle, such as the revelation that a couple of Old Firm footballers had been present, albeit they had remained safe upstairs in the VIP area of the gallery that overlooked the dance floor. They offered no comment other than to stress that they had got themselves out via the backstairs as soon as they saw what was going on. A 'glamour model' was more obliging, milking some exposure with accounts of what she had witnessed from the gallery in descriptions that read suspiciously like they had been cribbed from the existing reports.

Anthony wondered why a gang fight in a club got more play than a young woman's murder, or than a killing on the street in the vicinity of half a dozen other nightspots. Glamour side by side with danger, perhaps: a curious symbiosis of aspiration and disapproval.

Coincidentally, coverage of the Julie Muir murder trial cropped up in the period covered by the second spool. The killer's name was Teddy Sheehan, a mentally deficient oddity with a prior for exposing himself to school kids, whose move into the big league no doubt worsened the lot of every neighbourhood's local weirdo. At the close, there was a quote from a senior detective – one who probably had bugger all to do with the actual investigation – saying he hoped Julie's family would have some peace now.

Anthony doubted it. Everybody else could rest knowing the killer was behind bars, but not them.

Inheritance

Jasmine pulled up in front of Josie's house with a mixture of anticipation and guilt. She was looking forward to seeing her great aunt
for the first time in ages, but that gap was itself the source of
discomfort, particularly in combination with her true motivation
for finally picking up the phone and announcing her intention to
visit.

Josie was the younger sister of Jasmine's grandfather, Bruce, and
of Jim's mum, Isobel, both of whom were now dead. She had
sounded frail on the phone, her voice weak and unsteady, which
had made Jasmine feel all the worse about neglecting her promise
to come and see her more often, made when they were both at a
christening last year.

Growing up, Jasmine had enjoyed a special rapport with Josie:
the favourite auntie who would take her on day trips, which always
featured lovely cafés or posh tea rooms, and the one person who
was allowed to take her to (gasp) Glasgow for the panto at
Christmas. Sometimes Josie would turn up with her friend Fran,
and sometimes it was just the two of them together, Jasmine's ally
in a cosy conspiracy against the rest of the grown-ups. She was
flamboyant and energetic ('exhausting', quoth Aunt Isobel when
she didn't know Jasmine was in earshot), never at rest, and once
described by Jasmine's mum as being so skinny because she seldom
stayed still long enough to eat.

Josie's house was in fact a flat, forming the upper half of one
side of a semi-detached ex-council house built between the wars.
The building itself was grey and soot-blackened, but Jasmine
remembered the flat always being bright and colourful inside. It
was the one place she had ever been permitted to stay the night in
Glasgow. The first time had been because Josie and Fran were

taking Jasmine to Rothesay the next day and needed an early start to get the train to Dunoon for the ferry. That had been just before Jasmine started school. Then, when she was seven, she stayed with Josie and Fran for three whole nights because her mum was away on a course. In Jasmine's mind, the word was associated entirely with an army training facility she had seen on *Blue Peter*, so she had imagined her mum was spending three days climbing scramble nets and crawling through tunnels.

She parked the Civic in front of the house and walked to the front gate. The grass was in need of a cut, but not so much as to necessarily indicate neglect.

Jasmine climbed the outside stairs at the side of the building, wondering whether the ascent gave Josie problems these days. Before she reached the top, the door opened and her auntie was standing there with a huge grin. She looked absolutely fine, and Jasmine hurried up the last few steps impatient to hug her, relief opening the floodgates to a slew of other emotions. She was unable to prevent a few tears.

'Goodness, Jasmine, it's not *that* long since you last saw me,' Josie chided. Her voice was a little hoarse, but she didn't sound as though it was such a struggle to speak.

'I'm sorry,' she confessed. 'You didn't sound so good on the phone, and I was worried you might be in a bad way.'

'Och, it's nothing. I had a bad cold, but I'm on the mend. Come on inside.'

The flat seemed smaller than Jasmine remembered, mainly because most of those memories had been compiled when she was half the size. The effect now was to further emphasise how impeccably neat the place was, so much detail and variety squeezed into a tiny living room without it feeling cluttered. It was much as she remembered it, including the smell of pot pourri. The only marked differences were a DVD player beneath a flat-screen telly, and a picture of Fran on the mantelpiece.

Fran appeared in other photos on the walls, usually standing next to Josie. Jasmine remembered them being referred to collectively by family as Francie and Josie, after Rikki Fulton and Jack Milroy's legendary music-hall characters, something they tolerated with good humour. Individually, however, Fran was always just Fran, though it was usually prefaced with 'Josie's friend'.

It had only been after Fran's funeral that Jasmine deduced why this preface often sounded awkward in the mouths of relatives. She recalled being given Fran's room when she stayed with them, and wondering why there was little in it that suggested the personality of its occupant, in such contrast to the bloom of colour and vibrancy in Josie's bedroom. Furthermore, it had always struck her as unfair that her auntie had a double bed compared to Fran's single, not to mention a TV as well as all the nice cushions and knick-knacks.

'I saw you pulling up,' Josie said. 'That's a smashing car you've got. You must be doing very well.'

'Busy, though. That's why it's taken me so long to get in touch. Sorry. Excuses, excuses. What happened to your wee car?'

Josie used to have an old-model VW Beetle, the longevity of which played a large part in inspiring Jasmine's determination to keep her mum's early-nineties Civic running despite boasting hardly any of its original parts by the time of its fiery end.

Josie sighed.

'I just lost a wee bit of confidence. Had a couple of near things and didn't trust my eyesight the way I used to. I often regret it though. I'm sure I'd still be a far safer driver than half the head-bangers on the road today.'

Jasmine doubted it. Josie had always been a terrifying driver. She used to boast that she'd never had an accident, to which her mum would respond under her breath, 'Aye, but she's seen dozens in her rear-view mirror.'

'I make the most of my bus pass, but I miss the simplicity of my car. There's places I haven't been in years because it would just be too complicated.'

Wheels began turning in Jasmine's head, an idea beginning to appeal. It struck her that she would feel better about the mercenary element of her visit if she was also doing Josie a favour. It also might incline her great aunt to open up more if she wasn't stuck in her living room. It was a place where she would still see Jasmine as a seven-year-old, the temporary custody of whom always came with certain caveats regarding what she was and wasn't allowed to talk about.

'Like New Lanark, for instance?' Jasmine asked with an inviting smile.

'Och, don't be daft. I thought you were coming by for a quick cuppa. You must have things to do.'

All of which sounded a lot like 'That would be lovely.'

Josie had taken Jasmine to this place a couple of times when she was wee, so it seemed appropriate she should reciprocate now that Jasmine was the one with wheels and a licence.

'So, I get the impression business is booming, but how are you doing?' Josie asked, as they descended from the car park at a leisurely stroll. They had traded plenty of small talk and catch-up blether on the drive down, so Jasmine knew this was a specific and genuine enquiry.

'I'm okay,' she replied.

Josie nodded, understanding plenty from one word. She guessed Josie was okay too, in the same way, and that Josie could also make the following statement, verbatim, while talking about someone else.

'I miss her every day. I'm coping, I'm doing all right, but there's nothing in my life that wouldn't be better if she was still here.'

Josie didn't say anything; didn't need to. They both knew she understood.

'Perhaps the hardest part is realising I know so little about her. She had this whole life before I came along that nobody would ever talk to me about.'

They were approaching the rear of Robert Owen's house, a place where the whole world had once turned for the better, even if most people didn't know how.

Josie halted and regarded Jasmine with the look her relatives always gave whenever she attempted to broach this subject: pitying and regretful, but bound by oath.

'Your mum was always afraid of what might happen if you went looking for your father.'

'I'm not looking for my father, though,' Jasmine replied plaintively. 'I'm looking for my mother.'

The distant crash of the falls upstream was like the constant hum of an air conditioner in the background. It made all their words sound soft.

'I'm not afraid of hearing something I might not like. I've heard enough eulogies. I want to know everything about her, because these fragments are all I have left. I'd rather know her for *all* she really was than merely accept a version that's been deemed fit for public consumption. Surely you must understand that.'

Josie seemed a little rattled by her last remark, and in that moment Jasmine realised that this may well have been the first time anybody in the family had pushed her to acknowledge the truth about her and Fran. That was family for you: Josie may well have been 'out' in other circles but, for her or Fran's own private reasons, remained content to leave the issue politely untouched among her relatives.

Josie breathed deeply and cast a thoughtful glance over the buildings below.

'Tell you what,' she said, fixing Jasmine with a penetrating eye. 'Let's not go into the mills. Seeing as I'm here, I feel like taking a wee wander along to Corra Linn.'

They took a left past the schoolhouse, where a younger Jasmine had been allowed to write on a slate and glimpse what childhood looked like in the nineteenth century, and continued along the wooden boardwalk skirting the banks of the Clyde.

'What do you remember about Bruce, your grandfather?' Josie asked.

Jasmine felt a shock of apprehension. She had been steeled to hear all about her mum being caught up with villains, but with Josie's question she suddenly imagined a door opening to stories of abuse and realised she wasn't quite as ready as she assumed to hear every harsh truth. Especially as Granda had been a sweet old thing with a soft and cheerful voice, one of the few men in her early life and therefore all the more cherished for it.

'He died when I was six,' she said. 'So all I've got is impressions. He was nice. I didn't see him often. I don't think he ever kept very well.'

'Bruce had too gentle a soul for the time and the place he was born into,' said Josie, fondness and pity in her expression.

'What did he do? For a living, I mean.'

'Well, for a living . . .' the question seemed to give Josie a moment's pause. 'He was a painter.'

'An artist?'

'No, though he had his gifts that way. He was a painter and decorator: always his fall-back. He was very good, though, the steadiest hands you've ever seen. He could gloss your whole house and never a single drip.'

Jasmine thought of the steady hands she was complimented on at the shooting range, and wondered whether they were an inheritance. She hadn't been left much else by that generation.

'What was my grandmother like? She died before I was born, and my mum seldom talked about her.'

'She was actually Bruce's second wife,' Josie replied. 'His first wife, Maria, died in childbirth. The baby died too. He met Elizabeth some years later. She was an actress. There you go: a family profession. Or rather, she *had* been an actress. She was in her thirties by the time Bruce met her, and I think she had a bit of a past. She was still a looker, but already fading and she knew it. It had been a while since she had trodden the boards, but she had a lovely singing voice. That's how they met: Bruce was a talented pianist, and he became her accompanist.'

Josie took hold of Jasmine's arm. They had reached a tight bend in the boardwalk, where the waters were quite high alongside, though Jasmine was not sure whether that was the real reason Josie was hanging on right then.

'She never loved him,' she said calmly, though she sounded like she was reining in her true emotions. 'He couldn't see it. Well, he could see it, but he thought he could change it. Always the dreamer.

He was a good ten years older and worshipped her, but she just saw him as her consolation prize.'

'Is this the part where you say that they had a baby because they thought it would bring them closer together?'

'I don't imagine it was something that either of them thought through. It just happened. And as you anticipated, it didn't serve to change Elizabeth; not for the better, anyway. The poor thing endured what would these days have been identified straight off as severe post-natal depression. Back then, though, everybody just thought she wasn't fit for motherhood. And of course it didn't help that Bruce was always skint.

'That's why they ended up in Croftbank, which was a rough area even then. He did his best, but the harsh truth is that Elizabeth was drinking the money as soon as it came in. She had a bit of a drink problem even before she met Bruce, but everything got worse after Yvonne was born. She never got over her depression, and she didn't really bond with the baby. She came to see Yvonne as representing a life she didn't want, and a different life she had lost. That was why your mum was so determined to give you all of the love her mother never gave her.'

They had reached the hydroelectric power station. The falls of Corra Linn were just a few more minutes' walk ahead. Jasmine stared up at the twin pipes that ran down the side of the hill, and could sense the vibration thrumming through them. Or perhaps she only imagined she could sense it. Perhaps it was she who was thrumming as the deluge flooded through her.

'She never told me a hint of this. Not even that her mother was an actress. She said she was a housewife.'

'Technically, she was, but not much of one. Bruce doted upon Yvonne, of course, but it can't have been an easy house to grow up in, and they certainly weren't easy streets to grow up on either. You'll maybe have heard your relatives talking about how Yvonne "fell in with a bad crowd", but I don't think any of us has a clue about the truth of that. I think she just did what she had to in order to get by, and part of that was staying out of the house because it wasn't a pleasant environment.'

135

'I was given the impression that it was when she was older that she got mixed up with some bad people. You know, when she was a drama student and after that.'

'No, I think these were people she grew up around. I know that Bruce became very concerned about her during her teen years. She always had money, for instance, and Bruce was worried about where she was getting it: it certainly wasn't coming from him. It must have been hard to rein in a daughter's excesses while one of her parents was descending into full-scale alcoholism.'

'Did you ever see her at that time?'

'I made a point of it, yes. We had all heard that she was becoming a wild child but she was adept at giving a different impression when it suited her, so I only saw what she wanted me to see.'

They were approaching the first viewing point from which the falls were visible. Jasmine expected Josie to veer off the main path towards the railings and the little platform, but instead she kept on going towards the stairs.

'It's a bit of a climb,' Jasmine warned.

'It's worth it.'

They took it slow, stopping at each switchback. Jasmine was feeling it in her thighs, conscious that she spent way too much of her time sitting in cars and vans. She thought of Laura Geddes and her late-night runs. Air-rifle shooting wasn't going to keep her fit.

'Your mum left home when she got into drama school. She was still in Glasgow but she got a flat with some other girls, I think. I heard very little about her at that stage. I think Elizabeth's funeral was the only time I saw her in about two years, maybe longer. She seemed fine, but, you know, older.'

Josie wore a pained little frown as she said this last word, one from which Jasmine was invited to infer a great deal, but neither of them would ever know the details.

'Then perhaps a year later, out of the blue, Bruce tells me she's appearing at the Tron theatre. She had a job with a repertory company, one of those where one month you're on stage and the next you could be working with nine-year-olds in a community centre. Bruce was delighted. We all were. And then, just as suddenly, I heard she had quit the theatre company and left Glasgow.

'Everything was very hush-hush and rather fraught. Bruce wouldn't say where she had gone, never mind why. Then some months later he asked me to meet him in Edinburgh, and took me to the Simpson Maternity Unit, where I first laid eyes on you. I didn't even know Yvonne was pregnant.'

Josie's eyes filled a little now as she spoke, but for the first time since they started walking there was no sadness, no regret, only warmth.

'It was as I got my first wee hold of you that Yvonne explained the disappearing act. She didn't want the father to know about the baby. She didn't tell me who he was and I didn't ask.'

Corra Linn was in spate. Josie sat on a bench, Jasmine standing at the railing near by. They both stared, entranced, at the falls, arching like vast billowing drapes, an endless crash echoing around the rocks as a plume of vapour rose towards the skies.

Neither spoke for a long time. There was too much churning through Jasmine's mind, roaring in white noise like the waters. If she moved her eyes and focused a certain way, she could follow a small volume, seeing it hold its form for an instant as it plummeted into the next pool. In the same way, one thought held its shape in her head long enough for her to give it voice.

'Did you see her? At the Tron, I mean?'

Josie stared for a moment before responding, as though she required time to disentangle her mind from the spell of the falls.

'Oh, yes. She was Lady Macbeth. She was brilliant. For a while all I saw was my wee niece, but then Yvonne faded away and all I saw was the character. She seemed so young, and yet she played upon that, against an older Macbeth, like a young seductress who didn't anticipate what her powers would wreak, which only emphasised the tragedy.'

Jasmine's heart thumped as she ate up every word. Part of her had been waiting her whole life to hear this one account.

'I only saw her once,' Josie added with a sigh. 'At the time, I just assumed it was the beginning of her career, not the end. If I'd known that I'd have gone along every night, and to the matinees too.'

Josie gave Jasmine a sad smile as she noticed her tears.

'Och, come here, pet.'

Jasmine sat down beside her on the bench, where Josie ran a hand over her hair, like she had done when she was a girl.

Josie looked to the falls again and they both sat there in a silence for a while.

'I've got something for you,' Josie said. 'Remind me when we get back to the house. I meant to give it to you a while ago, but I was waiting for you to visit.'

'I should have come sooner.'

Josie took her to the room that was never really Fran's. It was cold, a damp chill in the air indicative of it having been a very long time since the radiator was turned on in here. Josie went to the wardrobe and pulled out some boxes, placing them carefully on the bed. They were all made of cardboard, but wrapped carefully in gift paper like presentation boxes.

Having found the one she was looking for, she popped off the lid and sifted through its contents. She removed an A4 envelope from a stack of binders and folders, then handed it to Jasmine.

Jasmine read Josie's neat and elegant handwriting in blue pen at the top left corner, and felt something inside her surge. It said simply: 'Yvonne Macbeth Tron'.

She opened it carefully and slid out the contents. They were black-and-white production stills, ten-by-eight publicity photographs taken during dress rehearsals. There were twelve prints, her mother in seven of them. She looked young, confident, vampish, angry, scared, forthright, vibrant, beautiful. Jasmine had been seeking forever for this treasure, imagining how she would feel if she ever found it. She had always assumed there would be tears, but none came. She just felt excited and proud, thrilled on her mum's behalf. This was the woman she had always known existed, the one her mum had been hiding from her.

'I offered these to your mother once, but she wouldn't take them.

She wouldn't even open the envelope. I realised that giving it all up must have been harder for her than she would ever let on, especially to you.'

'Thanks for keeping them,' Jasmine said. 'I'll treasure these.'

'You should have this stuff too, if you want it.'

Josie tapped the lid of another box on the bed, which now looked like the scene beneath a Victorian Christmas tree.

Jasmine pulled off the lid with undisguised impatience, like an excited child. She knew she didn't have to hide this from Josie.

It was full of old jotters, notepads and drawings, a time capsule from her mum's school years.

'I rescued this lot from Bruce's attic after he died. I offered it to your mum but she said to just bin it all. I didn't. I couldn't.'

Jasmine homed in on a makeshift scrapbook: an A4-sized unlined jotter with magazine cuttings, ticket stubs, flyers and photographs glued to its coarse paper pages. She was already looking forward to poring over its every detail when she got it home, but more immediately she couldn't help but scan the decades-old photos of her mum: Polaroids, prints and in some cases photocopies.

She had never thought she looked like her mum, but she could finally see a bit of a resemblance now that she was able to compare herself with the girl her mum had once been. Nonetheless, Jasmine wasn't exactly a mini-me. Who did Yvonne Sharp see, she wondered, every time looked at her little girl? Her own mother? Granda Bruce? Jasmine's father?

Then her eye was drawn to another face that she found familiar, and with a jolt she realised why. He appeared in a photo along-side her mum and a girl who featured in several other shots, obviously a close friend. They were in school uniform, on a class trip; from the background Jasmine guessed it was Kelvingrove art gallery, or maybe the People's Palace. The girls were side by side, posing for the shot, but the boy was engaging in what would now be termed 'photo-bombing': leaning over both their shoulders as he insinuated himself into the centre of the frame, laughing at his own buffoonery. The girls were aware of him; tolerant, vaguely amused.

Jasmine had been looking at a more recent photo of him yesterday, on the *Daily Record* website, where it reported that he'd been shot dead in his Bentley on his and her mum's birthday.

Stagecraft

Glen was sitting at a plastic table in the canteen, perched on a plastic chair, eating from a plastic plate with his plastic cutlery and occasionally sipping tea from a plastic cup. People talked about the indignities and deprivations of prison life, but nobody warned you it would be like living in Legoland. It was little things like this that really brought it home, far more than the locks and bars and uniforms. He missed the feel of metal in his hands, of tools in his hands. He missed the cold air of the outdoors, the wind on his cheeks and earth beneath his feet.

Only now was the true price becoming clear to him: the price of rashness, of letting his emotions cloud his judgment; the price of bad decisions he had made long ago; and the price of one truly good one.

He had his head down, as usual, trying not to engage with anybody. Since arriving in the remand wing Glen had been very careful about who he spoke to and when, paying particular attention to who might be looking on. Despite a few overtures, he wasn't looking to make any friends. It was nothing personal: he just didn't want to be responsible for anybody. In here, a friend was just something that could be used against him by his enemies, whoever they might be.

Stevie would have laughed to see him stranded in a sea of people and yet still dedicatedly alone. Big Single, Stevie used to call him. It came from his name sounding 'like a single malt' (hence Stevie also calling him Dram), but it was as much a reference to his preference for solitude.

He had found it difficult being surrounded at all times by so many people; so many *men*. It should have been second nature: he was used to being surrounded exclusively by males; aggressive and

141

tightly wound males at that. He was used to negotiating a landscape of latent threat. He was used to orders, protocols, routines; and used to watching his back. He was not so used to captivity. That was what changed everything. In his military days it was only ever temporary, and then he could fuck off into the badlands, into silence and shadow.

He was missing female company. Not just specific female company, but women in general: female voices, female thoughts, female perspective. The way they spoke, the way they looked at the world. The things they talked about, the things they *didn't* talk about.

He didn't speak much to the women at the refuge, but he liked to hear them talking nearby or around him as he worked. It centred him, made the world feel like a nurturing place rather than one to be survived.

This was not a nurturing place.

Somewhere up ahead a fight broke out, a sudden eruption of movement as two prisoners flew at each other. Plastic chairs began skidding on floor tiles as other inmates got clear or took up good positions to watch the bout. The screws moved in with steady purpose but a practised lack of hurry. Glen was reminded of the referee at an ice hockey game.

With all eyes turned to the unfolding action, Glen became aware of something else taking place in his peripheral vision; his eyes were drawn instinctively by another suddenness of movement and an accompanying spray of red. He saw a hand gripping a length of blue plastic plunge into a pocket, a figure turn and merge into the throng, job done.

An inmate held his face, blood welling over his fingers like he was trying to stem a burst pipe.

From the glimpse he had caught, the weapon had looked like a toothbrush, the head melted to mount a razor blade: a classic improvised prison chib. He didn't know whether the fight had been staged as a diversion or whether it had been an act of opportunism, but either way, the victim hadn't seen it coming, and neither had Glen, which was what really bothered him.

He felt vulnerable in a way he had never been in the field. The dangers were different here, and the normal rules of engagement didn't apply. He could scope out his environment, read the signs, listen to his fear, but he couldn't use his surroundings like he'd been trained. They would be coming for him, but he couldn't intercept them or out-manoeuvre them because he'd never know who they were until they were upon him.

He had a big target on his back and he could remember feeling this exposed only once before, back in Gallowhaugh. It was after he had taken down two local hard-cases who made the mistake of picking on Glen shortly after his sister died, when he was at his nadir of nihilistic teenage desperation. He was a soul in pain, he genuinely didn't care what happened to himself, and he had reached the stage where he achingly needed to damage someone else when the Egan brothers volunteered.

Unlike Glen, the Egan brothers had a lot of friends.

He was walking down Kerr Street when they appeared, scrambling from the waste ground like warlocks over graves. There were six of them, with axes, hammers, machetes, a bike chain. They had been lying in wait.

Throughout his youth, Glen had adapted to find a kind of security in his isolation. Being alone had become a refuge, a state that cultivated a stronger sense of self. But after his sister died, he understood what it was to be lonely. The absence of Fiona was like a void in the world, one he could never fill, but of late it had felt like it was himself who was disappearing.

He had no money. No job. No prospects. No ambitions. He lived in a shambolic and increasingly unkempt tenement flat with a broken husk of a mother. The one person he had truly loved was dead, and he was coming to understand that deliverance from their father had come too late for both of them. Glen was no longer subject to his father's violence, but his father's violence was in him now, a demon that had passed from one host to the next. He had taken a knife to the Egans, cut them up in broad daylight. What kind of future could possibly lie ahead after that? Not a long one.

He knew there would be reprisals, but it was not the prospect of brutality that disturbed him. He had known too much of that already for it to hold new fears. No, what disturbed him was the anticipation that when the attack inevitably came, he might accept his fate; that part of him was already inviting death. He would join Fiona in oblivion. Living always in violence, it seemed inescapable that he would meet his end in violence, but finally, at least, he would meet an end *to* violence.

That was why he'd been drifting, oblivious, off-guard. Part of him wanted this. Part of him wanted death. Another part just wanted mayhem, and didn't care if death was the price.

They were masked: nylon stockings pulled over faces, ski-masks improvised from reversed balaclavas with eye-holes torn out.

Instinct told him to run. Experience told him it would be pointless: if he got away today, they'd catch him tomorrow.

The demon told him he could strike before he fell.

Six guys don't attack at once, it whispered. One of them would be first. One of them would be that bit more resolute, that bit less apprehensive. Among the others, one, maybe more, would be hanging back, doubting himself, hiding his cowardice in the facelessness of a crowd, waiting for someone else to make the decisive move. His gait or his posture would betray him. If Glen could get his weapon in the early moments of the mêlée, then he'd soon see who really wanted this.

Glen scanned the six figures coming towards him. The demon lied. There was no gradual approach, no cautious steps to analyse. They were gathering speed, spreading out, breaking into a run, a charge. None of them was holding back, none of them showing any tell-tale lack of aggression.

This was a violence he had never faced before. Something, finally, worse than his father. He knew then that he wanted a future, any future he might carve; that even his faded sense of self was better than oblivion.

He wanted to live.

He heard a screech of tyres to his left and saw a white Ford Cortina shoot out of Milton Crescent. It slewed across Kerr Street and swung around until its tail was overhanging the pavement, the driver's-side rear door hanging open.

A figure was leaning across the back seat.

'Get in. Now,' he shouted.

He looked early twenties, shaven head, yellow tracksuit top. Glen didn't recognise him, but this wasn't the time to worry about climbing into cars with strangers.

Glen dived through the gap and the Cortina sped away with his legs still sticking out, the door flapping against his knees. He felt a weight on his back like a blow, then realised that the guy in the tracksuit was leaning on him in order to pull him all the way inside and get the door closed. Glen's head ended up in the footwell and, given his size, it took an awkward few seconds of manoeuvring to get himself sitting upright, not assisted by the speed at which the car was travelling and the way the driver was throwing it around corners.

'Thanks,' he managed cautiously.

The guy in the tracksuit glanced at him but said nothing in response.

'There's a man wants a word with you,' said the driver.

Archaeology

Anthony was sitting on the floor of the morgue surrounded by boxes, folders and yellowing pages, munching a McIntosh Red, the closest link to a computer in his immediate environment. He was down in the basement of HQ, where the more ancient case files were kept; dumped would be more accurate. These days such materials were carefully stored and indexed, some documents even available digitally, but for matters pertaining to quarter of a century ago he had to brave this cluttered oubliette.

The system gave a deceptive impression of order and efficiency. He had been able to do cross-reference searches from the comparative comfort of his desk, the computer listing files in a way that suggested they would be neatly and conveniently arranged when he went down to pick them up.

Ha. That had been hours ago. Or maybe days.

On the plus side, he could at least munch a couple of apples at his leisure without worrying about Zoe Vernon snaffling the rest of the bag.

A cross-reference on James Donnelly had unsurprisingly brought up several results; indeed Anthony would have expected more, but the most recent dated from only a couple of months after the nightclub fracas. Then he remembered McLeod mentioning that Donnelly was two decades missing, presumed dead, rumoured to have been murdered by Glen Fallan.

The unnamed source had been wrong, as it turned out, about nobody testifying. Despite James Donnelly claiming not to recognise – in fact not to have even seen – his assailant, Thomas Beattie was identified by multiple witnesses, and sentenced to three years.

Anthony had Beattie's file open on the floor too, and it was less coy about aliases. The son of veteran Gallowhaugh hard case Tam

146

Beattie, he was known as Tam Junior, but more frequently as Stanley, after his favoured means of leaving his mark. It wasn't simply a Stanley knife either, but a weapon comprising two blades taped together, kept apart by a fifty pence piece. This was so that the surgeons couldn't stitch the parallel wounds cleanly, guaranteeing a wide, ugly and very permanent scar.

Anthony got to learn Donnelly's nickname too, as well as confirming that he and his brother David, aka Doke, were Stevie Fullerton's cousins. Completing what the police believed to be the inner circle in those days had been Stevie's brother Nicholas, or Nico. Anthony had never heard of him, and it turned out he had been murdered back in 1987.

Also named on a list of known associates was Glen Fallan.

Stanley Beattie lasted less than a month after getting out on parole. He bled to death on the floor of a pub in Shawburn, ironically killed by what the coroner described as a defensive wound. He had held up an arm to stop a blade aimed at his face, only for it to open his wrist instead. Predictably, the investigation focused on James Donnelly. From this perspective it was clear that the reason he didn't name his assailant at Nokturn was because this was the only justice he was interested in.

Anthony looked at the photographs of Donnelly clipped inside one of the files, pictured before and after scar. He looked like a candidate for a boyband: handsome and cocksure. Sexy and I know it. He was reputedly a ladies' man. Also reputedly volatile, with a notoriously short fuse. According to statements, his temper often had to be reined in by his brother or the ever-pragmatic Fullertons. The Fullertons were all business, the file said. James, on the other hand, was all about James. He was spoilt, the good-looking baby of the family, used to getting attention. Not so used to hearing the word no.

The Shawburn Inn was precisely the kind of place somebody could be slashed without any of the drinkers or the staff being prepared to admit they saw anything. However, as fate would have it, the incident took place in full view of a sales rep from the brewery, a woman by the name of Linda Conway. As well as being able to describe the attack, and identifying Donnelly from photographs, she informed the police that the assailant had been in the company of a young woman.

Donnelly's alibi was that he had been at home with his girlfriend, but the file testified to the investigating officers' growing confidence that they could prevail upon her to come clean. They were sure the girlfriend was being pressured into lying out of a combination of loyalty and fear, and her story didn't stand up. They knew she was working at the local community centre, fifty yards from the Shawburn Inn, and the attack happened less than an hour after she clocked off.

When he read her name he almost choked on his apple.

Dust

Laura drove them past the railway station and took a left down a broad, tree-lined avenue, bordered either side by properties set back so far that only the occasional flash of sandstone could be glimpsed through gaps in the foliage. Then she turned right into a greyer, narrower street, a cul-de-sac that looked cut off from the blood supply that was richly colouring its surroundings.

Miner's Row was a tiny outcrop of (predominantly ex-) council housing on the verdant periphery of the enduringly affluent suburb of Capletmuir. It sat on the south-eastern outskirts of Glasgow, as the crow flies only a few miles from the schemes of Gallowhaugh, Shawburn and Croftbank, but a few light years in terms of social mobility. In fact, it might as well have existed in another dimension, and Catherine guessed Capletmuir's residents would have preferred that, particularly when it came to the premiums for contents insurance.

She was pretty sure Capletmuir was where Campbell Ewart had lived, or at least did when he was Under-Secretary of State for Scotland in the Thatcher cabinet. As she recalled, his home was often the subject of humorous comment because it was perilously close to the constituency border, back in a time when there was such a thing as a safe Tory seat in the west of Scotland; or indeed any Tory seats at all.

In those days, Capletmuir used to be known locally as 'the hamlet', an enclave of opulent villas built in picturesque meadowland during the early nineteenth century by the merchants of the empire. These days, so many new private housing developments had sprung up around it that it was the dowdy Miner's Row that was the isolated hamlet in their midst.

It seemed a good fit: Brenda Sheehan's number had been the

conspicuous anomaly on the list of Stevie Fullerton's mobile phone calls, a curious outlier among a familiar roster of known associates. Officers had been despatched to interview those who hadn't been contacted already, but Catherine didn't expect they would be any more forthcoming than their predecessors. This was why she had opted to tag along and provide corroboration when Laura spoke to Sheehan; that and the opportunity to share their confidential impressions of how the case was going, rather than the versions they presented to the squad and the brass.

They also had the list of Fallan's phone activity, which was unrevealing but for the curious fact that Jasmine Sharp had been in touch in the hours either side of his hitting Fullerton. What this indicated in the light of Beano's discoveries, she wasn't sure.

'It's been a longstanding nugget – and I think nugget is the appropriate word – of Glasgow bam lore that Fallan "disappeared" Jazz Donnelly,' Catherine told Laura. 'And that then Stevie Fullerton disappeared Fallan as payback for his cousin, albeit the latter's case of death turned out to be of the extremely rare "non-fatal" strain. I take the point that Fallan waited a very long time to commence the next round of "to me, to you", but his relationship with Jasmine Sharp might somehow have provided the catalyst. She was certainly the reason he finally blew cover a couple of years ago.'

'I'll admit I've been reluctant to rule out the idea that this was a paid gig,' Laura admitted. 'That Fallan was the means rather than the motive. But the fact that he got sloppy suggested otherwise. If somebody hired him to take out Fullerton, he wouldn't have made the mistakes he did. Using his own car, doing it in front of witnesses, mask or not: it seemed hurried, improvised. But if he was rash and reckless because of the girl, it starts to get clearer.'

'He's always been *very* protective of her,' said Catherine. 'And I don't just mean that as a figure of speech: I'm talking body language, like he's ready to take a bullet, or at least loose off a few.'

'You don't think . . .?'

'There's certainly something at the heart of that strange wee triangle: Donnelly, Yvonne Sharp and Fallan. Has your top-secret inside source turned up anything interesting?'

'Too early to say, but I'll keep you posted.'

Laura stopped right outside the address, there being no shortage of kerbside parking on Miner's Row. Most of the front gardens had been amended to include a driveway at the side, with Brenda Sheehan's one of the few falling into the non-monoblocked minority. They climbed out of the car into the autumn sunshine, Catherine immediately conscious of being monitored from across the road, where a wiry old woman in gardening gloves was peering over her hedge.

Sheehan's house was the left-hand part of a non-symmetrical semi, its drab roughcasting an almost absurdly stark contrast with the pointed brickwork of its right half. Indeed, the place was distinct in having a conspicuous absence of exterior improvements sufficient to suggest the council was still her landlord. Her grass looked in need of a cut, though it had not risen beyond the level that would have had Catherine nagging Drew. It was only marginally longer than on the postage stamp of lawn that remained next door, where the plot had been landscaped within an inch of its life.

The layout of Sheehan's garden probably hadn't been altered since the place was built: lawns front and back, with a grey path leading to the front door and around to the rear, the concrete slabs flanked by thinning gravel and punctuated by thicker moss.

Catherine had a glance up and noted that the venetian blinds were drawn over the first-floor windows. She checked her watch. George Osborne would not have approved.

Laura pressed the doorbell. Catherine guessed, just from the tone of it, that nobody was home. She had rung a thousand of these things in her time, and you could usually tell. Anything generating sound or movement inside could have a slight dampening effect to the experienced ear, but this was reverberating with absolute clarity indicative of silence and stillness within.

She strode across the lawn and had a peek through the downstairs windows. The venetian blinds were partially closed but she could still peer through the slits between, shading her brow with her hand against the reflected glare of watery sunshine. She saw discarded newspapers, full ashtrays and empty bottles, like the aftermath of a late but not particularly uproarious party.

'Ghosts of bottles past,' she muttered, quoting a song she had heard Drew playing the other day.

Laura gave the bell another try, but to neither's surprise there was no response. Sheehan hadn't answered her mobile either, the recorded message saying it was switched off.

Laura nodded to Catherine to indicate the approach of the woman in the gardening gloves, heading across the street with an inquisitive but purposeful expression.

'Think we're about to get chibbed by the neighbourhood watch,' Laura said.

'I reckon we can take her,' Catherine replied. 'Between us, anyway.'

'I don't know: those secateurs look badass.'

They both turned and walked out to greet the concerned-looking neighbour.

'Excuse me,' she said, 'would you be looking for Brenda? Brenda Sheehan?'

'That's right. We're the police. We were hoping we could speak to her,' Catherine said, guessing from her expression that the little lady had pegged them as polis as soon as they stepped out of the car, which was why she barely looked at the proffered warrant card. She wore a smile that was polite but tinged with worry, which didn't augur well.

'See, you don't like to be nosy, but the thing is, I haven't seen her in a couple of days, and those blinds have been the same all that time.'

'Do you see her quite a bit?' Laura asked.

'Oh, yes. I'm always out in my garden. I see her coming back from the shops most mornings. She goes to eight o'clock mass at St Stephen's, every day, and gets her shopping on the way home. That's why I was starting to get a bit concerned. I rang the door yesterday as well, but . . .'

Catherine and Laura traded a look.

'What's your name?' Laura asked.

'Mari. Lamont. Mrs.'

'Well, Mrs Lamont, we'll have a wee look and see what we can see. For just now, I'd recommend you go back to your garden and we'll let you know whatever we find out.'

'Thank you. I'd appreciate it.'

She retreated, looking all the more apprehensive than upon her approach.

'I think that's good enough reason to force an entry, what do you think?' Catherine asked.

'You're the boss.'

They took a walk around the back, where a cursory try revealed the back door to be unlocked.

Catherine went first into the kitchen, where she was immediately assailed by a rotting smell. It wasn't what she feared – not yet, at least. It was only food: unwashed plates in and around the sink, and the debris of takeaway and ready-meal cartons spilling from the top of an over-full bin.

She spied a twelve steps poster on the back of the door leading out of the kitchen, while on one wall hung a framed print of a burning candle above the legend 'One Day at a Time'. There was a sacred heart on the wall opposite, as well as a crucifix on a plinth sitting on the windowsill next to the sink.

There were also an awful lot of empties.

'Looks like somebody came off the wagon at quite a lick,' Laura remarked.

Catherine proceeded cautiously out into the hall, where the dust bunnies hugging the skirting boards looked like they were on steroids. In places the carpet crunched underfoot, with crumbs and other debris trodden into the pile. The place didn't look to be neglected, however: the walls were brightly painted and the carpet itself looked like it would scrub up well if it got some TLC from Mr Dyson.

She stepped into the living room for a clearer view, bracing herself for the possibility of finding Miss Sheehan lying dead behind the couch, out of sight of the windows. She saw nothing she hadn't seen when she spied through the gaps in the blinds. In keeping with the kitchen and the hall, she got the impression of a well-kept little home whose owner had recently undergone an unfortunate change in priorities.

'Partying solo,' Laura observed, noting the presence of only one glass on the coffee table, next to an empty vodka bottle.

Catherine took in the crucifix on the wall and the framed photos of the last two popes.

'I'm not getting a rock'n'roll vibe, though,' she observed.

They retreated back into the hall, where they stopped at a miniature holy water font mounted on the wall just inside the front door.

'Had to hold off dipping that and blessing myself,' Laura admitted. 'Pavlovian response. Not actually been to church other than hatches, matches and dispatches since I was about twelve.'

'I think it might be too late for prayers, though,' Catherine said as she began to notice the odour. 'You smell that?'

Laura wrinkled her nose then nodded grimly.

It got stronger as they climbed the stairs, and so did Catherine's resigned sense of dread. Being around dead bodies had long since ceased to bother her, but not knowing what sight was about to confront her didn't get any easier. Similarly, the smell was something she had become swift to identify but never got used to.

Sometimes she could smell it for hours later, imagining it must have adhered to her clothes. She couldn't help worrying what might adhere to her brain when she saw the source; how long might she have to sit outside in the driveway tonight in order to leave this sight in the car.

There was a bathroom at the top of the stairs, the door slightly ajar to reveal a lino floor and the edge of a towel rail. Catherine nudged it open with outstretched fingers, having to push harder than she had anticipated against a stiff hinge. It revealed a lemon-coloured bath suite, the tub dry, not even a hint of condensation on the surrounding tiles. It hadn't been used recently.

They proceeded slowly, reluctantly, along the narrow top hall, where three further doors were closed tight.

Laura opened the nearest, Catherine bracing herself for the olfactory onslaught. It revealed only a boiler cupboard.

Catherine stepped across the dusty carpet and gripped the handle of the door opposite, turning until she heard the click. Mindful of the stiff hinge in the bathroom, she gave it a good shove, but either it had been better oiled or had been planed in the past to

154

accommodate a deeper carpet, as it flew open and bounced most of the way back.

This was a mercy, the brief glimpse affording her and Laura a kind of thumbnail preview of the scene inside. There was less mercy afforded their noses.

Brenda Sheehan was lying on her bed, face-up with her head on her pillow. Her mouth was open, twisted into an endless silent scream, and her lifeless eyes bulged in terrified astonishment.

Catherine's eyes searched her for signs of injury, some physical testament to whatever had provoked this permanent gaze of horror. There were no wounds, no bruises, but there was dried sick on her chin and chest, with more spattered about the duvet.

'I'm not the expert,' Catherine admitted, 'but I think she may have choked on her own vomit.'

'And there was you saying you weren't getting a rock'n'roll vibe.'

Catherine glanced around the bedroom but neither of them stepped any further inside so as not to contaminate the scene. It was a modest little place, sparse and lonely: almost cell-like. There was very little in the way of personalisation, with a framed black-and-white photo on the wall the only item Catherine had so far spotted that didn't have religious or AA connotations. It showed a woman and a man standing next to what she recognised as the Astraglide chute at Blair Drummond Safari Park. Having spent many hours waiting at the foot of the thing over the years, she had little difficulty identifying it. The woman could have been Brenda Sheehan, she didn't know. She looked around forty, her hairstyle and clothes suggested it was the early eighties.

At first glance Catherine thought it wasn't a very flattering shot of the man, until a longer inspection indicated that his awkward and glaiket expression wasn't down to the camera catching him at a bad moment. He looked about forty, but was wearing a Yogi Bear T-shirt and getting his picture taken at the Safari Park with no kids in the shot. 'Learning difficulties' was the phrase these days. Special needs. Catherine wondered who he was to Brenda, and why this was the only picture of him on display.

More pressingly, she wondered what Stevie Fullerton could

possibly want with an ageing spinster who, until her relapse, appeared to have lived like a nun. She looked again at the photo, thinking she could see a resemblance between the pair: was he a brother?

Her eyes were drawn briefly to the dressing table close by, against the wall. Something about it bothered her, but she couldn't yet pin down what. Maybe it just reminded her of one a relative used to have: an old-fashioned piece with curved legs and a glass top.

In contrast to her own at home – not actually a dressing table, merely the top of a chest of drawers serving the same purpose – it bore very few items: a hairbrush, a hair-drier, a roll-on deodorant and a tub of talcum powder. Catherine had so much crap scattered on hers that Drew frequently complained about how long it took to move and replace everything when he was dusting.

That was it: there was no dust.

The carpet beneath looked as manky as downstairs, suggesting somebody whose retreat inside a bottle had not permitted any sorties to push the vacuum cleaner around.

Catherine looked at the skirting. There were grey clumps at the carpet's edges, same as in the top hall, but the tops of the boards themselves were spotless.

She got down on her knees and had a look under the bed. It was cleaner there than anywhere else: also, she would have to admit, in radical contrast to her own bedroom.

'What is it?' Laura asked.

'I'm not sure, but I think the late Miss Sheehan might not be the only thing around here that's starting to smell.'

Friends

'Heard my boys just got there in the nick of time,' Glen's host said, striding across an expanse of carpet in his vast front room. 'I'm Tony, by the way. Tony McGill.'

Glen knew who he was. Everybody did. He'd only been anything like this close to him once before, however. It had been at the Spooky Woods, back when Glen was about twelve. He had been out there one November night, wandering around just to stay out of the house, when he recognised his dad's Rover parked behind a black Jag.

He saw a man get out of the Jaguar's passenger side, a second figure remaining at the wheel. The man came around the rear of the car, removed something from the boot and then ambled around to the Rover, a polythene bag clutched in one hand, twisted at the neck so that the contents weren't dangling. His head was down, his face obscured. Glen knew he seemed familiar, just couldn't place him. Definitely not a polis, certainly not one of the usual crew anyway.

He climbed into the Rover on the passenger side and shut the door behind him. The inside light had come on in response to the door opening, then Glen saw an arm go up to the switch to ensure it stayed on once the door closed again.

He watched his dad lean forward, checking something on top of the dashboard. Money: he was counting money. Glen still couldn't see the other guy properly because he was turned around to face Dad.

The counting complete, the money went back into the poly bag and the light went out. Glen waited, expecting the man to exit, but he stayed in place. Glen saw his dad reach into the back seat and a few moments later they were both opening cans. They chinked them together – cheers – then began supping: big pals together, or perhaps toasting some kind of deal.

Glen believed in the polis back then. He needed to. At that stage he still wanted to be one. He knew his dad was a tyrant, but if there were criminals out there, then surely Dad was the kind of guy you'd want out there fighting them: hardline, punitive, uncompromising. It was the equation that made sense of his home life. Dad was the way he was because he had a difficult job: it made him tough at home because he needed to be tough out there on the streets. He held everybody to the letter of his law at home, just like he held the bad guys to the letter of the law.

Every little boy wants to believe his dad is a hero. Despite being repeatedly beaten and terrorised by him, and despite witnessing all that he'd done to his mum – maybe even *because* of all those things – Glen needed to believe that his dad was one of the good guys.

About ten minutes later the man got out, dropping his empty can on the grass. He walked with his head down towards the Jag, Glen still unable to see his face. Then there was a whistle and a flash as a bottle rocket streaked across the sky, launched from a nearby back green. The man looked up for the source and his face was lit by the rocket's final explosion, those tantalising hints of familiarity about him now made explicit.

If there was any spark of idealism left in Glen, then it burnt out in the flare of that firework and was equally extinguished by the time its remnants fell to earth.

And now Glen was standing in his front room.

He looked mid-forties, older than Glen would have expected, something paradoxically accentuated by the jeans and sweatshirt he was wearing, which looked like they belonged on a younger man. He seemed shorter and slighter of build than Glen had assumed, but this was resultant of McGill being light on his feet, like a boxer, a quickness and energy about him. There was a scar along the left side of his jaw, another on his forehead, but his expression was bright and lively, which gave him the appearance of a retired sportsman rather than a crook.

He offered a hand, giving Glen a firm but brief grip. Glen was grateful for the brevity. He didn't like shaking hands with anyone. It was supposed to be a form of mutual politeness, but to him it always felt like they were taking something from him, something he was obliged to give whether he felt like it or not.

'Glen,' he said uncertainly, pondering the redundancy of telling his name to someone who already clearly knew a lot about him. 'You sent them? How did you know?'

'You've been the talk of the steamie since you ripped the Egans. Doesn't take much to read the tea-leaves. You must have known it was coming.'

'I should have,' Glen admitted. 'I thought I'd given them reason to think twice.'

'Then you don't understand the game. It's like the laws of physics: for every action, there is an equal and opposite reaction; except in Glasgow it's a thoroughly *un*equal *over*-reaction. The Egans are a couple of heidthebaws, but they've got friends. Their old man that's in Peterhead, he was a pure psycho, but he was always pally with Tam Beattie. You heard of Tam Beattie?'

Glen looked him sharply in the eye before nodding. It seemed mutually understood that this question and response were an acknowledgment of what Glen knew about McGill as much as what he knew about his rival.

'The Egans do a few jobs for him here and there. What the polis call "known associates". So if you put doon two guys that do work for Beattie, then his people have to give it back ten times worse. Cannae let it get around that folk can take liberties. Which is why they'll come after you again – unless you've got friends too.'

Rate of Attrition

Jasmine had always imagined her mother attending school somewhere that looked like a set from a Dickens adaptation, but Croftbank Secondary had been built in the seventies and must have looked state of the art when her mum went there. It was showing its age in places, but its headmaster, Dan Quigley, was keen to impress upon her how, in certain other respects, it was in far better shape than ever.

He had insisted on giving her a tour, keen to showcase the place. He may have been under the impression that she was a reporter, a misconception Jasmine had courted on the phone to the secretary by choosing her words carefully and saying she was 'looking into the story' of a former pupil. She had added that this pupil was a contemporary of Stevie Fullerton, in order to provide context but so as to stress that the late drug dealer was not the focus of her enquiries.

'The cult of the hard man has been a blight on education in this city,' Quigley told her. 'I'm not from round here myself, but I grew up somewhere just like it. Kids need role models they can relate to, and for a long time that was sadly true of Mr Fullerton. When the best-known, and apparently most successful, guy who ever went to your school is a drug-dealing crime boss, it can't be much of a motivation to get the head down in geography, you know? But that's all changing now. We've got a former pupil who works at CERN. Another who's a CGI animator: she worked on the *Avengers* movie.'

'Guess it also helps when the hard men end up getting murdered in broad daylight.'

Quigley wore a strained expression.

'Guys like Fullerton were let down too,' he replied. 'Nobody raised their expectations.'

Jasmine had found another photograph of Stevie Fullerton with her mum and the other girl. It was loose, down at the bottom of the box, yellowed Sellotape folded over its corners from where it had perhaps once been stuck to a bedroom wall. It showed the three of them, along with another guy, sitting in a pub. Jasmine guessed her mum had been seventeen, maybe even younger, all dressed up to look old enough. They appeared excited, thrilled perhaps to be there: coming through the rite of passage of getting served, or at least not getting chucked out after the oldest-looking one buys the drinks.

'When something like this shooting happens,' Quigley added, 'there's a danger that it can reinforce people's perceptions of Croftbank, and that filters down to these kids. If you're writing about Stevie Fullerton, I'd like you to see the wider picture.'

'I'm not writing about anybody,' she corrected him. 'I'm trying to track down someone who was at school here with him.'

'So you're not a reporter?' he asked, a little confused, but curious rather than annoyed. 'What are you then?'

'I'm a private investigator,' Jasmine answered. She didn't feel so self-conscious saying that any more. It had long since started to fit.

'And who is it you're looking for?'

The girl's name was Ciara. Jasmine had established that from multiple captions in the scrapbook, having initially read her mum's teenage handwriting as Clara. Given that she had no surname to go on, she was very grateful that it wasn't Clare.

Jasmine took an envelope from her bag and showed him the picture from the school trip, telling him the first name. She didn't mention the other girl in the picture.

'I reckoned there couldn't have been many Ciaras at Croftbank Secondary back then, so I guessed this was as good a place as any to find out who she was.'

Quigley took the photograph in his hands and stared at it, fascinated. She guessed the sight of a young Stevie Fullerton was a source of prurient and morbid curiosity, all the more so in light of this week's events. Then she discovered that it wasn't Fullerton he was staring at.

'I don't know what her surname was back then, but I know what it is now,' he said. He was smiling. 'This is Ciara Flanigan.'

'How do you know?'

'She's my head of English.'

They sat in an empty first-floor classroom during the lunch break, Ciara grabbing bites of a sandwich and apologising, needlessly, for being so ravenous. It was just the two of them, ninety degrees to each other at a plastic-veneered desk.

Jasmine felt strange to be in her presence after spending so long staring at her image in those old photographs. It was like meeting the actress who had played a character in a decades-old TV show.

She had introduced herself to Ciara as 'Jasmine, I'm a private investigator,' before Quigley could give away her surname. She wasn't sure whether he would have remembered it from talking to his secretary; he certainly wouldn't have picked up on the significance, but the same was unlikely to be true of her mum's schoolfriend.

'So are you wanting to know about Stevie Fullerton?' Ciara asked. 'I was at school here with him, back in another lifetime, but I didn't really know him. Made it my business to keep out of his orbit, as I'm sure you can imagine.'

Jasmine placed the pub photograph on the desk and rotated it until it was the right way up for Ciara.

Ciara eyed her with a mixture of caution, surprise and self-consciousness. She had been caught out straight off the bat and Jasmine could tell she was rapidly reassessing the assumptions she might have made about the harmless-looking young woman she had agreed to speak to.

'Where did you get this?' she asked, both wary and curious.

'There are certain things I'm bound by client confidentiality not to reveal, but I can assure you that it's not your relationship with Stevie Fullerton that I'm interested in. I want to know more about his relationship with this woman. Do you remember her?'

They both knew she couldn't lie.

162

'That's Yvonne Sharp. My God, I haven't seen her in . . . Christ, is it really as long as that? Is she who you're working for? Or are you trying to track her down?'

Jasmine steeled herself.

'Yvonne Sharp is sadly no longer with us.'

She managed to say it without her voice faltering. It was easier that she was pretending to be someone else. But it wasn't over. She still had to watch Ciara Flanigan digest the news.

Ciara gave a little sigh, this inescapable revelation dropping an anvil on all the thoughts and questions that had only just begun to form.

'Pancreatic cancer,' Jasmine volunteered, though the question had not yet been asked. She just wanted to get the information out, get past this part. 'Three years ago now.'

'I always wondered what happened to her. We lost touch and every so often you mean to ask around. Think I even searched on Facebook once, but didn't find anything.'

Ciara picked up the picture and held it delicately in her fingers, as though touching brought her closer to the moment and the people in it.

'Spooky thought: I just realised I'm the only person in this photo who's still alive.'

'So this guy's dead too?' Jasmine asked, pointing to the other male in the shot.

'Yeah. He was murdered as well, back in the eighties. Some gangland tit-for-tat thing. So pointless.'

Jasmine felt her cheeks flush and hoped it wasn't obvious.

'Who was he?' she asked, trying to sound as natural and dispassionate as before. She braced herself for what she might hear: the two names she had tried to imagine him fitting as she stared at the picture last night, wondering whether she was looking at her father.

James.

Jazz.

'Nico. Stevie's older brother. I say older rather than "big", because Stevie was always the one calling the shots.'

163

She felt a small sense of disappointment, but a greater relief.

'Does the name Glen Fallan mean anything to you?'

Ciara shook her head.

'I know I'm in this shot, but I wasn't lying before. I wasn't in Stevie and Nico's circle, but I was friends with Yvonne. We were the two strange girls in class who did weird things like read books.'

'So how come she was in their circle? From what I can gather, they don't seem a natural match.'

'When you're living in the jungle, it helps if you have friends among the predators. Yvonne knew she would get less grief from other quarters if it was known she was friends with Stevie. I did too, to be honest. Stevie always had a soft spot for Yvonne. It went right back to primary school, something about them having the same birthday. And I think by the same token, Yvonne never saw Stevie quite how everybody else did. He showed her a different side. She wasn't ignorant of the fact that he was a headbanger, but she had less reason to be scared of him.'

'Was she . . . involved with him at any point? Were you?'

'Romantically?' Ciara gave a dismissive laugh. She indicated the photo. 'Even by those days we were still just wee lassies in the eyes of Stevie and his pals. These guys were already hanging out with older girls – women – and once they'd got used to what they could get from them, they would have seen us as too much hassle for too little payout.'

'Yet here you are, all together, down the pub. Not entirely staying out of their orbit here, are you?'

Ciara gave a curious little smile: part self-reproach, part despairing amusement at the choices she'd once made.

'They always had money, and they liked to show off. When you're that age, when you're dreaming of the high life and the previous best is a school disco or an empty at somebody's house, you can tell a few lies to yourself. Plus, it should be said, Stevie wasn't some volatile psycho. He was a crook and a hard case, but he wasn't a nutter. He was smart. If he'd been brought up in the stockbroker belt instead of Croftbank, he could have ended up a CEO in the City.'

'Except that the average drug dealer has more of a social conscience,' Jasmine suggested.

'And drug dealers are less likely to waste money,' Ciara added. 'That's what distinguished Stevie. He didn't mind a bit of mayhem, but he was principally interested in cash. Him and his pals were always into something.'

Jasmine glanced out of the window, through which she could see across the schoolyard and the playing fields. Kids milled and wandered around the concrete like particles in Brownian motion. Out on the grass, two separate games of football appeared to be in progress, one of which, Jasmine was pleased to note, featured several girls.

'I spoke to somebody who said Yvonne always had money,' Jasmine said. 'That her father was worried about where it might be coming from. Do you know anything about that?'

Ciara looked a little conflicted, like it might be disloyal to answer this, but she realised that the time for such loyalty was long gone.

'I don't know what she did, but I know she helped Stevie with something. She wouldn't talk about it. It wasn't when we were at school, though. It was later. Yvonne moved out as soon as she got accepted for drama school. She had part-time jobs and the like, and there were these insane socialist extravagances called student grants and student housing benefit, but she definitely had more coming in from somewhere.'

'So you still knew her after she left school?'

'Yes. Not so much when I first went to uni, because I still lived at home, but I shared a flat with her later on. There were three of us. Yvonne would pay more than her share sometimes, and that's when she had been doing whatever it was with Stevie. I think she felt guilty about it, which was why she was spreading the money around, but I don't think she felt she could tell Stevie she wasn't playing any more.'

Ciara shook her head and looked away, out of the windows. For the first time since Jasmine told her about her old school friend's death, she looked like she might be about to shed some tears.

'Can't believe it's been so long since it happened,' she said, swallowing to steady her voice.

'Since what happened?'

'Since Julie died. She was our flatmate. Julie Muir. She was murdered.'

Jasmine's mind whirred.

'Was this anything to do with . . .?'

Ciara shook her head dismissively, closing her eyes for a second as though blotting out a memory.

'No. It was just some weirdo. Not right in the head. She was just in the wrong place at the wrong time. Poor Julie.'

Jasmine was about to say how her mum had never mentioned this, but caught herself in time. Besides, she had: Jasmine recalled her talking about a flatmate who had died, though Mum never said she was murdered, and never said her name.

'We couldn't live in the same flat after that. I moved back home for a while and Yvonne found another place. That's when we drifted apart.'

Ciara looked at clock. She was wanting this to be over, and the bell was about to grant her wish.

'Among Stevie's people,' Jasmine asked, acting before time ran out, 'do you remember anybody called James? Or Jazz?'

Ciara concentrated for a moment, genuinely giving it some thought, but she didn't find anything solid.

'I don't really know. I honestly did try not to have much to do with them. There was a Jimmy that he and Nico were mates with, so he'd have been James. Jimmy McKay or McRae, something like that. Stevie and Nico also had some cousins they hung about with, but I never knew their names, just heard about them because they were mental. They didn't go to Croftbank, though. They were at St Joseph's.'

The bell rang and Ciara got to her feet. She was making a show of reluctance but Jasmine knew she couldn't wait to leave.

'Sorry I can't be more help,' she said, sounding relieved that this was the case. Nonetheless, she looked at the picture one more time.

'The person you really want to be talking to about all this is the woman who *took* this photo.'

'Who was that?' Jasmine asked, trying to sound professional rather than manic.

'The barmaid at the Bleacher's Vaults, where this was taken. That's where Stevie and his mates always hung out, and nothing went on under her nose that she didn't know about.'

'Do you know where I might find her?'

'I could point you in the right direction, but I don't think she'll be in much of a mood for questions right now. Her husband just got shot dead in a car wash.'

Crimeless Victims

Anthony could see Adrienne Cruickshank heading in his direction and immediately felt the tense grip of awkwardness and mutual discomfort that accompanied their mercifully rare encounters. The shift patterns had been kind that way, the pair of them rarely working at the same time in recent months. On the odd occasion that they did pass each other in a corridor they said nothing, the sum of their communication being a sheepishly regretful look on his part, and sometimes a flushing on hers; anger or embarrassment, he wasn't sure.

They hadn't exchanged a word since that night. The problem was that they said nothing the first time they ran into each other afterwards, and that made it harder to say anything the next time, and so on. It always felt wrong, but he didn't know what might be the appropriate way to put it right. As he stood there by the coffee machine he was aware that they both knew they'd seen each other, but it had become silently agreed etiquette that they would both pretend they hadn't. To Anthony, however, it just seemed to compound his discomfort, so for that reason he had mixed emotions as he realised that she wasn't merely passing, but heading specifically towards him.

'Beano, McLeod tasked me with something but I'm just going off-shift and she won't want it left hanging, so . . .'

'You need me to pick it up,' he replied. 'No problem. What is it?'

They sounded like two colleagues having a normal exchange, and there was a mutual relief as each understood that the other would remain a willing confederate in this self-deception. It was better than the silence, even if they were still pretending nothing ever happened.

It felt like progress. He was pleased to be asked for something, more so to have the opportunity to say yes. He wasn't sure why. It wasn't as though he had done anything he needed to make up for, but he felt a need to make up for it all the same.

'I've started a background work-up on Brenda Sheehan, this new vic. Well, she's not officially a vic yet, but, you know. McLeod and Geddes found her face-up in her bed, apparently dead from getting seriously jaked and choking on her own vomit, but they're treating the death as suspicious.'

'Sheehan?' he asked, thinking out loud because it gave him something more to say. 'Why do I know that name?'

'Don't know. It was on Stevie Fullerton's mobile records.'

That wasn't it, though. He hadn't seen those. It had tugged at something when she said it, a specific emotion. Something sad, irredeemably so.

'Anything interesting so far?' he asked.

'She's got a jacket,' Adrienne replied, handing him a folder, her expression indicating that this didn't constitute 'interesting' to any great degree.

She turned on her heel the moment he took hold of the folder, keen to extricate herself from the encounter as soon as he had picked up the baton.

He glanced at her again as she retreated up the corridor, sufficiently distracted by his thoughts that he almost walked away without lifting his drink from the machine.

He took the folder and the coffee to his desk and, having decided none of his emails were genuinely urgent, got straight to the background check McLeod wanted. Given what Adrienne had said about her having a jacket, he started by looking her up on SCRO, the Scottish Criminal Records Office database.

Sure enough, Brenda Sheehan had form, though not the kind that would make her a natural fit for Stevie Fullerton's contacts list. She had a string of convictions for shoplifting, drunkenness and public order offences, though the most recent was more than fifteen years back. He guessed she had been an alcoholic who got clean at some point around her fifties. Prior to that, she had compiled a classic jakey jacket, though surprisingly she hadn't served any time, just fines and admonishments.

He wondered about that: she was a repeat offender and yet she had stayed out of jail. Somebody somewhere must have put an understanding word in for her now and then, and perhaps this advocate had also been instrumental in getting her on the wagon.

Next, he keyed her name into STORM. It stood for Systems for Tasking and Operational Resource Management, but the awkwardness of the wording and the resultant fact that nobody who didn't already know would understand that it was referring to a computer database gave it the strong whiff of a backronym. It listed all contact a person had had with the police, from giving witness statements right down to phoning up about a car alarm going off and keeping them awake.

He hit Enter to initiate the search, whereupon his screen promptly hung, leaving him watching an hourglass icon. Only time would tell whether this was down to lag from heavy traffic, a user-end glitch requiring a reboot or a full-on system crash. As he waited, he wondered again why the surname had seemed recently familiar, and why it had resonated the way it did: with sadness, regret.

He got out his notebook and flipped back through the pages. Names jumped out in capitals from amid black slabs of his careful handwriting – Beattie, Donnelly, Nokturn, Sharp – but Sheehan wasn't one of them. Maybe it wasn't the name, he mused uncomfortably: rather, merely the act of talking to Adrienne that had prompted that response, the sound of her saying the word possibly echoing something she said that night, or even just her tone as she said it.

Christ. They had got on so well before.

DC Cruickshank was a divorcee and mother of two. She had previously worked in IT, but had jacked it in and joined the police after splitting up with her husband, a surgeon at the Royal. He had done the thing married men supposedly never do by shacking up with the nurse who had previously been merely his bit of fluff, bailing on his wife and kids, the older of whom was two at the time. Adrienne had come out the other side of a near-breakdown by throwing herself headlong into a radically new career. As another product of the ACDP, they had developed an affinity.

He thought they were both firmly in the friend zone. They could be flirty with each other, but in what he assumed to be the harmless way between two pals who knew it could never mean anything else. She was eight years older: it wasn't a huge age difference, but with everything she had been through and her raising two kids on her own, he just imagined she must see someone as immature as him as being almost a generation apart. As with many older women who engaged with him that way, for a long time he thought they were flirting with the aid of a safety net.

However, over time something was definitely beginning to spark between them. He was allowing himself to wonder, and among those wonderings was the crucial question of whether, just maybe, she was beginning to wonder too.

He should have asked her out, but he was too afraid of the consequences if he'd misread things. He didn't want to do anything that might make her feel uncomfortable and render things awkward between them in future.

Yeah, good job there, Beano.

If he'd just been less of a shitebag about it, it might all have gone differently.

They ended up sharing a cab after a works night out, a retirement do for somebody in CID. In retrospect, he realised that due to the geography of it, by 'ended up' he meant that Adrienne must have actually engineered it that way, as she lived nowhere near him. When the cab pulled up outside his building she invited herself in. He remembered her saying something about her mother staying the night to look after the kids, so she had a late pass.

She didn't say 'all-night pass'; they were both trading on ambiguities, implied invitations and fingers crossed behind their backs in case they needed to tell themselves they didn't mean it.

Or maybe that was just him.

Adrienne was a bit merry, but not pissed. He would never have let it go that far if he'd thought she was.

Anthony, for his part, was drunk enough to delude himself about what was going on, but not enough to go through with it.

They started kissing on his couch.

He went with it, willingly losing himself, still perhaps safely moored by the assurance that there was only so far it was likely to proceed. She had a late pass, not all night. This was the start of something; a little faster than he'd anticipated, but maybe they had earned the right to skip a stage.

He remembered that she undid a brooch across the neck button of her blouse, and what was understood in that gesture. He didn't remember who unbuttoned what after that, only that somehow they were both stripped of their top garments, as though they had evaporated. Then she reached behind her back and undid her bra, slipping the straps from her shoulders in a quick, unfussy movement.

Her breasts were large and full, slightly drooped, from suckling he guessed. He only glimpsed them for a moment before she pressed them against the skin of his chest, but that was when there could be no more delusion: that was when he knew how far this was truly going. This was a real woman, a mother, a divorcee, someone who had lived more life than him, for good or bad, and someone for whom the distinction between all night and late pass had always been immaterial to these purposes.

Which is to say that he was already getting spooked by the time she slipped a hand inside his belt.

'I'm sorry, I can't do this,' he said.

He had heard it over and over again in his head since, and it never sounded any better.

'What's wrong?' she had asked, concerned.

'It's just too soon. I'm sorry.'

His MP3 player had shuffled to 'Tree Bursts' by Admiral Fallow. He remembered it playing in the horrible eternity of non-communication that followed. He couldn't listen to it any more without being back there, which effectively meant he couldn't listen to it any more full stop.

He saw such mortification in her face, turning to pain and confusion.

He was still appalled to contemplate what she imagined he saw or thought in that moment the spell was broken. Did she beat herself up about seeming desperate, insinuating her way into his taxi, his flat, then throwing herself at him, lunging for his cock in the hope that she could take things past the point of no return before he sobered up? Please, God, no. It wasn't her. She didn't do anything to be ashamed of.

But more appalling was when he imagined what *she* might have thought. Would she think it was because of the kids, that he had slammed on the brakes when he realised what he might be getting dragged into? Or even worse, that he hadn't liked what he saw when she took her clothes off. Oh Jesus: the very idea of her thinking that left him all twisted up inside.

He should have explained, but *how* could he explain? While she was pulling her bra back on and wiping away tears of embarrassment was hardly the time to tell her this was the closest he had come to having sex in four years, never mind the reason why.

The screen finally refreshed itself, the STORM search page replaced by the results for Brenda Sheehan.

Sheehan was her maiden name: she had never married. He jotted down her date of birth and worked out that she was sixty-three when she died. She had lived at the same house in Miner's Row since the seventies, and there was a rash of call-outs to the address during the eighties, mostly concerning harassment and vandalism. Notes indicated that the target of these incidents was her brother, one James Edward Sheehan, for whom, rather strangely, she was listed as legal guardian. The incidents ceased around the end of the decade.

He wondered what changed; perhaps the local neds found something else to do, or the ringleader moved away. Then he found out.

The next listing detailed a police dispatch, eighteen years ago, to give her what they called the death message. Her brother had died.

In prison.

Anthony returned to the SCRO database and keyed in the name, the results appearing this time after a short delay. The brother had a conviction for public indecency, after exposing himself to some schoolgirls. That was probably what led to the harassment, but it was what ended it that answered why the surname had chimed in his head.

It was James Edward Sheehan who had murdered Julie Muir, in the case he'd read about at the Mitchell.

He flipped through his notebook again and found the page where he'd written down which months Fullerton had been checking out on the microfiche. That was when he realised he'd screwed up.

He hadn't been able to work out what Fullerton was looking for in the first spool, and having found the accounts of the riot at Nokturn and its fallout, he had focused on that instead. However, Julie Muir's killing had appeared on both: the first spool featuring the discovery of her body, and the second covering the trial.

Fullerton had been researching a decades-old murder case, and had recently been in telephone contact with the killer's sister. Now she, her brother and Stevie Fullerton were all dead.

He reached for his phone and speed-dialled McLeod.

Guest of the Government

Glen paced the narrow channel that was his cell and his mind was taken back to the sight of a polar bear he'd once watched in San Diego zoo, shambling up and down the edge of its tiny pool, shaking its head back and forth in distress at its confinement. How long had it taken for the thing to go nuts?

Glen considered how much he had seen of the world, and what his world had now been reduced to. He could probably paint all four walls and the ceiling without taking a step.

He remembered the first time he ever had a flat of his own, after he moved out of his mum's house. All grown up. Sorting out the connection of his phone and other domestic utilities had fallen somewhere between rite of passage and pain in the arse. For the first time in his life he had bills to pay, and ordinary, mundane, *adult* responsibilities.

In the movies, you never saw the criminal trailing round the shops to buy dinner plates or a settee. It wasn't all tedious, though: he could also kit himself out with his own choice of telly, video and hi-fi. No green screens, diagonal lines or knackered vertical hold for him any more. Brand new, best of gear, state of the art, and not because he was flush, but because it was free. During this floundering first encounter with utility paperwork combined with the mandatory labours of nest-building he had identified an opportunity, one which Stevie expertly refined.

Looking back, it was a wonder the credit crunch took so long in coming. Shops had targets to hit. They needed to shift units, rack up sales, and they didn't care where the money came from: your pocket, your credit card or a finance company, it was all the same to them. In fact, across a lot of chains, their preference was to sign you up to their storecard, so that not only would you walk out the door with a £250 telly, but £750 in credit should you want to come back for a video, a fridge and a microwave as well.

All they asked for was a bank card and a utility bill for proof of address.

These days, with it being computerised, a stolen bank card would flag up the moment you tried to refer it, but back then it was all being done on handwritten forms and sent by post.

Glen or Stevie would get on to BT, Scottish Gas and the Electricity Board and tell them they were taking up the service at a property they knew to be lying empty, always choosing one in a well-off neighbourhood. Back then, you didn't need bank details or credit cards to get a service. You signed up, they sent you a bill, and if you didn't pay it they cut you off.

They would sign up using names that corresponded with a stolen card or one of the many phantom accounts Stevie had opened using false ID. Then they would give the postie a back-hander to pass on any mail bound for their bogus name at the vacant property.

Each name and address could bag them a card for several different chains: Currys, Comet, Dixons; to say nothing of department stores.

It wasn't as simple as just turning up with the paperwork and a shopping list, however. Stevie knew that how you presented yourself was crucial. You didn't just need the right image, you needed a story and, in his case, a scene-stealing co-star.

Her name was Yvonne.

Glen had no idea how Stevie knew her, as she seemed to belong to another world. It wasn't just as if she came from a different background socially or geographically, more like she was of a different species. She carried herself with this unique grace, as though she was aware everyone in the room was looking at her and that she was simultaneously invisible. Glen had never seen anyone like her, not up close. When she wanted to, she could seem as glamorous as one of those women on *Dallas* or *Dynasty*, at a remove from your reality, yet at other times there was an everyday normality about her that could set you at your ease. It was as though she was unapologetic for her presence, but not brash; cooperative but not compliant; complicit but not beholden.

She and Stevie would go into the stores pretending to be a recently engaged couple who were moving in together. Stevie dressed smartly: a suit if it was a weekday and they were making out they had met up for a shopping trip over their lunch hour; expensive but non-flashy gear on Saturdays. It was almost incidental because the shop assistants, male or female, all ended up just looking at Yvonne.

It was the first time Glen understood what people meant when they said of someone: 'she wears the clothes, the clothes don't wear her.' Weekdays or weekends, Yvonne never looked glammed up; or crucially never like someone *trying* to glam up. She looked businesslike through the week, and understatedly elegant on Saturdays, with the air of someone who could look smart in bin-liners if you gave her five minutes and some paperclips.

Glen's role was confined to heavy lifting and driving the van, but his presence was explained airily by Yvonne as being her brother, along to help with the flitting and 'to make sure *he* [being Stevie] doesn't skimp on the spending'.

She could probably have said Glen was her indentured servant and nobody would have paid it much heed. All they ever saw was Yvonne, remembering nothing of Stevie or Glen; and if the polis were ever to investigate, the shop assistants would describe a girl who didn't exist, as outside of those jobs she never dressed that way, wore her hair that way, even walked that way. It was a complete performance, carried off so convincingly that Glen realised he had no way of knowing whether the person she presented to him and Stevie bore any resemblance to the truth either.

They didn't merely kit out their own pads, or flog the extras out the back of a van. Stevie had buyers who would come up from Manchester and Birmingham, paying for bulk loads. It would be sold as new on the floors of independent shops, and the prices reflected that.

They raked in thousands, scoring credit from electrical stores in every retail estate and high street across central Scotland. Stevie kept a log of where they had been and when, as well as the names of the people who served them. Staff turnover – or simply coming in on somebody's day off – meant they could hit them again once they had worked their way back to the start of the list.

Stevie always thought ahead, but nobody anticipated just how far ahead.

He raised a few eyebrows by starting a car-wash business. He rented a disused petrol station in Shawburn on the north side of the dual carriageway, a place that had gone out of business when BP opened a garage half a mile up the road. It must have cost him buttons. Hardest part was probably finding out who still owned it.

Stevie hired a bunch of wee shavers and a couple of older guys he could rely on to keep them in order, and kitted them out with buckets, sponges and chamois leathers.

Tony McGill was at a loss as to why an accomplished thief and fraudster such as Stevie thought such a venture worthwhile, and nearly choked when he found out he had set it up as a legit company, declaring profits to the tax man.

'It's a cash-only business, for Christ's sake,' Tony reasoned. 'Have you gone doolally?'

'That's how they got Al Capone,' Stevie replied. 'Unpaid income tax.'

'Aye, and he died of the clap as well,' Tony replied. 'Since then we've worked oot ways of avoiding both those problems.'

'Death and taxes catch up with everybody in the end,' Stevie argued. 'As you say, it's a cash-only business. We're not selling anything in quantifiable units: no stock to account for, and no way of knowing how many folk have come through here and paid to get their motor cleaned.'

'Ahhh,' said Tony. 'So the tax man doesn't need to know how much money you're really clearing, and you've got a legit income if they start asking how come you've got a nice motor and what have you. I get it.'

But he didn't.

As Stevie explained to Glen, paying tax wasn't a problem: it was the purpose of the exercise.

'Once you've paid tax on money, it's legitimately yours, no matter where it came from. All the cash I'm bringing in from jobs, I can put that through the books. Claim my wee car wash is doing a roaring trade, and every last fiver I've grafted, even if I rifled it out of somebody else's till half an hour ago, becomes, in the eyes of the law, officially mine. Or my company's, rather: corporate tax rate is smaller than personal.'

'But you've still got to pay the tax on it,' Glen pointed out.

'Like any expenditure, it's not what it costs, it's what it's worth. Tony cannae see what I'm buying with my taxes.'

'Whit, Trident?'

Stevie laughed.

'Naw. Tony McGill is a millionaire yet the man doesnae have a bank account. If the polis had the balls to raid his hoose, they'd find tens, maybe hundreds of thousands in cash stashed aboot the place, and they could do him like Capone because he cannae prove where it came from.'

'Tony's not afraid of that. He's paid out his own worthwhile expenditure to make sure he's protected.'

'There's no guarantees, though, not with the polis. But it's not about protection: it's about restriction, about limitations. You think these yuppies driving Porsches in London have got piles of hard currency hidden under their floorboards? The more money you make, the less cash you physically touch, and there's things in this world you cannae buy with a sports bag full of fivers.'

'Like what?'

But Stevie just grinned and tapped his nose.

Passing Glances

'As I said, I have to stress that at this stage we are merely treating the death as suspicious,' Catherine told Mrs Lamont, standing in her living room in a spot that afforded a clear view across Miner's Row to Brenda Sheehan's house opposite. The number of police and ancillary vehicles parked along what had commonly been an empty stretch of pavement indicated just how suspicious they were treating it, but she had to maintain the distinction.

Mrs Lamont carefully put down a tray bearing a matching teapot, milk jug, cups, saucers and even sugar bowl, complete with tongs for the neat wee cubes. The little girl still inside Catherine trilled with a daft excitement. There was even a strainer. Loose leaf, no less.

She had asked if they wanted tea and Laura had looked askance as Catherine said yes. They weren't supposed to, but Catherine didn't think there was much risk of Mari here pissing in the pot or trying to poison them. She reckoned they would get more out of her by accepting, reasoning that Mrs L probably didn't get as many visitors as she would like, and probably became more garrulous when she was showing off the good china. Besides, she didn't think it would wash to offer the usual polite excuse that they had just had one. Catherine guessed that Mrs Lamont's eyes had seen plenty, but had the further impression that they didn't miss much, especially through her living-room window. Thus she would have seen Catherine and Laura when they were across the road, and known there was no way they had got a cuppa at the Sheehan household.

They had been over there talking to the crime scene manager, DI Tariq Yunnis, and getting early feedback, all of which was supporting Catherine's suspicions.

'They'll need to do analysis, obviously,' he told them, 'but one of the Forensics techs said just from looking at it, the fluff and dust on the carpet had come from inside a hoover bag; maybe more than one. She reckoned somebody emptied the stuff about the place and then tramped it into the carpet.'

Catherine had watched an officer cart a big crate of bottles out towards one of the vans.

'We're getting those dusted,' Tariq explained. 'See who else touched them. See whether the *deceased* actually touched them.'

'Why do you suspect she didn't?' Catherine asked.

'Shopping bags,' he replied. 'She kept them in a wee dookit in the kitchen: disposable and canvas. There were still receipts at the bottom of some of them.'

'Not taking advantage of those tempting supermarket booze offers our politicians get so exercised about?'

'Not so much as a can of shandy. Time-stamps on the receipts indicated she usually shopped first thing, too, before they're allowed to sell alcohol.'

'Mrs Lamont, the lady across the street, said she went to the shops after eight o'clock mass,' Laura told him.

'That tallies. But the clincher is the neighbours on the other side of the semi. They said that three nights ago, about eleven, they heard a jangle of glass, like somebody was taking out a load of empties. My guess is somebody was actually bringing them in.'

'So it's looking like she was still on the wagon?'

'That would be my impression so far, but if you want it from the horse's mouth, we found the details of her AA sponsor. Zoe Vernon is away to interview her.'

Mrs Lamont poured tea through the strainer with practised delicacy and no little pride. It was, as Catherine had predicted, a pleasurable ritual, even in circumstances such as this. Nonetheless, despite being starved of company, it was her guess that Mari hadn't extended this hospitality to her neighbour from over by. Those remarks about not wishing to be nosy, and seeing her with her shopping of a morning: these depicted two women on polite-greeting-over-the-garden-fence terms, not afternoon-tea-with-the-good-china terms. Given that the alcoholic Brenda may well at one time have been the neighbourhood nightmare, this probably wasn't surprising, but equally it could have been Brenda who kept her distance during those days. Alcoholics could go to great trouble to hide their habits, which made Catherine wonder how much Mrs Lamont knew.

'Did you know Miss Sheehan well?' Catherine asked.

'Ach, no,' she replied regretfully, as though things might have turned out better had she taken an interest. 'Just to say hello to, really.'

'How did she seem to you recently? Did she appear stressed, worried, different in any way?'

'No. Just . . . normal, I suppose. She was a creature of habit, which was why I got a bit worried when I didn't see her coming back from mass as usual.'

'Were you aware she had a drink problem?'

She looked confused for a moment, genuinely taken aback.

'Well, yes, of course,' she said. 'But that was a long time ago. She's AA now. Has been for years and years.'

Catherine watched her stumble and pause on her misuse of the present tense, giving a sad little shake of the head by way of correcting herself. They weren't close, but Brenda had clearly been a fixture in her little world for a very long time. At times like this, your instincts struggled to grasp this wasn't a temporary absence.

'So you had had no reason to suspect that she was back on the drink?'

'Absolutely none,' she replied, both adamant and incredulous, as though this was to impugn both Brenda's honour and her own powers of observation.

Catherine wasn't shy about impugning either.

'Do you mind if I ask what you would have been looking for?'

Mrs Lamont gave her a demonstrably patient look: polite, but unmistakably intended to convey that patience had been required.

'Well, I haven't seen her being sick in the street or falling down unconscious on her front lawn for at least fifteen years, but perhaps the signs got subtler.'

And that's me tell't, Catherine thought.

'So you saw her at her worst,' she suggested.

'No, dear. I think I saw her at her most drunk. I don't think anybody saw her at her worst, as she bore a great deal of difficulty alone.'

'What do you mean?'

She sighed and took a sip of tea, glancing across to Brenda's house.

'I never knew the family; Brenda and her brother Teddy moved into that house after her mother died. The father absconded way back: he was a no-user, by all accounts. The mother died quite young – I think she was only in her fifties – and that left Brenda responsible for Teddy. He was, you know, mentally handicapped. I don't know if that's considered rude these days, so forgive me.'

'Not at all. Do you know what was wrong with him?'

'No. They'll have a name for it now, no doubt, but back then they'd have just said he was simple. As far as I'm aware, Brenda already had a problem with the drink before her mother died. I think the mother may have too, I don't know. But it can't have been easy, burdened with Teddy when other women would have been having families and careers and what have you.'

'Was he, I mean, was she what would now be called a full-time carer?'

'I suppose. Teddy went off to some kind of day centre – you'd see him at the bus stop – and Brenda did some cleaning work in between times.'

'So he had some degree of autonomy?' Laura asked.

Mrs Lamont gave them both a pained look. There was a yes and no answer coming, but the level of equivocation was way above the floor model.

'He did. He was out and about on his own quite a lot. Brenda could send him for a pint of milk, you know, but there was no guarantee he wouldn't give the change away to somebody on the walk home.'

'Was he vulnerable, then?' Catherine asked, wondering about the unmistakable impression she had developed that Teddy wasn't around any more.

Again the pained look, and a long pause.

Mrs Lamont glanced out of her window, as though worried who might be watching, then dropped her voice to speak.

'He got into trouble with the police. They said he was interfering with himself in front of wee lassies. I must say, at the time I wasn't convinced it was what they said it was. I've no doubt he was maybe footering with himself, because you'd see him do that, but I would have been surprised if he was aware of anybody watching, or even entirely aware of what he was doing. These weren't primary school girls, you see. I think there was an element of mischief because he was regarded as the local weirdo. And of course after that it got worse. The local kids gave poor Brenda a torrid time. Shouting abuse and throwing eggs, putting things through the letterbox.'

She looked across at the house again, shuddering at the memory. Or at least that's why Catherine thought she was shuddering, until Mari corrected her.

'I thought he was harmless. Just shows you how wrong you can be.'

'Why, Mrs Lamont?' Catherine prompted, as a pause threatened to become a silence.

'He killed that young girl, didn't he?' she said, as though Catherine ought to know. 'But of course, it would have been before your time. You forget as you get older. Twenty-five years doesn't seem so long any more.'

'It was before my time as a police officer, certainly. Who did he kill?'

'Her name was Julie Muir. She had just got off the train up near the big houses. He strangled her.'

She put the cup to her lips and stopped, then put it down again. Bad memories, bitter tastes.

Catherine watched Laura write down the name. They'd find out the details back at HQ.

'If there was any kind of silver lining, you might have thought it was that at least Teddy was off of Brenda's hands, but I don't think she regarded it that way. You seldom saw her out and about

184

once he went to prison, and on the odd occasion you did, she'd cross the street or avoid catching your eye.'

'What happened to him?' Catherine asked, calculating that he ought to have been released long since, unless he was sectioned.

'He died in prison. I don't know if it was anything to do with his condition, I just know he died. Of course, someone like Teddy, you'd always be afraid one of the other prisoners would do something to him, but that wasn't what happened.'

Mrs Lamont seemed to change her mind about the tea and drank down the last of it, as though drawing a line under something.

Catherine's phone rang: Zoe. She excused herself and took a walk out into the hall, leaving Laura to take over for a minute. She heard her ask about when Brenda got cleaned up, and the beginning of Mrs Lamont's answer, something about Teddy's anniversary.

'Hi, Zoe. I gather you're talking to Sheehan's AA sponsor,' Catherine said, so that Zoe could take a few things as read.

'Yes, ma'am. Sponsor's name is Agnes Nisbet. She's a retired teacher. She's known Brenda for fourteen years, sees her at least once a week, most recently five days ago. Absolutely no hint she was coming off the wagon, and I'm guessing she'd know what to look for.'

'Had she come off before?'

'A few wobbles over the years, yes, but Agnes said you could see the build-up to them from miles out.'

'So I take it she was on an even keel recently.'

'More than that. Agnes said she had been a bit burdened, as she always was at this time of year.'

'Is this about the brother?'

'Yes. You know about that?'

'We're with the neighbour across the street. Getting filled in on local history.'

'Okay. So she gets kind of burdened when it comes around to "the anniversary", as Brenda described it.'

'The brother's death.'

'Except that this year, Agnes said Brenda came out the other side of it early and in good shape. She was religious, wasn't she? A Catholic?'

'Tim to the brim,' Catherine confirmed, thinking of all the crucifixes and holy pictures. 'Why?'

'It's just that Brenda told her sponsor she was in a good place, mentally and spiritually, because she had "finally made her confession". Agnes kept using the word "burdened", so I got her to clarify that this was Brenda's term. It sounded like there was something she seriously needed to get off her chest, and she felt a lot better about herself afterwards.'

'Aye. Until a little while later she's surrounded by all this alky debris, having apparently drunk herself to death.'

Catherine walked back into the living room, where Mrs Lamont was talking with admiration and regret about Brenda's efforts to literally put her house in order, her endeavours to tidy up her garden being particularly appreciated by the neighbour who had to look at it every day from her own.

'Mrs Lamont, did you notice whether Brenda had any visitors recently?'

She gave it some thought, gazing across the road as though trying to picture the scene without all those polis vehicles cluttering it up.

'Not in the past few days, no. Although, hang on, there was a chap maybe a couple of weeks ago. I noticed him because I saw his car going along very slowly, like he was looking for a particular house, and I was very curious to see where he was going to stop. He got out and went in to see Brenda. He was there a while. I saw him coming out again.'

'And did you see Brenda? Did she seem upset or anything?'

'No. They seemed to part on quite polite terms.'

'Do you think you would recognise him if I showed you a picture?'

'I don't know. I'd be happy to try.'

Catherine reached into her bag and looked out the mug shot she carried for control purposes. It was of an actor from the Pantechnicon, posing as a con.

'Is this him?'

186

Mrs Lamont pored over it for barely half a second and shook her head.

'No. Definitely not. Too young, for one thing.'

'What about this one?' she suggested, presenting a picture of Glen Fallan.

'The age is closer, but no.'

Catherine swapped it for a shot of Stevie Fullerton.

'And how about this guy?'

Mrs Lamont reached for the picture and began nodding enthusiastically, pleasantly surprised at her own certainty.

'Yes. This is him. I wasn't being nosy. It was just that I couldn't help but be curious as he had such a fancy-looking sports car.'

Face Value

'Tick tock,' said a voice from behind Glen as he jogged along the edge of the sports field, savouring the outside air and maximising his exercise time.

He turned and, as he expected, saw only a group of inmates standing watching the football match that was in progress, none of them making eye contact.

It wasn't the first time he'd heard it, though each time the voice had been different. Somebody was trying to put the fear into him, playing on the facelessness of the place and the fact that he'd never know who to look out for when the time finally came.

The only person he at least knew *not* to look out for had been the first guy to vocalise the threat, because he was the only one who said anything face to face. It was somebody he vaguely recognised from way back when, twenty-five years and in this prick's case about twelve stone ago.

'You're deid, Fallan,' he had said, leaning over Glen as he lay back, using one of the weight-training machines. 'You're fuckin' deid.'

'I've been deid before,' he replied. 'I'm developing a tolerance.'

Glen knew he could discount him as a threat because the people he was truly worried about wouldn't be identifying themselves. Nor would they be giving him any warnings.

Glen heard a sudden babble of voices from over by the entrance, and saw one of the screws bark orders to his colleagues as he hurried towards the source. This time Glen immediately checked his surroundings, watching for a blindside attack like the one that had claimed the slashing victim in the dining hall. This wasn't a diversion, however. Whatever was going down had happened inside.

Exercise time was extended by twenty minutes because they were still cleaning up the corridor when the standard hour was up.

Word spread fast in a place like this. Before he had even made it back to his cell, Glen had learned that the victim this time was the slasher from the other day. He'd been stabbed in the throat with a sharpened hairbrush. He had been rushed to the infirmary, but the rumour was he was already dead.

Tit for tat. Back and forth. The endless cycle.

He thought of Stevie, and a cycle Glen thought he'd ended long ago, but he'd been wrong.

Nokturn.

It was a place on West George Street called Night-Tek, which Stevie renamed, after a club he'd been to while on business in Holland. The main interior was square, overlooked by a mezzanine level on three sides, meaning most of the seating areas were secluded beneath the upper platforms, with the dance floor in the centre. Up on the mezzanine, there was a further elevation of two steps at one end, forming a golden-rope-cordoned VIP area. This was where Stevie held court among friends or received special guests, such as the occasional footballer, boxer or model: sometimes comped in, and in other instances paid to put in an appearance.

Glen didn't like pubs but he did enjoy nightclubs. He liked the music, the volume and power of it, and he especially liked the fact that it was too loud for anyone to bother speaking much. People seldom tried to make conversation with him, and this made it easier to just melt into the walls and observe.

Jazz had been at the bar, almost certainly pulling rank to get served ahead of the queue, but that wasn't what led to the carnage. This was premeditated and carefully planned. An unholy alliance of the Egans, the Beattie mob and assorted other Gallowhaugh miscreants had slipped in, separately and quietly, and on a pre-arranged signal commenced wrecking the joint.

The pre-arranged signal was Stanley Beattie slashing Jazz, opening his face from his cheekbone to his jaw.

Downstairs descended into mayhem instantly, as the assailants took advantage of the panic among the revellers to start tearing up the place. They primarily attacked known faces associated with Stevie, but if they couldn't find one to hand, they just went for anybody who didn't get out of the way fast enough. Tables and chairs flew, as did fists, boots, bottles and glasses.

Glen accompanied Stevie as he ran to the balcony. Even amid the chaos, the darkness and the flashing lights, it didn't take him long to suss what was going on. Doke and Haffa went barrelling into the mêlée, the club's bouncers also charging in from all sides. The music went off and the house lights came up, but neither prompted a breaking of the spell: they just provided a clearer view of the violence and made the sounds of screams, wreckage and collision seem all the louder.

Glen tried to restrain Stevie from his efforts to get downstairs. 'Let your boys handle this,' he urged.

Glen saw it for what it was: a jealous, impotent act of destructive defiance, like a doomed peasants' uprising. Stevie should have ignored it, gone back to the VIP area and sipped champagne until the perpetrators had all been chucked out onto West George Street, or even presided over it serenely from above, recognising that it represented a form of triumph.

'They're just trying to drag you down to their level,' Glen told him. 'They want a shot at you, on their terms.'

Stevie stared at him in consternation, then wrestled his way past. Glen could probably have stopped him, but it wasn't worth it. Stevie wanted it too much.

Looking back, Glen's reasoning hadn't stood a chance, and the latter gambit had probably been the most counter-productive thing he could say. As he began to understand, gazing down and watching Nokturn's new owner wade into the fray, Stevie was always on their level. Stevie had been holding court in his new kingdom, sipping champagne in the VIP section, then two minutes later he was brawling in the dirt with nobodies, and what this told Glen was that Stevie, in keeping with all his crew and all the guys they were fighting with, would *rather* be brawling in the dirt than lording it in the VIP section. They only wanted to be sitting there as a fuck-you to their rivals anyway.

Despite being ahead in his thinking, and having the vision to see a world beyond Gallowhaugh, when it came down to it, it was still all about face, all about being on top. If somebody wanted a shot at Stevie he couldn't walk away from it, like he couldn't stand even thinking they'd put one over on him. He also loved the violence, loved the mayhem, a strange corollary to his meticulous sense of organisation, his command of systems and plans.

Glen saw nothing he could use or enjoy in this. He watched for a few minutes and then slipped away out the fire exit, the sound of sirens carried on the blast of cold air that greeted him as soon as he opened the door.

Bad Blood

The car park outside the Old Croft Brasserie was surprisingly full for this hour of the morning, Jasmine thought. It was just a little past ten and yet it looked like it could be lunchtime; an upscale business lunchtime at that, going by the array of pricey rides lined up across the tarmac. Her beloved red Civic was only a year old and in her eyes still immaculate enough to grace any showcourt, but it looked almost dowdy, not to mention minuscule, alongside so many Q7s, X6s, Cayennes and Range Rovers.

She had heard the place was very trendy, but hadn't anticipated that it would be attracting such a crowd for morning coffee. At least this meant it was open, as she wasn't sure whether the mourning period was officially over.

She was trying to stem a sense of trepidation as she walked towards the main entrance, and thought of how her mum might have felt as she approached the same building back in her teens. Was she excited about the prospect of a night in the pub? Was she apprehensive about getting knocked back? Was she conflicted about being in the company of the Fullerton brothers, aware of the protection their patronage conferred, but equally conscious of being marked by association? It was impossible to know, and not much easier to picture. They'd spent a fortune renovating the place, so much so that her mum might not have recognised it.

Jasmine could see movement through the glass doors, hear the hubbub of voices and the clack of heels on a hard floor. Still she couldn't shake this feeling of exposure and vulnerability, hitting her all the harder for it being so unaccustomed. Doorstepping strangers was what she did for a living. It always put her a little on edge – and arguably that was where she needed to be in order to do it effectively – but she had grown used to how it felt.

This was something different, and in that action of reaching for the door handle, she understood why. The difference was that normally at this point she was pretending to be someone else. It was both her gambit and her shield: that moment of walking through the door and representing herself as someone she was not was the moment she stepped into character and left the real Jasmine outside. This morning, the only card she had to play was the truth; being herself the only valid passport to the world she needed to explore.

The door held firm, resisting her attempts both to push and pull. She tried the handle on the other one but fared no better. They were locked. However, her ineffective rattling at least attracted the attention of someone inside. A tall, heavy-set middle-aged man in a suit approached the doors, a tired expression on his face. He looked like a bouncer but she thought it a little early in the day for such personnel, and couldn't think of ever encountering one at a restaurant.

He opened the door just a little, certainly not by way of inviting her inside. Close up, she revised her bouncer impression. The suit was too expensive-looking, and in conjunction with the scars and tattoos she estimated she was dealing with management rather than employee; but not necessarily restaurant management.

'I'm sorry, we're closed the now,' he said.

Jasmine made a point of gazing inside, where she could see roughly twenty people seated at tables or standing around the bar.

'It's a private function,' he explained. 'Family only.'

This was when she had to play her card, and in so doing cross a point of no return.

'I *am* family,' she said.

His features compressed into an expression of terse consternation; not mere puzzlement, but the aggressive certainty of someone who expected to know every face present at this gathering today.

'My name is Jasmine Sharp. My mother was Yvonne Sharp.'

She could see the whole process in his eyes: information being sourced from some mental archive as he sought to retrieve the name, then the tiny but unmistakable flinch as he deduced the significance and possibilities presented themselves. Nonetheless, he still wasn't quite getting there, and thus he still wasn't quite ready to open that door.

'I never met my father, because he died before I was born. But I'm told his name was Jazz.'

She tried to make it sound like she knew this was her all-access pass, but her voice faltered on the last word, feeble and appellant. This was the conversation her mother never wanted her to have, the world she had gone to extraordinary lengths to protect her daughter from.

The man on the door didn't look like someone who was ordinarily rocked on his heels by anything less than a baseball bat, but he seemed slightly dazed by what she had just said. He stared at her, startled for a moment, then turned his head to look inside. Jasmine couldn't see who he was looking to, but a few moments later a petite female figure emerged from behind a table and began pacing towards the entrance.

He held the door open for Jasmine now, looking at her as though he couldn't be sure she was real, as if she might suddenly vanish and turn out to have been an apparition.

'Jazz Donnelly?' he asked.

Jasmine couldn't confirm this, as it was the first time she had heard someone give her father a surname.

'Hence Jasmine,' she replied.

'Jesus. I'd no idea. I'm Jazz's big brother, David.'

He held out a hand, uncomfortable in the gesture as though aware of how inadequate and ill-suited it seemed to the occasion. Jasmine gave it the briefest and most awkward of squeezes. It felt warm against her skin, cold from driving. His hand was large and strong, but the grip was weak, reflecting the uncertainty of what was passing between them.

The petite woman had made it to the door. She looked early fifties, smart but a little over-dressed, especially for the time of day. She was lavishly made-up, but it couldn't disguise tired eyes and a harshness to her features. She was smaller than Jasmine but exuded a latent aggression like it was a force field. This, she guessed, was Sheila Fullerton, the person she had come to see.

'Sheila, this lassie says she's Jazz's daughter,' David explained, sounding like he needed somebody else to judge the veracity of it for him. 'Says her ma was Yvonne Sharp. Mind ay her?'

Sheila looked Jasmine up and down, cold scrutiny failing to disguise an almost fearful astonishment at what she was being asked to rule upon.

Jasmine decided to speak before the verdict was in.

'Are you Sheila? Who worked here when my mum used to come in? It's just . . . she told me absolutely nothing about those days, and I've heard you might be able to help.'

Sheila continued to stare, wide-eyed and a little stunned.

'You say . . . Yvonne . . . Sorry, *was* . . . Do you mean your mum . . .?'

'She died three years ago. But I gather she was born on the same day as Stevie Fullerton, and they used to come here together. He was your husband, right?'

The hubbub continued in the background, but in that moment it felt to Jasmine like she and Sheila were entirely alone, and locked in silence. She honestly had no idea whether she was about to be beckoned forth or frogmarched back out through the double doors.

Sheila glanced to David, then back to Jasmine.

'Come on through,' she said. 'We'll go somewhere quiet we can talk.'

All The Perfumes Of Arabia

Glen hefted a beige-coloured grille that he identified as having once been part of a vacuum cleaner, moving it from the chaotic melange in front of him and placing it carefully into a marked hopper. All around him, other inmates were carefully and unhurriedly getting on with the same thing, either side of four long tables piled high with smashed-up stereos, monitors, domestic appliances, toys and packaging.

All plastic. More bloody plastic.

Tons of it were delivered to the prison's recycling workshop every day, to be hand-sorted by the inmates then sold on to a reprocessing firm who would refine it into pellets for re-manufacture. Given the sentence he was looking at, Glen estimated that if he worked here every day, by the time he got out he would have enough carbon offset points for a guilt-free trip to the moon.

He took in the scene of unfussy diligence all around, imagined what the well-meaning social reformers might make of it. To them it might prove that gainful and dignified employment was what all men needed, that they wouldn't turn to crime if they were given a useful role and a shared sense of purpose.

Maybe, Glen thought, but you'd need to get to them early. After all, the gainfully employed didn't suddenly turn to a life of crime simply because it paid better. Most criminals of Glen's acquaintance had never known anything else. They were second- and even third-generation, people to whom it would never have occurred to look for honest work. They grew up looking at the world with different eyes, seeing different kinds of opportunities, different kinds of obstacles. They envisaged treasures behind every locked door yet imagined many of the open ones were somehow impenetrable to them.

These plastics could be reprocessed and turned into something else. It wasn't so easy for the people sorting them. Glen understood that better than most. Where others had been conditioned by growing up with crime, Glen had been conditioned by growing up with violence. It had shaped him into an instrument that wrought more violence, an instrument from which ruthless men had profited. It shaped him so completely that he had lost sight of any other self he might have been.

That was until he had his epiphany, watching Yvonne playing Lady Macbeth at the Tron.

It was haunting, watching her so fully become someone else, an effect that served to further remind him that he had no idea who the real Yvonne was. She looked older, burdened, so dark and so consumed with an inner want, with anger and ruthlessness and a dozen other things that were not Yvonne at all. To Glen, it was spellbinding.

Then she drifted across the stage like she was disconnected from it, eyes open but dead, face expressionless.

'Lo you! here she comes. This is her very guise; and, upon my life, fast asleep. Observe her; stand close.'

'How came she by that light?'

'Why, it stood by her: she has light by her continually; 'tis her command.'

'You see, her eyes are open.'

'Aye, but their sense is shut.'

'What is it she does now? Look, how she rubs her hands.'

A sharply focused lighting gel bathed only her hands in red, and Glen watched with growing disquiet as he understood what she was trying to wash away: a stain that wasn't there, and yet could never be cleansed.

'Yet who would have thought the old man to have so much blood in him.'

As Yvonne rubbed her hands with increasing desperation, he saw the blood pouring from a hundred wounds. He saw it spilling on the floors of pubs, of restaurant kitchens, in living rooms, bathrooms, garages, alleyways, streets, gutters.

197

'Here's the smell of the blood still; all the perfumes of Arabia will not sweeten this little hand.'

So much blood. So very much blood, all spilled by his hands, his deeds.

Yet what set him on edge as he sat in the darkness of the theatre was not that he saw his reflection in Yvonne's horror, but that he felt the scale of its *absence* in himself. As she rubbed her hands in the eerie red glow he apprehended the horror he ought to be feeling, but simply did not, could not.

Why did he feel nothing? He could feel Lady Macbeth's guilt, feel moved by it though it was merely a fiction, but could not feel a revulsion of his own. Yes, there was guilt – a gripping, twisting, unsleeping torture – for what he had done, but not for the deeds themselves, not for any of those he had killed. He knew he could kill again – he knew he *would* kill again – and feel none of what Yvonne was depicting on that stage.

'What's done cannot be undone.'

He couldn't change what he was, but he could change what he did. He had to put this instrument into the hands of men who might use it constructively. He had to pay the proverbial debt to society, but he chose to do it on his own terms. It was good enough for the big corporations.

He noticed one of the screws glancing his way a couple of times, then begin to make his way towards him. Glen wondered what kind of petty shit he was about to get picked up on, but instead the guy just told him to go and get a fresh bin for cable offcuts, as the one currently on the go was getting full.

The guard seemed strangely apprehensive about giving this order. It wasn't as if Glen could refuse.

He put down the smashed computer printer he had just lifted and made his way towards the fire doors that led outside to a partially covered courtyard. This was where the empty hoppers and bins were returned to once the reprocessing firm had dealt with their contents. The big hoppers ran on castors, but various colours of wheelie bin were used for collating smaller items, such as discarded circuit boards and, in this case, lengths of wire and cable.

Glen was ambushed moments after the doors swung shut at his back. They converged from behind as he entered a narrow channel between two rows of skips full of unsorted plastic, appearing all at once, as though from nowhere.

Glen recalled his first real kicking at the feet of a young team in Gallowhaugh. 'Polis boy,' they had called him, in reference to his dad. They were led by a sadistic wee piece of work called Joe McHaffey, whose oldest brother ended up one of Stevie's trusted lieutenants.

He remembered lying on the ground, cowering in a ball, the repeated impacts of his forearms being driven against his head. That wasn't satisfying Joe, though.

'His nose isnae burst yet.'

Glen would never forget those nasally wee words, as he instructed his mates to grab his arms and expose his face.

Joe wanted to see blood.

These guys were after much more than that.

Last Man Standing

Jasmine was led through the restaurant, conscious of a drop in the volume of discussion as those gathered noted the new arrival. She felt almost every eye in the place take her in, and from this rapidly deduced that everybody here knew everybody else. They were all similarly over-dressed for the time of day, though the women's colours were generally sober. It looked like a wake, but she knew that Fullerton's body would not yet have been released. This was some kind of informal memorial that was being hosted in the meantime.

Despite the upmarket décor and the name of the award-winning chef boasted on the menu she still couldn't picture her mum in this place, even in its present incarnation. To put it politely, these were not her mother's kind of people. It was a strangely paradoxical effect that to put a suit or a posh frock on certain individuals only served to emphasise the less presentable elements of their appearance. It was like prefixing the term 'businessman' with the word 'legitimate'.

There were women drinking glasses of wine and men downing pints, and it wasn't yet half-ten in the morning. Jasmine could smell the alcohol off the spillage traps on the bar and felt queasy. She recalled Josie's voice whenever she encountered jakeys on the street supping Special Brew or Buckfast while she was still digesting breakfast: 'I can't say the sun's quite over the yardarm.'

The mum who brought her up belonged to Josie's world. How the hell did she ever end up in this one?

She was led to the brasserie's compact but high-ceilinged private dining room, where several mirrors contributed to an artificial sense of space around the single long table. It was a neat trick, important not to make a group paying through the nose for the VIP treatment feel like they were being shoehorned in. Nonetheless,

Jasmine feared she was going to be feeling pretty claustrophobic in here before the end.

Sheila pulled out a chair for her, significantly on the other side of the table from the exit, then sat down opposite. David, or 'Doke' as Sheila called him, remained standing against the wall, close to the door. Jasmine got the unmistakable impression that she was very much under scrutiny, and quite possibly under their guard.

Jasmine produced the photograph of her mum with Sheila's late husband.

'I believe you took this,' she said, placing it on the table and turning it around to face her hosts.

She watched Sheila place a hand over her mouth at this ancient artefact that had found its way to her here and now as though through a wormhole in time. Doke leaned over to examine the photo also, letting out a surprised chuckle.

'Jesus. I remember her right enough,' he said, a tinge of pleasure creeping into his voice. 'That's Stevie and Nico.'

Sheila looked a little more haunted by the image, the sight of her late husband in his youth perhaps cutting a little too deep right then.

Her eyes lifted from the picture to regard Jasmine once more.

'You don't look like her,' she said, but it sounded more like an observation than a scorn upon her claim.

'She often said that. I've seen pictures of her as a younger girl: there's more of a resemblance in those. People would sometimes say I must look like my father, but to be honest that usually led to her getting off the subject.'

Jasmine tried to picture Doke as a younger man, searching for a sense of what her father might have looked like.

'We had no idea Yvonne was pregnant,' he said. 'She just disappeared.'

'Aye. "Just disappearing" was catching back then,' Sheila said pointedly, though Jasmine couldn't tell whether the jaggy end was aimed at her or Doke.

There was a light knock at the door, and a waitress appeared

201

carrying coffees for the three of them. Jasmine took a sip in silence, wondering whether her cheeks were as red as they felt, with two pairs of eyes still examining her so intently. She had little doubt that they believed her, but knew that wasn't the biggest question on their minds.

'She needed to get away,' Jasmine said, aware there was no point in sugar-coating this. 'She didn't want Jazz knowing she was pregnant. She wanted a clean break from her life in Glasgow.'

'Where did Yvonne go?' Sheila asked. She glanced down at her side, where Jasmine guessed her phone sat in her right palm.

'Edinburgh. Not exactly the ends of the earth, but far enough.'

'And she raised you herself, or . . .?'

'On her own, yeah.'

'Did she work?'

'She was a drama teacher.'

'And what is it you do yourself?'

Sheila's eyes narrowed just a little more as she spoke, and Jasmine couldn't help but feel she had just been checkmated.

'I have my own business. I'm a private investigator.'

Sheila sat back in her chair and sighed with a grim satisfaction. She held up her iPhone, on which a web page was visible.

'Private investigator, Jasmine Sharp. You're the one who helped put away those bent polis who were working for Tony McGill.'

'That's right.'

Doke's face darkened.

'You're the lassie that was cuttin' aboot with Glen Fallan when he showed up back from the dead two years ago?' he demanded, his voice low, like storm clouds rolling in. Jasmine could tell it wouldn't take long for them to break. 'The same bastard that just shot oor Stevie? The bastard that . . .'

'Doke,' Sheila cautioned. 'Keep the heid. The lassie's no' done nothin'.'

'Do you have any idea who Glen Fallan is?' he asked, incredulous. 'Did he tell you about the good old days?'

'He told me enough,' Jasmine replied. 'I know he killed people, but—'

202

Doke leaned over, slapping a hand on the table.

'He killed your fuckin' father. He killed Jazz. Did the cunt fuckin' tell you that?'

Jasmine looked up at the boiling anger in his face, then at her coffee. She picked up the cup and had a long pull at it, swallowing slowly. She wasn't trying to look nonchalant, she just needed something to physically occupy herself for a few moments while his anger receded, as she feared any kind of immediate verbal response would be incendiary, regardless of the content.

She didn't answer his question, reckoning her lack of surprise was answer enough.

'Nothing about this is straightforward,' she said. 'Yes, he killed my father. And yet, when my mother was in her last days, she had Fallan tracked down so that she could see him again before the end. *That's* what brought him "back from the dead". Was it to forgive him? I don't know. Was it to ask him why he did it? I don't know. I want to find out what happened back then. Like it or not, we're related, all three of us, but unlike you, I've never seen my father's face. I've never even laid eyes on a photo.'

Doke let out a very long sigh, the sound of a storm blowing itself out, if perhaps only temporarily. He sounded frustrated, like this would have been a lot easier to deal with if it fitted into the paradigms he understood. Sheila remained harder to read, still shutting herself inside and assuming the weather outdoors was bad.

'There's not many pictures of Jazz,' Doke said, sounding more reflective. 'At least, not from around the time he was seeing Yvonne.'

He looked at Sheila as he said this. There was clearly something unspoken in his latter remark.

'Didn't like getting his photo taken,' she agreed. 'He had this scar, right the way down his face, from forehead to jaw.'

She touched her own face as she spoke, looking away as though she could see Jazz in one of the mirrors.

'How did it . . .' Jasmine inquired tentatively, feeling she was on delicate ground.

'This sneaky wee cunt Stanley Beattie slashed him one night in a club, out of nowhere,' said Doke. His voice was tinged with an anger that still sounded raw, decades after the fact. It drew a warning look from Sheila: keep a lid on it.

'Jazz was a looker, and he knew it,' she said. 'He had a face that would get a jelly piece at any door, as my mammy used to say. Always had women wrapped around his pinkie, and he took a few liberties.'

She and Doke traded a look, Sheila telling him not to bother denying it.

'Aye, he flung it aboot,' Doke admitted. 'He was different after the slashing, though. Quiet. He'd calmed doon.'

'He wasn't calm, he was angry,' Sheila countered. 'Suffering in silence.'

'Either way, he did change,' Doke said. 'Yvonne wouldn't have went near him before that. Not that way, I mean: she'd known him for years, like, but she knew he was too much a Jack the lad to get involved with him. She must have thought he was calmer.'

'Some women are drawn to a damaged man,' Sheila said. 'They think they'll be able to put him back together in a way they prefer. Doesnae work out like that, though. We all thought Jazz was calmer. Truth is, he was just bottling it all up and eventually it was gaunny explode.'

There were a few seconds of quiet, which in this context Jasmine knew not to mistake for a moment of calm. Something hung in the air between these two that was not precisely blame or accusation, but definitely a cousin of both. Sheila seemed to be leaving it to Doke to continue, but he remained silent, his eyes straying to the photograph and back to Jasmine.

'Jazz killed Stanley Beattie as soon as he got out the jail,' Sheila said.

'He didnae mean to kill him,' Doke stated adamantly. 'He went to slash him and the guy put up his arm; Jazz ended up opening his wrist. It was an accident.'

Sheila said nothing, just gave Jasmine an arch look as though to say, 'How do you respond to that?'

It was a first glimmer of a different alliance that might emerge here, between the two women against a male mentality rather than between Stevie's two relatives against the interloper.

'He never moved on from the slashing, that's the point, Doke. We thought he had changed but the whole time he was just waiting to even up the score. It's why he's no' here any more. It's why Stevie's no' here any more.'

'Naw, that cunt Fallan's why they're both no' here any more,' Doke thundered, glaring at Jasmine.

'Aye, because *none* of you can ever move on,' Sheila retorted. 'Look at this photo: what does it tell you? Nico, Stevie, both gone. You should be happy, Doke: under these rules you're the winner if you're the last one left standing.'

'Fallan's still standing,' he reminded them darkly.

'Why did Fallan kill my father?' Jasmine asked quietly, almost apologetically.

'What did he tell you?' Doke replied.

'Nothing. Only that my father's death made it easier for my mum to escape. He wouldn't tell me why he actually did it.'

'Nobody knows for sure,' Sheila said, 'but it happened after Jazz battered her.'

She gave Doke a look, warning him against any denial based on misplaced filial loyalty.

'He thought she was swithering about being his alibi,' Doke admitted.

Finally Jasmine was seeing something other than defiance and anger in his expression when talking about his brother.

'She had been with him when he killed Stanley, but she told the polis he was with her somewhere else at the time. The polis were leaning on her because they knew she was lying and she was the weak link.'

'So he thought beating her up would engender a deeper loyalty?' Jasmine asked, barely masking her outrage.

'He wanted her more afraid of him than she was of the polis,' Sheila explained. 'But Fallan found out, and it never went well whenever Fallan found out about a guy beating up a lassie.'

'Well, you would know,' Doke muttered. 'You've nae problem with evening the score when it suits you, eh Sheila?'

Sheila stared down at the table for a moment, then continued as though Doke hadn't spoken.

'Fallan's da used to leather his maw,' she said. 'Used to leather everybody in the hoose. But because his da died before he could stand up to him, Fallan was always looking for surrogates, you know?'

Jasmine thought of the place she had first found him, at a domestic violence refuge where he was handyman, gardener and courier, among other services. Rita, the woman in charge, had alluded to what happened when abusers turned up at the place. The police would warn the blokes off, escort them from the premises, but once they knew their wives or partners were there, they always came back; except when Fallan was around.

'When he warns them off,' Rita told her, 'they never come back.'

'Jazz just went out one night and was never seen again,' Doke said, his lips thin, eyes narrowed too. 'That bastard killed him, dumped him somewhere and then lied to us about it. We never got to bury him, never had a proper funeral. *That's* what Fallan did to your father.'

The waitress who had brought the coffees returned looking for the empty cups and perhaps to see if anyone wanted anything else. She got as far as popping her head into the doorway and very swiftly read the atmosphere, hurriedly turning on her heel.

'He told me he owed me,' Jasmine said, feeling like it was incumbent upon her to respond, though she didn't know who appointed her Fallan's spokesperson or apologist. 'He said he owed me a debt.'

'You're not the only one he felt he owed something,' said Doke. 'It just wasnae so much settling a debt as payback.'

'For what?'

He and Sheila shared a look, like he knew she wasn't going to be happy but he couldn't be bothered with her disapproval any more.

'Fallan tripped himself up, for once. He told us he helped Jazz pack and fly away to Spain to lie low. Problem was, Stevie had contacts in the polis, and he found oot that Immigration had no record of Jazz leaving the country. That's how we knew he'd killed him.'

'What did you do to him?' Jasmine asked, steeling herself.

Doke rolled his shoulders, his posture straightening. All of a sudden he looked like he was answering in court.

'What happened after that, I cannae say for sure, because Stevie was fly, a born schemer. Unlike Jazz, he didnae just blaze in and worry aboot the consequences later.'

Doke's face shone as he warmed to the tale.

'There was a few of us he knew he could rely on. He gave each of us an envelope, which we werenae to open until we were alone. In it was a message telling us a time and a place. Some folk turned up to wherever it said and found one other member of the crew. Their instructions were just to stay there until they got the shout that it was done. Other boys had instructions for getting Fallan.'

'What did they do to him?'

'I was one of the folk that ended up just sitting around, so this is second hand. They ambushed him. They put a sack over his head and arms, and pinned him like that with a rope, then they got into him with hatchets and hammers and all sorts. I heard even a sword. They assumed he was deid when they left him, and for two decades that's what everybody assumed.'

'Why the business with the envelopes?' Jasmine asked.

Sheila looked down at the table, evidently not sharing Doke's pride in her late husband's resourcefulness.

'It was in case the polis ever tried to get somebody to turn. Only the folk who were there knew who else was involved, and the rest all had cast-iron alibis. I never even knew for sure whether Stevie was one of the ones that went – until Fallan turned up again and shot him.'

He gave her a look of contempt as he said this, like she had cheapened him by forcing him to explain all this to her. He also seemed to think it was the last word, the irrefutable clincher. If so, Jasmine was still missing something.

'I spent a lot of time with Fallan,' she said, 'and he never talked about grudges or settling scores. He had left that all behind for twenty-odd years. Why would he suddenly decide to kill Stevie now?'

'Beware the vengeance of a patient man,' Doke replied. 'That's what Stevie always said. Didn't he, Sheila? Well, now we know whose vengeance he was afraid of.'

Blunt Instruments

There were four of them. Two had stepped in from behind, cutting off his escape route to the recycling workshop. Two more had emerged from between the big skips, standing in front of what was anyway a dead end.

He didn't recognise them. As anticipated, they had not previously made themselves known, and the bloke who had threatened him directly was not among them.

They all had improvised weapons. They had blades. They had clubs.

They had no chance.

He had chosen his first target and struck before any of them were even sure he'd noticed them. He collapsed the guy's windpipe with a fingertip blow to the throat, disarmed him and used his falling body to block off the man next to him as he stepped sideways through the narrow channel.

In less than two seconds, Glen was standing with his back to the doors and nobody behind him. He was still facing three of them, but he had a length of pipe in his hand and it wasn't plastic.

He was the one cutting off *their* exit.

Christ, he thought, was this all they could muster? Or had his reputation so diminished through his prolonged absence that they thought this shower, plus the element of surprise, would be enough to take him down? It wouldn't have been enough twenty years ago, and that was before he had been taught to fight by military professionals.

It certainly hadn't helped them that there *was* no element of surprise.

Glen had long ago learned how to truly listen to his instincts. He understood how fear, the insistent sense that something was

209

wrong, emanated from parts of the brain that predated language or even cognitive thought, and thus operated a million times faster. He had needed no such primal instincts today, though: the awareness that he was about to be attacked didn't precipitate in the fraction of a second before the first blow was attempted. It came when the screw came over and told him to get a fresh bin for the offcuts.

It was all over the guard's face: a draining anxiety about what he knew was about to go down. More than that, he was thinking beyond it too. This guy was already worried about the inquiry later, unsure whether his arse was covered, concerned for his job. Glen could tell this wasn't a backhander to look the other way. There was pressure from somewhere else.

How far did it go, he wondered. Were the cops in on this too? He'd soon find out.

He rendered two of them unconscious as swiftly and cleanly as he could. He didn't want the aftermath getting complicated. The third one he left wide awake. Glen needed him to talk.

Glen had known this was coming, not merely since he'd noticed the state of that guard. He'd known it was coming since the moment he entered the prison.

Glen hadn't spoken a word to the cops, but that didn't matter. It was the golden rule of assassination: kill the assassin before he can tell anybody his version of events.

Sooner or later, he knew, they would make their move, and that was when he might finally catch a glimpse of who they were.

'Who arranged this?' Glen asked.

The guy answered pretty fast. He had expected this to be an easy gig, but now he wouldn't be getting whatever he was promised, and clearly there were no contingencies. Whoever put him up to this hadn't warned him what he was really getting into, so he wasn't feeling particularly loyal. Especially when Glen asked him if he had ever been curious about what his own spleen looked like.

'Doke,' he replied pleadingly. 'Doke Donnelly.'

'Shite,' Glen spat.

'It's the truth,' the guy said, panicking. 'It was Doke. He said to tell you it was payback for Stevie. And for Jazz.'

The guy had misunderstood why he swore. It wasn't because Glen didn't believe him: he did. He swore because this was the worst possible answer. Doke was loyal enough and stupid enough to have ordered this attack, but these were also two solid reasons why he couldn't possibly be behind the other thing.

Confession

'Knew I shouldn't have worn these,' Laura mourned, glancing down as her otherwise comfortable and work-practical suede shoes sank into the sodden turf, their soft tops spattered further with every step she took.

'And I bet you said no when the nice woman in the shop offered you the can of that spray-protector too.'

A fairly scunnered look told Catherine she had just added a layer of regret to Laura's discomfort.

They were making their way across the Shawburn municipal playing fields towards one of several pitches where football matches were in progress, the failing light indicating that none of them could have very long left to play.

Their route along a cinder path had brought them up behind one goalmouth of what had been indicated as pitch seven. It was here that Catherine ruined Laura's mood – and quite possibly her shoes – by proceeding around the touchline towards two groups of men gathered near the halfway mark. All but two were dressed in tracksuit tops, shorts below, indicating that they were substitutes. The exceptions she took to be the respective coaches or managers, though there was no discernible age gap between them and many of the participants.

When she'd been told where she might find Father McGhee, Catherine had assumed the priest must be in charge of the team, but she quickly realised that he could be anybody here. It was far from a youth game, and the fitness levels clearly weren't exacting either. She reckoned Laura would be able to comfortably outrun all of them, even in her suede pumps, while trying to keep pace with Zoe Vernon would have had them chucking up their guts.

Laura and Zoe would need their speed, though, were they ever imprudent enough to get involved in a game like this. In the time it took to walk halfway around the pitch, Catherine had seen two tackles that merited the production of her warrant card, never mind one from the referee; followed by an elbow-strike to the face like something out of the WWE. This last left its victim flat out in the penalty box while his team-mates raged at the ref, who had apparently missed it.

'We're looking for Francis McGhee,' Catherine said by way of announcing herself to the nearer of the groups on the touchline.

The one guy not wearing a tracksuit and shorts turned to address her.

'Do you see that guy with the number eight jersey? The one who just clothes-lined that boy a second ago?'

'*That* was Father McGhee?' Laura asked, appalled.

'Naw. But keep watching him, because your man's gaunny put him up in the air in aboot thirty seconds.'

Sure enough, as soon as the offending midfielder next got possession he was blindsided by a sliding lunge that could only have been described as 'late' by anyone naïve enough to believe that the ball played any part in the perpetrator's calculations. The tackle was, to Catherine's eyes, bang on time.

The referee hurried across to the aftermath, thrusting a red card at the silver-haired assassin, who responded with a resigned but disgusted wave of his hand.

'Aye, well seeing the blind cunt spotted that,' complained one of the subs.

'To be fair, he could hardly fuckin' miss it,' said the coach. 'Only bastart who never saw it coming was the buckled walloper in the number eight jersey.'

Catherine watched the offender leave the field. After a red card, the verb of choice for describing the dismissed player's gait was normally 'trudged', but this guy sauntered, head high, like he was out for a walk and the game just happened to be going on behind him.

He was in his fifties, she reckoned. He had a full head of hair, swept back in a severe-looking quiff. His face was weathered, lines

213

accentuating every angle, like he had walked out of a Howson painting. He reminded Catherine of Samuel Beckett, except she had never seen Samuel Beckett scissor-kick somebody from a horizontal position, following through with the trailing leg.

'Is that him suspended next week?' somebody asked.

'Aye, but he was going his holidays or away with the school or something anyway.'

As he neared the touchline, silver hair gave a cursory shrug of explanation or apology to his coach, like he knew neither was truly necessary.

'Franny,' the coach said, jerking his head towards Catherine and Laura. 'Polis here tae see ye.'

They hadn't identified themselves as such, but with certain types you didn't have to, and they liked to let you know it too.

'I'm Detective Superintendent Catherine McLeod, and this is Detective Inspector Laura Geddes,' she said, producing her card.

'Was the tackle *that* bad?' he asked, with a fly smile towards the boss.

'I was always given the impression that Jesus said turn the other cheek,' Catherine suggested.

'Jesus never had to play holding midfielder in the Shawburn and Gallowhaugh District League,' he replied.

'We need to talk to you about one of your parishioners.'

'Sure. It's a long way back to the pavilion: walk up with me. Gary, you got the key to the dressing room?'

The coach reached into his jacket and tossed McGhee a key with its end wrapped in red electrical tape.

'I'm only giving you this because these ladies will make sure you're not in there dipping pockets.'

'Aye, very good. I'll catch you after full time. You think we can close this one out with ten?'

'Gaunny have to, aren't we. But six-nothin' up, aye: I think we can cling on.'

They walked with him back along the edge of the pitch and on to the cinder path.

'Not exactly the beautiful game,' Catherine observed.

'Naw,' he replied with an arch grin. 'It's an ex-offenders team. Keeps folk occupied, which is important when you're unemployed. Gives them something to belong to, team-mates who'll look out for each other on and off the park. That's why I had to clean that boy out. It was so Eddie, the bloke that got elbowed, knows I've got his back.'

'Looking out for mind, body *and* soul.'

'The Lord's work is never done, and sometimes it requires a two-footed mucking out. But you're not here to talk about fitba, so what can I do for you?'

'It's about Brenda Sheehan,' Catherine said.

McGhee nodded solemnly, maybe even relieved that it was about who he had expected and not some new difficulty.

'How long did you know her?'

'More than twenty years. Since I came to the parish. She was AA, as you may know. One of the twelve steps is putting your trust in a higher power.'

'So you'd have seen her recently. How did she seem?'

'Grand. She was a troubled soul, and she seemed that wee bit more, I don't know, happy in her own skin, or in her own head maybe.'

'So it would surprise you to learn that she was found surrounded by empties, apparently having aspirated her own vomit?'

McGhee literally stopped in his tracks. He seemed to calculate something, then resumed walking.

'I'm guessing you wouldn't be here if you didn't think it would surprise me.'

'We're treating the death as suspicious, yes. What do you know about her brother, Teddy?'

'I conducted his funeral. That was how I got to know Brenda back in the days when she worshipped the great god Smirnoff and seldom saw the inside of the chapel. I hadn't been at the parish long, so I only got the history second hand. It was a truly miserable affair. I mean, I've seen some horrendous funerals, heart-breaking circumstances, but in its own way that was the saddest, because she was so alone. There was hardly anybody in the church; even some of the regulars who turn up to mass every day gave that one a bodyswerve because of what he'd done. Fuckin' holy wullies, bane of my existence.'

Catherine had to remind herself that she was talking to a priest. It wasn't just that he was dressed in muddy football kit, but his language and even his metre jarred with all her previous experience. The others she had met tended to slip into this auto-piety register that seemed an attempt to imbue their mundane and frequently asinine contributions with some deeper meaning and authority.

'How did he die?'

'He went off a roof at Bailliehall prison.'

McGhee arched his brow. Clearly there were layers to this.

'Officially, it was an accident. Death by misadventure, failures of supervision, blah blah blah.'

'But unofficially, you think something else?'

'I don't *think*: I know. It was a suicide. The prison authorities didn't want it official, though, as that would have triggered all sorts, and they could argue there was no definitive way of knowing. Either way, it happened because he was somewhere he shouldn't have been, and that was the part they wanted to address: their own procedures, not what was going on in the guy's head. Heads rolled, arses were kicked, new procedures instigated.'

'But if there was no definitive way of knowing . . .' Catherine prompted.

'There's enough of a difference between definitive and reasonable doubt to give autocrats all the wiggle room they need. But I got the inside story, including details that weren't supposed to leave Bailliehall.'

'Who from?'

'The prison's Catholic chaplain. He made a point of letting me know.'

'Why would he do that, when it was supposed to be confidential?'

'Because he was a cunt.'

He slowed his stride, looking her in the eye so that she and Laura both understood this wasn't coarse flippancy, common

216

disrespect or McGhee trying to come across as a bit of a character. This was something that ran deep.

'His name was Cawley, Father Pearce Cawley. He was a dinosaur, which I imagine you'll appreciate is really saying something when we're talking about Our Thing here. One of those bastards who got a dodgy Bible: all the pages about redemption and forgiveness were missing, you know?'

'Don't they end up cardinals rather than chaplains?'

'I'm saying nothing. But what you need to know about the Catholic Church: it's changed noo, but back then, if you committed suicide, you couldn't be buried in consecrated ground, and there could be no mass said for you. That miserable auld fucker knew Teddy Sheehan had jumped, and he wanted me to know too, because I was planting him.'

'Did he have it in for Teddy? Did he have a specific interest in the case, or a falling out?'

'No. He was bloodless: somebody with no imagination, no empathy, no compassion. He knew what the rules were but it would never have occurred to him to look beyond them, you know?'

'You're asking a polis that?'

'Naw. Just checking you were the type who understood that this was a bad thing.'

'So what did you do?'

'I went with the official version. Boy deserved a proper burial. Brenda deserved it.'

'So, hang on,' Catherine said, winding back. 'You couldn't be buried on consecrated ground if you committed suicide, but you were good to go if you murdered somebody?'

'Aye. If you had sought absolution.'

'And had Teddy?'

'I took it as read. He'd confessed to the crime. He didn't need to confess to me.'

'What is confession, exactly?' Catherine asked. She knew fine, having asked Laura for her lapsed-Catholic take on it, but she wanted to nudge McGhee on to the subject.

'It's a waste of fuckin' time, mostly,' he replied, which differed quite markedly from Laura's answer. 'Seriously, ninety-nine point nine per cent of it is actually absurd: wee folk like Brenda who have next to nothing in this world, who have hurt nobody, but they still need to sit there and tell me all the ways they *think* they've been bad.'

'So why do you do it? Is it because you signed up, it's part of the job and now it's your shift?'

'I do it, like many other apparently daft things in this game, for the exceptions rather than the rules. For the zero point one per cent that really need it.'

'But what is it they need? What can you give them?'

'I cannae say for sure that I've ever given them anything. I can only say what they need: forgiveness. They ask it from God because they can't get it from the person whose forgiveness they need most.'

'Themselves,' Catherine said.

He looked at her for a moment, long enough for her to worry about what he saw.

'I've been there myself,' he said softly, the studs of his boots crunching as they crossed on to concrete. 'I think most of us have, at some point. You ask for absolution from something higher because you hope that will give you permission to forgive yourself. Are you a believer, officer?' he asked.

Catherine shook her head. Saying no seemed wrong somehow, diminishing, and she resented the way it was phrased, not specifying what she may or may not be a believer in.

'Didnae think so,' he replied with a wry smile, almost conspiratorial. It was as though he didn't bloody believe it either. 'When somebody like me talks about a higher power, I know that turns some folk off. But I'm closer to your position than you'd imagine. I think we all have a need to believe in something greater than ourselves, and to make our lives a contribution to that. Some might call it God. You might call it the greater good.

'But what I take from it, what I know, is that the greater good needs you to cut your guilt loose so you can get on with making a contribution. It needs you to forgive yourself.'

They were nearing the pavilion: a grand, Victorian-sounding

word for a dull, seventies-built grey concrete box. It was time for the money shot.

'Brenda Sheehan's AA sponsor told us that the last time she saw her, she seemed happier, less burdened. She said she had made her confession. Father McGhee, I realise that it's supposed to be confidential, but I need to know what she told you.'

She braced herself for the self-righteous bit about violating the sanctity of the confessional. Instead he fixed her with a curious look, scrutinising and almost relieved.

'I can't do that,' he replied, politely apologetic.

'But she's dead, Father,' Catherine argued. 'And if anything she told you might be in any way related to what brought that about—'

'You don't need to sell me justice, officer,' he interrupted, that strange look still glinting in his eyes. 'I'm as pragmatic as they come. But you weren't hearing me earlier. I already told you: Brenda Sheehan was not one of the zero point one per cent, remember? I can't tell you what she confessed because there's nothing *to* tell. If Brenda made the kind of confession that liberates a soul, then she didn't make it to me.'

With that, he walked off towards the changing rooms, leaving Catherine in no doubt that he was telling the truth. It was that look of something close to relief: when she told him they were here about what Brenda might have confessed, he understood that he wasn't going to be compromised or conflicted, because he knew he couldn't help them.

She watched him unlock the door and was moved to start after him before he disappeared inside. She trotted up the short flight of steps, leaving Laura down on the concrete.

He heard the sound of her shoes on the stairs and turned around.

'Father, for what it's worth, I wanted to say I admire what you're doing, you know, as a priest getting involved with the football team. I don't see a lot of feel-good rehabilitation stories in my average week, but that doesn't mean I don't think it happens.'

'So you believe in redemption?'

'Some days that's harder than others, but I try.'

'You and me both, hen.'

219

She was walking back down the stairs when she heard him call after her.

'By the way,' he said, his foot keeping the door from closing. 'I didnae join the team because I'm a priest.'

It took her a moment to suss what he meant, then it all fell into place.

'What was that about?' Laura asked.

'That's no shepherd,' Catherine replied.

'What?'

'I'll tell you another time.'

A Woman's Work

She found herself at the chopping block once more upon another cool, clear morning, the first real frost of autumn underfoot. It was early November, hoar coating the edges of the brown leaves scattered untidily about the place, one more job nobody had time enough to do. They were piled up like snowdrifts against the wooden wall of the stables, its doors bolted and locked. Demetrius had been sold months back, another luxury they could no longer afford. The sacrifice was lessened by the fact that nobody liked going into the stables any more, and Lisa hadn't ridden him after that horrible day.

She placed a short log on the block and hefted the axe two-handed, splitting the firewood with a practised stroke. She wore only a T-shirt despite the cold, knowing that it would be enough once she got swinging. It might be the warmest she felt all day, given the temperature inside the house, where the central heating remained steadfastly off, every drop of oil an extravagance. The wood she was chopping was for the living-room hearth, but that was only ever lit at dusk, leaving the house chilly all day.

It helped to be busy, keeping her hands occupied as a means of distracting her mind, and when that was impossible, at least it passed the time while she waited for news. She got into a rhythm: placing, swinging, splitting. Sometimes this kind of exertion helped work out her frustration. This morning she could feel it having the opposite effect, as though it was instead summoning up more anger as her arms unleashed harder and harder strokes until she felt tears run down her cheeks. She stopped to wipe them away and blow her nose, looking back towards the empty house.

Dad had been doing three people's jobs since he was forced to lay off Donald and Michael, no longer able to pay them due to a sharp recent increase in overheads. They weren't the only farm to have this problem, they knew. There had been whispers and allusions in certain circles: that was why on that first day her parents had grasped so quickly what it was all about. There were rumours and stories, yes, but nobody admitted that it had happened to them. Money was tight, they just said. These were hard times. Fear and shame kept it secret. They seldom even gave it a name. When it was referred to at all between farmers, it was done so obliquely and briskly, like they were hurrying past a road accident, and there was no question whatsoever of it being mentioned to anyone outside of their own four walls.

The first Saturday of each month, he would come by to collect: the cadaverous grey man in the BMW. The younger man in the polo-neck had only returned once, replaced after that by a squirrelly looking wee guy always dressed in a tracksuit top above a pair of jeans with a tartan-effect pattern through them. They had been trendy for a few months about two years before, but had by then reached the final, irredeemable phase of the fashion cycle whereby they were practically the uniform of the style-oblivious. He was restless and fidgety, constantly sniffing and flipping his too-long greasy side-shed away from his right eye. She reckoned he might as well have the words 'SNEAK THIEF' embroidered on his tracksuit top, instead of FILA. Any plain-clothes store detective who didn't stick to this chancer from the second he entered their shop should be sacked for negligence.

He didn't just collect, though. On each visit Cadaver would announce an increase in the rate for their 'protection'. He was bleeding them dry as ruthlessly and rapidly as a beheaded chicken over a bucket.

Through a combination of wounded pride and desperate bloody-mindedness, Dad was nonetheless determined that the girls continue their education, despite their demands to be allowed to find full-time work or to just stay home to help him run the farm. Lisa had gone on to university, as planned, but remained living at home while she attended Glasgow. Lisa maintained that it was all the same to her, but she still kept her acceptance for Cambridge in her bedside drawer, a memento of the other life she could – and should – have had.

There was no vet school and no Laurel Row any more, school fees being out of the question. She had failed to get the grades she needed in her Highers, though she did fare better than she initially feared given the state she was in around the time she sat the exams.

Now she was in sixth year back at Calderburn High. The UCCA guide showed that there were some vet schools down south that would take her if she got an A in her Higher physics re-sit and at least a B for SYS chemistry, but how could she realistically think about going away to uni when Lisa hadn't been able to? How, in fact, could she think about the long-term future at all? There didn't seem to *be* a long-term future any more, only an on-going struggle to make payments that went up every time the grey man visited. She knew they couldn't go on like this, yet she kept asking herself where it would end.

An unmistakable pointer towards the answer presented itself when Dad collapsed while cleaning out a feed-trough. He had looked very pale the previous morning, having worked through a very heavy cold during the week, in the face of constant entreaties from Mum that he should be in his bed. She winced to think how long he may have lain out there – and in what condition he would ultimately have been found – had it not been for the vet, Harriet Chambers, who spotted him from where she was working in the dairy shed.

They endured an aeon of not knowing in some grotty hospital waiting area, purgatory with plastic chairs, and when they did finally get to see him he was behind glass, a tube in his mouth. His eyes were open but glazed, unfocused. This was due to sedation, a doctor assured them. His signs were stable, they were getting fluid into him and would maintain observations overnight. It was a polite and well-intentioned invitation for them to go home and get some rest.

She barely slept, though more than Mum, no doubt. Everyone was awake before dawn, even the normally unrousable Lisa, all impatient for information. There had been no phone calls in the night, at least; she understood that no news was good news, or at least not extremely bad news.

Despite her aching need to see him, to be there to hear whatever the doctors had to say, she also knew she had a duty – a very important duty – to remain behind.

'There's a thousand things needing done,' she told her mum.

Mum knew she was right. Nothing stopped because Dad was in hospital. In fact, the workload had just multiplied.

'We'll go in shifts,' she said. 'Lisa can drive home later to spell me and I can go up in the afternoon. I've got my licence now, remember.'

'Of course,' Mum nodded. She had passed her test over a month ago: teaching her to drive being yet one more task her dad had taken upon himself rather than fork out for a third party. It was no doting indulgence, though; it was imperative that all of them were able to fetch supplies, and even taking the tractor to the top fields required a stretch along the open road and therefore a licence to do so.

Satisfied that she had enough for tonight's fire, she was carrying the wood inside to the living room when the phone rang.

It was Harriet Chambers, phoning to ask if there was any news and to say that in her hurry yesterday she had left a bag in the dairy shed recess. She told Harriet the situation and said she'd keep her posted. She offered to drive the bag over later, but Harriet said it wasn't urgent; she'd come by on Monday morning to pick it up.

She tramped back outside feeling deflated, trying to block out a pessimistic thought that this had been merely a precursor to a far worse instance of getting her hopes up only to be let down. However, the phone rang again before she had got halfway back to the dairy shed, and this time it was Mum.

'It wasn't a heart attack,' she said, able to name that fear for both of them now it could be discounted.

'But how is he?'

'He's asleep just now. The tube's out. He's on the mend. Well, the staff say it'll take a while, but . . .'

'What was wrong?'

'Exhaustion, the doctor said. He's got a viral infection which brought matters to a head, but it's mainly just, you know . . .'

'Overwork,' she said, her relief that it wasn't a coronary already fading. An infection had precipitated his breakdown, but there were no antibiotics for his true ailment.

'The doctor says he needs rest. Weeks, he's talking about.'

'He'll need to write a prescription for battleship chains.'

Mum gave a quiet little laugh, but they both knew it was no joke. He needed to rest, but he couldn't and he wouldn't.

'Oh, God: there's something else. I forgot, with all that's going on; just remembered when I was talking to the doctor.'

'It's okay, Mum. I know. First Saturday of the month. That's why I volunteered to stay behind.'

'Why didn't you say something?'

'Because I knew you would wait around here when you needed to be up there by his side.'

'Your father never wanted either of you to have anything to do with—'

'I know. But we're big girls, Mum.'

She heard a crackle on the line as her mum sighed in resignation.

'The envelope is—'

'In the drawer in the kitchen, the one next to the cutlery. I know. Lisa and I both know.'

'You girls know so many things you shouldn't have to.'

There was an insistent beep on the line.

'My money's running out. I'm about to get cut off. When he turns up, don't let him in the house. Just hand over the envelope.'

'Don't worry, Mum.'

'Lisa will be coming home after and you can come u—'

The line went dead, a click and a moment's silence followed by the dialling tone.

She went back out to the dairy shed to resume her cleaning-out, feeling like she just wanted to lie down somewhere. She decided she'd best retrieve Harriet's bag while she remembered. The lack of sleep and the efforts she had already exerted that morning were starting to sap her muscles, the thought of the second milking around teatime enough to make her want to cry. There was just so much to do. Even if by some Herculean effort they could hold things together while Dad recuperated for a few weeks, they'd just return to the start of the cycle, and what then?

You'll work yourself into an early grave. Mum used to say that to Dad all the time, back when it was just an expression. She hadn't said it for months, though. Too close to the bone.

The bag was on a shelf in the recess, as Harriet had said. It was sitting open, a pair of rubber gloves beside it. The vet hadn't even begun her first examination when she saw Dad collapse outside.

She reached inside and took hold of a pair of ear-marking pliers, the first instruments that came to hand. She held them up to the light through the translucent plastic windows, balancing them delicately in her fingers, and thought about where she was supposed to be by now, where they were all supposed to be. Plans and ambitions truncated, shorn off brutally and without warning, the wound still raw. Everything taken away by low-life parasites.

She felt the pain of her dad's impotence. He couldn't stand up to them because they had zeroed in on his biggest vulnerability. If he stepped out of line, they wouldn't go after him, but hurt him through his daughters. She didn't doubt it either. She had seen what they did to Lysander, and knew that anyone capable of that was capable of anything.

Parasites.

Animals.

She felt the rage boiling up inside her again, threatening to turn to tears. She had to stay in control. She would not let any of these scum see her cry.

She placed the pliers back inside the bag, which was when she noticed the tranquiliser gun, along with a flat grey plastic case full of darts.

She took out the pistol and held it in her right hand, cocking it with her left against surprising resistance. Pointing it at the far wall, she found herself wondering whether it might change the picture if it turned out those daughters weren't as vulnerable as everyone assumed.

She pulled the trigger, feeling the spring drive the bolt back home with a force that trembled right up her arm.

Yes, it just might.

Parallax Perspective

Jasmine had her left eye closed, and through her right she could only see the target: grey and white concentric circles staring back like some mesmerised eyeball, a watery unreality about the image as it was refracted through the optics. She watched the crosshair drift in front and concentrated on her breathing, relaxing into a rhythm, gradually becoming accustomed to the motion. She was using the gas rifle, so she prepared her body *not* to brace itself for the kick.

It had taken her a long time to realise she was doing it, and not just at those times after she had recently been using the spring-powered gun. Going right back to that first experience at the hotel in the Borders, some part of her was always waiting for the recoil. It could affect her breathing, her posture, even her trigger action, all in the tiniest way, but this was entirely about tiny margins, hugely magnified at the other end.

The gas rifle didn't kick. The only movement she'd feel was the trigger slipping through the hammer release as she squeezed it. Everything had to be smooth, everything had to be fluid.

She could hear the air issues and the impact plinks of other shooters; hear them and yet not hear them. She could block them out, turn them into white noise, like the wind or the drumming of rain. Somewhere nearby she could hear someone's mobile phone ringing. She blocked that too.

She had talked to Fallan about it once. He seemed to know a lot about the subject. He told her he had learned in the army, but didn't elaborate.

'If you need quiet to shoot, you're useless,' he told her. 'Because you won't *get* quiet to shoot. You need to create your own quiet, and learn to inhabit your own silent place where noise can't reach you, even sudden, unexpected sounds. You have to crawl into that place and stay there. Doesn't matter if it's seconds or hours: you don't leave until you've taken the shot.'

The mobile was outside her place, as though it was ringing behind thick glass. She could hear a voice too, just as muted, just as detached. Then she felt a hand on her shoulder.

'Haw, Jasmine, for fuck's sake, you gaunny answer that or whit?'

It was Eric, one of the other regulars at the range. He was pointing to her shoulder bag, where the mobile was still ringing.

'You might be in the zone, hen, but it's doing every other bugger's heid in.'

'Sorry,' she said fishing for it in her bag, though by the time she had located it among all the junk she kept meaning to 'rationalise', the caller had rung off.

She hadn't realised it was her own phone because the ringtone was unfamiliar. She had this crappy wee thing as a substitute while her handset was out of commission, and still wasn't sufficiently familiar with the sound for it to have established a Pavlovian discipline.

The morning after discovering that Ned Untrusty had performed a secret sim transplant, she had gone to a shop and got her provider to issue her a new card, one that would restore her old number. She installed it in a cheap handset, the other one now quarantined.

She asked the guy behind the counter to take a look at the foreign sim, though he clearly thought she was mental when she explained that he wasn't allowed to remove it from the clear plastic pouch she had brought it in. He identified it as a pay–as–you–go sim, and when he scanned it into his system it came up as holding ten pounds of credit. This was so she didn't notice the switch due to a sudden inability to make phone calls.

If it had been another provider, as soon as she looked at the screen she'd have noticed that the network name was wrong. This meant that either Ned had got lucky, or he had turned up with a stack of sims, all bearing credit. He hadn't looked the type to be regarding such expenses as the cost of doing business. This was a steal-to-order job.

She had taken the phone apart wearing disposable latex gloves, still having a box of them left from one of Fallan's visits. They had been talking about guns, Fallan explaining how no amount of technical instruction or practise on the range would necessarily empower you to shoot the enemy, as armies worldwide had discovered over the past century.

He told her about the phenomenon of non-firing combatants: how a tiny percentage of individuals had been responsible for shooting fatalities in the Second World War; how in Vietnam it was estimated that millions of rounds had been fired per actual hit; how in the First World War most of the trench warfare kills had been the result of ordnance. Soldiers found it easier to throw a grenade into a hole full of men they couldn't see than to look a fellow human in the eye and pull the trigger. That was why sniper kills were the easiest, he explained. The further away you got, the less you were confronted by the reality of your actions.

Up close, that was where you found out if you really were a killer.

A little later he went out to the shops, returning with two pumpkins and the box of latex gloves. At the time, she didn't realise she was under instruction: she thought they were cooking. He cut a number of small circles out of the pumpkin's skin, then got her to thrust her thumb inside, directing her to twist it upwards then back and forth, pulping the flesh and carving out a channel.

She was very tentative at first, but he made her do it over and over, faster and faster, until it was all one motion, practically a reflex. Her thumb was aching by the time they were through. It would have been worse without the gloves, he explained, as they prevented the pumpkin flesh from getting under her nail.

Then he told her what she was practising. She almost threw up.

The wee shite at the Alhambra had to have left prints, she reckoned. She had handled the phone plenty before discovering that it had been tampered with, but not the places he'd have needed to touch: the back cover, the battery and the new sim itself. All had been removed at her kitchen table wearing latex gloves and sealed in air-tight plastic, as was the phone itself, for what it was worth. Leaving her with this shitey effort.

She hated to admit she was missing functionality that not so long ago she'd have scorned, but that's how it was. Her phone had become an indispensable personal assistant, a conduit through which she ran almost every aspect of her daily life. However, as she thumbed laboriously through the cheapo handset's labyrinthine sub-menu system just to see who the missed call was from, she realised that being Thoroughly Wired Millie had brought its own vulnerabilities.

If her phone had been targeted specifically, then the thief would have needed to know she'd be at that concert. Conveniently for him, that didn't require any feats of mind-reading or even surveillance. All it would have taken was for him to check her Facebook page or Twitter feed, neither of which were protected, as it wasn't like she was live-tweeting her investigations, just chatting to friends.

Perhaps when she got home she should check whether she'd recently been followed by @badguy.

The missed call was from Laura Geddes. Jasmine switched the phone off in case she tried again. She didn't want to speak to her. She had nothing to give her; or at least nothing that she wanted to. Almost everything she had discovered so far just seemed to be nailing Fallan's motive: doing the cops' job for them, as she'd feared.

She put the rifle to her shoulder once again and took up position, finding the target, relaxing into her breathing rhythm. The outside world faded and dimmed, and she was back in her quiet place. A place she could think.

Why didn't she want to talk to Laura? Why was it so hard to accept the obvious conclusion that all of the evidence was pointing to? Was it simply because of what they had been through that she trusted him, that she liked him? Was there anything concrete supporting her doubt, or just emotion and instinct?

Tit for tat. An eye for an eye. Family loyalties. Your classic cycle of violence. It all made perfect sense, apart from the timescale. *Beware the vengeance of a patient man*, Stevie Fullerton had said. But could that vengeance truly have waited her entire lifetime? So far every witness statement and every hard fact pointed to this being the case. The only thing even remotely hinting at anything else was the business with the phone.

She wasn't giving that to the cops right now though, because it was the only card she had to play and she didn't trust them with it. If they ran the prints and it only gave them the name of some no-mark ned, how motivated would they be to follow that up?

Instead she had given it to Harry Deacon at Galt Linklater, whose police contacts meant he could get the prints analysed through back channels. It was going to take a while, but it kept the information under her control.

She needed more, though.

The crosshairs steadied, their bobbing reduced to a steady, minute and predictable path. She squeezed: a little too early, a little too low and to the left.

It didn't help that she hadn't been able to contact Fallan. He still wasn't talking, not even to her. The cops had him on remand and he was refusing visitors.

Jasmine reckoned she knew why.

She thought of how she'd spent her morning. That thick-necked gorilla, with his scars and tattoos and his ostentatious, wear-the-price-tag suit, was her uncle. He had sat there simmering with rage, alluding to her mother being a criminal and laying down the very gory details of her unknown family history. This was the world Fallan had sworn to keep her away from; the world her mum had gone to great lengths and great sacrifice to escape.

She took another shot, a hiss of gas followed by the plink as her pellet rattled the back of the catcher. Low and left again. She was still squeezing too early, another hangover from the slower action on the spring rifle's trigger.

Fallan wouldn't see her because he didn't want her drawn into this, and now she knew the reason. It wasn't just because of what it would expose her to: it was because the risk wasn't worth the reward. She had finally found out who her father was, but there was no satisfaction in it, no hint of filling a lifetime's absence. It was just a name. She hadn't known Jazz Donnelly, and nothing she had learned about him made her feel any kind of a connection.

Heredity was meaningless. It wasn't about flesh and blood. It was about thought and deed. That was why she felt closer to the man who had killed her father than to a dead thug named Jazz Donnelly.

There must have been more to him than that, though she was never going to know. Her mother had lived a strange and evidently dangerous life once upon a time, but she'd never have been some daft moll hanging off the arm of a gangster.

She guessed he must have been charismatic and exciting, as well as attractive, but Sheila had suggested Mum was wary of getting involved with him until after he was slashed, whereupon he was perceived – wrongly – to have slowed down his normal act. Sheila had also implied that her mum was the type drawn to damaged men, perhaps thinking she could change a guy like Jazz. There must have been something she saw in him: someone like herself, perhaps, shaped by difficult circumstances but who might yet be reshaped into someone who could rise above them. Or maybe that was merely something her mother *needed* to see, something she was projecting.

There was so much Jasmine had merely glimpsed during her uncomfortable morning at the Old Croft Brasserie: matters they weren't prepared to elaborate upon, and others still about which they clearly didn't know enough.

It had been suggested that Fallan might have killed Jazz because he had beaten up her mother. Jasmine wasn't sure she could believe that, but this didn't matter so much as what lay behind the fact that others considered it a possibility.

Fallan was not merciful in dealing with men who attacked women. Rita had hinted at it, Sheila confirmed it, and made reference to the reason why.

Fallan's father, a notoriously brutal and corrupt cop, hadn't just beaten his wife, he had terrorised his family.

'Everybody in the hoose,' Sheila said.

That seemed to suggest there was more than just Glen and his mother under his fist. Who else was in that house? Who else had Iain Fallan 'leathered'? And why had Glen never mentioned them?

233

Jasmine loosed another shot, ripping through the paper faster than she could blink. It was still low, but wide to the right. Though barely conscious of it, she had altered her breathing, thinking too much about having been early on the trigger.

Just breathe, she told herself.

'You've nae problem with evening the score when it suits you, eh, Sheila?'

Sheila had been the barmaid way back when, a few years older than the young drinkers in that photograph. A trawl through online news reports had told Jasmine Sheila's age, as well as the fact that she was Fullerton's second wife. Perhaps there had also been a first husband. Had he knocked her about? And had Fallan intervened on her behalf?

Stay with the rhythm. Keep everything fluid.

There was something else there, some element of Sheila's manner that had gnawed at Jasmine every time she thought back to it. She had been far slower than Doke to accept Jasmine's story, keeping those shields up, not looking to make new friends. Her pain was bleeding out of her all over the carpet. She was a tough woman who implicitly understood the nature of the world she had found herself in, but that didn't mean she liked it. She was angry over the death of her husband, but her anger went broader and deeper than that. She was angry at Stevie, at Doke, at all of them, for keeping up their endless rally of vengeance.

Jasmine thought back to Sheila staring at the table as Doke spoke about Stevie and his carefully orchestrated attack on Fallan.

Sheila didn't want to hear about it. She knew there was no option not to listen, but she looked like she wanted to be somewhere else. Doke had warmed to the subject of Stevie's ruthless ingenuity, spelling out his clever plan to protect his men from the consequences.

Jasmine thought it just sounded mob-handed and cowardly. Maybe Sheila did too, as well as being aware that it had sown the seeds of Stevie's death.

That wasn't it, though. Sheila had been bitterly vocal when she felt scornful of Doke's pig-headed hard-man ethos, but when he talked about that she hadn't even wanted to look anyone in the eye.

And suddenly Jasmine thought she understood why.

She let all the parts of her body move as one, a single motion uniting her eye, her lungs, her arms, her index finger.

Plink.

Dead centre.

'*Beware the vengeance of a patient man. That's what Stevie always said. Didn't he, Sheila?*'

Why that prompt? Why her reluctance to agree? It couldn't have been that Stevie never said it; that would have been simple to dispute.

She kept with the motion, stayed fluid, held the rhythm.

Plink.

Dead centre.

A sack to blind him and a rope to restrain him. '*Hatchets and hammers . . . Even a sword.*' Beaten and broken and stabbed until his assailants assumed he was dead: it was hard to imagine such a horrible, brutal, sustained and vicious attack; easy to imagine a thirst for retribution.

When Stevie learned Fallan had shown up still alive two years ago, he must have been terrified. Sheila too.

Breathe. Squeeze.

Plink.

Dead centre.

Now Jasmine finally understood what was wrong; what it was about Sheila that hinted all was not as it should be.

She wasn't angry at Fallan.

Throughout their entire discourse, the person she should have borne the most hatred had failed to spark her ire, and Jasmine could think of only one reason why that should be. In light of all that had gone before, and in the face of so much hard evidence, it couldn't merely be gut feeling or instinct that caused her to harbour any doubts.

Sheila Fullerton had something more solid than that.

From on High

Beano appeared at Catherine's office door, an apologetic, if frustrated look on his face, and, significantly, nothing in his hands. She checked her watch: it had been a good hour and a half since she sent him on this errand, and if she had been aware of how long had passed she might have sent out a search party.

'I can't find it,' he told her.

Catherine was used to hearing this from Duncan and Fraser, whose efforts to locate whatever they had lost seldom extended beyond the reach of their arms, or looking in more than one place. Beano, she knew, was at the other end of the scale. He was as diligently resourceful as he was boyishly reluctant to disappoint, plus his familiarity with the morgue where old case files were stored was second to none these days. Over the past week, he had spent so much time down in the depths that they ought to start calling him Gollum.

'Shit.'

'I searched among the files from around the time of Sheehan's death too, in case it had been taken out and put back around then, but no dice.'

Catherine had only very occasionally seen the inside of the morgue, and had been vaguely reminded of the closing image in *Raiders of the Lost Ark*. The materials pertaining to thousands upon thousands of closed and prosecuted cases were boxed up and stacked in no particular order, just wherever somebody had found a space. There were clusters and patterns: rows and stacks reflecting some kind of chronology regarding when they were placed there, but there was no preordained system of organisation. Plus, if somebody had for instance taken a 1995 box out ten years later, it would more likely have been returned among the 2005 files rather than put back where it had been found.

'I can go back and keep looking,' he offered. 'I just wanted to check whether you'd prefer I did that, because it might be a waste of time and there might be something else . . .'

'No, no, you could be there for ever. And you're right: there is something else I need you to do. I want you to go back and take another look at Fallan's and Fullerton's computers. We weren't looking for anything related to Brenda Sheehan before, so we might have missed—'

'I'm all over it,' he replied, scurrying away.

Dear Lord, she thought, please don't let Beano ever grow up and get a life. He's far too useful. But not infallible, unfortunately: she had sent him to retrieve the Julie Muir case files.

Catherine picked up the phone and dialled Moira Clark. She wasn't sure whether her old boss had any direct involvement in the Muir investigation, but if not, chances were she'd at least know who did.

Moira answered after eight or nine rings, just before Catherine was about to give up. Her voice came through against the sound of dozens of voices reverberating in the background, and Catherine pictured her in the main lobby at the Scottish Parliament, fetching her mobile out of that cornucopian shoulder bag she carried.

'Catherine,' she said. 'Good to hear from you, my dear, but whatever it is I'm afraid you'll have to make it quick.'

Catherine was ready for this. She was just grateful to have Moira even answer the phone these days. The woman was still on the committee for bloody everything, but on top of that was increasingly involved in consultations at Holyrood. Given that the Justice Minister had her on speed-dial, it seemed remarkable she would let Catherine clog up her line, but that was Moira for you. She was the kind of woman who would keep the *First* Minister on hold while she finished giving advice to a probationer.

'Sorry, I hope I'm not disturbing you. Are you at a conference?'

'No, I'm at Terminal Five going my holidays and I'm in the queue to board.'

Catherine knew she could skip the small talk.

'I need to know about a murder from before my time. Julie Muir.

She was strangled by a guy named Teddy Sheehan. We can't find the files.'

She heard Moira let out a dry laugh, recognising the complaint. 'Do you remember the case?'

'Yes. The girl had got off a train at Capletmuir station on a Saturday night.'

'That's the one. Do you know who I can talk to about it?'

'Well, I know who worked it. Who you can talk to might be a wee tad more delicate.'

There was a mordant amusement in Moira's tone, forewarning some complication that invoked her sympathy but which nevertheless, as a connoisseur of police irony, she couldn't help but savour.

'Oh God. What?'

'It was one of the first murder inquiries to feature the talents of a promising young CID prospect by the name of Mitchell Drummond. Whatever happened to him, eh?'

Catherine winced. Drummond was the Deputy Chief Constable, and the polar opposite of Moira: the type of self-important autocrat who, even if he did have time to talk to you, might not answer the phone in order to underline just how busy he was.

'Oh God. Please tell me you remember who *else* was working the investigation.'

'Aye. That's where it gets worse. Drummond was riding shotgun with Bob Cairns.'

Catherine was on her way upstairs towards the DCC's office when she encountered Beano heading down in the opposite direction, carrying Stevie Fullerton's laptop. By her watch he should have been off shift half an hour ago.

'Where are you going with that?' she asked. 'Actually, more to the point, where have you *been* with it?'

He arched his brows, like he knew the answer wouldn't please her.

'Had to get it back from LOCUST. Thought I'd nip up so it's where I need it when I'm back on-shift. They were all over it like, well, locusts.'

He gave her an apologetic smile, barely hoping that it would stem the tide of outrage.

Maybe it was Beano's expression, or maybe it was the realisation she had had this conversation with Abercorn too often already, but something made her decide she wouldn't rise to it this time. She needed her head to be in the right place for this meeting.

'Did Abercorn give you the "it was sent to us by mistake" patter? Because that didn't wash the last time.'

'I didn't see Abercorn. I spoke to Paul Clayton, and he got snotty on Abercorn's behalf instead. It's nice to see that they delegate in that department.'

'What did he say?'

'A quality whine about us not sharing with the other children: how we couldn't expect to have a senior drug dealer's computer at our disposal without them champing at the bit. To be fair, we'd had the thing for days.'

'Aye, and if we'd found anything of interest we'd have forwarded it. Eventually,' she added, with a hint of a smirk. 'Did he put up a fight about handing it back?'

'No. Just seemed peeved that they had needed to come over and thieve it. Understandable, given how generous they are whenever they happen upon resources and intelligence.'

'They must have been finished with it then. I can't think what they were hoping to find: Fullerton was too careful to store anything juicy on a computer that could be traced to him.'

'It wasn't anything juicy about Fullerton they were checking for,' Beano told her. 'It was anything juicy about LOCUST. Clayton said the brass are always shitting themselves in case anything ever comes out about how they do business.'

'Letting Off Criminals Under Secret Trades.'

'So ever since we went into Fullerton's house, they've been getting pressure from above to make sure nothing damaging leaks out.'

'If they're happy to give back the laptop, that means they can't have found anything compromising.'

'Aye. Or else they've deleted it.'

239

Beano hurried on down the stairs and Catherine resumed her ascent.

She had made a call to Graeme Sunderland and asked him to request a meeting with the DCC on her behalf. She knew that Sunderland not only spoke Drummond's language, but was closer to his rank and knew how to handle him. Thus Sunderland had established that Drummond had a window to chat before admitting that it wouldn't be himself who was doing the talking.

As she reached the landing and turned left through the swing doors she was beginning to question the wisdom of this, doubts assailing her as to whether this was a conversation that she needed or wanted to have. She liked to think she had a good track record of speaking truth to power – perhaps at cost to her advancement on occasion – but there was a voice in her head asking whether this was an exercise that unnecessarily put her in harm's way.

In a jungle of political animals, Drummond was an alpha predator. He was shrewd, calculating, slippery and ruthless, an arch strategist who had hidden agendas inside his hidden agendas, and an ear for the subtext in every statement. He was so much in his element among the upper echelons of management that it was almost amusing to think of him once upon a time out conducting inquiries, taking statements, getting bodies. The very notion was like seeing unearthed footage of a cabinet minister working behind the bar as a student.

He was on the panel that interviewed her for the LOCUST job. She had always assumed Abercorn made sure Drummond recognised one of his tribe, but only now was she contemplating how that might only have been part of it. Just as big a factor could have been that Drummond had taken a dislike to her.

He wasn't someone you wanted to get on the wrong side of. Abercorn, for all his machinations, gave the impression of having very little ego. It was all in the game to him, which was why he was so thick-skinned about LOCUST's unpopularity. Drummond, by contrast, was self-regarding and spiteful.

As Moira put it, 'it's always about him: that's his weakness and his strength. If you never lose sight of that, you'll be fine.'

Catherine was grateful for the advice, but suspected that in order to be fine she'd need a lot more than that.

She'd have been wary of mentioning the subject of Bob Cairns with the DCC even before she learned they had worked together. His name was well up anybody's list of Things We Don't Talk About, but to Drummond, a man who was inclined to take embarrassments to the force as a personal affront – as though people had cooked it all up just to make *him* look bad – then you'd better have a bloody good reason for bringing it up. It would be like going up to Michael Barrymore and saying, 'Hey, can we talk swimming pools?'

In fact, Catherine was wary of mentioning Bob Cairns to any cop over a certain age, because even if they never knew him personally they might still be inclined to harbour a vicarious resentment towards her for putting him away.

Cairns had a charge sheet of murder and corruption going back thirty years, a paid lieutenant of the notorious Iain Fallan in his bloody pact with the self-styled Gallowhaugh Godfather himself, Tony McGill. If he had been in any other line of work she'd have been fêted for a bloody good collar. Unfortunately, when it came to unmasking bent cops, the messenger always got shot. Everybody knew you did the right thing, but nobody was going to thank you for it. Most of them wished it all had never happened, which was fair enough, but others were clearly of the belief that it would have been better if it all had simply never come out.

The question was which camp Drummond fell into.

Catherine pictured herself outside the headmaster's office as she knocked at his door, expecting to hear 'Come!' barked out in response. Instead, Drummond appeared at the door and held it open for her, beckoning her inside. He seemed approachable to the point of solicitous.

She wondered what she had done to deserve this welcome, then she remembered that this was part of his game. Like any politician, you wouldn't get far unless you could turn on the charm, and carefully control which face you presented to any given audience.

It was a timely warning. No matter what they discussed,

Drummond would be polite, professional, calm and measured; and he would give no outward hint that she was being blacklisted for ever, right then and there.

She would have to pitch all of this with meticulous judgment, aware that simply by having arranged this meeting at all – even by requesting it – she was already starting at a deficit.

He showed her to a chair but remained on his feet. He took position behind his desk, framed by large windows offering a view north-east from Govan towards the city. Look at my domain, he was saying. He didn't need the cheap psychology to emphasise his stature. He was very tall, if rather awkwardly so, reminding Catherine of her image of Steerpike in *Titus Groan*.

His hair was grey all over these days, in contrast to the conspic-uously monochrome black dye job he sported for way too many years when he was vain about still appearing youthful. He had obviously decided that in senior management it was better to look distinguished, which made her wonder whether he was the only guy in the building to actually dye some of his hair grey in order to maximise the look.

'So,' he said, demonstrably ready for business now that he had composed the situation. 'DCI Sunderland said you wanted to speak to me about the Fullerton case?'

He pitched a tone of inquiring puzzlement, as though he didn't see how this could possibly be so and was curious to discover how.

'Actually, sir, it's a related matter that I was hoping you could help me with. Shortly prior to his death, Fullerton appeared to be taking a pronounced interest in an old murder case, one that you played a part in investigating.'

'Oh, right,' he said, still sounding unsure where he might fit in. 'And is your area of interest not covered in the files?'

Catherine concealed a wince, aware that, only moments in, the deficit had already increased. She wasn't just in danger of looking impertinent, but incompetent too.

'We can't find the files, sir. The case is a quarter-century old, and I don't know when you were last in the morgue, but . . .'

He gave an impatient nod.

'It's like a fractal experiment down there, I know,' he acknowledged, though this concession didn't necessarily mean he accepted her excuse. 'What was the case?'

Catherine took a breath.

'Julie Muir. She was murdered by a man called Teddy Sheehan. I believe the investigation was led by Bob Cairns.'

So there it was: out. She had reasoned that there was no going back now, so she ought to dive straight in. Any fannying about regarding the Cairns part was to imply that she thought Drummond had reason to be uncomfortable, and she really didn't want that.

Drummond stared at her for a long moment, leaning forward, both his forefingers and thumbs resting on his desk, little arches at the ends of his arms. Then he nodded and stood up straight again.

'What's important to remember about Bob Cairns is that the revelations about his criminal activities do not automatically suggest that everything he did was corrupt, or that all of his police work is automatically suspect.'

Catherine opened her mouth to acknowledge his point, but clearly it wasn't her turn to speak yet. Far from it, in fact.

'And although it in no way excuses any of the dreadful things he did, it remains true that Cairns would not have survived in the job as long as he did were it not for the fact that he was a highly competent investigator. Indeed, I worked with him, and indeed I learned a few things at his side but, like everybody else, I had no inkling about the other aspect of his character.'

He went on in that vein for a bit, laying it all down, speaking like he was the one who had called her here to talk about it. That was when something struck her about his manner, never having been one on one with him before: he spoke like he was giving a press conference. Everything he said was considered, neutral and precise. And as Moira said, it was always about him.

Catherine wondered what he was like with the wife of a morning, over breakfast.

'What needs to be stressed about this coffee is that though the milk itself has turned, this in no way reflects upon the quality of the beans, and should not be allowed to colour people's impressions of the croissants or the jam.'

Catherine waited until the official statement on the DCC's lack of contamination by Bob Cairns was over, before reminding him of what she was actually here to discuss.

'Do you remember much about the case, sir?'

He glanced out of the window, a calculated pause to add gravity to his next pronouncement.

'I remember *too* much about it. Even if it hadn't been one of my first murder cases, I'm sure it would still have stuck. It was just one of those dreadful affairs, tragedy upon misery; no closure, just completion. A young woman was murdered, her family devastated. We got the killer, but there was no satisfaction in that. He confessed and the evidence was uncomplicatedly irrefutable, but nobody was buying trebles to celebrate a result, you know? I mean, we've both had cases where you feel it in the gut, almost a sense of elation that you put the bastard away, but this wasn't one of them.'

He looked down at his desk, regret weighing heavy upon his features. She could only spy it from a certain angle, but it was the most human emotion she had ever seen on his face.

'Sheehan died in prison a few years later, did you know that?' he asked.

She answered with a nod.

'There were conflicting accounts, rumours it was a suicide,' he stated quietly. 'I don't think it matters either way: it was one tragedy compounding another.'

When he raised his head again, he was composed once more, back in press-conference mode.

'Should he have been in the general prison population? A place like Bailliehall? I don't think so. Was he competent to make that confession? I'm not sure; it wouldn't even be procedurally legal these days and a competent lawyer would be able to drive a coach and horses through the whole thing. Did we get the right man? Absolutely. That was the only consolation. It was as nailed on as the one you're dealing with now, with Fullerton and this Fallan character. How is that coming along, by the way?'

244

'Well, sir, our efforts right now are centred on what Fullerton might have done to precipitate his death, which is why I'm here. We know he visited Sheehan's sister Brenda, and he was at the Mitchell Library looking up old press reports of the murder. To that end, can you think of any reason why Fullerton might have been interested in the Julie Muir case?'

He was shaking his head before she finished speaking.

'I honestly can't. There was no gangland connection, so—'

'Unless you count Bob Cairns,' she interjected, instantly regretting it.

Drummond didn't bite, though. Rather, he looked like he was considering it.

'I still can't see where it would fit together,' he said. 'Was there any other link between Fullerton and Brenda Sheehan? And how lucid is she, these days? That was another tragic element to the whole mess: the poor woman was—'

'She's dead, sir.'

Drummond looked shaken. He was a man used to pretending nothing was news to him, even as he was learning it, but his gifts were failing him now.

'But you just said Fullerton . . .'

'We found her two days ago. She had choked on her own vomit. The autopsy hasn't been completed yet, but I think she was murdered. She hadn't touched a drop in years, but her house was staged to make it look like she was back on the drink with a vengeance.'

Drummond put a hand to his mouth. There were no prepared statements to be read out on this one.

He turned away and gazed out of the windows. He didn't want to look at her, and quite possibly didn't want to be seen right now either. Catherine had feared raising the spectre of Bob Cairns, but now Drummond looked haunted by a different ghost.

This press conference was over.

All the Small Things

Glen often heard murders or other acts of violence attributed to gang wars, drug wars and turf wars. Indisputably, gangs, drugs and territory were factors in these incidents, but they were never the primary cause. In Glasgow, folk didn't plan ahead when it came to bloodshed. They didn't go in for campaigns and strategies. Vendettas, yes. Feuds, absolutely. Tit for tat. Grudges. Vengeance. There were wars of attrition that could span decades and even generations, but they were never over anything so abstract as a commodity. It was always personal. Always petty.

Petty. From the French *petit*, meaning small. Small things, small men. It was said that a person was only as big as the smallest thing that annoyed them, and no matter how high they climbed, none of the criminals Glen knew was ever bigger than the most trivial slight. None of them was ever wise enough, secure enough, to just walk away. When they went to war, no matter how history dressed it up, ultimately it was over their own fragile egos.

Pish wars. That's what they truly were, but that didn't read so well in the newspapers and the true-crime best-sellers.

Looking back, it was inevitable that Stevie Fullerton and Tony McGill were going to clash. Stevie was as ruthless as he was ambitious, and while he wouldn't have gone out of his way to make an enemy of Tony, if Tony got between Stevie and what he wanted Stevie would never have been shy of the fight. Tony, for his part, had that endemic Glaswegian affliction whereby he just hated seeing somebody else getting on. The sight of somebody younger and sharper, making plans and making money, bothered him more than losing money himself or his own plans going awry. Their interests didn't need to run contrary in order for Tony to feel threatened. He was a middle-aged man still kidding himself that he was in his prime, that the best was yet to come, and everything he saw in Stevie told him otherwise.

Stevie bought a pub over in Croftbank, where he grew up. This was when Glen began to understand what he meant when he said there were things you couldn't buy with a sports bag full of fivers. He had already got the lease on Nokturn, but he wanted bricks and mortar. He was empire-building, and starting close to home.

Too close to Tony's home.

Croftbank was three miles along the dual carriageway from Gallowhaugh, past Shawburn and closer to the city. The pub was called the Bleacher's Vaults, where Stevie had been drinking since he was old enough and bold enough to get served, and which had latterly functioned as his unofficial HQ.

The official licensee was still Donny Lawson, the same guy whose name had been on the paper for a decade, but both the business and the premises were separately owned by Stevie through two shell companies, one of which also owned the 'company' that owned his car-wash business.

Stevie moved his money like a magician working the cup-and-balls routine: just when you thought you knew what he'd done with it, you realised he was up to something else. A pub, being largely a cash-only business, was another good way of turning dirty money into legitimately accounted profits, but the car wash was still adequate for what Stevie needed laundered at that stage. Clearly, he anticipated having larger revenue streams to process in the very near future.

Maybe Tony understood these ramifications and maybe he didn't. Either way, he decided to put down a marker by offering to supply the Bleacher's Vaults with spirits. He was sleekit about it too: sent his new bag man, Arthur, to talk to Donny Lawson, who was happy enough to meet the prices being quoted.

This was how it got murky, entirely in keeping with Tony's intentions. Some might say he was disrespectful in going behind Stevie's back rather than talking to him directly, but Tony could claim he was according Stevie a certain status by showing that he regarded purchases such as this as matters for their respective underlings to deal with. However, this latter interpretation over-looked the widespread understanding that Tony 'offering' drink to a pub or a restaurant made a very strong statement about the nature of his relationship with that establishment's proprietor.

Egotism. Pettiness. Pish.

Tony wasn't trying to do Stevie a favour or work out a mutually beneficial arrangement; nor was he struggling for outlets for his supplies of smuggled and stolen drink. He was telling him: know your place.

Equally, it was in Stevie's gift to humour the older man, take his cheap booze and let him kid himself he was the Gallowhaugh Godfather if he wanted to. Stevie didn't need to make Tony an enemy until he *was* an enemy, and that was how Stevie played it – on the surface at least. In reality, by dipping his fingers into his business Tony had not only infuriated Stevie but had inadvertently made it clear that he would present an obstacle to his ambitions.

Stevie said nothing about the booze Tony was supplying. He appeared to take it in his stride, even inviting Tony to the Bleacher's Vaults for the official Under New Management re-opening party, where he gave him all the deference the older man felt he was due. Stevie played the part of the eager and ambitious up-and-comer, a man with plans and new ideas but who knew he could still learn from a master like Tony.

In fact, the party was an appropriately auspicious occasion for him to break the news of an opportunity that could vastly benefit both of them.

'It's early days, and I could be getting ahead of myself, but I think I might – might, okay? – be on to a supplier.'

They were sitting in a horse-shoe booth in the main lounge, Stevie gulping a pint of lager, Tony sipping malt poured from a bottle of twenty-one-year-old stuff that his host had presented to him. Glen was standing close by, holding a can of Irn-Bru. He didn't drink alcohol and he didn't much like pubs, but Stevie had invited him along. As ever, he blended into the background: saw more than was seen, listened far more than he spoke. He may have been the only observer to read the true significance of Stevie's gift to Tony, having previously heard him disparagingly refer to whisky as 'an old man's drink'.

'A supplier? Of what?' Tony inquired, trying to sound only mildly curious.

'H.'

Tony nodded, then a strained look came across his face, the expression of someone who has seen this lassie flash her knickers a few times but never given up the goods.

'It's not local,' Stevie went on. 'No pre-cut bags of powder you'd be better off sticking in your washing machine. This stuff's coming off a boat pure. That's the problem, in fact. I've not quite got my foot in the door because I'm not quoted. I can raise the money, but these guys are looking at the big picture and they're not interested in doing one-off deals with second-division outfits. Not only is it piecemeal, it's risky for them too, because I could be anybody. I could be polis. They want regular purchases and they want names they can trust. Names that carry weight. So what I've got to ask you, Tony, very politely, with lots of very pretty pleases, is whether I can give yours.'

It was a couple of weeks before Stevie was able to report back; time enough for Tony to grow sceptical over whether Stevie knew where this door even was, never mind his chances of getting his foot inside it.

'That boy says more than his prayers,' was how he put it, his growing impatience and disappointment betraying how much he wanted to believe Stevie's claims.

Eventually, though, Stevie made a trip to Liverpool and returned with a sample. Tony wouldn't have known pure from Persil, but for a man who had 'fought to keep drugs out of Gallowhaugh' he wasn't long in getting it into the hands of someone who could analyse it for him.

The quality was verified, the price deemed acceptable and – eventually – the split agreed. Stevie was fronting eighty grand, Tony a hundred and sixty, with the merchandise to be divided seventy-thirty in Tony's favour. Stevie was authorised once again to make representation and confirm arrangements down south. However, this time when he returned, there was a major stumbling block.

'They're jumpy,' Stevie reported. 'They're about ninety per cent ready to back out. They say they're getting polis vibes from somewhere. My contact says they can be like this; reckons they're paranoid because they've never dealt with anyone in Glasgow before.'

'I thought you said my name would carry weight?' Tony protested.

'Aye, a wee bit too much as it turns oot. The problem is, the name Tony McGill is synonymous with . . .'

Tony looked white as he faced the prospect of several decades' worth of chickens – or should that be stoolpigeons – coming home to roost.

'Polis? They're getting a polis vibe off *my name?*'

'I'm no' saying that,' Stevie corrected hurriedly. 'But you've carved a fair old reputation for keeping drugs off your turf, and let's just say they're finding it difficult to believe you're willing to buy.'

Tony sighed with frustration, and no doubt a modicum of relief. It was a misunderstanding: that was all. Nothing that couldn't be cleared up, especially if—

'What if I spoke to them myself? Can you set that up?'

'I can ask,' was all Stevie could promise.

Six days later, Tony travelled down to Liverpool with Stevie, accompanied by Glen for security and Arthur for his counsel. Arthur had moved up the pecking order a couple of years back, when Walter and a headcase called Sweenzo both got found shot dead in a field in Ayrshire.

Glen drove, at the wheel of Tony's Jag. They met Stevie's contact in a pub on Chapel Street and he led them to a warehouse at Waterloo Dock. There were three other vehicles outside: two Granadas and a Merc. The place was disused, the dock itself in its dying days. It looked to Glen like the kind of place they always filmed the showdown scene in *The Sweeney*. When they got inside, this impression was further enhanced by the sight of two blokes standing at the foot of an iron staircase packing semi-automatic rifles: HKs, serious kit.

They exchanged uneasy nods of recognition with Stevie's contact, a Mancunian named Sammy who asked the Glaswegian quartet to wait while he went upstairs. He returned a tense and silent few minutes later, and announced that Tony, and Tony alone, could go upstairs.

Tony looked to Stevie, as though seeking assurance that this was the standard procedure.

'I've never been here,' Stevie confessed quietly. 'Never even seen these guys. I told you: I'm not quoted.'

Tony glanced at the hardware momentarily, then a stony composure settled upon his face before he mounted the stairs. There followed another long, silent and increasingly tense wait, until the sound of laughter rang out from above, replacing the indistinct hum of guarded voices.

Tony emerged after another half an hour, leading them wordlessly back onto the broken-cobbled street.

Glen opened the Jaguar's rear door for him, keeping an eye on the warehouse entrance. Sammy came out not far behind, heading back to his Chrysler Sunbeam as Tony climbed into the back of the Jag.

Tony waited until everyone was inside and the doors all closed before making his announcement.

'It's on. Two weeks' time. They'll contact Stevie with the time and location, but it's me that has to make the buy personally. Just this first time, they said. After that they'll deal with Stevie.'

'Ya dancer,' Stevie declared. 'You are some man, Tony. You are some man.'

Tony just smiled with quiet satisfaction, contemplating his bright new future all the way back up the road.

Open Wounds

This is what tragedy looks like twenty-five years on, Catherine thought. She and Laura sat in Sam and Audrey Muir's living room, watching the pair of them grip each other's trembling hands as they huddled together on their settee, surrounded by the modest mementoes of the life they had led together.

The usual metaphors of wounds and scars could not adequately describe their condition; what she saw was not the remnant of old pain, or enduring numbness where the damage had been so great as to cut off feeling. This was a phantom limb.

They looked afraid, even before Catherine had got past the formalities and broached the subject. They were scared because they knew that was why she was here. They knew what this was going to feel like.

It always annoyed her when the papers described people as 'brave' when what they really meant was tragic: 'Brave widow's tears for war hero husband'; 'Brave little Annie loses her battle with cancer'. It was a kind of platitudinous courtesy towards those who had suffered greatly but whose suffering had been appropriated as media property. Bravery implied a choice, and in the above cases, what was the non-brave alternative?

Sam and Audrey Muir were brave. They didn't need to do this, yet here they were, reliving the worst thing that had ever happened to them.

This wasn't where they had learned about their daughter's death. She didn't know why, but Catherine took some comfort from that. It would have felt that bit harder to ask this of them if they had been in the home where Julie grew up, even the room where they had been told to sit down when the police arrived at their door.

This place was new: a modern semi built this century. She

wondered when they moved, whether there had been another place in between. It seemed smaller than the life the pictures offered glimpses of; retirement down-sizing maybe. There were photographs of grandchildren everywhere: three of them, Catherine reckoned, snapped from infanthood through school years and, in the case of the eldest, a graduation gown. They were on the mantelpiece, on the walls, on occasional tables: haphazard collages, framed triptychs, even a digital display, fading new shots in and out every few seconds. Catherine deduced from some older images of a gangly teen in a mullet and late-eighties Rangers top that the doting father of the three grandkids was the Muirs' son.

She spied only one picture of Julie. It sat on the mantelpiece, crowded by other photographs. Catherine had once read why it eased the pain to rub a part of your body that had just been hurt: the added sensory information sent to the brain diluted the signal coming from the point of the injury. That's what was going on here. It was as though they could only glimpse Julie amid an overload of information about the good things that had come later.

There must be other photos hidden away: lots of them. She was beautiful.

'She was always in such a hurry to grow up,' Audrey said.

'Twelve going on twenty,' added her husband.

'She always wanted the trendiest clothes, and we used to argue about what was appropriate for a girl her age to wear.'

'Clothes and records, that's all she was interested in. And, of course, we never had the money.'

'Nobody did,' said Audrey. 'Not in those days. Julie understood that: that's why we'd go fifteen rounds over what she was and wasn't allowed to wear. If we could only afford to buy her something new once in a blue moon, then she'd be determined it was the trendiest thing possible and I'd be concerned about how many times it would survive the wash.'

'She was a grafter, though,' Sam said. 'She always had part-time jobs right through her teens. I remember driving to pick her up at midnight from Safeways at Shawburn every Thursday and Friday night because I didn't want her walking home at that hour.'

Catherine watched him wince, the memory of his fears coming back to him, the things he had endeavoured to protect her from only for his efforts to be in vain.

'She couldn't wait to get away from home.'

'That's not true,' Audrey insisted, as though defending both their honour.

'I don't mean away from us. I mean out of Croftbank, where we lived. And if I had been in work more regularly, I'd have got us all away from there, but what could you do? It was the Eighties. Thatcher and her "economic miracle",' he added bitterly.

'Julie wanted to live in a Duran Duran video,' her mother said with bittersweet recollection. 'And it would have been hard to imagine anywhere further from that fantasy than Croftbank. She was nineteen when she moved out.'

'Barely nineteen, though she'd have passed for twenty-five. We couldn't stop her. She had about three jobs when she was still living here: shifts in different clothes shops in town. Then when she was eighteen she could do bar work in the evenings as well.'

'What kind of bars?' Laura asked, looking for where a young Stevie Fullerton might fit into this picture.

'Only trendy places,' Audrey replied. 'Same with the clothes shops. She wouldn't have worked anywhere she didn't want to shop, and she wouldn't have pulled pints anywhere she didn't want to drink. I couldn't even tell you the names of them. They'll all be long gone, turned into other things.'

'So where was she living, after she left home?' asked Catherine.

'She shared a flat with a couple of other lassies,' Sam answered. 'They were a few years older than her but she knew them both from school. It was off Victoria Road.'

'Only twenty minutes on the bus from Croftbank,' said Audrey, 'but to her it was another world. She was what she wanted to be, all grown up.'

Audrey suddenly broke down, Sam placing a hand around her shoulder. Catherine could picture the same scene twenty-five years ago, and imagined it played out frequently over the intervening decades. He produced a hanky and she dabbed at her nose and eyes, apologising for herself, everyone else in the room telling her it was okay.

They all meant that the apology was unnecessary. Little else was actually okay.

'It's just the tiniest things sometimes,' she said. 'You never know what's going to bring it back. Even at the time, I remember getting fixated about wee things that just weren't that important.'

Sam nodded, his face like rainclouds, dark and troubled, barely holding back precipitation.

'You focus on wee stuff,' he agreed, 'because you cannae cope with the rest: it's too much.'

'Like the ring,' Audrey said. 'Julie had this ring I gave her for her sixteenth birthday. It was my great-grandmother's, and it got passed down through the family, mother to daughter. It never came back. The police returned her earrings and her wristwatch, and I remember getting completely obsessed by the fact that the ring never came back.'

Catherine had heard similar tales before. The missing item didn't even need to have that kind of family significance: anything that didn't return could come to symbolise all that was lost in the eyes of the bereaved.

Audrey shook her head, a couple more silent tears seeping out as she briefly closed her eyes.

Catherine addressed her next question towards Sam, as if to let Audrey know she could take a moment.

'Do you remember her ever mentioning somebody called Stevie Fullerton?'

'I know who Stevie Fullerton was,' Sam replied, something stern and defensive creeping into his expression. 'What has he got to do with Julie?'

'He seemed to have taken a recent interest in the case and we're trying to work out why. He visited Brenda Sheehan not long before his death.'

Catherine opted not to share the fact that Brenda had been murdered. This pair were barely clinging on as it was.

'That fucking cow,' Audrey suddenly spat, appearing to almost startle herself with the hatred in her tone.

'There, Audrey,' Sam cautioned. 'Don't get . . .'

'I'm sorry,' she said, more composed. 'It's just . . . she tried to cover for him, and I can't forgive that.'

'She did the right thing in the end,' Sam reminded her. 'Nobody wants to believe that about their . . . their family.'

'I know, but she lied for him. Said he was at home with her. Doesn't matter if she admitted it later: she still lied.'

Sam gave Catherine a helpless look. It was a needless apology; she could see what was going on. Brenda's lie was like the ring: another totem drawing a disproportionate response. In a strange way it was easier to be angry at Brenda for lying than to be angry at Teddy for doing it, as the latter was just too overwhelming an anger to tap into.

'Just to come back to Stevie Fullerton,' Catherine said softly. 'Is there any connection you can think of from back then?'

Sam shook his head.

'You're asking the wrong people,' Audrey answered. 'She never told us what was going on with her socially, even before she moved out. You'd be better speaking to her flatmates.'

'Do you remember their names?' Laura asked, notepad at the ready.

'Sure,' Audrey replied. 'There was Ciara Flanigan. That's C-I-A not K-E-I. She was training to be a teacher. Somebody said she's at Croftbank High, back where she started. And the other one, I don't know what happened to her. Her name was Yvonne Sharp.'

Catherine and Laura looked straight at each other, utterly failing to keep their responses inconspicuous.

Masks

There had been a power outage cutting the streetlights along Shawburn Boulevard. It made the Old Croft Brasserie stand out like a beacon, the floods illuminating its car park apparently fed off a private source. Through the windows Jasmine could see that the place was full, as though the reservations had piled up and the diners been hovering impatiently during its temporary closure.

It was a different crowd from the private function the other morning, fair to say. All that money and effort cultivating an image and a reputation for her restaurant: Sheila knew implicitly what the people she was pitching for wanted, what they expected, how they dressed, how they conducted themselves. Stevie's crowd were so not it. She wondered how Sheila felt whenever a party of them pitched up of an evening, and how good she was at hiding it.

Jasmine could see her as she stepped though the double doors. She was in hostess mode, showing a party of four to their table, two staff in close attendance to take coats and hand out menus. She was in a neat black shift dress, her appearance smart but not flashy, as though she knew she had to look good for her clients but not more dressed up than they were. Her hair and make-up evidenced time and care, flattering but not overdone. She looked in her element: busy, genial, authoritative; the hostess into whose care the diners eagerly delivered themselves, as much the face of the business as the hot-shot chef was the driving force.

How many of the clientele would know she had just been widowed, or under what circumstances? How many would now be aware that she had been married to a notorious Glasgow crime boss?

There was certainly no evidence of a morally motivated boycott. Maybe it was like Starbucks: the product on offer was sufficiently tempting that most punters would rather swallow their principles than go without swallowing the fare they had come to crave.

Jasmine watched her smiling, like the place had been shut for a few days over a burst pipe. Nobody at any of the tables would have a clue how she really felt. She couldn't hide it from Jasmine, though. She hadn't finished her drama training, but she was enough of an actress to recognise when another one was practising her art.

Jasmine waited to be noticed, standing next to the corralled station where the bookings ledger and the phone sat next to a computer running the table-management and billing systems. A waitress glanced her way, burdened by a tray of plates, looking around to see if someone else could help. She spoke, directing her boss's attention.

The mask failed for just a second, a look of concern flashing across Sheila's face, followed by a brief glimpse of the defensive aggression that had greeted Jasmine previously. Then the hostess was back, calm and politely approachable, albeit not smiling.

'I'm afraid we're full,' she said, breezily apologetic, as though she'd never seen Jasmine before. 'And unfortunately I don't think I'll be able to offer you anything for the foreseeable future,' she added, making play of flipping through the ledger.

'I get the message,' Jasmine told her. 'But I just have to ask you one question, and then I'll leave you alone.'

'As you can see, we're extremely busy just now, and I don't have time to—'

'One question,' Jasmine repeated. 'Woman to woman, nobody else party to the conversation.'

This time, Sheila got the message.

'And what would that question be?'

'What makes you think Glen Fallan didn't kill your husband?'

Seduced and Abandoned

In keeping with the complexity of the overtures, the buy was no straightforward handover.

'I told you they were jumpy bastards,' Stevie told Tony. 'They'll accept the payment from me, but they'll only hand the merchandise to you. I hand over the cash, and once it's verified they make a call and authorise their man to release the goods to you. Separate locations, that's the way they like it.'

'Why?'

'Means if anybody's picked up a tail there's no transaction for the polis to witness. Plus it means no mad rocket gets tempted to try blowing everybody away and walking off with the gear *and* the cash.'

'So how does that work? You just hand over a case full of money at point A and hope they're nice enough to return the favour to me at point B? What if they just take a gun to you and piss off with two hundred and forty large while I stand there like a fanny waiting for a bus?'

Tony seemed to think he was the wise old head outlining a legitimate concern. He didn't realise that even his fears were based on his limited perspective and obsolete thinking.

'Do you think pulling something like that would be worth the grief to these guys?' Stevie asked him. 'For the sake of less than a quarter mill? They've got half a dozen buyers giving them that kind of money four and five times a year. This is big-time, Tony.'

'Well, if you're happy enough, fine. It's you that's taking the risk, and just so we're clear, it's you that's liable for the money if anything goes wrong.'

Stevie assured Tony that nothing would, but nonetheless requested that Glen accompany him to his end of the handover rather than Tony's. It was a request to which Tony was more than content to accede. Indeed, before the two vehicles set off on their respective runs, Tony took Glen aside and made sure he understood his job.

'Protect my money,' he told him. 'That chancer's expendable – my money isnae. If this goes bad, the debt is his, but if he doesnae make it, the debt is yours. Get me?'

Glen thumbed his lapels, letting Tony see the Steyr nine-mill he had recently added to his arsenal.

'Got you.'

Stevie seemed very nervous throughout the drive. He kept checking his watch and was equally attentive towards the rear-view mirror of his MR2 to make sure Tony and Arthur were still following in the Jag. It was an utterly uncomfortable ride for Glen all round, as he felt like a deckchair folded up inside the cramped little Toyota.

Both cars stopped at a service area outside St Helens for a final check by payphone that everything was still on. The call lasted mere seconds, just a formality. Stevie simply said 'Yeah, it's me, we're set,' then paused a moment before responding: 'Okay.'

They had an hour to kill, so the four of them grabbed a coffee and a fry-up, then got in their cars and went their separate ways, to their very different fates.

Tony and Arthur returned to the warehouse at Waterloo Dock for the pick-up, while Stevie's drop was supposed to be at Lime Street station: public but anonymous, and close to payphones for the authorisation.

Stevie barely uttered a word after leaving the services, which struck Glen as all the more uncharacteristic for a guy with his gab. It wasn't every day you drove around with that kind of cash in your motor, right enough, to say nothing of what the goods would be worth in the long run. Still Stevie kept glancing at the time – all the more, in fact, now that he couldn't alternate it with checking Tony and Arthur were still around.

Stevie pulled his MR2 into a multi-storey and switched off the engine. He sat restlessly, fingers fidgeting, then eventually turned the engine back on so that he could listen to his Simple Minds cassette. His face seemed a little pale, but more noticeable was the fact that the tips of his ears were glowing red, like he'd been outdoors in freezing wind and just come inside to the warm. He stared out of the windscreen at nothing in particular, his fingers now occupied by tapping a rhythm, and seemed to drift away in his thoughts.

Glen checked the clock himself after a while, and noticed that the appointed drop time was only two minutes away.

'Shouldn't we be getting a shift on?' he asked.

Stevie came out of his reverie with a start, then looked again at the clock.

He nodded, almost reluctantly, where Glen would have expected him to spring out of the vehicle.

They walked around to the station, Glen keeping a vigilant watch fore and aft for anything amiss, not least some chancer of a bag-snatcher who might score the spawniest grab of his life.

'I don't see Sammy,' Glen observed, scanning the concourse.

Stevie said nothing, just checked the time yet again and led Glen towards a bank of payphones, where they stood in wait.

They waited two minutes, which became five, which became seven, ten.

Glen kept scanning the entrances, but Stevie only had eyes for the clock. That was when Glen realised that Stevie wasn't really expecting to meet anybody.

He was about to ask what was going on when one of the payphones began to ring. Stevie dived across to answer it, giving fright to some old dear who had been approaching the thing when it went off.

'It's me,' was all he said.

He stood there gripping the handset, listening intently, his eyes focused on some indeterminate point, a relegated sense.

Stevie listened for only a few seconds, then replaced the handset gently, as though it or the cradle might shatter. He placed a hand on the silver trunk of the payphone, steadying himself, then let out a slow sigh before straightening up.

'Are we okay?' Glen asked.

Stevie just nodded, the tiniest tremor of his head, then began to walk away.

'What's up? I thought you said we were okay?'

'Not here. I'll tell you in the motor.'

Stevie was sweating by the time they were both back inside the MR2, and not from the exertion of a brief walk. His breathing was weird too: he kept letting out these protracted exhales. His hands were gripping the steering wheel even though the engine was off, and Glen could see his pulse ripple the skin on the inside of his right wrist. The guy's heart was thumping.

'What's the script?' he asked. 'Why did the drop not happen? Is it still on?'

Stevie swallowed, then turned to face Glen.

'Tony and Arthur have been lifted,' he told him.

Glen felt something tighten inside him, a sense of danger, a fear of being trapped. He always felt a twinge of this when he heard someone he knew had been arrested, but this was pure-strain.

'On their way to the warehouse? What for?'

'Naw. *Inside* the warehouse. There was a raid.'

'A raid? So the filth *were* on to these other guys? Nae wonder they said they were getting a polis vibe. Tony and Arthur will be fine, though,' Glen reasoned. 'They never made a purchase. Wrong place, wrong time, that's all.'

Stevie shook his head.

'They were lifted in possession. Enough H to send them down for all day.'

Glen couldn't work it out.

'But you never made the drop.'

Stevie let out another huge sigh, throwing his head back.

Then he saw it: the nervousness, the heart rate, the sweating, checking the time, checking the rear-view.

Glen pulled out the Steyr and levelled it at Stevie's ribs, out of sight below the dashboard.

'You set him up, didn't you? You grassed him.'

Glen cocked the hammer, his thumb unlatching the safety.

'I asked you a question.'

Stevie turned and looked Glen in the eye.

'They say it's not polite to answer a question with a question, big man, but you should indulge me, because this one's a stoater. Tell me: who puts on a mask to give somebody a doing?'

Glen didn't follow. He was still reeling from the news, and he couldn't begin to see where Stevie was going with this.

'I ask you again, Dram: who in Gallowhaugh, or anywhere else in Glasgow, puts a stocking over their heid, or a balaclava over their face, to give some poor dick the message?'

'Somebody who doesnae want caught?' Glen ventured.

'Naw, Dram. The answer is: nobody.'

Glen was about to counter, which was when he saw it, the mirror he was preparing to hold up turning back into sand.

They had come for him: nylon stockings pulled over faces, reversed balaclavas with eye-holes torn out.

'Heard my boys just got there in the nick of time. I'm Tony, by the way. Tony McGill . . .'

Glen felt the little MR2 come loose from the world and drift, unanchored in time and space.

'They'll come after you again – unless you've got friends too.'

He closed his eyes for a moment, trying to stop his head from spinning, the images and memories from crowding him, all glimpsed in new light, altered meaning. When he opened them, he was back in that Liverpool car park, back in reality, but it would be a new reality.

'Were you there?' he asked.

Stevie said nothing, which was a yes.

Glen uncocked the gun and let it rest in his lap.

'What happened today, Stevie?'

Stevie stared ahead again, across the concrete, where a woman was folding up a toddler's buggy to fit it into her boot.

'I beat him at his own game, that's what happened. Did what he's been doing for years: fed him to the polis. Scaled it up, though.

I wasnae dealing with CID no-marks and chucking them wee tiddlers. I removed him from the picture and I took him for a hundred and sixty grand in the process.'

'Why?'

'He was in the way. He's a fuckin' dinosaur. All this "keeping drugs out of Gallowhaugh" pish. He should have retired gracefully and left us all to it, but he still wanted to be the big man. He sealed his fate when he sent Arthur round to Donny Lawson. That's when I knew he needed tell't.'

Glen thought about everything that had happened since the re-opening party. Stevie being the man with a contact, dangling the bait, making it look like it might all fall apart so that Tony would be all the more eager to grasp it. He thought of the first trip to Liverpool, the warehouse, Sammy, the guys with semi-autos. Heckler & Kochs. Serious hardware.

Preferred *police* hardware.

'This has been a set-up all along, hasn't it?'

'There's somebody far bigger than me that Tony's pissed off,' Stevie replied. 'He's been shagging somebody he shouldn't. The wife of somebody *very* connected.'

'There was never a source, was there?'

'Naw. Tony won't know that, though. The plan was that there would be a bit of a mêlée: the kiddy-on suppliers get away, but Tony doesnae and he's left holding all the H. A lot more H than two hundred and forty grand would buy. And in order for them to have handed it over, as far as Tony knows, I had to have made the payment. The suppliers took the cash, handed over the merch, then the roof fell in. Jolly bad luck, old chap.'

'He'll know. He's not daft.'

'He's finished. He'll get thirty years.'

'He'll still have reach. Friends on the outside. Tony junior, for one thing.'

'They'll be too busy fighting over their share of the carcass.'

'Even so, Teej will have to come after you if he wants to take over the reins. He'll look like a nobody if he doesn't.'

'Aye, well, that's why I'm sitting here talking to you, big yin. I want you on side. I was never meeting anybody at the station today, remember? I didnae need you for protection, Dram. I was keeping you away from the jaws of the trap.'

But Glen knew Stevie too well to accept the purity of this motive.

'Naw, you were tying me into your side of it. Nobody would believe I walked out of this clean without being in on it.'

'Aye, you're tootin' there,' Stevie conceded. 'But it's a done deal noo, so what are you gaunny dae? You could shoot me here in this motor and prove your loyalty to that two-faced auld prick, or you can come in with me and make some real money. Starting with forty grand right out of that briefcase.'

Glen flipped the Steyr's safety back on.

'Eighty,' he said.

Believe in What You Want

Sheila stood with her back against the wall, one foot tucked up flat to the brickwork, blowing smoke into the cool, dark air. She looked like a schoolgirl having a fly fag behind the bikesheds, rather than the proprietor of a thriving restaurant taking a break to enjoy a cigarette around the back of the kitchen.

She had told Jasmine to wait there, and as time drew on Jasmine had begun to wonder whether it was just a subtle way of getting rid of her. After about a quarter of an hour, however, she had appeared where she said she'd be.

She was aware that it was fifteen minutes in which Sheila could coach herself to get her story straight, or even decide she didn't owe her an answer. The sooner she spoke, the less reliable Jasmine estimated her testimony would be.

In the event, she just stood there and smoked, like she was waiting for Jasmine to make the first move.

Jasmine remained silent and waited her out.

'What makes *you* think I've got my doubts?' Sheila eventually asked.

'*Beware the vengeance of a patient man*,' Jasmine replied. 'Stevie wasn't talking about Fallan, was he? That's not who he was worried about. When he showed up again, back from the dead, despite everything he had done Stevie wasn't scared of reprisals from Fallan, and neither were you. I think we both know why.'

Sheila allowed herself a strange smile, at once seemingly wistful and yet bitter, and took another drag.

'I *was* scared,' she said. 'I've spent thirty-odd years being scared for folk I know, folk I care about. But Fallan was the reason I stopped being scared for myself. I married young, too young. Married the bastard that ran this place once upon a time. He was

266

eleven years older than me. Donny, his name was. I was naïve, but he was . . .'

She took a draw on the cigarette, looking blankly away into the darkness of the unlit Shawburn Boulevard.

'He'd have killed me,' she stated evenly, but Jasmine could see her bottom lip tremble.

It suddenly struck her how small Sheila was, shorter and slighter than Jasmine. The image of a grown man hitting this tiny woman flashed into her head before she could stop it, and she felt queasy.

'In the end, he'd have killed me. I still wake up nights and get shaky thinking about what could have happened.'

'Did Fallan . . .' Jasmine considered how to phrase this, what she might reasonably allude to. '. . . make him go away?'

'In a manner of speaking. He wasnae in much of a state to dispute the terms of the divorce, let's just put it that way.'

'And was that when you and Stevie got together?'

'Christ, no. This was before you were born, hen. Stevie and me never got together until a lot later. Properly, I mean: seriously. We got up to all sorts under Donny's nose. Too close under his nose, as it turned out. He leathered me because he knew he couldnae try anything with Stevie. He was good at hiding it, and good at keeping me feart so I wouldnae tell anybody. He couldnae hide it from Fallan, though. He knew the signs too well.'

Sheila took one final puff then ground the butt under her heel. She blew the last of the smoke out in a long, sustained exhale then turned to look at Jasmine.

'I was like your mother with Jazz: I wouldn't have let myself get involved in a real relationship with Stevie when he was younger. He was too fast, too wild, and he wouldnae have been very interested in me either. I mean, Christ, you should have seen his first wife.'

Jasmine had. The papers and websites had run the Nineties modelling pics, but even in the more up-to-date shots she exuded poise, if not exactly taste or understatement. She was married to a millionaire nightclub owner now.

'We were pals down the years, and you could say we had a

267

professional relationship, with him owning the Vaults and me ending up landlady. But it was only when he was in his late thirties that we got close; or that I let myself get close. I saw him different from how I used to: he was mature, he had this air of control about him. It was like he'd moved on from all that.'

'All what?'

Sheila gave a dry, joyless laugh.

'Exactly. I never put a name on it, what it was before, so it was easy to kid myself about Stevie later. I'm no' sayin' I was in denial about what he was involved in, just that I could kid myself about what it might one day bring to the door.'

She lit another, folding her left arm across her chest as her right hand held the cigarette to her mouth.

'When I looked at him I didn't see violence. He was a businessman. He wasn't interested in violence, he was interested in money. Stevie said all the violence he'd ever been involved in was about young men with something to prove, and if it hadnae been over drugs they'd have been fighting about something else.

'Nobody in Stevie's game thinks they're being bad. Doesnae matter whether the polis are onto you: after a while the polis just becomes like the weather. Some days it's sunny and clear, other days it's pissing down. We'd often talk about drugs, about how daft it is that the government are telling you what is legal to put into your body. Stevie always said there was only violence in the drugs game because the drugs were illegal. I lapped it up. You believe what you need to, don't you?'

Jasmine didn't reply, and worried for a moment whether her silence itself sounded judgmental.

'When you're scared, though, that's when you cannae kid yourself any more. That's when you're forced to face up to reality. When Fallan reappeared I was climbing the walls. I'd heard all about what Stevie had done, and I knew what Fallan was capable of too.'

She took a long drag, like she couldn't get through what was to come without it. It reminded Jasmine of a labouring mother on Entonox.

'At first Stevie just told me he had protection, and said if Fallan was gaunny do anything he'd have done it by now. None of it made me sleep any easier, but Stevie didnae seem worried. I thought he was acting the big man, kidding himself, being like the guy I wanted nothing to do with twenty year ago. We had a huge fight aboot it, and eventually he told me the truth. That's how much Stevie loved me. That's how much he *trusted* me. He wouldn't have told another soul on earth.'

Jasmine didn't need to ask what Stevie had told her. She had worked it out for herself on the firing range.

'For twenty years, there were only two people in the world who knew,' Sheila said. 'And the saddest part is that in all that time, nobody questioned it. All that cloak and dagger stuff about envelopes and alibis: eejits like Doke just lapped it up.'

'You believe what you need to,' Jasmine replied, echoing Sheila's own words.

'Whereas you heard it one morning and you'd seen through it by teatime.'

'I had a few clues you and Doke didn't.'

'Don't sell yourself short,' Sheila told her, a tiny hint of warmth in her voice for perhaps the first time. 'You're smart. It's well seeing your name's Sharp, because you never got that from Jazz Donnelly.'

'I had the benefit of context. Sometimes the longer something is staring people in the face, the harder it is for them to see it.'

Sheila narrowed her eyes and regarded her intently again, examining Jasmine in detail, but no longer with suspicion: it was more like there was something specific she was looking for.

'Maybe not quite as sharp as you think, though.'

'Why, what did I miss?'

Sheila shook her head, a neutral but implacable firmness to her face.

'Naw, naw, hen. You've had all you're getting from me. Just be very careful what you do with it.'

With that, Sheila reached for the handle and pulled open the door to the brasserie's kitchen.

'Please, I've just got one last question,' Jasmine implored. 'If it wasn't Fallan that Stevie was talking about, then who's the patient man?'

Sheila looked incredulous that Jasmine hadn't worked this part out.

'Tony McGill,' she said, like it was self-explanatory. 'The man was inside for fifteen years. It was Stevie that put him there, to get him out the picture . . . Stevie and Fallan.'

VIPs

'This is about Stevie Fullerton, isn't it?' asked Ciara Flanigan with a weary amusement Catherine found difficult to read.

Ciara had walked into the reception area carrying a plastic tub of pasta salad and a spork, her decision to take her lunch with her suggesting that she suspected it might not be a quick word. She was around Catherine's age, maybe a little older, and Catherine had to rein in that unworthy competitive instinct that started looking for evidence that the other woman wasn't wearing quite so well as herself.

'It's related to the late Mr Fullerton, yes. How did you know?'

'You're not the first to ask. I had a private detective in here the other day asking about him. I didn't think you actually *got* private detectives except in the movies. She certainly didn't look like Humphrey Bogart.'

'She?' Laura confirmed, giving Catherine a glance.

'Yes. They say you know you're getting old when the police start looking younger, but if the same extends to private detectives then I really am getting on a bit. She looked like she could be dogging school.'

'Why was she asking you about Stevie Fullerton?' Catherine enquired.

'Mostly she was asking about an old flatmate of mine, Yvonne Sharp. She's dead now, unfortunately. I didn't know that. We'd lost touch a very long time ago. We were both at school with Stevie Fullerton: this school, as it happens. She was interested in how Yvonne and Stevie knew each other.'

'So she didn't mention her surname, this investigator?'

Ciara searched and came up blank.

'Actually, now you mention it, I think I only heard her first name: Jasmine. How did you know that?'

'Because her surname is Sharp. She's Yvonne Sharp's daughter.'

Ciara's mouth briefly formed an 'o', then she gave a rueful sniff of a laugh.

'I never saw it. She sat in front of me all that time, asking about Yvonne, and I never saw it. To be fair, it's been twenty-five years, but it's not like she didn't jog my memory. She even showed me a picture from back then. So she's not really a private detective then?'

'Oh, she's real enough. A real pain in my arse sometimes. What did you tell her?'

Ciara spoke for a while, recounting their discussion, then Catherine moved on to the main reason for their visit: Ciara's other flatmate.

'Julie worked behind the bar at Nokturn,' Ciara said. 'That's how she ended up sharing with us. Yvonne recognised Julie from school and they got talking. We needed somebody else to share the rent and she wanted out of her parents' house.'

'Why was that?' Catherine asked, curious to hear a different perspective. She didn't get one.

'Bright lights, big city versus Croftbank? The city's not that big and the lights not that bright, but everything's relative. Julie wasn't to be contained. It could be knackering, to be honest, because although on the surface she was all glam and sophisticated, inside she was still quite immature. I don't mean that in a bad way – you know, selfish or huffy. I just mean she wasn't as grown up as she thought she was.'

'Do you mean she was vulnerable?'

Ciara thought about it.

'She was streetwise, like you had to be in Croftbank, so she wasn't some ingénue, but there were ways she was naïve. A bit of a dreamer. That was partly why the guys were doe-eyed over her: she wasn't cynical.'

Catherine watched the hurt and regret pass across Ciara's face like a cloud, blotting out the sunshine brought by the pleasure of her recollections.

'So she got a lot of attention from the men?'

'Oh, yes. She didn't stay behind the bar for long. Stevie made her the hostess for the deck and the VIP area. It was waitress service only up there, with prices to match. Lots of champagne. It was quite a moneyed crowd. Old Firm players, models, pop stars. If a band was playing Glasgow, that's often where they'd end up. I danced with the guitarist from Effervescence one night and on another I got off with Matt Black, the comedian. Wear the right dress in the right place and suddenly anything's possible.'

'But equally, you can be wearing the wrong dress in the wrong place too,' Catherine reminded her.

Ciara nodded darkly.

'What was Julie doing out in Capletmuir of a Saturday evening?' Catherine asked. 'If she lived just off Victoria Road, and Nokturn was in the city centre . . .'

Ciara looked uncomfortable in a way that had not been precipitated by previous discussion of ostensibly more sensitive subjects. Catherine recognised the genus right away: she was afraid of what she could or couldn't safely say.

'Don't you know this stuff?' Ciara asked, shifting in her seat. Not a practised liar, the teacher squirming like she was a first-year covering for his mates.

'Just assume for this purpose that we don't.'

Ciara chewed on a mouthful of nothing.

'Well, that's tricky for me, isn't it? Because up until now it's been me that had to pretend I knew nothing about it.'

'I don't follow.'

'I'm asking whether you really don't know or whether you're just making sure I remember my lines.'

Catherine sighed with impatient curiosity.

'I really don't know. We can't even find the bloody case files.'

Ciara frowned, as though deciding whether this was a wise idea. She didn't appear to have reached any conclusions but ploughed ahead anyway.

'She was seeing a guy from out that way. Well, he had a flat in town, but that's where the family home was. His name was Gordon Ewart.'

Ciara said this with a note of contempt, and Catherine got the impression that there was supposed to be something self-explanatory about it. There wasn't, as far as she could see.

'All mention of him and his family was kept out of the court case, and I got an unambiguous warning from the polis to watch what I said. They told me that if it leaked to the papers they'd know where it came from. It wasn't germane to the case and it would cause a lot of unnecessary difficulties. It's a sight to behold when you see the establishment mobilised. Nobody was quite so concerned about the Muirs.'

'The establishment?' Catherine asked sceptically, conveying to Ciara that she sounded like she was in the hinterlands of tinfoil hat territory here. Then the surname clicked and she remembered who had lived in Capletmuir, in a big posh house on the border of his constituency.

'The establishment, yes,' Ciara insisted. 'His dad was *Campbell Ewart*. He was a cabinet minister: Under-Secretary of State for Scotland. So you can maybe see why I got leaned on not to go blabbing that it was his son Gordon's nightclub-hostess girlfriend who got strangled and left in the woods.'

'He was one of the rich kids you mentioned.'

'He was a regular at Nokturn. Him and his hooray pals.'

'Champagne Charlies,' Laura suggested.

'An apposite choice of words,' Ciara responded pointedly, though Catherine guessed the choice had not been fortuitous. 'It wasn't just the fizz and the ambience that kept them coming back, or why Nokturn was the "in" venue for a certain crowd. Back in those days it was *the* place to score coke.'

'Was Julie doing it?'

'I don't know. Probably. Julie would try anything.'

'And Gordon Ewart?'

She looked from side to side, as though checking it was okay to go on.

'For sure. He wasn't that discreet, and neither were his wanker mates.'

'Risky business when your dad is a junior minister.'

'That's the thing, though: privileged folk like that think they're

274

invisible, partly because they've got people looking out for them. There's no way the press didn't know. I'm sure deals are done to keep that kind of thing quiet.'

'Undoubtedly,' Catherine agreed. 'In the press's eyes though, "MP's son snorts coke at nightclub" isn't really a story. It's a bargaining chip: "We keep this quiet and you give us something else."'

'It would have been a story if they knew about him and Julie. That's why I got leaned on. A connection to a murder case, even painting him as the grieving boyfriend, would have been the ideal vehicle for the papers to go to town. And it wouldn't just have been Gordon they went to town on.'

'What do you mean?'

'Well, don't forget about his mum. She was a raging alkie back then: it was the biggest open secret in Scottish politics.'

Catherine recalled the awkward allusions in the media to Philippa Ewart being 'unwell', and the bristling disapproval that met any attempt at humour or innuendo in the public discourse. As a consequence, she had developed the impression of the unfortunate MP's wife being some feeble and pathetic specimen, her alcoholism debilitating and confining her like a cripple. In sobriety, Philippa had turned out to be a formidable and quite admirable individual, dedicating much of her time to alcohol and drug charities. In these she was not content to merely play the part of fund-raising figure-head; she was also a notoriously pushy lobbyist. And for a Tory wife – or more accurately ex-wife – she was refreshingly light on the judgmental rhetoric, having been down there herself.

'I think the press tend to exercise some discretion on that because alcoholism is recognised as an affliction,' Catherine suggested, still not inclined towards the idea that the Illuminati were scrambling all resources to protect a mediocrity like Campbell Ewart, even if he did come from aristocratic stock.

'Yes, but what about the *reason* she was an alcoholic? All those affairs Campbell Ewart had been having, the stories that only emerged after he got turfed out in 1992 – the press must have known about that stuff all along.'

'Probably,' Catherine conceded. 'I think the significant part is that it wasn't open season until he lost his seat. He was being protected before that. You say you were leaned on. By whom?'

'I don't remember their names. I'm not sure I even heard them. They weren't the same cops as interviewed me for the murder case. They weren't Glasgow CID. Whoever they were, they weren't there because of Julie. They were there because of Campbell Ewart.'

'So was Julie and Gordon a serious thing?' Catherine asked.

'It was starting to look like it. I thought he was a dick, but Julie said he was different away from his friends. It was never going to last, not that I could see. I'm not sure Julie did, though. That's what I meant by naïve.'

'And had there been anybody else in the picture? Anybody that might be jealous?'

'The only other person in the picture wouldn't have been jealous. She slept with Stevie a few times, but it was mutually understood to be nothing serious. There may have been some overlap at the beginning, but that was before she and Gordon got close.'

'So how did Stevie take it when she died?'

'I don't know. Everything kind of fell apart after that. I couldn't stay in the flat any more. That was the beginning of the end for me and Yvonne in terms of staying in touch. I never went back to Nokturn. I saw him at the funeral, though.'

'And how did he seem?'

'Glasgow tough guy. How do you think he seemed?'

'We're just trying to work out why he would be taking an interest in Julie Muir's murder all these years later. He was looking up news archives, talking to Teddy Sheehan's sister.'

'I've no idea. Julie's funeral was the last time I spoke to him. He wasn't buying the official line, though. He thought there was something iffy about it.'

'Iffy how?'

'Girlfriend of a cabinet minister's son gets murdered and the polis conveniently lock up the local weirdo for it. I gave his speculations precisely zero credence: to a guy like Stevie, everybody the polis put away was a fit-up job.'

Something must have given him renewed belief in his theory though, Catherine reasoned. Otherwise Brenda Sheehan wouldn't be lying on Cal O'Shea's slab.

The Driving Seat

Jasmine pulled away from the brasserie car park and stopped at the T-junction, indicating right, where the promise of light a quarter of a mile ahead beckoned her in the direction of home. To her left was blackness, the occasional glow of oncoming headlights only seeming to emphasise how dark the boulevard was, more like a country road at night than an urban dual carriageway.

To the left was where Stevie Fullerton had gone on that fateful morning, into his own final darkness. She decided to retrace his path, see for herself the spot where this man, whom she had now learned was a relative, had spilled the last of the blood they shared. She endured no belated sense of loss at his death, but she now understood what he meant to Sheila, whose pain was adhering to Jasmine like the smoke from her cigarettes.

She drove along slower than normal, passing joggers and dog walkers, disturbed by how close she got before she saw them alongside. The road led from Croftbank, through Shawburn and on to Gallowhaugh: the one-time domain of Tony McGill.

Fallan had worked for him, Stevie too; indeed, according to local myth just about everybody involved in criminal enterprise – and plenty supposedly involved in preventing it – had been on his payroll at one time or another. As Fallan had put it, Tony McGill's network was like Facebook for criminals.

Local myth also told that he was the man who 'kept the drugs out of Gallowhaugh', but according to Fallan this had been purely a self-serving strategy for shoring up his power base. An old-school gangster who built his broad fiefdom on rackets, robberies and contraband, he didn't have a supply line for heroin when the game started to change, so he had applied his muscle to the Canute-like pursuit of driving the dealers off his turf. Not only did it slow the consolidation of his emerging rivals (for a while, at least), but it conferred upon him a quite absurd air of civic respectability, with him painted as some kind of redoubtable community leader. Fallan said it was like when Nixon appointed Elvis as an anti-drugs figurehead: those in the know were utterly staggered at the ignorance among the well-meaning high and mighty.

McGill craved respectability as much as he craved money and power, Fallan told her.

'He even fucking voted Tory.'

This compounded the ignominy when McGill went down for his part in a massive drug deal, the size of the haul testament to how jealously he craved a slice of the dominant new business. The McGill myth maintained that he had been set up, and according to Fallan this part was actually true, 'just not by the cops'. He hadn't elaborated, so this was the first Jasmine had learned of what he meant – and how he knew.

McGill's sentence was commensurate with the scale of the haul, and he served more than half of it. When he first got out he had found himself yesterday's bam, and for a few years had struggled to rebuild his powerbase, but these days he was right back at the top of the tree. Same as it ever was; he had climbed up there on the shoulders of some bent cops, who had got rid of a major rival for him and thus opened a gap in the drug market that he was well placed to fill.

Some said the best revenge is living well, but Jasmine didn't imagine that memo had reached certain parts of Glasgow. If somebody screwed you over and you ended up in jail for more than fifteen years, living well when you got out was never going to be enough.

Jasmine reached the roundabout where the boulevard was transected by Capletmuir Road. The streetlights were functioning on the other side, running on a different circuit. A little past it was the ancient, disused petrol station that had been transformed into a car wash by Stevie Fullerton. A cash-only operation, the kind of business where the number of transactions was impossible to audit and thus a facility where it wasn't just the vehicles that came out nice and clean on the other side.

There were cones blocking the entrance, so she pulled up on the pavement alongside the low boundary wall.

For a place dedicated to making things gleaming and spotless, the premises itself was pitifully shabby. She guessed it looked very different by day, when it was open: suds and spray and glinting chrome catching the eye and distracting it from signs of chronic neglect.

It had only been closed down a few days, but it already looked abandoned and imminently derelict. The islands where motorists used to fill up appeared conspicuously denuded of their pumps, and the sad little office was bereft of the posters, news hoardings and other paraphernalia that would have advertised a petrol station as a going concern. It seemed like the car wash had been a temporary commercial squat, a parasite business attached to its predecessor's corpse.

The only paint that looked like it had been applied this century was on a single slab that denoted the far side of the exit back on to the dual carriageway. This, presumably, was the slab the gunman's vehicle had struck on its hurried exit, according to witness accounts. It was on the left-hand side as you drove out, which tallied with what Laura Geddes had told her regarding Fallan's Defender sustaining damage and paint transfer to its left flank.

Jasmine would never forget her first time sitting up front in that rickety, bumpy, diesel-smelling monstrosity, the place she had first conversed one on one with the man who was at that point insisting his name was Tron Ingrams. She could vividly picture the encounter still, not least because it ended in gunplay. There were still nights when she woke up shivering, her traitorous subconscious reliving the experience in her dreams: the shotgun blasts, the breakneck driving, the handbrake turns, the skid, the crash, the fear.

What was particularly weird was that frequently when she recalled the incident she would remember herself and not Ingrams as driving, and the reason for that was also what was wrong with this picture.

Fallan's Land Rover was a left-hand drive.

He had purchased it overseas, and thus it was Jasmine's memory of sitting on the right-hand side during the shoot-out that

280

sometimes confused her recall into thinking she had been at the wheel.

Laura had definitely said the scrape and the paint were on the left flank, and were sustained on the way out of the car wash.

Jasmine stared again at the white slab.

Its counterpart on the other side of the gap had enjoyed no such pampering, and nor had the slabs at the entrance. It was as though it had been painted for no other purpose than to be struck by a Land Rover Defender on its getaway from a shooting, leaving a distinguishing mark that would identify the culprit.

Our Betters

'Should we have a wee sign with his name on it?' Laura asked. 'Flowers and balloons maybe?'

'I think my warrant card will suffice,' Catherine told her.

They were standing at an arrival gate at Edinburgh airport, waiting to intercept Gordon Ewart after he disembarked his flight from Heathrow. Catherine had made several fruitless attempts to contact him throughout the day; he was steadfastly ignoring the messages she was leaving on his mobile, and she had been consistently rebuffed by his secretary to an extent that made her suspect the woman was under explicit instruction to do so.

He would be in meetings all day, she said: that was why he was away in London. He was back down south in two days' time, and had a full programme in between. Catherine didn't even get offered an intentionally discouraging 'how about a week on Thursday?' The message was that he was incredibly important and immeasurably busy. But what was also implicit, and rather intriguing, was that he appeared to believe that if he stalled long enough, Catherine would give up and go away.

'I feel like we're paparazzi or reporters or something,' Laura said, as the first passengers began streaming from the airbridge.

'If we were reporters, they wouldn't have let us down to the gate without a boarding pass.'

'Can I still get duty free?'

Gordon Ewart was a senior executive for Cautela Group, on whose board his father still served as a director. It was a security-to-logistics behemoth, and Catherine was conscious that looking like a reporter might actually be worse than looking like a cop, given how skittish its senior management tended to be of late.

Cautela Group were the latest megafirm to be accused of

'aggressive tax reduction' strategies in the UK, a charge that carried all the more sting given how much of its business came from government-awarded contracts. Their suits wouldn't be in the mood to answer questions from strangers, but Catherine had little doubt the firm would ride out the storm comfortably enough. Nothing succeeds like success, they said, but Cautela sat alongside the likes of Capita and G4S in proving that, for a connected few, nothing succeeds like failure also. It seemed no matter how many fuck-ups or embarrassments they were responsible for, the contracts just kept rolling in.

It probably helped if you had good government contacts. Such as having a former Tory cabinet minister and his son on the payroll.

She spotted Ewart striding briskly from the mouth of the airbridge, a tall figure carrying himself with absolute confidence. He was deep in conversation with another expensively suited middle-aged male, both of them bearing briefcases in one hand and their mobiles in the other.

They didn't cast a look towards anybody as they marched in step, the thrusting gait of two men with places to be and who expected everybody else to recognise this and get the hell out of their way. Thus when Catherine and Laura stepped deliberately across their paths, they both flashed looks of annoyance at these impertinent females, but didn't glance long enough to notice the badges.

'Mr Ewart,' Catherine began, but he waved her off brusquely and muttered something about having no comment to make.

Catherine fell into step and identified herself.

'This is not *Dispatches*. I'm with Strathclyde Police. I need to ask you some questions about Stevie Fullerton.'

Ewart turned and glared at her in confused indignation, but he didn't slow down.

'You have got to be joking,' he said. 'You have really got to be fucking joking.'

According to Wiki he'd been a boarder at Strathallan. From the accent she guessed he hadn't spent a lot of his holiday time beyond the periphery of his father's house, never mind the periphery of his father's constituency.

'No, I'm not joking and this isn't a bloody strippergram either. I am investigating—'

'I know what you're investigating. Jesus Christ, I thought this was sorted. I literally don't have time for this and it would be in both our interests, believe me, were you to leave me alone *right now.*'

He strode on, his face flushed. His companion looked uncomfortable to be witness to this, Ewart no doubt furious at the embarrassment. He was showing no intention of stopping.

How about some more awkward, Catherine thought.

'It's concerning two different murder inquiries,' she said loudly. 'Three if we include Julie Muir.'

Yeah, that bloody stopped him.

'You'd best go on ahead,' Ewart told his pal. 'I'll catch you up later.'

The other man nodded and hurried away, glancing back and gesticulating with his mobile.

Ewart let him gain some distance then resumed walking just as briskly. No suggestion that they find a seat or a quiet corner: this guy wanted away, and he didn't expect to be detained.

Catherine had been a cop twenty years, so she had to delve deep to remember what it felt like to encounter a police officer as a civilian. She recalled always being cautious and wary, polite and cooperative, ever conscious of the potential dangers when power met caprice. Most people she met were at least the first two, even the hardened crooks. The sense of entitlement emanating from this prick was quite staggering.

'We've been speaking to a witness who told us that your relationship with Julie Muir was suppressed at the time of the investigation.'

'Christ, are you detectives or archaeologists? And if you're researching ancient history you must *know* it was suppressed, though that makes it sound far more conspiratorial than the truth. It wasn't deemed relevant; or at least not sufficiently relevant as to be worth exposing my father to the fallout.'

'When it comes to murder investigations, I'm seldom sure what

284

is or isn't going to prove relevant in the final analysis, no matter who gets exposed to "fallout".'

His pace had slowed a little, Catherine reckoning this was so that it didn't appear to onlookers that he was trying to get away; better that it just appeared he was chatting casually to two more suits, albeit cheaper ones.

'Julie was murdered on her way to my parents' house, but her intended destination was deemed incidental once it became clear what had happened. She never got there that night because of that fucking mong.'

Ewart bared his teeth as he said this, almost daring her to object to his terminology. His aggression was palpable, but was it principally aimed at Sheehan or Catherine?

'I was interviewed and my relationship with Julie was made known to the investigation. Once Sheehan had confessed the Procurator Fiscal's office concurred with the police that there was no need to bring me into the court case. My father's position meant it would have been a sideshow everybody could do without. If my father had been just anybody, then no, I doubt such a courtesy would have been extended, but the fact is that my father wasn't just anybody.'

'What about your relationship with Stevie Fullerton?'

Ewart visibly seethed, gripping the handle of his briefcase as an inconspicuous outlet for his anger; just not inconspicuous enough.

'Don't you bloody people speak to each other? Because believe me, if you're out on your own your feet won't touch—'

'Forgive me, Mr Ewart,' Catherine told him. 'There was an announcement over the PA, so I didn't quite catch what you said, and I *know* I can't have heard it properly because it sounded like you were threatening me.'

They had reached the domestic arrivals area. Catherine could see Ewart's companion waiting for him near the automatic doors leading out to the car parks. Ewart clocked him too, and stopped walking. He turned to face the way he had just come. He didn't want anyone who knew him to be witness to this discussion.

'I came forward voluntarily,' he said. 'This was all supposed to be cleared up.'

'You came forward voluntarily about what?'

Ewart sighed.

'Fullerton had been phoning me, threatening to kick up a stink about my wild days. It was blackmail: sheer opportunism. Cautela had been all over the media and he must have thought I'd pay good money to avoid further bad publicity.'

'Your wild days?' Catherine asked, curious to see how much he would cop to. The more candid he was, the more it might suggest he was trying to divert attention from something else.

'If you've spoken to a witness who knew about me and Julie, then I'm sure you already know what Fullerton was alluding to. My association with the notorious Nokturn nightclub: sex, drugs, Fullerton's own gang connections. Throw in Julie as well and he thought he had a classic tabloid cocktail, light on detail but heavy on innuendo.'

'So you contacted the police about this?'

'Yes. And *before* Fullerton was killed, I hasten to add. I got in touch again after that happened, in case anybody was stupid enough to think I had a motive.'

'You did have a motive,' Catherine reminded him.

'Hardly. I told him to fuck off. Called his bluff. He kept at it though: he thought *I* was bluffing. The bastard phoned my mother as well, hoping the potential embarrassment might milk her too. That's why I went to the police. I made sure I was eliminated. Fullerton's whole intention was to drag me into the sleaze, and I was damned if he was going to achieve it posthumously. This was all taken care of,' he added impatiently, like she was being particularly obtuse.

'Stevie Fullerton's murder is my investigation, Mr Ewart. Nobody can eliminate you from that except me.'

He gave a humourless, scornful laugh and looked at her with open contempt.

'What rank did you say you were, officer?'

'Detective Superintendent.'

'Then you ought to be asking yourself how far above your pay grade all this happened for it not to have seeped down to your level. And I'm guessing you'll find yourself a lot lower still by the time this is all over.'

With that, he turned on his heel and marched off towards his business-class buddy by the doors.

'A real charmer,' Laura said. 'Hard to see why he's been divorced twice. I've never seen somebody so sure his arse was watertight. Who the hell has been telling him that it's all taken care of?'

'Especially if Fullerton had been calling the guy making threats shortly before his death,' Catherine agreed. 'Which makes me extremely confused as to why this is the first *I'm* hearing about these threats.'

'I'd heard nothing either,' Laura assured her. 'His name never came up before Ciara Flanigan mentioned it. Hang on, though: Ewart said Fullerton phoned him – repeatedly. Why didn't his number appear on Fullerton's phone records?'

Catherine suddenly pictured the USB stick she had received, eventually, from the Intelligence bureau via Sunderland.

Via Abercorn.

Laura's mobile rang. She glanced at the screen then held it up for Catherine to see.

'I need to take this.'

Laura did a lot of listening, not so much speaking. She glanced across to Catherine every so often, eyes wide, palpably frustrated that her reaction was as much as she could immediately convey, but her expression implied it was worth waiting for.

'That was Jasmine Sharp,' Laura reported.

'Your secret source.'

It had been Laura's idea to bring Jasmine into play, figuring she might be able to wheedle a little more information via angles otherwise closed off to the investigation. However, it had been Catherine's idea that Laura should pretend she was going behind her boss's back, estimating that if Jasmine thought she was working at cross purposes to Catherine it would motivate her to dig all the deeper.

Catherine had taken a disproportionate and perhaps unworthy satisfaction in thus playing the girl, as it felt like she was evening the score. She harboured an enduring, powerful and instinctive suspicion that Jasmine had in some way screwed her regarding a previous case. She didn't know quite how and she didn't have any proof, but she was in little doubt that something about it reeked of deceit.

Jasmine might have an innocent face and look like she'd have difficulty staying upright in a stiff breeze, but she was a sneaky, duplicitous and thoroughly sleekit wee bitch, which was why Catherine had agreed it would be useful to have her *inside* the tent on this one.

'She claims she can prove Fallan was set up. Sheila Fullerton told her that the story about Stevie and his crew attacking Fallan and leaving him for dead is bollocks. It never happened, so there's no grudge, no motive – and that's according to the widow. Jasmine also pointed out that the Land Rover just happened to scrape against the only freshly painted slab at the car wash, conveniently marking it for later identification.'

'So what?' Catherine asked, not yet sharing Laura's sense of portent.

'The witnesses said the slab scraped the Defender's passenger door. Fallan's is a left-hand drive.'

'Yeah, they *said* passenger side,' Catherine argued, 'but presumably they just meant the left-hand side as it was facing the road.'

'Presumably? Did anybody go back and check which side the gunman was sitting in those CCTV images? The gunman who had taken the precaution of wearing a skull mask and a hood, but was driving to and from a daylight hit in his own car?'

'I didn't notice what side he was driving,' Catherine admitted. 'In fact, I don't think I even heard anyone mention that Fallan's vehicle was a southpaw.'

'How hard would it be to fit fake plates, or to scrape the side of your patsy's Land Rover with, say, a half brick painted white? Then your hitman makes sure he bashes that nice white slab on the way out—'

'Except the paint transferred from the brick wouldn't chemically match the stuff on the slab,' Catherine pointed out. 'The paint on Fallan's vehicle did.'

'It would match if it came from the same tin: that's what Jasmine's saying.'

Catherine got out her mobile and dialled.

'Zoe? Do you have the CCTV shots of Fallan's Land Rover to hand? I need you to look at them and tell me which side of the vehicle the guy in the skull mask is sitting.'

'Just a sec, boss.'

The line went silent for a few seconds, then Zoe picked up again.

'The usual. Right-hand drive. Why?'

She recalled Abercorn's words when challenged about the USB stick.

Look, Catherine, not everything I do is a fucking conspiracy, okay?

No, but this was starting to look a lot like one.

The Point of no Return

Anthony glanced up from the laptop and spotted Adrienne walking along the passage between the first row of desks and the individual offices. He was sure she saw him too, but they were both adhering to the etiquette of pretending otherwise, kidding themselves but fooling nobody. It was ridiculous when he considered how much could be observed from the tiniest glimpse, how few milliseconds it had taken for him to notice movement in his peripheral vision, look up and then positively identify her. Yet here they both were, feigning obliviousness, an absurdity compounded by the fact that they were both polis and supposedly professionals at taking cognisance of their environments. Nonetheless, what anyone chose not to see remained a prerogative that everyone tended to respect.

She knocked on McLeod's door and then stepped inside her office, still visible through the open slats of the blinds.

He wondered what she was doing in at this time, and felt a tingle of anxiety that a change in the shifts might have them working alongside one another again. He couldn't say whether the anxiety was piqued by the possibility of this happening, or that it would not.

He was forgetting his own shifts had changed as of today. He had been in here since stupid o'clock and lost track of time as he trawled fruitlessly through Stevie Fullerton's laptop. He was starting to think he would have preferred to be back in the morgue, having another crack at exhuming the Julie Muir case files. At least down there he knew there was something specific he was tasked with tracking down. The past couple of days had been a soul-wearying exercise in not being sure what he was looking for, and hoping that he'd recognise it if he saw it.

He had begun to nickname Fallan's computer 'Procrastination', as it was the thief of time. It was a Frankenstein's monster of a PC, a buzzing, humming abomination sporting several different internal hard drives, each of which was partitioned, and each partition of which booted a different operating system. Even a simple search using dates as a filter to bring up recently accessed files had to be repeated multiple times, as certain documents and programmes were only recognised by certain OSs. A perverse part of him wanted to lock some Mac-zealot friends of his in a room with the thing, just to see how long it was before they started to cry.

Adding to the sense of futility was the knowledge that anything worth looking at was probably inaccessible. There were whole areas protected by encryption software that was literally military-grade. Anthony didn't even dare attempt a password guess in case some blokes in black ski masks came belaying through the windows in response.

Fullerton's laptop was a simpler affair, but no less frustrating. It was messy but clean: the digital equivalent of an overstuffed suitcase, but so far not one in which anybody had found so much as a smuggled cigarette. There were so many icons on display that it was difficult to see the wallpaper: every add-on, shortcut and useless piece of bloatware it had ever downloaded still sitting proudly on the desktop.

The cache bore testament to browsing habits that suggested he and his wife shared the machine; either that or Stevie was a secret shoe fetishist and commercial tableware enthusiast.

A long, slow scroll down a truly colossal Internet Explorer history did at least throw up a number of search results pertaining to the Julie Muir murder case, but he found no text or other documents with 'Muir' or 'Sheehan' in the search string. As Paul over at LOCUST had also concluded, Fullerton simply wouldn't have stored anything sensitive on a machine he shared with the missus. If there was treasure to be found, it was stored elsewhere, on a detachable drive or these days just as likely off site, though the browser history hadn't thrown up any login pages for FTP or cloud storage.

Anthony recalled that the gunman had taken Fullerton's phone, so perhaps there was something important on there, but that seemed even less likely than keeping anything compromising on a laptop, as the mobile was more likely to be misplaced or stolen. Nonetheless, there had to be a strong motive for taking it, as a hitman wouldn't run the risk of tying himself to the murder for the sake of the extra hundred quid he might raise by flogging the handset later.

He was about ready to run up the white flag and tell McLeod he'd struck out yet again. LOCUST could have it back if they wanted, though that desire would probably only last until they realised McLeod had been pulling their chain; and if not it would be parcelled off to be gutted by the division's IT geeks.

He heard McLeod's door open and looked up instinctively. Which instinct was that, though? He already knew who was coming out of there, so it wasn't caution or curiosity, neither of which would, furthermore, demand that his gaze lingered.

Adrienne emerged and looked his way also. Their eyes met for a short moment, both of them managing an apologetic wish-it-were-otherwise smile, then she started to walk away.

She had a background in IT, Anthony remembered. There were maybe things that she would know to do that would never have occurred to him. He wasn't sure whether he believed this was likely to make much difference to his efforts, or whether it was just a pretext to get her over here. He wasn't sure whether it mattered either.

Adrienne began to hit her stride, heading back the way she came. She would soon be out of reasonable 'hey, while you're here' range.

He almost waved, almost called.

A couple more paces took her past the point where a wave would catch her attention. He was conscious of the very moment she passed the event horizon, the point when he knew the opportunity had been lost. It was also the point when he realised how much he had wanted it.

He got off his arse and ran, calling her name before she reached the lifts.

She turned around, a little surprised, a little curious, a little apprehensive.

'Have you got a minute? I'm going mental hunting through a laptop here, and I thought a fresh pair of eyes . . .'

'Sure,' she said.

She didn't smile but her eyes seemed bright. They both knew what this was.

It was only a matter of yards, but Anthony's heart was thumping by the time he got back to his desk, as though he'd run up every stair in the building. He sat down in his chair again, Adrienne hovering at the side of the desk.

'It's Stevie Fullerton's laptop. I'm looking for anything linking to Julie Muir or Brenda Sheehan, but I'm at the end of my tether. I was about to jack it in and hand the machine in to PC World.'

By this he meant send the laptop in to the division's tech geeks. They called it that because the experience was much the same as putting a PC in to the store for repair: it took so long to get results that by the time it came back you had usually done whatever you needed to without it.

'I suspect if he was using it for anything interesting, then the files are off-site, but I can't even find links to cloud storage or anything.'

'If we can find out who he's got a web storage account with, we can put in a request to the provider, but that's a message-in-a-bottle job,' Adrienne replied. 'If it's UK-based we'd be in with a shout, although it'll take months, but if it's overseas, forget it. It's not good marketing for IPs and storage outfits if it gets around that the authorities can crowbar open your online vault.'

She wore a rather unhopeful frown, and he thought she was about to walk away. Instead she wheeled over a free chair and took a seat next to him.

'Budge up,' she said, her hands falling on the keyboard, her foot brushing his ankle just for a second as she nudged him to move aside.

She opened a control panel and set the machine to compile a list of all installed programmes. It took a while, as it was cluttered with all manner of auto-installed and unnecessarily bundled crap.

'Okay,' she said, having apparently seen what she was hoping to. 'He's got Firefox installed, but despite there being icons spammed all over his desktop like confetti, it isn't one of them. It's not installed where it normally defaults to either. We could be in business here.'

'I don't follow.'

'It's nothing to geek out over. This isn't IT expertise you're seeing here, it's divorcee expertise.'

'I'm intrigued either way,' he replied, suddenly aware that he sounded disproportionately excited. It wasn't about what she was doing with the laptop; it was because they were talking to each other the way they used to.

She began opening system folders, digging her way down to where the Firefox.exe was inconspicuously tucked away.

'My ex, Phil, did most of his browsing on Internet Explorer. But when I had become suspicious that he was playing away, I had a wee snoop one night and found that he was also running Firefox. Just like Fullerton's laptop here, you wouldn't have known the other browser was even installed. I only found it because I was searching unlikely folders for where he might have stashed photos or whatever.'

Adrienne clicked on the bookmarks. To Anthony's disappointment, it displayed the default URLs that came with a clean install. Adrienne nonetheless ran the cursor down the list, hovering briefly over each entry.

She smiled, but he couldn't see why. She pointed to the bottom corner, where the corresponding address was displayed, so that the destination could be seen without clicking.

'You can give a bookmark any name,' she said. 'No matter what the URL actually points to.'

Adrienne clicked on Help and Tutorials in the Mozilla sub-menu. A moment later they were looking at the login screen for 'E-Vault Back-up and Storage'.

Her smile grew wider and Anthony simply gaped as he looked

294

at the login fields. Fullerton's username appeared in the top one, above a line of black bullet points, the 'Remember Me' box ticked by default underneath.

'Same as Phil. He hid the car where nobody would look, but left the keys in the ignition for convenience.'

She clicked the login button.

Sins of Omission

Catherine looked at the two different printouts, carefully laid side by side, page for page, for the purposes of comparison. At a glance they were identical: same headers, same layout, same logos, same tagging. You would really have to know there was something missing before it would even occur to you to look for it, which was why it never struck anyone to be suspicious of the original.

She had asked Intell to send Stevie Fullerton's phone records a second time; or rather, Adrienne Cruickshank had asked on her behalf, as Adrienne had a good contact over there who could fast-track the request and, just as crucially, make sure it came to Catherine and Catherine alone. To that end, the new file came in by email rather than on a flash drive. Catherine had expected its predecessor to arrive that way too, but somebody had gone to the trouble of making sure that didn't happen.

She wanted to be absolutely certain before she confronted Abercorn: wanted the evidence to be right in front of her, indisputable. Not that evidence being right in front of her was any kind of guarantee around here, she reflected, casting a glance towards the CCTV stills that mocked her from elsewhere on the desk.

Every year, at the squad's Christmas night out, she announced the Wood for the Trees Award, for the piece of evidence that it took them the longest to realise was staring them in the face. It was a good-humoured exercise, focusing on the article of evidence itself rather than pinning blame on anybody. The purpose was to remind them all how easy it could be to miss what was three feet in front of them when their focus was on the minutiae.

Last year it had been an apparent suicide, the victim having slashed both her wrists in the bath. It had taken an embarrassingly long time for anybody to wonder how she had managed to grip the knife for the second cut, having severed all the tendons in her other arm.

There were a few weeks left before Christmas, but it would be fair to say that the Land Rover had this year's title in the bag.

She took a pink highlighter pen and put a thick stroke through each entry displaying Gordon Ewart's phone number. They had been carefully deleted from the version Abercorn passed on to her, though as it was an Acrobat document this couldn't have been straightforward. The original subscriber check must have been Photoshopped and then the adulterated image saved as a PDF again.

A bit less of a giveaway than a big black marker, but he'd been caught nonetheless. And now she was going to nail his balls to the wall.

He appeared at her door within an hour of being called: new league record. Abercorn seldom responded to the first or even fourth request to talk, but she had been a little disingenuous in her summons. Rather than phone him up and say she needed a word, she had got Beano to phone Paul Clayton and let slip that they had unearthed something LOCUST had missed on Stevie Fullerton's laptop. When, inevitably, Paul had begged Beano to say what it was, he had claimed it was now out of his hands and that the laptop was irretrievably in Catherine's possession.

As far as she knew, Beano hadn't found anything. In fact, he had apparently spent yesterday lost in the labyrinthine hell that was Fallan's PC, and was only getting around to looking at Fullerton's laptop this morning. Nonetheless, merely the suggestion that he had unearthed something tasty proved irresistible LOCUST bait.

'I'm told you put in your thumb and pulled out a plum,' Abercorn suggested with an eager smile, rapping on the inside of her door-frame. His winning manner was intended to disguise the fact that he was (a) crapping himself and (b) livid about the prospect that something damaging had fallen into Catherine's hands.

She watched his eyes gobble up the room, scanning anxiously for the laptop.

'I've discovered an interesting file, yes,' she said.

'On Fullerton's laptop?'

She feigned confusion.

'No. On a USB stick that you gave me. You'll remember: it was accidentally sent to LOCUST.'

Abercorn looked wary. He could sense the ambush coming; he just didn't know from where.

'I got Intell to send me the same subscriber check this morning and I've been playing a wee game of spot the difference. Maybe you'd like to join in. As a wee hint, the redacted phone numbers are in pink.'

Abercorn stared at the printouts on her desk: they were upside down from his perspective but he didn't need to see the fine details. He had a look on his face like he'd just given his first blowjob and nobody had warned him what happened at the end.

'You'll be wondering how I found out. Allow me to enlighten you. Yesterday evening I had a very unsatisfactory conversation with a thoroughly unlovely specimen who seemed to be under the impression that he had been eliminated from my investigations, despite his only coming to the attention *of* my investigation a matter of hours before. This individual also made a point of stressing to me that these matters had been decided so far above my rank that I'd be giving hand shandies to probationers by the end of the month if I didn't drop it.'

Abercorn stood up straight, like he was on parade awaiting inspection.

'I can only apologise,' he said. 'I appreciate that from your perspective this is inexcusable, and I don't expect you to be anything less than outraged. The nature of my remit means that there are unavoidable compromises, and occasions when the purview of an investigation overlaps other ongoing inquiries. Sometimes we get away with it, sometimes nobody notices. But every now and then we're going to get our dicks caught in the zipper. This is one of those times.'

It was a disarmingly open and unequivocal *mea culpa*, the kind she never thought she'd live to hear from Abercorn. But that in itself told her something wasn't right. As she had mused just the other day, Abercorn was thick-skinned about LOCUST's unpopularity: sometimes infuriatingly so. He never apologised, because he didn't believe he had anything to apologise for. In a way, this was almost a backhanded compliment to counterparts' professionalism that he expected them to understand – even though they didn't like it – why he had to go about his business the way he did.

Then it occurred to her that he had been unexpectedly conciliatory when she first challenged him about the USB stick. He had even asked around on her behalf to garner some more information on the symbol.

Abercorn never did favours, not without subtly guaranteeing that he would get something bigger in return. He had behaved, she realised, like someone who had making up to do: like a man with a guilty conscience. Except, as she had just considered, Abercorn never had a guilty conscience about anything he did professionally. It was all in the game, nothing personal. Why would he suddenly be feeling conflicted over this?

Then she worked it out.

'Whose phone number is this?' she demanded, pointing to one of the pink streaks.

'Let's not play games, Catherine. We both know whose number it is, but I am not in a position to discuss the matter any further.'

'You're not in a position to discuss it because *you* don't know. You're covering for somebody.'

He remained standing to attention, but seemed to shrink away from her. She could tell he was thinking about how best to stage his retreat, so she got up and closed the door, putting herself between it and him.

'Who gave you the stick, Dougie?'

He stiffened again, composing that famous poker face of his. But she had already seen his hand.

'I know you won't give up your superior, and I respect you for that, but something's rotten in the state of Govan and your loyalty is helping the wrong people. Somebody's fucking with my murder investigation and you're going to tell me who. You don't need to name names: just look into my eyes and tell me it wasn't Drummond who gave you the flash drive.'

His mouth said nothing but his eyes blabbed like a supergrass. He couldn't tolerate her gaze.

Abercorn reached past her to grab the door handle. She didn't get in his way but did follow him out into the corridor. She observed his retreat but to her surprise did not relish the sight of him defeated. Whatever was going on, he wasn't part of it: he had merely covered for his boss because he thought that was his duty.

As she watched him walk away she became aware of somebody waving to her from a nearby desk. It was Beano, sitting next to Adrienne. The sight surprised her. The two of them had seemed all pally-pally for a long time and then suddenly they were never to be found together, like matter and antimatter. Catherine had seen it before, two people like those battling tops you used to get: they spun around in each other's orbits, closer and closer, then when they finally touched it threw them violently apart.

Something was uniting them at the moment, though. They both looked like they were about to wet the seat.

'Boss, you really have to see this.'

Reality TV

Catherine was looking at Brenda Sheehan sitting in an armchair in her living room, gazing back from the screen as though gazing over Adrienne's shoulder and out through the blinds. She was dressed in a baggy green sweater beneath a blue housecoat, a garment that always piqued Catherine's curiosity as to where such unflattering and anachronistic items were still on sale. Watt Brothers, probably.

Brenda looked a little timorous and unsure, but not uncomfortable, not afraid. Her eyes were slightly bloodshot from crying some time recently, a scrunched-up hanky in her right hand further evidence of this, but otherwise she seemed in good health. She was certainly keen to talk, tripping over herself as she spilled out her recollections.

Her living room was looking better than the last time Catherine saw it too. It was a tight shot, framing Brenda fairly closely, but she could see enough to be struck by the order and cleanliness of the coffee table. There was no hint of the alcoholic dereliction they had witnessed; no hint of alcohol, in fact. There was a mug of tea and a presentation tin of chocolate biscuits in front of her, perhaps brought by her visitor.

'Take your time, Brenda,' said a male voice, its tone patient and sympathetic. 'Just tell me again what we talked about before. Forget about the phone: just look at me.'

'We're guessing that's Fullerton,' Beano said, pausing the playback. 'He doesn't appear in the shot, but . . .'

'It is,' confirmed Catherine. 'I've spoken to him. You found this on the laptop?' she asked, amazed.

'No, it was remote storage,' Adrienne answered. 'Fullerton uploaded it to a site called E-Vault and we found his login details.'

'Did you find anything else?'

'Just this. According to the user settings, he set up the account the same day this file was uploaded. We're guessing this wasn't put here to keep it hidden: it was a back-up, in case the original file got lost or deleted. This video might well be why the gunman took Fullerton's phone.'

'But if he uploaded a back-up from the laptop, why wasn't there a copy *on* the laptop?'

'We have a theory,' Beano said, 'but it contains spoilers.'

He clicked to resume play.

Brenda looked concerned.

'I'm no' sure where to begin,' she admitted.

'Doesn't matter,' said Fullerton. 'Just say what you were saying before. Say what you remember.'

She nodded, taking a moment.

'First thing was, I suppose, hearing about the lassie. You know, hearing that they'd found a body up near the footpath next to the railway. You just wouldn't expect anything like that here, in the hamlet, especially not back in those days. You always felt safe here. It was that quiet. When I first heard, I thought it must have been somebody hit by a train.

'When I saw the polis car pulling up in front of the house, to the door, I thought they were coming to ask if we'd seen anything. I thought they'd be chapping every door in the street. But they were there to take Teddy away.'

'Who was "they"?' asked Fullerton.

'Cairns was the one in charge: Bob Cairns. I knew him because I'd had a wee bit of bother before. And there was a younger one, a big lanky boy. He wouldn't have farted without Cairns telling him to. Cannae mind his name, though. It's gone right out my head.'

'Was it Drummond?'

'Aye. That was it: Drummond.'

Catherine was aware of both Beano and Adrienne looking towards her when this name was confirmed. This was why Beano had suggested they take the laptop into her office rather than watch it at his desk. They were all acutely aware that the stakes just went up.

'When they lifted Teddy I assumed it was a mistake. I thought maybe they'd got a description of somebody that looked like him, or there was a mix-up over the name. Teddy's full name was James Edward Sheehan, so I was thinking there must be somebody called James or Jimmy Sheehan that they're after, and it would all get cleared up. But no, it was oor Teddy they wanted right enough. They had him away for days. Teddy wouldn't have known what was happening to him. He didn't know his rights, so he wouldn't have known to ask for a lawyer. He'd have been putty in their hands.'

'But you gave a statement, didn't you,' Fullerton prompted. 'You gave him an alibi.'

'That's right, son,' she answered, her lips wavering, her expression threatening tears.

She took a sip of tea and swallowed, finding her voice again.

'I told the police that Teddy couldn't have done this, because he was here with me that night. I can't remember who I gave my statement to. It wasn't the ones who arrested Teddy. I told them Teddy was seldom out of the house in the evenings. Now and again he'd go for a walk in the summer if it was a nice evening, but usually after he'd had his tea he'd be in front of the telly or doing a jigsaw. He loved jigsaws.'

These last few words came out as a strangled whisper, a fond memory turning to pain.

'I had been drinking that night,' she admitted. 'I drank every night, back then. But he was here, Teddy was here.'

She wiped her eyes with the sleeve of her housecoat, apparently forgetting about the hanky gripped in her hand.

'Do you need . . .?' Fullerton asked, though they couldn't tell what was being offered. Perhaps another hanky.

'No, you're all right, son. I just need a minute.'

'Take your time, Brenda.'

She gulped at her tea, a tentative sip becoming something more needy, more urgent. In that moment Catherine glimpsed what it might have been like when the vessel in her hand contained vodka.

'They came back,' she said, putting down the mug. Her expression was grim but stonier, less weakened by uncertainty.

'Who did?'

'Cairns and the other one. Drummond. They got me to change my story. Or to "revise my statement". That's the words that'll follow me to the grave. The words St Peter will read out when I have to answer for what I've done.'

'Did they threaten you?'

'No. Well, I suppose they did, but it was more subtle than that. Cairns didn't challenge me or call me a liar or anything. He said he thought I was mistaken. He knew I'd have been drinking that night, so he told me my memory couldn't be clear. He started off planting wee seeds of doubt. Then he got talking about my drinking, about the troubles I'd had. My arrests. Shoplifting. God forgive me, son, I'm so ashamed of it now, but back then money was always tight, especially with Teddy's big mouth to feed, and his clothes and his bus fares.'

'There's none of us lived perfect lives,' Fullerton said, prompting a few exchanged glances.

'Cairns was sympathetic,' Brenda went on. 'He got me talking about Teddy, about how I'd been landed with him when other women were meeting husbands and making lives for themselves. Said it was no wonder I drank. But he also said it wasn't fair on Teddy either, having been left in the care of somebody who couldn't cope. He said the social would have been liable to take him away if they knew the states I was getting myself into, and that's when Drummond brought up the charges.'

'What charges?'

'The shoplifting. I was due in court in a couple of months, and he said it was likely to be a custodial sentence this time. Teddy would be getting taken into care if I went inside. But Cairns said it didn't have to be like that. He could make the charges go away, said I deserved a fresh start: a new beginning. He said Teddy had done a terrible thing, and he knew why it was hard for me to believe that, but that Teddy might be dangerous, and how would I feel if I stood by my drunken alibi and Teddy killed somebody else?'

She looked away, down at the table, and closed her eyes for a painful few seconds. Catherine anticipated another breakdown, but when she opened them again there was something darker in her expression, something that would not allow tears. Tears were a sign of self-pity, and in Brenda's face Catherine saw only shame.

'It wasn't the threats, or the pressure. It was me. I was weak. I wanted rid of him. I wanted a life of my own, a new beginning like Cairns was offering. And I didn't want to go to jail. I couldn't face the thought of doing without drink for however long I got sentenced.

'I let myself believe it. Cairns made it easy for me. I knew I had been drinking that night, so I told myself my memory could have been wrong. I knew Teddy had been out for a walk one of the evenings around then, but I couldn't have said for sure which one, so I told myself that maybe it *was* the Saturday night. Or Teddy could have been out while I thought he was upstairs doing his jigsaw . . .'

Brenda put a hand to her forehead and leaned into it, as if her head would roll off without the support. She didn't speak for a long time, maybe twenty or thirty seconds.

Catherine could vividly imagine the scene in that same living room, twenty-five years earlier, and in particular she could picture the view from inside Drummond's head. Brenda wasn't the only one allowing herself to be seduced by a lie. The witness was confused. She had been drunk, she was being instinctively loyal to her brother; and besides, her alibi was going to be worthless in court anyway because she was a hopeless alcoholic.

'The worst lies are the ones you tell yourself,' Brenda said, 'because you'll never find forgiveness for those.'

She gazed down again, then looked back at her confessor, for Fullerton was undoubtedly the one she had been referring to when she spoke to her sponsor.

'He told me Teddy would get taken care of in prison, that he would be somewhere special, like a hospital.'

Brenda's face crumbled, the self-reproach giving way to uncontainable sorrow. She broke down, the words 'God forgive me, God forgive me' repeated over and over until they were swallowed by her sobs.

The file ended there, the words 'Play again?' in the centre of the screen reading like a dare under the circumstances.

'This is toxic,' Catherine stated.

'No shit,' agreed Beano, his tone acknowledging that an ordinary day at work was in the first throes of turning into a major crisis with ramifications for all their careers.

'This doesn't prove anything in and of itself,' Catherine said. 'The DCC can plausibly argue that all it shows is that he was present as the junior partner while his senior colleague persuaded a witness, who may conceivably have been lying or mistaken – certainly unreliable – to alter her story.'

'Aye, but given that Brenda Sheehan and Stevie Fullerton are now both dead, and the case files are missing . . .'

'Quite,' Catherine answered.

'You asked why there isn't a copy of this video on the laptop,' Beano reminded her. 'I think there probably was, until very recently. Paul Clayton said they were getting pressure from upstairs to make sure there was nothing compromising to LOCUST on Fullerton's computer. I'm guessing that pressure was coming from Drummond in order to get the laptop away from us.'

'But what if *they* found the video file?' Adrienne asked.

'LOCUST wouldn't have looked twice at it, especially if a glimpse just showed an old woman talking. Nor would they have been particularly suspicious if the DCC said he wanted a wee poke through the laptop himself.'

'We'll never know,' Catherine admitted. 'But if it's true, it's not the only thing he's tried to erase.'

She indicated the printouts sitting beneath the laptop on her desk.

'Stevie Fullerton's phone records were amended by Drummond. He removed the number of Gordon Ewart, Cautela Group senior executive and son of Campbell Ewart, the former Under-Secretary of State for Scotland. What is less well known about Gordon Ewart is that he was dating Julie Muir at the time of her murder. Ewart told us that Fullerton had been blackmailing him, threatening to make a stink in the press over his coke-sniffing wild years and his connection to the killing, but I'm starting to think Stevie was threatening to expose something bigger.'

'Cairns and Drummond had an educationally subnormal suspect in custody for however long they needed,' observed Adrienne. 'No lawyer, no witnesses, no tape recorders back then.'

Catherine recalled Ciara Flanigan's words, the conspiracy theory Stevie Fullerton was hawking at Julie's funeral: *Girlfriend of a cabinet minister's son gets murdered and the polis conveniently lock up the local weirdo for it.*

'We all need to take a breath here,' she warned them, 'and step extremely cautiously from this point forwards. Like I said, this video proves nothing. On its own, it's more dangerous to us right now than to the DCC. Especially as we don't know what his role in all of this is.'

'So how do you want to play it?' asked Beano.

'I want to light a fire under him and see how he reacts, but I'm not going upstairs to chap on his door. I don't think I need to stress that we'll be flying under the radar here.'

'Secretly investigating the Deputy Chief Constable? No boss, you don't need to stress that. What do you want us to do?'

'I want you to compare both versions of these phone records, find out if there was anyone else Drummond didn't want us to know Stevie was speaking to. And as it's unlikely we're ever going to see the investigation files again, I want you to look through the court records of the case. I'll ask Dom Wilson at the Procurator Fiscal's office if he can get somebody to dig them up. I'll be speaking to him anyway.'

'Why?'

'Because I'm going to get him to release Glen Fallan.'

Blind Alley

It was close to noon when he finally emerged from the close, the blue doorway tucked between a late-night kebab shop and a grim-looking computer repair and game-exchange joint. Clearly he had been up at the crack of half-eleven, ambling bleary-eyed along the street at an unhurried pace.

It was going to be a foot follow, which wasn't ideal on her own, but less conspicuous than a vehicle pursuit. Jasmine had always suspected it would be a foot follow. Somehow she couldn't picture Ned Untrusty having his own wheels, other than for the brief period between stealing them and fencing them off at the nearest chop shop.

She climbed out of the surveillance van and got into step roughly twenty yards behind him. She was dressed in what she considered her Velma costume, intended to make her look inconspicuously dowdy. Her hair was tucked under a beret chosen for its complete lack of aesthetic merit, and she had donned an equally drab overcoat and a pair of glasses to complete the look. This guy had to have studied what she looked like in order to ID her at the Alhambra and make his move. She couldn't afford to be recognised as she would only get one shot. If he made her, it was over.

Jasmine was aware that she was disproportionately fixated upon this. It wasn't some amazing lead, yet she had been almost giddy with the rush when the information came through from Harry Deacon's contact in print analysis.

'The chancer who stole your phone is called Billy Darroch,' she was informed. 'He lives upstairs from PC Clinic at 248 Carswell Road.'

She finally had a name for the slimebag who had swiped her sim, which meant she had a possible link to whoever was behind the Fullerton shooting. It was tentative at best, but as long as she was pursuing it then that meant the investigation wasn't over, and she achingly needed that to be the case.

She had spent yesterday on a shift for Galt Linklater, sitting in a van outside a house in Pollokshields, watching for a subject who never emerged. His curtains didn't even open. Bastard must have cosied up with a duvet and a DVD boxset while she sat there and stared at a never-changing scene. To be honest, it was a bit of a result: it was money in the bank and she wouldn't have been on her game had a follow been required. She had been listless to the point of depression, bereft of energy and feeling at best numb, at worst hovering constantly on the verge of tears.

She felt assailed by a crushing sense of disappointment and anticlimax. This quest she had been on for most of her life had ultimately led her to an empty place, from where there appeared to be nowhere else to go. She had pulled back the curtain and discovered the true nature of the Great Oz. For so long she had been desperate to know who her father was, and to find out the truth about her mother's life before she was born. She had finally discovered the answers to her questions, but had learned nothing that changed how she felt.

On top of that, there was the inescapable conclusion that she'd been had. When she called Laura Geddes with her findings, if she was being honest, she didn't know how she expected to feel. She wasn't looking for a junior sheriff's badge and a pat on the head, but as soon as she imparted the information she felt hollow, suddenly aware she had eagerly handed over the fruits of her labours and got nothing in return. Laura had sounded intrigued and grateful, but her manner was markedly different from when she had visited the flat.

'I'll pass this stuff on right away,' Laura had said. 'I'm with Catherine just now. She'll be very interested in what you've just told me.'

Catherine, not McLeod. She didn't sound cagey and tense, concerned about her boss going off the rails. She sounded energised and confident, eager to receive her own pat on the head.

That was when Jasmine sussed that she'd been played. It seemed embarrassingly obvious now, but kudos to Laura for her performance. There was no way she was ever going behind her boss's back, but Jasmine had bought it, and she'd paid for it with a load of unbillable hours, doing McLeod's job for her gratis. McLeod must have been in on it from the start, the torn-faced fucking cow.

This was why she needed to follow Billy Darroch. It was the only angle she had left, the one thing she hadn't handed over to the cops. This would keep her foot across the threshold of the investigation, just enough to stop the door closing.

He was not a taxing subject. Short of wearing a hi-viz vest, there was little else he could have done to improve his visibility. He was dressed in a crimson hoodie: Little Red Riding Ned. Not only did it make him easy to eyeball from distance, but the hood restricted his peripheral vision so he was unlikely to catch a sideways glance. Plus there was something conspicuous about his gait, a gallus waddle like he owned the pavement, all elbows and bobbing head. If only all of her marks were this easy.

A wee bit less slick and sneaky when you're not the one preying on the unwary, eh Billy?

He headed into the low-level station just past the new Nando's, buying a ticket at the window. His nasal voice was horribly familiar as he asked for his ticket, giving her a shudder as it took her back to his disingenuous solicitude at the Alhambra.

She followed him down to the platform and got on to the same carriage of a train bound for Lanark. He had bought a Roundabout day pass, so she had to remain close as she didn't know where he would be getting off. Central Station probably, either to change trains or for a wander through the town. She tried not to think of what kind of afternoon might lie ahead of her, following him around a tour of various Cash Converters and second-hand electronics shops; or of how unlikely it was that he'd meet with anybody involved in setting up Fallan.

He didn't get off at Central though, or Argyle Street. He stayed on as the train passed beneath the city centre and continued southeast. She looked at the list of stops along the line taking the train

310

ultimately to Lanark: among them Croftbank, Shawburn High St, Shawburn East, Gallowhaugh.

Darroch alighted at the first of these, making a call on his mobile as he ambled along the platform. Jasmine kept her distance as only a handful of other passengers had got off here, so she wasn't close enough to earwig what he was talking about.

Croftbank: this was where her mother grew up, where she had gone to school with Stevie Fullerton, where Stevie and his crew had drunk in the Bleacher's Vaults, and where the Bleacher's Vaults had become Sheila Fullerton's pride and joy, the Old Croft Brasserie.

Darroch made his way out of the station's main exit and turned right, in the direction of the Bleachfield Centre, about half a mile away. It was a massive new shopping development, combining a make-over for an existing seventies-built horror with a modern extension. The Bleachfield Centre was dominated by a new Tesco but also accommodated several thousand square feet of retail outlets, many of which showed true pioneering spirit in coming to this part of the planet. If Billy was off for lunch at Wagamama, Jasmine thought, then the world truly no longer made sense.

She maintained her distance as he proceeded with no deviation, definitely heading for the shopping mall. There were very few pedestrians, most people arriving at Bleachfield by car, but he remained oblivious of her pursuit, yakking away into his phone.

He took a right turn down a narrow gap between a warehouse and the high concrete perimeter wall of a light industrial unit. Shit. It was a shortcut and she'd have to take it too as she couldn't afford to be too far behind when he ventured into the throng of the Bleachfield Centre at lunchtime.

Fortunately there was a transit van with its rear doors thrown wide so as to take up most of the narrow alley, and Darroch was almost past it by the time she made the turn. It meant that she could use the vehicle as cover by walking closer to the far wall, Darroch having walked alongside the near. There was a chubby guy in overalls standing to the left-hand side, blocking the passage, but he closed the door as she approached and stepped back against the wall, gesturing for her to pass.

Darroch came back into her line of sight once again, nearing the junction at the far end as she reached the rear of the van. Then she felt two strong hands at her back and she was driven forwards through the open door on the right-hand side of the vehicle's rear. The tailgate hit her at thigh level and she tumbled forward onto the plywood floor, scrambling and spinning as the man in overalls came barrelling in after her, pulling the other door closed at his back.

She had just about righted herself and climbed on to all fours when he sent a heavy arm forward and launched his fist into her face. She saw a blur of movement, her eyes unable to focus as her head whipped to the side at a ferocious pace, then felt a second blow as her shoulder slammed into the wall.

He was on her again even as she bounced against the metal, sending three more punches into the same side of her head. She could taste blood and feel something solid rattling around inside her mouth as she collapsed, then sensed the van begin to move just before she passed out.

Marionettes

By Catherine's estimate, Fallan's shoes would barely have hit the pavement before she got the call from the DCC, demanding to see her in his office. She had known that news of this development would get back to him swiftly, as that had been her intention, but she was trying not to think of what this said about how long she might hope to keep certain other undertakings from his notice.

Ordinarily, she would have taken the stairs, giving herself time to clear her head and prepare for the imminent confrontation, but his tone warned her that anything other than the express route would be interpreted as insubordination. Ignoring the logic that making him wait was going to be the least of her transgressions, she opted to take the lift.

She felt an instinctive reluctance to step inside when its doors slid apart, revealing the empty chamber within. The silence of it and the sense of isolation further added to the feeling that she was being conveyed automatically towards her judgment. Keep the heid, she told herself, shouting down the voices that were asking what the hell she was doing, warning her that she was poking a very big tiger.

I've poked bigger, she reminded them.

Adrienne had discovered three more numbers deleted from Fullerton's mobile phone records. One, as anticipated, belonged to Gordon Ewart's mother, Philippa. A second had been traced to the name Colin Morrison, but as it was a common name and they hadn't yet been able to get in touch, that was all they had on him so far. But the third deleted number had provided no such impediments. It belonged to one Mitchell Drummond.

Catherine had been peremptorily summoned, but the DCC was

mistaken if he thought she was coming up there for a smacked bottom and a telling off. He was the one who had a lot of explaining to do. She wasn't holding all the cards, but she had a pretty good bluffing hand, particularly given his knowledge of what might be out there.

She just had to hold her nerve. Same as any interview: you keep the suspect talking and eventually he'll give himself away.

She knocked on the door and was greeted by a gruff 'Come in.'

Catherine stepped inside, leaving the door open to imply that she didn't anticipate being here long, a butter-wouldn't-melt gambit.

Drummond stood behind his desk with his arms folded. She was struck by the contrast with Abercorn in her office, back straight, head up, taking his licks. Drummond's head was forward, subtly aggressive, spider to her fly. He had come a long way from the 'big lanky boy' Brenda Sheehan had described.

'Close the door,' he told her. 'Sit.'

She complied, keeping her expression neutral, allowing a flicker of confusion to play across her face. She wasn't doing any of his work for him.

'You've released Glen Fallan,' he stated, his voice welling up with suppressed rage. He actually had to swallow before he could go on. 'Would you care to explain why?'

'The PF's office has dropped the charges.'

His response was staccato, jaws clenched. Only a few words at a time could escape his bared teeth.

'And why. In the name of fuck. Would they. Fucking. Do that?'

Catherine thought of the breezy and solicitous manner with which he had greeted her the last time, his considered and precise delivery, those press-conference answers. Despite Sunderland not telling him what it was regarding, he had known it would be about Julie Muir. He'd been ready and prepared: even asked her why she hadn't looked up the case files.

Played, sir.

But contrast all of that with the way he had responded when she told him Brenda Sheehan was dead, probably murdered. He hadn't known that in advance, and it left him genuinely spooked. She was dealing with a frightened man, which meant she might be able to reach out to him.

It also meant he could be all the more desperate and all the more dangerous.

'Because Fallan didn't do it, sir. It wasn't Fallan's vehicle at the murder scene: it was a similar model bearing duplicate plates. Fallan's vehicle is a left-hand drive. We re-interviewed the witnesses and they all confirmed that the gunman got out of the right-hand side of the Land Rover, something backed up by CCTV images. It became clear to us that he had been set up.'

'Fallan was apprehended by armed officers and had a pistol in his possession,' Drummond argued.

'But not the murder weapon.'

'He and Fullerton had a history. The way I heard it, Fullerton tortured him and left him for dead.'

'We have subsequently learned, from Fullerton's wife, that the story you're referring to was just gangland whispers. This case isn't about Glen Fallan, sir. It's about Julie Muir.'

Any further protests he wished to make about Fallan's release evaporated with the mention of this name. The rage subsided too, revealing itself to have been nothing but bluster. He was no longer on such solid ground, and less confident about the wisdom of going on the offensive.

He stared, waiting to hear what she had to say, ready to assess the ramifications.

'Brenda Sheehan initially told the investigation that her brother was home with her on the night of the murder. She later retracted this alibi, leaving poor Teddy to twist in the wind. We have reason to believe Brenda Sheehan told Stevie Fullerton she was threatened and intimidated into changing her story.'

Drummond gave her a dubious look, as if to say 'is that all you've got?', but he was over-heavy on the scorn. She could tell he was worried.

'Brenda Sheehan was a hopeless alcoholic who by her own admission was drunk on the night in question,' he said. 'She wasn't intimidated any more than you'd pressure any witness into backing down from a lie.'

'I think telling her she was going to jail for shoplifting if she stood firm, but that all charges would be dropped if she sang your tune, constitutes something more than mere pressure, sir.'

'Oh, for Christ's sake, you're believing that garbage? Brenda Sheehan is the very definition of an unreliable witness. Her testimony would have been as credible in court then as her latter-day revisionism sounds now, especially as it's bloody obvious she was being coached all the way by Fullerton.'

Catherine gave it a moment, waiting to observe whether he'd realise what he'd just said. She could see the first glimmer of it, the frantic internal reading back of the transcript.

'So you've seen the video, sir?' she asked quietly.

Drummond stood with his eyes wide, nostrils flaring involuntarily. He seemed paralysed, no longer merely standing behind his desk but trapped there.

'A man called Gordon Ewart told me that he had been eliminated from my investigation, apparently before I had even learned his name or the fact that he'd been Julie Muir's boyfriend at the time of her death. This part had been kept out of the court case with the blessing of the investigation. Mr Ewart gave the impression that he had very senior police connections.'

She was expecting anger, even hate, but saw something soulless instead, like he was barely present any more.

'Gordon Ewart's number was deleted from the subscriber check I ordered on Stevie Fullerton's phone records. So was his mother's and, very significantly, so was yours. Why was Stevie Fullerton calling you, sir?'

Drummond didn't respond. He continued to stare, but his eyes seemed less intent, as though he was looking past her, or unable to focus.

'Who is Colin Morrison, sir?'

Drummond sat down behind his desk and sighed. There was something discomfortingly languid about his movement, resigned and yet somehow automated. The energy and fortitude with which he normally carried himself was gone, and it was as though some emergency back-up system was keeping him in motion.

He rolled open a drawer in his desk and reached down into it. Still saying nothing, he placed a brown folder on to the worktop, flipped it open and turned it around.

Inside was a single sheet of paper and a sealed envelope. On the sheet of paper was a drawing of the symbol that had been daubed on Fullerton's head, the symbol that had become a gangland meme. The symbol whose origin nobody seemed to know.

Drummond pushed the envelope towards her and tapped it twice. She could see her name printed on the front. His face remained stony, his manner still strangely distant.

Catherine opened the envelope and slid out a single sheet of paper. She unfolded it, revealing it to be a photocopy of an A5-sized handwritten page, the shadows at its edge indicating it to be from a notebook. It was a ledger, listing names, addresses, dates and amounts. About two-thirds of the way up she saw the name McLeod next to the address of the farm where she grew up. The date was burned into her mind.

Above this line, all of the entries ended with the word PAID. The most recent of these had been lodged the day before. There had been no collections after that.

Catherine felt the room swim.

'Who gave you this?' she asked, as a lifetime's fears began rattling the gates.

Drummond shook his head in a way that allowed her no hope that he could be prevailed upon to answer.

'The individual who gave it to me said that you would understand its significance. He wished to stress that he understands its significance also, and that right now he is alone in this regard. This will change considerably in the event that you should prove uncooperative.'

He sounded absent, and she worked out what was going on with his manner, his body language. The revelations of what she knew had moved things out of his control. He could no longer contain the situation, and was now reduced to being the vessel for someone else's will.

Somebody had the goods on him, like they had the goods on her.

'You will cease all unauthorised inquiries pertaining to the murder of Julie Muir, which I would remind you was resolved to the satisfaction of this department and of the law courts twenty-five years ago.

'You will also stand down the investigation into the death of Brenda Sheehan. The autopsy report shows that the deceased aspirated on her own vomit following a resumption of the binge-drinking habits that blighted much of her life. The obvious conclusion is accidental death, and this should not be affected by the understandable dismay of those whose disappointment at Brenda's return to alcoholism may have led them towards hysterical feats of speculation and projection.'

He kept talking, sounding like he was reading from a prepared statement, in an anaemic imitation of his ebullient press-conference idiom. This stuff almost sounded like it had been lawyered.

'You will continue to diligently investigate the murder of Stephen Fullerton, pursuing the existing, solid lines of inquiry centred around Fullerton's former associate, Glen Fallan. This has been an extremely difficult undertaking, complicated by the reluctance of certain criminal elements to cooperate with the investigation, and under these circumstances your failure to ultimately resolve the case would be understandable. It may, however, lead you to reconsider your own position.'

She felt like she was sinking into the carpet and the walls were looming over her. His words faded into the background as her sense of self began to dilute but some part of her mind was still functioning as stenographer.

He was telling her he wanted Fallan for the Fullerton killing, regardless of all she had learned. Acknowledging that this was a tough sell, an acceptable second would be for the case to remain unsolved and go cold due to her incompetence, over which she would resign.

'Who is doing this?' she asked him, fighting tears.

He didn't answer, didn't even shake his head, didn't look her in the eye.

318

Table Manners

She felt her stomach lurch as she saw the BMW approach, hurtling along the single track that led from the main road with a haste that was reckless to the point of nihilistic. It was how Squirrelly always drove that thing: showy, self-important and loud. Too late, she realised how easy it might have been to just roll the tractor into the lane as he took that last blind bend at the usual speed: a tragic accident, a harsh price but a lesson to all those exuberant urban drivers about the dangers of those seemingly empty country roads.

A different lesson would have to do.

She steadied herself, pictured it in her head once more. She felt sick all of a sudden, now that the time had come. It would be so much easier just to hand over the envelope, forget about this. Don't let him into the house, wasn't that what her mum had commanded? She pictured that instead, her meekly saying nothing, simply pressing the manila parcel stuffed with bank notes into Cadaver's hand as he stood on the doorstep, watching him walk away, climb back into his vehicle and drive off. Vividly, she flashed forward to how that would feel, and knew that it would be far worse than this, far worse than any fear or apprehension or self-doubt.

She was doing this.

She walked briskly to the kitchen, where she pressed play on the radio-cassette and turned up the volume. The chorus of 'Send My Heart' by The Adventures all but covered the sound of the reverberation of the BMW's engine against the dairy shed. The doorbell rang a few moments later. She ignored it, firing up a gas burner beneath the kettle. Another ring followed, the angry extended double-push almost funny in its impotence, like Morse code for 'Don't you know who I am?'

She ignored that too, and composed herself to appear busy and distracted when inevitably they arrived at the back door. She took her place at the sink and began to peel a potato. Her hands were trembling.

The back door opened without even a knock. Cadaver entered with his best hard-ticket scowl on his face, by way of registering his displeasure that he had needed to come looking for an answer rather than be received at the front door. Catherine feigned fright and surprise at the intrusion, pretending she had been too caught up in her task to notice his approach. It was something of a method performance, as she was already wan and tremulous in anticipation of his arrival and what might lie beyond it.

'Get your da,' Cadaver ordered, the words issuing from between lips that barely moved. No niceties, no faux politeness; there was a violence in his issue, an intent to unsettle and intimidate.

'Pardon?' she replied, instinctively bristling at his manner despite her fear.

'I says get your da,' he growled. 'Move.'

'That's no' nice, you,' Squirrelly interjected. 'We'd like to speak to your daddy please,' he said to Catherine with a patronising smirk.

'He's not here,' she told them, putting down the potato peeler and reaching for a dish towel to dry her hands. 'Nobody is.'

Cadaver took a moment to process this.

'That's all right,' he replied. 'We'll just take a wee pew here and wait for him. Come on,' he said to Squirrelly. 'The lassie's getting a brew on. Two sugar and milk in mine.'

They both helped themselves to a seat.

'Where is he?' Cadaver asked. 'Will he be long?'

'A wee while, yes,' she said tersely. 'He's in hospital. He collapsed yesterday. Doctors say it was exhaustion. Personally, I think he's been suffering from parasites.'

She felt her voice waver as she spoke this last, her indignation driving the thought but her fear sapping its vocal conviction.

'Aye, boo hoo,' Cadaver responded. 'Where's the fuckin' money?'

'Here, come on you,' Squirrelly reprimanded, though he was

320

giggling as he did so. He turned to Catherine. 'Sorry about the language, doll. That's pure out of order, so it is. And you about to make the pair of us a cuppa tea as well.'

He was smiling, trying to look friendly, but in it Catherine felt an even greater sense of humiliation. It was worse than being merely patronised: he was underlining her powerlessness, rubbing it in as he smirked and giggled and sniffed.

'Never mind the tea. She knows what we're here for. And you better have it, hospital or nae hospital.'

'I've got it,' she assured him.

'See? The lassie's brand new,' said Squirrelly. 'He's murder, in't he, darlin'? Got to forgive him, but he's a bit on edge cause he's got the cold. He's feeling a little horse, you know what I mean? Or do you neigh?'

He let this out in a whinny. He did this every time he saw her, crowbarring some kind of horse-related jokes into whatever he had to say.

She felt her face redden in hatred.

Something amused Cadaver about this and he emitted a guttural, wheezing laugh, like the winning gag on a TB ward comedy night.

'Two sugars as well for me,' he said without looking at her, instead sharing a smirk with Squirrelly.

'Haw, say please you, ya'n ignorant tube.'

'Please,' he acquiesced. It was more calculatedly insulting than when he was merely spitting staccato commands, and her hatred grew accordingly.

She turned her back so that they couldn't see her face, close to tears, her cheeks burning, and found herself reaching for two mugs from the tree largely because it was a disguise for the real reason she had faced away. The next track started on the cassette player: no less than her favourite song. She tried to concentrate on the music, let it take her somewhere else.

'Oh, and if you've any Abernethy biscuits,' Squirrelly suggested, hauling her back to the humiliation of the here and now. It prompted a wheeze from Cadaver and a snottery guffaw of delight from

Squirrelly utterly disproportionate to the remark; some private joke between them, her exclusion from it part of the humour, part of the sport.

She made them each a mug of tea, her hand shaking as she poured the kettle, now more from rage than fear.

They were sitting there, in her family's kitchen, relaxing like they owned the place while the man who truly did was in hospital – put there by these people. Squirrelly had his back to where she stood spooning sugar at the slate worktop. He was sitting at ninety degrees to Cadaver, the pair of them now talking like she wasn't even there, as though she were a waitress or a skivvy.

The arrogance.

The complacency.

They will try to burn you down, went the song on the cassette. *But what they say can make you strong . . .*

She was doing this. She knew she wouldn't be able to reload fast enough after the first shot, once the element of surprise had expired, but she had deduced that she wouldn't have to.

She placed their mugs in front of them on the kitchen table, along with a packet of Rich Tea biscuits. Neither of them said thanks, continuing to chat away like she was invisible. Squirrelly was telling a story about something that had happened in a pub the night before, acting like every line of neddish patter in an overheard exchange was Oscar Wilde. Cadaver nodded appreciation, emitting his consumptive laugh every so often.

'I'll just get you what you're owed and you can be on your way,' Catherine announced, ahead of leaving the room.

'Oh, I don't know, hen,' said Squirrelly. 'This place is spiffing for tea. What's it like for lunches?'

She went to the living room where she had stowed Harriet's bag. The cash envelope was sitting inside it, above the pistol, which was primed and loaded. She took them both out, removed another dart and practised the manoeuvre. She tried it first with the left hand, the gun in her right, but it felt weak and awkward. She transferred the gun and tried with her right hand. Yes. That felt strong. That would do it.

322

She carried the bag back into the kitchen, barely eliciting a glance as she returned to her previous place at the worktop, between the fridge and the range.

She could still back out of this. They would never know what was in the bag. She wasn't past the point of no return. But as she reached for the envelope full of the money that was tearing her family's lives apart and listened to Squirrelly's sneery nasal laughter at her kitchen table she realised the true point of no return would be the one whereby they walked out of here and her chance to act was gone.

She placed the envelope down on the table roughly halfway between the pair of them. Neither reached for it, another arrogant gesture of confidence, further conveying the message that they were in no hurry and would leave only when it suited them.

She turned away from the table and reached into the bag with her left hand, retrieving a dart from her pocket with her right, her body blocking Cadaver's line of sight to what she was holding.

This was it. She took in a silent breath, large and long but not sharp, then turned on her heel and drove the dart between Squirrelly's shoulder blades as they stuck up above the seat-back. She struck with a downward stabbing motion, the point thrusting through the synthetic fabric of his tracksuit top like paper and embedding itself right to the chamber.

She then took a step back from the table and raised the gun with her left hand, holding it by the barrel as she brought up her right to grip the stock. She hesitated for only a fraction of a second to steady her aim, keeping her focus on the target of Cadaver's trunk, consciously avoiding looking into his eyes. He reacted with surprising speed in getting to his feet, but had barely begun to push the heavy wooden chair back from beneath him when she pulled the trigger. The dart's coloured tail sprung up suddenly upon his left breast like a corsage.

It was as he stood staring at the dart that she realised she had thought through how to strike but neglected to consider an exit strategy. Her position had allowed her to exploit the vulnerability of them both being seated and Squirrelly having his back to her, but as he climbed also to his feet, she saw that she had painted herself into a corner. Squirrelly was between her and the hall, Cadaver well placed to block her escape to the back door. How long did these things take to work? She hadn't even checked the strength or dosage: they could have been optimised for bringing down a distressed Highland terrier.

Right at that moment however, neither of them seemed intent on pursuing her. Squirrelly was grabbing around his back with both hands, trying in vain to reach between his shoulder blades, while a darkening shadow on Cadaver's charcoal trousers betrayed that he had wet himself. She understood: she thought he'd got up to come after her, but he had in fact been trying to flee, because he'd caught one glance and thought she was holding a real gun.

Squirrelly dropped, smacking his head off the slate worktop on his way to the floor. Cadaver slumped back into the chair that he had only partly slid away, his legs evidently having given out, his face drained and his expression disoriented. His head must be swimming, she assumed, as he was grabbing at his upper arm even though she had shot him in the chest. He then rolled over as though turning on his side in bed, and fell to the floor, the chair toppling beneath him. Catherine heard him gurgle and splutter for a few moments, then he was still.

Paralysis

Jasmine didn't know how long she was unconscious. It felt like everything was blank only for a moment, but the coming-round part took ages, as though her senses were reluctant to report for duty given what they were going to be asked to deal with.

She opened and closed her eyes several times, her surroundings swirling sickeningly in the first few instances. There was a ringing in her ears and a host of different kinds of pain: shooting, throbbing, aching, searing.

She lifted her head and saw that the man in the overalls was sitting in a crouch against the opposite wall of the van, rocking with its motion. He looked early fifties, maybe older: portly but imposing, strangely baby-faced features above a jowly jawline, like someone who wasn't genetically built to carry fat but had piled it on nonetheless.

'You fuckin' sit still and don't make a fuckin' sound, right? You fuckin' make a sound, you get another fuckin' slap, right?'

His eyes blazed with intent as he spoke, giving the impression he'd prefer it if she didn't comply. There was no danger of that. She was shaking with fear, shivering like she'd been dunked in the North Sea. Nothing in her was ready to defy this person. She would do whatever was required to prevent him from hitting her again.

A slap, he called what he'd done.

Her face was beginning to swell, her lip leading the charge. She could feel blood stuck to her cheeks and taste it in her mouth. Her tongue probed a ravaged section of gum, springing back like she had licked a battery. At least one tooth was gone, possibly two. She suspected she may have swallowed them.

Amid so much other pain, she was still able to feel a sting too. They must have been on her even before she got to Darroch's

325

address, and she had been so intent upon her surveillance that she had failed to notice that she was the one being tailed. She thought of his constant yakking into his mobile. He was getting instruction all the way, maybe before he had even left his flat.

Darroch had led her into a trap. Adding insult to multiple injury, he had made himself an easy mark, implying that he or his confederates didn't rate her detective skills enough to have faith that she wouldn't lose him on the follow.

She had no idea how long they travelled. She had a watch on but didn't dare look at it, didn't dare do anything that the pudgy man in the overalls might not like. She felt the van brake and accelerate, swaying as it cornered. She heard the hum of engines as vehicles passed outside, brief pulses of oncoming traffic and longer rumbles of cars overtaking.

For all she knew they could have been going around in a big loop. She could see nothing.

At one point she could hear the voices of pedestrians outside while the van was stationary, presumably stopped at lights. She thought for half a second about shouting for help or banging on the walls. She looked up at her travelling companion and saw him staring back. It felt like he could read her mind. She found herself shaking her head as though in answer to an unvoiced accusation: I'm not planning to make any noise.

Please don't hit me again.

Please don't hit me.

Artefacts

It was impossibly calm and quiet where Anthony sat, the sound of turning pages amplified by being the only affront to the silence of the room, though even that noise was swallowed by the insulation of a thousand leather-bound volumes lining the walls. There was no reverberation, no sound from outside, and a stillness to the air as though even the motes of dust had been ordered and alphabetised.

He could hardly imagine a greater contrast to the chaos of the station, where several phones were always ringing and voices constantly raised merely to stay above the din of each other. In this chamber at the Procurator Fiscal's offices he felt like he was sealed off from the world, but inescapably prominent in his thoughts was the fact that he had been sealed off along with Adrienne.

It occurred to him that this was the first time they had been alone in a room together since that night. That they had been here for an hour before he realised this had to be a good sign, given that it wasn't any ordinary room: it was like an awkwardness stress-test environment. Granted, they had some compelling reading matter to distract them, so he couldn't gauge for sure what was going on between them in this sustained silence. Did this mean they were comfortable in each other's company, or were they each immersing themselves in the task at hand because it helped them pretend like the other one wasn't there?

He couldn't speak for Adrienne, but he was happy she was here. Apart from anything else, he needed some solidarity right now. The sense of complicity made what he was doing feel a little less like career suicide, though maybe this only meant that it was a suicide pact instead.

He glanced up at the walls and bid himself a wry smile. Maybe there was another reason they called him Beano: he spent so much time in print. So if he was going out, he was going out his way: sitting in a library, cramming at a desk, the fast-track graduate hitting the books and fast-tracking himself right out the door.

It was an unusual feeling, to knowingly pursue something even though he was aware that it would get him in serious trouble if the boss found out. Anthony had never done anything wanton in his life. As a kid he'd always worked hard, learned his spelling, got his sums right, done his homework, listened in class, never answered back. But sitting here right now he understood that he hadn't done those things because he was afraid of getting a telling off from the teacher. He had done them because that was how he was brought up. This was *about* getting his sums right. It was about finding the correct answer, and he was moulded to do that in a way that deferred his consideration of consequences to the point of negligence.

It was easy for him, though. If he got bagged because of this then fuck da police: he'd move on. He'd moved on from worse. He'd be mightily angry about it, sure, but he wasn't gambling with anybody else's chips. Adrienne, by contrast, was a single mother with two kids to provide for.

'Do you think this makes us maverick cops?' he had asked her on the short drive over here.

'No, I think it makes us *ex*-cops if we're not extremely careful,' she replied, leaving no doubt that she was aware of the stakes.

As per McLeod's request, Dominic Wilson had looked out the records of the Teddy Sheehan prosecution, retrieving the files from the PF's equivalent of the morgue. Anthony was aware that it was not a small favour. There was something between Wilson and McLeod, some quiet bond of trust, the confidentiality of this undertaking reflected in his also granting them this windowless chamber to peruse the documents. Nonetheless, the PF's office was as gossipy and leaky as any cop shop, and it was hard to do anything out of the ordinary without somebody taking notice. You never knew who was watching, and you never knew who they'd tell.

There hadn't been a murder trial per se. Teddy Sheehan's lawyer had submitted a guilty plea on his client's behalf at the hearing following his hundred-and-ten-day lie-in after being charged. Subsequent hearings had been to determine the severity of the crime and the minimum term to be served under the statutory life sentence. The materials Dom Wilson had fished out were what would have formed the basis of the prosecution had there been a not guilty plea and the case gone to trial. Consequently, many of the documents were duplicates of the ones Anthony had been looking for back at Govan nick. Once again, Drummond's efforts to erase the evidence had been thwarted by the existence of a remotely stored copy.

There were police statements, interview statements and, of course, the confession. It was tempting to skip to that first, but given that it was likely to be the least reliable document in the box, Anthony decided it would actually be most instructive to read it last. Just like a live case, it was important to put together both a chronology of the investigation and a chronology of the events, developing a wider picture so that every piece of evidence could be valued in context.

Julie Muir's body had been found on the Sunday morning by Capletmuir resident Malcolm Vickers, who was out walking his dog. It was discovered among a waist-high crop of wild garlic, evidently dragged there out of sight. Mr Vickers rushed home and called the police.

Bob Cairns and Mitchell Drummond were first on the scene. They had happened to be in the area attending an incident in nearby Gallowhaugh.

There were crime-scene photographs, black-and-white ten by eights. Anthony spotted these as he lifted the document that had been on top of them, glimpsing enough to recognise what they were before concealing them again. Tentatively, reluctantly, and feeling uncomfortably voyeuristic, he uncovered them once more and forced himself to look.

To his relief, he was largely spared her face. She was lying on her back, her head turned to one side, her long hair draped over her features. There were close-ups of the marks on her neck, the tight pattern of bruising and abrasions. These were easier to look at: they were just skin, just shapes. They could be anybody. It was the personal details that always got to him, the notes of uniqueness still sounding out through the cacophony of white noise that murder made as it turned the individual human form into anonymous and interchangeable shapes. It was the stories suggested by an unusual pair of shoes, an esoteric tattoo, a striking piece of jewellery. In Julie's case, it was a ring. Her hand was resting on her chest, like a virgin in a medieval painting, drawing Anthony's attention to how out of place this olde-worlde-looking item seemed against her trendy clothing.

According to the confession, Teddy Sheehan encountered Julie Muir on the pathway adjacent to the railway line, close to where she was found. He had gone out for a walk because it was a dry night, though not so dry back at home, where his sister was reportedly asleep on the settee having necked half a bottle of vodka. She was frequently asleep at that time, the statement said, though she would often wake up and continue drinking until passing out again or until the bottle was finished, whichever came first.

Julie smiled at him as she passed, which apparently made him aroused. He turned and caught up to her again further along the path, where he took off his belt, dropped his trousers and exposed himself. Julie got upset at this and began to scream. Startled by her response, Teddy grabbed Julie and put his hand over her mouth, trying to keep her silent. As she struggled, trying to scream louder through his muffling hand, he became more concerned about getting into trouble and dragged her into the wild garlic. Panicked and confused by the strange state of excitement in which he found himself, it was here that he looped his belt around Julie's neck and strangled her.

Anthony marvelled at the phrasing of the confession, the insights it offered into Teddy's mind, the little notes and minor details intended to lend authenticity to the narrative. It was a case study in why the polis weren't allowed to pull this shit any more. Cairns had written down precisely the version he thought would play best if it came to trial, and got this befuddled, frightened and quite possibly beaten educationally subnormal suspect to sign at the bottom.

He thought of Brenda right at the very start of the video, rambling but impassioned as she poured out her heart to her guest, before Fullerton let her compose herself and told her to take it from the top.

'Oor Teddy wouldn't hurt a fly. Everybody knew that. All those wee bastards that used to call names and throw stones: he always ran away. Never so much as turned around and told them to shut it. And when I finally got to see him on remand . . . He was scared, so scared. I asked him if it was true, if he'd done it, and he said he wasn't allowed to talk aboot it. What does that mean? Not allowed? By who?'

Anthony could guess.

What did they do to you, Teddy, he wondered. What did they tell you would happen if you didn't stick to the script?

'Jesus,' Adrienne said, the first word either had issued since they began poring over the contents of the box.

'What?'

'She was pregnant.'

'How do you know?'

'Pathologist's report. Nobody else seems to have been aware of this. None of her friends or flatmates mentioned it in their statements. Her parents didn't know either.'

'Did her boyfriend?' Anthony asked pointedly.

There had been a statement from Ewart in the file, with a note to say it was strictly confidential. Supporting the contention that his relationship with her was of little relevance to the case was his claim that he hadn't even been at his parents' house that night, and had no idea Julie was planning to drop by. She had only visited the place once before, for a dinner party a few weeks previously, but he'd driven her there.

'Can think of poorer pretexts for a surprise visit,' Adrienne suggested, 'than to confront your boyfriend with the news that you're up the duff in front of his scandal-wary parents.'

'Can I see the report?'

Adrienne handed him the pages, which he traded for the confession.

331

There it was, in the clinical bloodless prose that reduced all that was once Julie Muir to a technical read-out of her final state.

The victim was approximately three months pregnant at time of death . . .

He scanned the rest of the report, the precise description of the injuries to her neck, the corresponding condition of internal organs, the estimated time of death.

The ligature used to strangle her suggested a combination of metal and a softer material, probably leather. This was consistent with Sheehan's confession that he had used his belt.

She had not been sexually assaulted.

Anthony was about to put the report back down when he saw it.

'Fuck,' he announced.

The most vital piece of information in the entire document was at the very top, and they had both bypassed it in their hurry to get to the details.

'What?'

'The pathologist's name – it's Colin Morrison.'

Journey's End

The van had maintained a steady pace for a long time, indicating progress along the open road, and Jasmine hadn't heard any other traffic for a while. She had no way of verifying this, but she felt a growing sense of becoming further and further from anywhere populous. Thus when the van began to decelerate fear seized her, letting her know that her previous terror had been a mere overture. Truly, it was better to travel hopelessly than to arrive.

The van stopped and she heard a door open from the cab, though the engine was still turning. A fist banged on the side, close to her head, causing her to start.

'Right,' said the pudgy man, opening one of the doors. 'Come on.'

She emerged into a gathering gloom, rainclouds darkening the skies and making it difficult to gauge the time of day. She was outside an isolated cottage, hills and woodland stretching away behind it. She couldn't see any other houses. By a rough estimate of how long she had travelled, it could be Perthshire or it could be the Borders. She had no idea.

The van drove off again as soon as she was clear. She hadn't seen the driver at any point.

She was led towards the cottage, trembling with every step. She wanted to run, but it was as though she was caught in a tractor beam, paralysed by the knowledge that she would be caught and punished.

She took a closer look at the building as she walked across the weed-strewn path. The windows seemed strange: reflective and yet completely opaque. It took her a moment to realise that they were all covered from the inside by aluminium foil.

A cloying, chokingly fetid smell filled her nostrils as she stepped inside, and she was struck by a fierce, humid warmth at odds with the absence of carpets or indeed furniture.

Nobody lived here. Nobody had lived here for a long time.

She could see light spilling from slightly open doorways either side of the hall, dazzling to eyes that had grown accustomed to the dimness of the van and the glowering conditions outside. It was too bright to look directly into the rooms at first, but down at floor level she could see wide plastic tubing running through the gaps between the doors and the frames, leading along the downstairs hallway and disappearing through a hole cut in a wall at the rear. It was a makeshift ventilation system. Her eyes caught a glimpse of foliage as she was directed up the stairs. It was a cannabis farm.

In the top hall she passed two more rooms turned into nurseries, before being led into a starker chamber. It was a single bedroom, though it didn't contain anything to lie down on. The floorboards were bare, and the only wall covering to speak of was a rampant outbreak of mould resultant of a humidity not normally found at this latitude. In the centre of the room was a wooden table with two foldaway chairs on either side.

The room had a single window, possibly the only one in the house not lined with foil. It gave a view to the rear, showing the rain begin to fall on the stark hillside behind the cottage.

She took a couple of paces forward, not knowing where to put herself. It looked like a cell, but for some reason she was relieved that it didn't have a bed.

Pudgy closed the door and stood just in front of it.

'Take your clothes off,' he said.

Jasmine froze, revulsion over-riding the defensive impulses that ·had previously compelled her to obey. Instinctively she gathered her arms about herself. Pudgy took a surprisingly speedy step forward and punched her again.

She fell to the ground amid another explosion of light and pain, all of her previous hurts revisited and amplified by this further blow.

'Take your fuckin' clothes off and put them in a pile,' he shouted.

He backed away again as she struggled woozily to her feet.

Her hands were shaking so much that she could barely grip the buttons on her overcoat. Slowly, she managed to remove it, fold it over and place it on the table.

'Come on,' he said impatiently. 'Get on with it.'

She became conscious of the little assurances she was giving herself: *he's* not taking my clothes off; he's keeping his distance; there isn't a bed in here. Any time she caught herself doing this, she recalled what Fallan had taught her.

We don't listen to fear properly. We feel it, but we try to explain it away. When we rationalise it, we're looking for reassurance. We're looking for reasons why it's going to be okay.

This was not going to be okay.

She had to listen to her fear, but equally she could not let her senses be overwhelmed by it. She could not give in to panic and desperation. She had to stay in control.

She undressed as commanded, placing all of her clothes in a pile on the table. Pudgy watched her, arms folded. She tried not to catch his eye, aware he was watching her the whole time. He was detached from what she was doing, but only in the physical sense. He was an intent voyeur, empowered by feeling no need to disguise his gaze. She was the one afraid to be caught looking.

He remained against the wall until she was finished. She flinched and backed away when she sensed him move, but he only came as far as the table to pick up the clothes. Then he retreated from the room and locked the door.

She was left standing next to the table, naked, scared and confused. Instinctively she went to the small window, driven by thoughts of flight. It looked paint-stuck, but she could use a chair to break it. What then, though?

This was why he'd asked her to undress; or at least she hoped so. No need for ropes and restraints when your prisoner is one storey up in the middle of nowhere and hasn't a stitch to cover herself against the November rain.

A moment of despair was dispelled by further panic as she heard footsteps announce his return. He unlocked the door and stepped inside, placing down a mug full of water and a chipped bowl.

'Water in, water oot,' he muttered, smirking to himself, then withdrew once again.

Outside the rain grew heavier.

Jasmine sat down on one of the folding chairs, hugging her arms to herself though the room was stifling.

She was too scared even to cry.

Gutted

'So if we're secretly investigating the DCC,' Anthony said, climbing the stairs to Colin Morrison's flat, 'is it ripping the piss to be pulling overtime on it?'

'This could be our last ever pay packet from the force,' Adrienne replied. 'Might as well try for a heavy one.'

They were joking about it but they each knew how deep they were in. Neither of them had slept well, and both of them had lied about why, as if a refusal to name their fears would somehow ward them off. Adrienne said it was because one of the kids had woken her in the night complaining of bad dreams. Anthony suspected that it wasn't her daughter who had been visited in the darkness by demons from her own subconscious.

Anthony claimed his bleary appearance was down to playing *Team Fortress 2* online until the small hours. Truth was he had tried, but he couldn't concentrate. He had logged on to a server and joined the blue team, but he wasn't sure whether he truly was on the blue team any more.

They were both nearing the end of their shift by the time they had finished up at the Fiscal's offices and tracked down an address for Colin Morrison, but there was little question of them clocking off. It was easy enough for him, but potentially more of an issue for Adrienne.

'Have you got to get back for the kids?' he asked.

'It's okay,' she replied. 'I've got a nanny, and I always check with her before a shift starts, to make sure she can stay on if work gets complicated. This definitely qualifies.'

'So she scores overtime too. Everybody wins.'

'Or it's one more person on the bru if this goes tits up.'

Morrison's flat was on the second floor of a tenement in Cathcart, two to a landing. The close was immaculately kept, its walls lined with green tiles to roughly shoulder height, above which was crisp and regularly re-coated blue paint. There were planters on each half-stair turn, a bay tree in the first, a healthy ficus in the second. It always amazed Anthony how different one tenement could be from the next. He had shared a flat just around the corner from this place when he was a student. The buildings looked identical, but the only organic life he'd ever encountered on the common stairs was a jobbie laid overnight by some manky bastard who couldn't wait until he got home.

Adrienne rang the doorbell but Anthony wasn't any more optimistic about getting an answer than when they had tried Morrison's landline. The flat had a wooden outer door comprising two halves meeting in the middle. They looked robust, heavy and unwelcomingly closed. Contrastingly, across the landing his neighbour's outer doors were open, tucked back to form the walls of a shallow porch.

Adrienne tried the bell again and waited a little longer, but there was no sound of movement from within, and no light from the glass panel above the semi-doors. She tried the handle and, to their mutual surprise, it opened.

'Not locked. Shit, look at this.'

The inner door's lock had been punched out: a pro-looking job, fast and quiet, probably executed with the outer doors closed for concealment. Whoever had done it had closed everything over again upon exit, not wishing to advertise the fact that the place had been hit.

Adrienne opened it and stepped inside, then promptly stepped back out again, pulling the door behind her.

'What?' he asked.

'We're going to need face-masks. At least a hanky or something.'

Anthony's stomach lurched. He wasn't sure he was ready to be first on scene at the discovery of another body, especially as it would necessitate an inescapable admission of how they had come to find it.

'Oh shit.'

'No, it's not a smell. Not yet anyway. It's just . . . You ever see

338

that film *Sunshine*, the bit where they find the spaceship that's been dead and drifting for decades?'

Adrienne reached into her bag and produced a pack of wet wipes.

'New use number two thousand, seven hundred and twelve,' she said, placing one over her nose and mouth and proffering the packet.

Anthony followed her inside, where he was grateful for the wet wipe but could have done with a pair of goggles as well. As the thick clouds of billowing particles stung his eyes, he tried not to think about how in the movie Adrienne just mentioned the dancing dust was disintegrated human flesh.

'Single men,' she said disapprovingly. 'They never think to lift a duster or push the hoover around once in a while.'

Anthony had never seen anything like it, and given that he'd lived in a few student gaffs, this was saying something. The closest he'd witnessed had been when his parents were getting their dining-room floor sanded, and he'd made the mistake of sticking his head around the door while the bloke was running the machine.

'What the hell is this?' he asked, but as he looked past Adrienne and further into the flat he could see the answer through every open door.

The place had been torn apart. Anything that could be opened was ripped asunder; anything that could be broken was in a thousand pieces; anything that could be turned inside out had been disembowelled. The air was choked with fibres from every seat cushion, every pillow, every duvet, the stuffing pulled out and dumped on the floor. Picture frames lay broken at the foot of every wall, their canvases slashed and discarded. Skirting had been tugged from the walls, carpets lifted and rolled back, floorboards worried at with tools.

'Do you think they were looking for something?' he asked.

Adrienne turned around very slowly. He couldn't see her mouth over the wet-wipe, but her eyes told him his patter was rotten.

'At least this means we're not going to find a body,' she said. 'If Morrison had been here they'd have made him tell them where whatever it is was hidden.'

'Unless he came home and interrupted them,' Anthony mused, eyeing the one closed door off of the chaotic hall.

'Flip you for it?' she asked.

Anthony was having a heated internal dialogue regarding the price and value of chivalry when the doorbell suddenly rang from eighteen inches above his left ear. He had a mental image of himself as Scooby Doo leaping into the arms of Adrienne's Shaggy, so chivalry probably wasn't going to edge the debate.

'Hello?' said a female voice, following up the ring with a knock on the frame of the door.

He pulled it open to reveal a woman in her late sixties or early seventies, dressed in a paint-spattered smock, further pigment flecking her hair. Behind her across the landing he could see that the front door was open on the flat opposite. This was the neighbour. She had a brush in her hand, a fine, pencil-thin item indicating that she was working on canvas as opposed to slapping a fresh coat of emulsion on the ceiling.

'Oh my God,' she said, taking in the sight of two strangers and the devastation at their backs.

Anthony produced his warrant card as quickly as he could, before she might flip out in the fear that she'd caught the bad guys in the act.

'Police, ma'am.'

'Oh no. There's been a break-in. Oh, God, that's awful. Poor Colin. What a dreadful sight to come back to.'

'Do you know Mr Morrison, Miss . . . Mrs . . .?'

'Alva. Margo Alva. Mrs. I live across the landing. But this is just dreadful. Poor Colin, after everything that's happened. I just hope he's having a nice holiday.'

She was very precisely spoken, reminding Anthony of his Great Aunt Vera who would not tolerate a glottal stop within the walls of her Kelvinside abode.

'Everything that's happened?' asked Adrienne. 'Has Mr Morrison had some trouble recently?'

'Hmm, well, not that recently perhaps. Honestly, where does the time go? He lost quite a bit of money in that credit crunch business. Back when he was still working, he used to joke about retiring to the sun. Now he's just grabbing it a bit at a time, I suppose.'

'So Mr Morrison is away at the moment? Do you know where?'

'No, I'm afraid not. I just saw him leaving on Tuesday afternoon.'

Anthony and Adrienne shared a glance. Tuesday afternoon: when the news had broken about Stevie Fullerton going off in his Bentley to the great car wash in the sky.

'He was on his way down with his suitcase as I was coming up the stairs. I teach a still life class at the Botanics on Tuesdays, you see. He said he was going abroad for a wee break but he didn't say where. He didn't stop to speak. I think he was maybe worried he was going to miss his plane. He certainly seemed to be in quite a hurry.'

The Price

Catherine sat in the kitchen staring at the rain as it lashed the windows, her barely touched mug of tea long since gone cold on the table in front of her, surrounded by the dishes she hadn't been able to motivate herself to clear. She had thought she might cry once everyone else had gone out and there was nobody left to hide her tears from, but the truth was that now she was alone she just felt numb.

Less than an hour ago she had been seated here at the dinner table with Drew, Duncan and Fraser, eating from the same roast chicken, drinking from the same jug of water, listening to the same music on the speaker dock, but she felt like she was observing it all from behind a wall of glass. She could reach out and touch them, hear their conversation, respond to their remarks, but she wasn't feeling any of it, only pretending to them that she was.

She was wearing a mask, one that it seemed incredible they could not see through. Every smile she gave them felt conspicuously false, every laugh hollow, and the more she faked the further away the three of them became. Yet she could not afford to let them see that she was in turmoil, that she was clinging on by her fingernails. When she first got home she had sat outside in the car for only a few moments before concluding that the ritual would be futile in this instance: the only way she wasn't bringing this inside with her was if she stayed out there all night. There was no way to escape from it, only conceal it.

She thought of all those occasions when she *had* worn her pain on her sleeve: short-tempered, unapproachable, volatile; or palpably disconnected, uncommunicative and withdrawn. It had been the single greatest ongoing point of tension between her and Drew.

'*There's this dark place you go . . .*'

He thought it was the job that took her there, away from him and from the boys. But the truth was that the dark place had been there long before she joined the force. Doing the job was what had kept the darkness from swallowing her for ever.

Until now.

The irony doused salt liberally about her wounds. The darkness had tracked her down, followed her into her house, bared its fangs in readiness to devour her family, and yet she was drawing on her every strength to conceal that there was anything wrong.

Duncan was losing it at Fraser, a sustained campaign of minor irritations finally breaking through the dam and delivering the reaction his little brother had sought. He bellowed at him, his cheeks reddening, fists and jaw clenched with shuddering forces of pressure. She could see tears of frustration, a familiar sight in Duncan, as he struggled to contain the torrents of emotion that could erupt from within.

She glanced warily at the cutlery gripped in his hands, ashamed of her own fears and yet unable to prevent herself from feeling them.

Drew intervened, apportioning equal blame: that time-honoured parental arbitration that was unsatisfactory to both parties but without alternative. Nonetheless, they reined it in with no dissent, as Drew had a nuclear option tonight. He was taking them to see the WWE tour at Braehead; they had been looking forward to it for months – almost as much as Drew wasn't – and they wouldn't do anything to jeopardise it this close to the prize.

The spat was swiftly forgotten. Conversation turned to what their favourites were going to do to each other in the ring, and then to what they had been doing to each other in the wrestling video game they got last Christmas. Their play was all fantasies of violence. Their table talk was of nothing but violence. Then they were going out to watch this absurd pantomime of simulated brutality.

Catherine had to hide how she felt beneath feigned vicarious excitement, her protests silent behind this wall of glass. She was with her husband and her boys, sitting in the kitchen, present but not quite connected. Was that how it was going to be now? Was that the price?

What really hurt – what always hurt most about this – was that she couldn't tell Drew what was wrong. He was the first one she went to when she needed to unload, to pour out her troubles and be shown they weren't so awful now that they weren't flapping around manically inside her skull like a bird trapped in an attic.

She had been missing him, even as he was sitting right beside her. It had been this way many times down the years, but tonight she had experienced a far more acute version of it, and found herself facing an entire future of feeling this way.

How could she tell him about this, though? And if she couldn't tell Drew, who could she talk to about it?

It would not be accurate to say that over time she had made her peace with what she did, but she had learned to live with it. Every so often it crept up on her again, but she drew strength from her family: her need to conceal this providing a constant force, like magnetic repulsion. It was a self-sustaining symbiosis: she endeavoured to repel the darkness from them, but drew the power to do so by bathing in their light.

Now she would have to live with other crimes, greater sins, in order to continue shielding them from the truth. For what was the alternative?

What would it do to them if she was taken away?

What would it do to them simply to know?

She didn't want to find out. To be with them, to be here for them, that was all that mattered. And yet she would never fully be present. It would always feel like this. There would be times when it faded into the background and she would almost forget, but it would always come back, always be with her. She would always be afraid. She would always be disgusted with herself. She would always be stuck here, behind a mask, behind a glass wall.

This was the price now, the hidden price of her sin. To keep her family together she had no choice other than to pay it, but the cost was not merely what she would always know about herself. The greater part was that the men behind this would go unpunished. They would thrive and they would prosper, and inevitably, when the time came, they would ask her for more.

Was this how it started, she asked herself? Was this how you became Bob Cairns?

She thought of Drummond in his office today, hostage to his own transgressions, rendered soulless: a vessel for another man's will.

Whose will, though? Gordon Ewart? His father?

Her phone buzzed, skidding sideways along the table like a tiny hovercraft. It was Beano again. She picked it up and hit Ignore, feeling just a little more shitty about it, as she had done incrementally on each of the past three times today. She was leaving him hanging and it was cowardly, she knew, but she couldn't speak to him because that would formalise a decision she wasn't yet ready to make. As long as she remained incommunicado, then what she had discussed with Drummond wouldn't bleed into Beano and Adrienne's world.

The rain continued to patter against the window, like a fairytale malefactor drumming his evil claws against the glass. At some point she was going to have to move, get up from this chair and start clearing these plates.

'Just leave them,' she had told Drew, so that he could get the boys organised and off to Braehead.

Part of her had wanted them out of the door as soon as possible, so that she could stop pretending.

The doorbell rang, its benign electronic chimes incongruously unsettling, like the playing of a music box in a horror movie. Surely Beano hadn't come here, she thought. It was possible, though: she had roped him and Adrienne into this and then cut herself off.

Worse still, what if it was Drummond?

As she raced through further possibilities, she rapidly realised that there was precisely nobody she wanted to see right now, not even Drew and the boys. She had only once felt so lonely in her life, and she couldn't say for sure that this wasn't worse.

The chimes sounded again, accompanied by an insistent banging on the door. Whoever was out there knew she was home, and wasn't going away. She lifted herself laboriously from her seat and walked slowly from the kitchen, through the hall towards the front entrance. There was a shape moving behind the bevelled glass panels, their warped opacity further occluded by the rain.

She stopped in her tracks and opened the cupboard under the stairs, from which she retrieved an old police twin-handled night-stick that she kept just in case. Then she proceeded towards the door, tucking the baton out of sight. One hint of threat and she'd crush the bastard's windpipe before he could touch her.

She undid the lock and pulled the door slightly ajar. Through the narrow gap she found herself face to face with Glen Fallan.

The Last Kindness (ii)

The car had surely never been driven so carefully or politely, as Catherine took every precaution to avoid doing anything that might attract the attention of the police. She did entertain a lingering worry that this in itself might inadvertently draw suspicion through the sheer incongruity of a typically ostentatious BMW doing things such as indicating, observing lane discipline and maintaining a distance of more than eighteen inches from the car in front, but it was a smaller risk. Besides, nothing was surer to bring the police into the equation than getting into a prang, so she was proceeding with all caution, and unavoidably extending an unintended and undeserved courtesy to the two passengers locked in the vehicle's boot.

It certainly hadn't looked a comfortable way to travel so much as around the block, never mind a couple of hours down bumpy and winding South Ayrshire back roads, so they ought to be grateful that the car wasn't being driven in the manner it normally was.

She was sweating profusely by the time she had managed to heave them both inside, trussed at the wrists and ankles, and having feared that they wouldn't fit she felt she could give the manufacturer a glowing testimonial regarding the car's boot capacity. Its occupants might not be quite so glowing in their testimonials, not that either of them had voiced an objection at the journey's outset.

The worst moment had been when she first tried to move Cadaver. Rolling him on to his back, she had felt a shock at the dead weight as she tugged at his arm to turn his face sideways out of the puddle of drool that was pooling beneath it on the cold stone floor. She had a moment of panic as she feared the whole plan would fall apart through her inability to move him a few feet, never mind all the way through the house, out the front door and into his car. Then she recalled moving some heavy sacks of winter feed on

Wednesday evening, and deduced that the wheelbarrow would do just as well for a heavy sack of something else.

She had used a wooden board as a ramp at the back steps, then again at the rear of the car. What with the ravages of the board and the metal front edge of the barrow as she tipped its awkward load, she made a right mess of the BMW's paintwork. Shame. What was it Cadaver had said? *Aye, boo-hoo.*

As she drove she heard a bump from behind her, then another, then a flurry of them. The sounds shook her as surely as had they been beating against the back of her seat, but she knew they would cease once their futility had been established. It took a while though, possibly because it would take longer for two people to give up trying to escape than just one alone. What she didn't want to admit to herself was that she was hoping it *was* two people trying to escape.

She was close to her destination. The thumping did indeed tail off after a short while and she resumed rehearsing in her head, as she had been for most of the journey: going over and over what she was going to do, what she was going to say. She'd open the boot and let them struggle their way out, all the time keeping her dad's rifle trained on them.

'You're getting nothing more from this family. Tell your boss and whoever else is in on this racket: you ever come back to our farm, it's this rifle you'll be getting shot with, not a tranquiliser. We'll bury you in the fields and you'll never be found.'

Over and over in her head. She knew where she'd stand, knew what she'd say, and had worked out her exit strategy this time. She was better prepared than back in the kitchen, yet there was one discordant note telling her that none of what she had pictured would happen. It was a thought she was trying to shout down, drown out with her prepared speech: 'You're getting nothing more from this family . . .'

The puddle of drool on the kitchen floor. Cadaver's eyes rolled back, not fully closed.

No. It was just the effects of the drug: tranquilisers hit different subjects in different ways.

'We'll bury you in the fields and you'll never be found.'

Then she was going to drive away, leaving them on the edge of a cliff on the South Ayrshire coast.

Have fun walking back from there, boys.

They'd have no money for a bus or even to a call from a payphone, as she had cleaned out their pockets. Their names were Walter Russell and Paul Sweeney, according to, respectively, a bank card on Cadaver and a video club membership on Squirrelly. She'd leave the car on the double yellows at Calderburn Station, where it would get a pricey ticket, maybe even towed away by British Rail.

These people were bullies. That wasn't to say they weren't strong, weren't dangerous, but their modus operandi was to prey on the cowed and vulnerable. She was letting them know they'd find easier pickings elsewhere.

She turned the car off the narrow B road on to a sliver of a single track, the turn-off for which was all but camouflaged by a bend in the road and a copse of trees. Ayrshire was full of such isolated arbours, like huddled clumps of daisies that had been missed by some giant lawnmower. The track was paved by crumbling concrete for the first thirty or forty yards, then gave way to compacted earth rutted by tractor wheels. She could see gulls ahead, soaring on the updraught where the sea met the cliffs. Ailsa Craig was a grey blur, shrouded in the clouds that had swept in from the west. There was no sign of human life in any direction.

They used to come to this place for picnics when she was wee: days out beneath blue sky, her and Lisa drinking Creamola Foam from plastic cups, nothing more sinister to worry about than wasps. It felt like the four of them were the only people in the world. Nobody else ever came here. Her mum knew about it because she had grown up only a few miles from the spot, a farmer's daughter also, who spent her childhood days walking and cycling every track and path just to see where they led.

She stopped the car and killed the engine, pocketing the keys. The thumping resumed a few moments later, in response to the vehicle being silently stationary and therefore not merely stopped at lights or a junction.

Catherine reached into the rear footwell and lifted the canvas bag, from which she removed the rifle. She fed four rounds into the breech and slid the bolt: up, forward, down, back. A shot over their heads or into the vehicle would drive the point home. The noise alone would have them jumping out of their skins: people who had only seen guns on the TV were always literally shaken by the real report of a live round.

She opened the door and walked around slowly, the rifle's strap slung around her shoulder and the barrel steadied by her left hand. There was a bracing wind whipping in from the water, a smell of sea and a tang of salt borne upon it. She checked the ground underfoot at the rear of the vehicle, then popped the boot and took a couple of swift but measured steps backward, taking hold of the stock in her right hand and levelling the rifle.

There was a grunt and a scuffing sound, then the lid of the boot flew upwards with a speed that almost caused it to rebound all the way shut again, that absurd spoiler threatening to crack the rear window. The squirrelly one, Sweeney, clawed his torso over the mouth of the boot and flopped awkwardly to the ground. He had worked loose the bonds around his wrists, but not quite disentangled the rope from his ankles.

When he raised his head and looked up, his eyes were wild, terrified, his pallid face drained of its cheeky assuredness and his body shaking as he hyperventilated in spluttering panic.

'Jesus Christ. Jesus Christ.' His eyes darted around as he spoke, focusing on random areas of his field of vision. 'Jesus Christ. Jesus Christ.' He looked at Catherine a couple of times, but in those first disoriented moments she seemed to be of no greater significance than anything else his restless eyes alighted upon.

Catherine wasn't focusing entirely on him either, her gaze constantly drawn to the still-gaping mouth of the boot, from which nothing else had yet emerged.

'Jesus Christ. Jesus Christ.'

His eyes fixed on her again and this time he finally seemed to see her.

She was trembling herself now, her mind going blank, the

350

beginnings of a descent into panic. Grasping for a hold on something stable, she remembered what she had rehearsed.

'You're getting nothing more from this family,' she tried to say, but her mouth was dry and quivering and her ill-formed words seemed swallowed up by the wind.

Still she gazed past him into that blank, gaping mouth. Still nothing issued from it but a silent accusation.

'You're getting nothing . . .' she tried again, but her throat seemed to swell from within and choke her words. If she could say it, say her piece, she'd be back in the plan, it would all be the way she pictured it.

'You've kill't him,' Sweeney screamed, as though he sensed her denial like a sheet of glass in front of her and was trying to shatter it with his voice. 'Ya fuckin' cow, you've fuckin' kill't him.'

The glass disintegrated into a million fragments that could never be put back together. She knew he was dead as she tipped his body into the boot. Knew he was dead as she tied his ankles and wrists. Knew he was dead as she hauled him off the kitchen floor. She had shot him in the heart with a horse tranquiliser. She did know the strength and dosage because she knew where Harriet Chambers was supposed to be going before Dad's collapse changed her plans: to Garrowfoot Stables, where a yearling colt had gashed the cannonbone of its right foreleg and wouldn't let anyone near itself.

She had killed him, and locked his colleague in a car boot with his corpse.

'You're getting . . . you're getting . . .'

She saw again the future they had all seen for her father on that awful first day, when he came storming down the hall with the rifle; except this time it had happened, this time there had been no one to grab the gun and stop it. The process was in motion, one that would end with her in jail and her family torn apart, her parents crushed more devastatingly than by anything these crooks had wrought.

Sweeney meanwhile began climbing to his feet, coils of rope falling away as he raised one leg and let them drop. Then she saw the flick knife.

'Put the gun doon or I'll fuckin' cut ye,' he vowed, his disorientation replaced by trembling anger.

She tightened her grip on the gun, though she couldn't have said whether this was to steady her aim or because one part of her was trying to wrestle it away from the other, like she and Lisa and Mum had done to Dad in the hall.

She backed away a step, two steps, but as she retreated Sweeney began advancing, the knife gripped in front of his face.

'I mean it. I'm gaunny fuckin' slice you, hen.'

She witnessed the fury in his eyes, heedless of the weapon. The fear was gone. He saw no threat in front of him, only vengeance.

Catherine didn't remember making a decision to pull the trigger: only an impulse, a signal from her brain to her finger and the bang, muted in the wind, blown away like the smoke from the muzzle.

Sweeney flew backwards as though jerked on elastic, landing in a crumpled sitting position with his shoulders against the back of the BMW's left rear wheel arch. He appeared dazed and startled for a moment, even as his hands reflexively pressed against the wound below his ribcage, then he looked up incredulously at her, his breathing a series of laboured, agonised moans.

'Oh God, I'm sorry,' she said.

She dropped to her knees on the dirt, the rifle falling into her lap, still hung around her shoulder by the strap. Her vision clouded as her eyes filled up.

'I'm sorry. I'm sorry.'

The blood spread across the front of his tracksuit, spilling through the gaps between his fingers; that awful laboured moaning beginning to take on a despairing, panicked quality. From inside she suddenly felt bile rise like something within her was being purged by a greater force than her body could muster. She vomited harder than she could ever remember, but at the end there was no sense of catharsis.

The rifle suddenly felt heavy and shameful, diseased. She had to get it off, get away from it. She staggered to her feet and unslung it, letting it drop to the earth next to the puddle of sick, then she turned and began to walk away. She didn't know where, didn't think beyond each step, knew only that she had to put distance between herself and what lay behind her.

That was when Sweeney managed to speak.

'Don't go,' he said, a groaning, heartfelt plea. 'Please stay with me. Please stay.'

The words halted her like a brick wall across her path. She still wanted to flee, perhaps even more so, but she could not. She did not want to turn back, to confront what she had wrought, but she knew she would, knew she had to. Not for absolution, for she knew he could not give her that even if he wanted to: this was hers to carry always. She turned back to Sweeney, who had stolen from her family, tormented her, humiliated her, because it was how her father had raised her. This was the last kindness she could give him.

She knelt down next to him, her back also against the rear of the car, and gently pulled his shoulders towards her until his head was resting on her chest. His breathing was irregular, sometimes jolting, sometimes long and slow.

'I'm scared,' he said. 'I want my mammy.'

Catherine cried silently. He couldn't see her face and once again she didn't want him to know she was in tears, but this time because it felt like something she wished to spare him, rather than deny.

His eyes looked to be losing focus, gazing blankly into space as his lids fell halfway to closing. The moaning had all but fallen away, his breathing shallow now, shallower with every breath.

She placed a hand on his head and stroked his lank, greasy hair.

'Is that you, Mammy?' he asked, his voice a broken whisper.

Catherine swallowed to prevent a sob, replying in a whisper of her own as her voice would have broken had she spoken properly.

'I'm here,' she replied, feeling the warm waters run down both her cheeks.

'I'm sorry,' he breathed. 'I'm sorry, Mammy.'

'It's all right,' she whispered.

She shuddered as his right hand suddenly moved, reaching just a few inches to grip one of hers.

'I'm cold,' he said, then she felt the weight of his head shift slightly, and in that moment she knew he was gone.

She remained there for a time, just in case it wasn't over, in case he still needed her, and because it delayed the rest of her life that had to follow. Then she gently let his head come down to rest on the earth and crouched by his side. She stared at his face, peaceful and still, a ghost of the cocksure and restless visage that had walked into her kitchen only a few hours before, and she looked at the bloody mess beneath his chest.

She felt the stirrings of panic about how her mind was going to cope with this. It seemed so big, so terrible, so frightening, something she couldn't contain, like what she had vomited out but so, so much bigger.

Something took control, something deep within. She dabbed her index finger in his blood, held it above his forehead and flicked it, marking him with a short spray. Then she dabbed it again and drew the arc.

Sitting back to look at it, she felt calm and in control. In the ritual she found not absolution, but understanding: the knowledge that this was how it had to be. She had killed him so that her family could survive.

We're taking this creature's life to preserve our own. Killing something is a sacrifice — it's always a sacrifice, and a sacrifice should be solemn. We'll live off this creature today and tomorrow too. We owe it our gratitude and we owe it our respect, our courtesy . . . and our kindness.

Leverage

Fallan looked tortured and fraught, restlessly animated like a fly bashing itself against a window in confused desperation. He was soaking wet, dressed in jeans, a T-shirt and a light jacket, nothing in the ensemble designed for a night like this. She realised he had to be kitted in the clothes he'd been wearing when they lifted him. No wheels either, as they wouldn't have surrendered the Land Rover to him yet.

'Why did you release me?' he demanded.

He sounded like an anguished ghost, blaming her for his exile from eternal rest.

'We know you didn't do it,' she told him. 'Jasmine Sharp spotted that the Defender at the car wash was a right-hand drive. You owe her big time.'

'But why did you bring her into this?' he asked, in a manner that had Catherine adjusting her grip on the nightstick.

'That's not something I can discuss with you. She came through for you, that's the important part. What's your problem with it?'

'Because they've taken her.'

'Who's taken her?' Catherine asked, but Fallan didn't appear to be listening, or didn't consider it worth an answer.

'I was keeping her out of this. That was the deal. I take the fall and they leave her alone.'

'What deal? Who are you talking about?'

'The day Stevie died I got a text, purporting to be from Jasmine. It said she was in trouble and asked me to get to Glasgow right away. When I phoned, it just rang out. I dropped everything and drove. It wasn't her, though: it was so I didn't have an alibi. I was on my own, in my car, when Stevie got shot.

'They phoned me after he was dead, again using Jasmine's number.

355

They were using her as leverage. They wanted me to go down for Fullerton, and if I took the fall they'd leave her alone. That's why I said nothing, even when I saw the stills of the Land Rover. But now I'm out and Jasmine's missing. They've got her.'

'Have you told the police?' she asked, then promptly realised it was a stupid question. There were police in on this, and Fallan had to know that. 'Why have you come here?' she added.

'Because you're a part of this.'

'I'm not a part of anything,' she protested, wondering how crazed and paranoid Fallan might be. She edged a foot against the door, ready to close it if she felt the need.

Fallan reached forward to one of the glass panes and drew a shape in the rain and condensation. It was crude and runny, but she knew immediately what it represented.

'They've got leverage on you too. They hung this thing around your neck like a choke chain from day one, and I'm guessing they've started to tighten it. That's why you're the only person I can trust.'

The rain continued to batter down, running off Fallan's hair and on to his face.

'You know what this means?' she asked him, indicating the rune. He nodded.

'Who's they?' she asked again, her insides turning to mercury. 'Who's got Jasmine? Who's doing this?'

Fallan's face looked like a gravestone.

'Tony McGill.'

As soon as he said the words she could see that it had been in front of her all the time. Bob Cairns and Tony McGill went way back, and he must have been promoted to McGill's principal tame cop following the death of Iain Fallan.

What she couldn't see was how McGill fitted into the Julie Muir killing, given the absence of any known connection between McGill and Drummond. She knew Fallan was right, though: knew it like you know winter is on the way.

'How can you be sure?'

'Can I come inside?' he asked.

'No,' she told him. 'If you know what this symbol means, you'll

356

understand why I'm not going to invite you over my family's threshold.'

'I'm not a fucking vampire.'

'No, it was others who did the blood-sucking. You're something worse.'

She grabbed a jacket and lifted her keys. 'We'll talk in the car.'

'Aye. Cannae be having a killer in the house, can we, McLeod? That would never do.'

Truth and Reconciliation

Anthony feared he was running out of time to say something.

He was driving through the car park of the sports club looking for a space, the Vauxhall dwarfed among rows upon row of SUVs. Reassuringly he spotted Cal O'Shea's Land Cruiser tucked between an Evoque and a Q7. Cal's partner David had told them he was down here playing tennis, but he wasn't sure how long Cal would be or where he was headed afterwards. Fortunately it looked like they would catch him.

The club was in Hamilton, and Adrienne lived nearby in Motherwell. Anthony was going to drop her off at home after this last call, then take the Vauxhall back to Govan where his own car was parked.

They were getting on fine, though it was difficult to say whether this was in spite or because of the situation in which they found themselves. It felt good to be talking again, to be working together. Nonetheless, he couldn't help but feel they were approaching the point where they either had to acknowledge the elephant in the room or they were mutually accepting that they never would. Beyond that point, they would both be entering another silent pact to pretend it never happened, and for some reason he just didn't think that was good enough. It felt cowardly and dishonest, and though he knew it would keep things comfortable between them he also knew that it would also keep them at a distance too. It would mean they weren't past it, and nor would they ever be.

How did you bring up something like that, though?

He had been looking for the right moment, but it never seemed to come. It wasn't like they had nothing else to talk about. The end of the day seemed an appropriate time, but he wasn't sure he wanted to do this parked outside her house. It would be too much like he was making a play, as though he was angling to be asked in or something.

So maybe there would never be a right time; or maybe he just didn't want it enough.

He pulled into a space at the far end, next to a jogging trail, and killed the engine. The light smir of rain that was blowing around occluded the windscreen now that the wipers were off, causing the world outside to blur.

Adrienne reached down into the footwell for her bag, and it was as she moved to grab the door handle that he forced himself to speak, feeling like it really was now or never.

'Adrienne, sit tight a second.'

'What is it?'

He sighed, which felt like such a conspicuous overture that she surely had to see what was coming: the three words neither of them had yet been able to bring themselves to say.

'About that night.'

'Oh, God, look, just don't,' she said, grabbing the handle and tugging it open.

Anthony reached out with his left hand and gripped her wrist.

'I need to explain myself,' he implored.

She looked aghast, like she desperately wanted out of the car. Something kept her there, though, and for that he was grateful.

'I'm the one who needs to explain myself,' she protested. 'I'm just mortified. I was a bit pissed and I threw myself at you. I'm sorry. I must have looked totally desperate.'

'You didn't. It was me. I just wasn't ready for things to move that fast. I thought I was, so I'm sorry I led you on.'

'I didn't need much leading.'

'It's not that I didn't want something to happen, it's just . . . It had been a long time. Not a lot of match practice, you know?'

'Me neither. Why do you think I was throwing myself at you?'

'I don't just mean, you know, the physical. It's a long time since I've been involved at all.'

'How long?'

He sighed. After so much tension over the months, this

conversation had been surprisingly easy. They were both almost giggly with the relief of getting it out in the open. But now came the truly difficult part.

'About four years,' he told her.

'Four years? But you're only in your twenties.'

'I was in a relationship for a long time.'

'Painful break-up? I hear you. Four years, though. Must have been a pretty bad one.'

'The worst kind.'

'What kind is that? Because you'll have to go some to match me, pal.'

Anthony swallowed. He'd come this far, laid the groundwork. Only a few more words now.

'The kind where she dies.'

The rain was growing heavier. A gust of wind rattled a volley of drops against the windows, like it had tossed a handful of gravel at the car.

Adrienne squeezed his hand and gave him the look that he'd been praying for: the one that told him he didn't have to say anything else for now.

'You win,' she said quietly.

Fellow Travellers

The lights changed to green and Catherine steadily pressed the accelerator. The beams of her headlights ventured ahead hopelessly like cannon fodder into battle, swallowed by darkness and rain. It was not, by anyone's measure, a fine night for a drive.

'Where are we going?' Fallan asked.

'Nowhere. I just want to be moving.'

'Helps you think?'

'Yes. Inasmuch as previously all I could think about was getting you as far as possible from my house. Now I can think about something else. Like how do you know what this . . . leverage is that they've got on me? Have you always known?'

'No. That time you came to gatecrash me and Jasmine having breakfast a couple of years ago, I realised I recognised you but I didn't recall from where. All my wee guilt neurones were firing – I do have those, by the way – but all I knew was that you must have been there in the background when I was doing something I'm not proud of.'

'I'm guessing that didn't narrow it down.'

'Not exactly, no. It was when you showed me the symbol in the interview room that it all came together, like it was the primer for a code. Even the name resonated suddenly. You kept it when you married, didn't you? Until then I had assumed McLeod was your husband's name.'

'I've always been Catherine McLeod. Except when I was Cassie, which was what my big sister called me when I was a baby because she couldn't pronounce Catherine.'

'When I saw the symbol on the page I could picture it on the ground at a farm long ago, blood on frosted grass. I remember stopping to look at it that morning with old Walter. He was Tony's collector.'

361

'You weren't just there that morning though, were you?' she stated, stealing a glance across to the passenger seat. 'You were there the night before too.'

'No. That wasn't me. I wouldn't do that. Christ,' he added, giving a dry laugh of exasperation.

'What?'

'I was about to say I couldn't harm a defenceless animal, which is true. Just pondering why that is, when I've never had a problem harming the higher mammals.'

'You and the ALF. So who was there the night before? Who was the psycho who slashed my horse?'

'Sweenzo. Paul Sweeney. A headcase, right enough: like a permanently shaken-up bottle of ginger. Probably a putative serial killer, but we'll never know, seeing as he was shot dead and left in a field with a weird symbol painted on him in his own blood.'

Catherine changed up, hitting a slip road on to the motorway. She wanted to move faster, and it was better lit.

'Are you telling me Sweeney did it because you think it will make me feel better, or because it's true?'

Fallan ignored this.

'Why did you do it?' he asked.

'They were killing my family.'

Catherine had replied before she could even think about it. The words just spilled out, a reflexive response.

'I didn't mean to kill them. I wanted to scare them off, let them know we weren't easy meat. I shot them with tranquilisers and drove them out into the middle of nowhere. But when I opened the boot, the older guy was dead. Then the other guy came at me, and . . .'

Her mouth became dry, though moisture wasn't going to be a problem for her eyes.

'I'm not like you,' she said, struggling to steady her voice. 'It was self-defence. I shot the older guy as well so that it looked like a hit. I did what I had to in order to survive.'

'I meant, why did you draw the symbol on them?' Fallan clarified neutrally. It was like the killing talk was the epitome of mundane to him, but *this* part was intriguing.

'I needed it to mean something. I needed to connect it to something else. It made some kind of sense at the time, but when I look back it's like it wasn't me who was doing the thinking.'

Catherine kept her misting eyes on the road, but she was conscious of Fallan nodding. She wasn't sure how she felt about getting the impression that a guy like him understood where she was coming from.

'You've never told anybody about this, have you?'

'Nobody.'

'That's a lonely place to live. Not even your husband?'

'Especially not my husband. I never wanted anyone to know. That's why I'm vulnerable: I'd do anything to keep it from Drew. But now Tony McGill knows. I don't know how, but you're right: it's being used to keep me in line.'

'Same as me, he only worked it out recently. He knew about the symbol at the time, but no more than that. The cops must have leaked it to him: Cairns probably. McGill assumed it was one of his rivals making a move against him, guy called Archie Cutler. So when he got somebody to do one of Cutler's people he was found with the same symbol drawn on him. Then back and forth and back and forth, the Glasgow way.'

'And was that "somebody" you?'

'No. I didn't leave bodies. I think it was Stevie's brother, Nico; or maybe Nico killed the guy that killed the guy that . . . you get the picture.'

'I've *seen* the picture, Fullerton's brother lying in an alley with that sign painted on the wall.'

'Nobody knew what it meant or where it came from, though. When I saw it I never connected it to your farm. Glasgow gangsters are unimaginative wee neds: they don't get deep into the semiotics. Like everybody else, I assumed it was bam on bam. I thought the symbol must have been in a film, and that whoever drew it on the ground at the farm had copied it from the same source as whoever killed Walter and Sweenzo. That's until you handed me a copy and it all fell into place.'

'So how does McGill know?'

363

'While I was inside I heard that Walter's widow died last year, and when his son, Alec, was renovating the house he discovered a hidey-hole behind a skirting board. Apparently Tony was very pleased about something Alec found, but wasn't telling anybody what or why.'

'He sent me a page of a ledger,' Catherine said, 'showing the date when my family were due to make our next payment. At the time I was terrified somebody would come back, looking for money or revenge. I thought it must be obvious what had happened. They never did, though, and I could never work out why.'

'Ironically, it was their own system that protected you,' Fallan told her. 'Deniability. Walter handled that whole protection business, and Tony never knew who he was collecting from. It was so if the cops ever took an interest he could honestly say he'd never even heard of these people. Problem was, when Walter died nobody knew where he hid the list of 'customers', as he called them. Even if they'd had the list, they'd never have guessed it was some civilian fighting back. And besides, Tony had other priorities after that. He found himself fighting on a lot of fronts.'

Catherine came off the motorway and on to the dual carriageway that bisected the sprawling schemes of Croftbank. She hadn't had a destination in mind when she set out, but the more they talked the more her instinct took her towards Gallowhaugh, where Glen Fallan had grown up, where his father Iain had ruled his own personal fiefdom, and where Iain's ally Tony McGill had preposterously been credited with 'keeping the drugs out'. Gallowhaugh, Shawburn, Croftbank: that was the world where this had all started, and something told her that was where it must end too.

That world had a satellite however, connected and yet distant: the hamlet of Capletmuir, where a bright young woman with her whole life ahead of her had been murdered on her way to the home of the Under-Secretary of State. It remained outside the main picture, held in a remote orbit, but like gravity, Catherine couldn't see the force that was keeping it there.

'What makes you sure it's McGill who's got Jasmine?' she asked.
'You'll have heard about how Tony got fitted up by the cops

when he went down in a big drugs bust? Well, it wasn't the cops who fitted him up. It was me and Stevie. We didn't frame him: he *was* there to buy the drugs. We just made sure he showed up where the cops wanted him to. Poetic justice, we thought, given how many folk Tony had dobbed in to the polis as part of his you-scratch-my-back arrangements with the likes of my dad. But he's been waiting a long time for his revenge. Killing Stevie in his own car wash and having me take the fall probably seems doubly poetic to Tony.'

'What's poetic about a car wash?'

'It's symbolic. Stevie was something of a criminal protégé under Tony, and the car wash represented him not just him outgrowing Tony, but moving into things Tony didn't understand. Stevie even tried to explain it to him, but he still didn't get it. Stevie thought Tony was yesterday's man, and the car wash must have been a totem of that in Tony's mind. He has a long memory.

'The poetic thing about framing me for the shooting is that I was never jailed. I was too careful: the guy who always got away with it. The irony would be in me finally going down for a killing I *didn't* commit.'

Catherine took a left at the roundabout and pulled on to Shawburn Boulevard. They would soon be passing the Old Croft Brasserie on the left-hand side.

'This is about more than revenge,' she told Fallan. 'There's an angle to it that you don't know about. Fullerton was digging around, asking questions about a murder that took place twenty-five years ago. The victim's name was Julie Muir. She worked at Nokturn. Fullerton believed that Bob Cairns and Mitchell Drummond, who is now the Deputy Chief Constable, by the way, fitted up a special-needs case called Teddy Sheehan for the killing. This ringing any bells?'

'I remember it happening. I knew who Julie was but I didn't know her. Any time I found myself in Nokturn, it would be fair to say I was a wallflower. One thing I've always done well is blend in to the scenery.'

'Her boyfriend was Gordon Ewart. His father is Campbell

Ewart, the then MP, and his mother is Philippa Ewart, the drugs campaigner. Gordon's now a big noise at Cautela Group, and he's highly connected. Drummond's been keeping Ewart's name out of the case, same as his name was kept out of the spotlight when Julie died. Fullerton was in touch with him shortly before he was killed. Ewart says he was blackmailing him, threatening to tell the press about his links to Julie and his coke habit back in the Nokturn days. Do you remember him?'

'Vaguely. I tended to mentally background the celebs and rich kids because they weren't the types I had to watch out for. I don't see what connects Tony to this Ewart guy, though.'

'Nor I, but McGill's the one cracking the whip for Ewart's benefit. He's squeezing me and he's definitely squeezing Drummond.'

'And now he's got Jasmine,' Fallan said with finality.

They came up alongside the Old Croft Brasserie and drove deeper into darkness, the streetlights ahead being out of service. Further along the dual carriageway was where Fullerton met his soapy fate. It occurred to Catherine that she hadn't seen any CCTV footage from this end of the boulevard, close to the restaurant, and wondered whether the power failure was related.

'Jasmine told us they stole her sim and spoofed her phone number on the day of the shooting. Is it possible they've done it again?' Catherine suggested, though she wasn't optimistic.

'No. They've got her. They let me hear her voice, told me to stand by, said they'd know if I went to the cops. The day Stevie was killed they just needed to put me where they wanted me. The stakes are higher now. They want to control me, and they know this is how.'

'Stand by for what?'

'I don't know, but making me wait is part of the game. It works best if you give the mark time to ponder what he might lose, because then, when you tell him what you want, he's only too glad to cooperate. This is textbook Tony McGill. See, Tony's old school: that's what people used to say. He might be a crook, but he's got a code of honour. You'll have heard the three golden rules of old-school Glasgow gangsters?'

Catherine wondered where he was going with this. She recalled

Moira mentioning it, and she also recalled that the only reason Moira brought it up was to underline that it was bollocks.

'They don't grass, they don't deal in drugs,' she began, then she understood. 'And they don't hurt women and kids. Jesus.'

'That was always Tony's true golden rule,' Fallan said. 'If you want people to be afraid of you, hurt what they care about.'

She was about to inquire how McGill knew that what Fallan cared about was Jasmine Sharp, but as soon as she asked herself the question she suddenly realised that there was a new front-runner for this year's Wood for the Trees Award.

Prisoners

Jasmine could hear a vehicle approaching, the splashing of tyres through puddles audible from somewhere outside. She switched off the solitary bare bulb that hung from the ceiling, the better to look out into the darkness, and moved to the window. There was a faint glow to her right, but she couldn't see the narrow road as her room was at the rear of the house.

She listened intently to the growing purr of an engine and the crunch of wheels on the loose gravel and broken paving. Then the engine was silenced and a car door slammed shut.

She could hear voices in the hall, low and gruff, fading as they disappeared behind a door downstairs. They were below and to the right, words muffled and indistinct. She thought she could make out the sound of a tap running, a chink of crockery.

Fuckers were sitting down to a cuppa.

They seemed in no rush. This suited her and tortured her at the same time. There was so much fear in not knowing what was going on, yet whenever she sensed movement from below, the possibility that somebody might be venturing upstairs, her heart raced.

Eventually, inevitably, she heard footsteps on the stairs. She got up from her chair automatically, something in her demanding a state of readiness, only for her to become more acutely conscious of her exposure. She shrunk back against the wall beneath the window, furthest from the door, then squatted down, balling herself up.

The footsteps grew nearer, striding steadily along the bare boards of the upstairs hallway. It was only one person. The gait was different from Pudgy: lighter in tread yet noisier in volume. Some reflexively analytical part of her brain told her she should expect to see a smaller man in hard-soled footwear, as opposed to Pudgy in his trainers. It didn't tell her anything that might make a difference.

The door opened and in walked a wiry figure wearing an expensive suit in a cut that was at least twenty years too young for him. She saw money, she saw vanity and she saw a man unused to having anyone around who might tell him he was kidding himself.

He was early seventies, but not early seventies like somebody's amiable grandfather. He was early seventies like Jimmy Savile: lean, strong, vicious and predatory.

The only pictures she had seen had been decades old, always from the same paltry selection the tabloids had on file, but she knew who she was looking at. This was Tony McGill.

'Come and have a wee seat, hen,' McGill said.

He walked over to the table and pulled a chair out either side, like he was inviting her to sit down in his kitchen. Like she wasn't his prisoner. Like she wasn't bloodied. Like she wasn't naked.

Jasmine didn't have a choice. She scrambled across the floor like an animal, trying to keep her breasts and crotch covered as she positioned herself on the chair. She knew there was nothing he wasn't going to see if he wanted to. The point wasn't to spare her own shame; it was to accentuate his.

McGill looked around at the mouldy walls and ceiling, the bare bulb, the tiny window, and finally at the bowl on the floor, into which she'd had no choice but to finally pee.

He shook his head and sighed.

'Not nice being shut away in a pokey wee room, is it?' he asked.

Jasmine didn't answer, didn't meet his gaze.

'You've only been here a few hours. Can you imagine what it feels like to hear a judge give you a sentence in *decades*? And can you imagine what it's like to know that you've been set up by people you trusted? People you took under your wing and gave a start in life?'

He didn't raise his voice. There was even a wry little chuckle in there, but it was hollow, rattling like chains on a wooden floor.

'Whole life ahead of you. All your plans, all the things you thought you had plenty of time to get around to. And then it's all taken away. Doesn't seem fair, does it?'

She couldn't muster a reply, and that wasn't good enough. He reached across the table and cupped her chin, forcing her head up, forcing her to look at him.

'You're awfy quiet, hen. From what I heard, I thought you'd have more spunk. Bet you'd more to say for yourself when you were fucking everything up for Bob Cairns and that lot, eh?'

Still she said nothing. She couldn't think of any words. His eyes burned right through her, not with hate or anger, but something else: something horribly eager, almost elated, yet at the same time joyless and cold.

This was not about her, and for that reason, no matter what he thought, it wouldn't satisfy him.

'Have you got plans? A boyfriend maybe?'

As he asked this, he broke off his gaze to stare conspicuously at whatever he could see of her tits.

'See, when I got banged up, I had somebody I wanted to be with. Somebody I loved. I know people look at me and only see a hard case, but that's not all there is. I had somebody special. And I don't mean his mother,' he said, gesturing below with his head.

She interpreted this to mean that Pudgy downstairs must be Tony Junior, or Teej as he was known.

'No, that was long over. I'm talking about a woman of class. Somebody who turned heads wherever she went, but wasn't appreciated where it mattered most. I appreciated her. We were going to be together, and Christ would *that* not have turned heads?'

He grinned, as though inviting her to join him in his reverie, but bitterness was already bleeding into it.

'Not to be. You can't ask anybody to wait thirty years minus time off for good behaviour, can you? No, if you love somebody set them free, they say. I set her free, and spent the time we should have had together locked up in wee rooms smaller than this, pissing in pots and wanking into hankies.'

He sat back with his arms folded, staring, lapping up the silence.

'You'd have to be angry about something like that, wouldn't you say?'

She didn't say. She was doing well to breathe.

He cupped her chin again.

'Do you know what this is about?'

He looked like he'd have been disappointed if she said yes. He needed to tell her.

'I was set up by the late Stevie Fullerton and by the formerly late but apparently not so late Mr Glen Fallan. And I've waited a long time to put things right. Things *need* to be put right, believe me, hen, or else you cannae move on. I wasn't in a hurry, though. I'd waited all those years inside: I could wait a wee while longer for the right moment to come along, and it did.

'Stevie gave me a wee problem, and as luck would have it Glen provided me with the ideal solution. A very satisfying solution, I thought, set up by me like I was set up by him. But the best part would be that he'd know he was stuck in there, in prison, where he could do nothing about the fact that I was out here. With you.'

McGill ran a hand down the side of her face, causing her to flinch. Then he sat back again and sighed, almost regretfully.

'Aye, Glen was always trying to be somebody's guardian angel, always looking to be the knight in shining armour to make up for that one damsel in distress that he wasn't able to defend.'

Neither fear nor caution could disguise Jasmine's response to this. She met his eyes inquiringly before she could even think to stop herself.

'You think I'm talking about your mammy? Naw, I barely knew her. I'm talking about way back, when he was in his teens. I'm talking about a nasty accident in his house. Well, that vicious bastard Iain swore it was an accident, but when you're never done laying into your family you cannae be surprised if it ends in tragedy.'

McGill reached into the inside pocket of his jacket, where she was sure she glimpsed the top of her phone in its pink sleeve. Teej had made her speak into it before, got her to say 'This is Jasmine'. She didn't get to hear who was on the other end, but she could guess. McGill produced a photograph, keeping the printed side facing him for the time being. On the yellowed back she could read the words 'Fiona and Glen, Kelburn Park'.

'Fiona got knocked over. I gather she was trying to stop Iain battering her wee brother. She hit her head on the fireplace. Nobody in that house was ever the same again. Iain was dead inside even before somebody finished the job. She was a lovely looking girl, too, wouldn't you say?'

McGill placed the photograph down on the table in front of her. It showed Fallan as a skinny teen, standing next to his older sister in front of a fish pond or boating loch. Jasmine stared at the girl's face, perplexed by its striking familiarity. For a confused moment she wondered if she was looking at an early picture of her mum, and her mind flashed with ramifications and consequences, tallying up everything Aunt Josie had told her and wondering how it could all be a lie.

Josie hadn't lied, though. The girl in the picture didn't look like her mother.

The girl in the picture looked like Jasmine.

A half-gasp, half-sob escaped from her mouth and she placed a hand over it, no longer mindful of covering her breast.

McGill was chuckling with grim satisfaction.

'Aye, it has to be said that boy Jazz Donnelly was a mad shagger. A *mad* shagger. Flung it about like you wouldn't believe. I once heard that he fucked three different lassies in the office of that Nokturn place in the same night, and then took another one home later. He must have pumped a hundred lassies before he got around to your mammy, so it's pretty amazing that none of them ever showed up claiming he got them pregnant. A fucking miracle, you might say. Unless it turned out the bold Jazz was firing blanks. What do you reckon?'

The Satellite

There was no let-up in the rain as Catherine reached the outskirts of Gallowhaugh. They stopped at a set of traffic lights, a wee parade of shops sitting to the left facing a road that ran parallel to the dual carriageway. She recognised it. A mid-level dealer named Jai McDiarmid had been found dead a couple of years back, behind what had then been his own tanning salon. The premises were boarded up now, nobody taking on the let. A couple of doors down there was a group of teenagers outside a chippy, huddled under the cover of an overhang, a scene Catherine guessed she could have witnessed here on any rainy night over the past four or five decades.

She noticed Fallan gazing fixedly out of the passenger-side window towards the parade, and wondered what memories were replaying inside his head.

'How did you come to be working for Tony McGill in the first place?' she asked him.

It seemed to take him a few moments to disengage from wherever his mind had been before he could deal with her question.

'It's a long story. In the simple version, you could say I was headhunted. Tony was an adept manipulator of people: he understood the many and various things that could motivate them, not just the venal ones. And it's testimony to his skills that I didn't realise I had been manipulated until I was already too far down the road to turn back.'

'You knew who he was, though? Growing up, I mean.'

'Everybody knew who he was. I knew who all the hard men and players were around Gallowhaugh, and I hated all of them. I had never met Tony McGill, but I hated him the most, because I knew he was in cahoots with my dad. When I was at a sensitive age, the one redeeming feature I believed my dad to have was that he was a polisman, fighting the good fight. I made a lot of allowances for his behaviour on that basis. Then I found out about him and Tony, and the last piece of façade crumbled. I finally saw what my old man was, but I suppose I must have transferred a lot of blame onto Tony.'

The lights turned to green. Catherine pulled away, staying on the dual carriageway. She still didn't have a destination in mind, and neither did Fallan. He was waiting for a call, and it felt right to be mobile.

'So what changed your mind?' she asked.

'Learning that nothing's ever that simple, especially in Gallowhaugh. One day I was walking through the ruins of what used to be a factory, when I saw six or seven guys coming towards me. They had axes, hammers, machetes, motorbike chains. They all had scarves over their faces, up to just below the eyes. That was unusual – round here, if you were going to give somebody a doing the whole point was that the victim, and everybody else, knew exactly who was giving out the message.'

'They were masked because it was going to be more than that,' she suggested.

'Fortunately I didn't have to find out. A car came screeching up and the back door flew open. Somebody told me to jump in, and I didn't wait to be asked twice. The driver told me "there's a man wants a word with you," and I knew who he meant.'

'Team Tony to the rescue.'

'Aye. The twist was, years later I found out what the scarves were for: it was so I didn't recognise that the blokes with the tools were Tony's people too. It was a set-up.'

'So that you felt you owed him from the off, and that he was on your side.'

'That and the opportunity for him to make an impression. They drove me to meet him, and not in some dingy pub or snooker hall. I got taken to his house, this huge place up in the hamlet. It was so he could come over as the benevolent ruler, show off his stature by putting himself in the context of a different world from the streets that . . .'

But Catherine had stopped listening after one key word.

'The hamlet?' she asked.

'Aye. It's what we called Capletmuir. Tony had this massive house—'

'Take me there,' she interrupted. 'Right now. Show me where it was.'

She did a u-turn through the first gap in the central reservation and accelerated back towards the junction as though it was an emergency.

It only took a few minutes to reach Capletmuir, the satellite place removed and yet connected to the world once ruled by Tony McGill. The car snaked between opulent new developments, culs-de-sac bending away out of sight either side of the main road, on past Miner's Row, where Brenda Sheehan had lived and died, towards the railway bridge at the crown of the hill.

Fallan directed her past the station, the road passing beneath the train tracks, then left, inevitably, on to the tree-lined enclave that was Silverbirks Lane. It was a narrow road, laid down long before the advent of the motor car, and the exclusivity of the neighbourhood was underlined by the fact that the subsequent upgrades in tar and concrete had not included the addition of a pavement. Walls, trees and hedges abutted the road, just shy of a narrow strip of grass banking.

The houses themselves could only be glimpsed, each of them set far back from the road and intentionally obscured by greenery. Fallan pointed to a set of huge wooden gates, set into the modern brickwork of a high wall, their automated hinges powered by electric servos.

'That was the place. The gates have had a revamp, but that was McGill's house.'

Catherine kept driving. The road bent around to the right as she slowly followed it, taking it further away from the railway line that ran parallel to the properties nearest the main road. On the lefthand side, about sixty yards after the place that had once belonged to McGill, she spied a gap between the tall housing of another security gate and the wall bordering the next property.

This was where the path came out: the path that led to the woodland behind the sprawling plots of Silverbirks Lane, trailing among the trees until it ran alongside the railway and emerged next to the station.

'What?' Fallan asked.

'Julie Muir's body was found just off that path, somewhere around what I now know to have been the back of Tony McGill's house. Can you see where he fits into this now?'

'Starting to,' Fallan replied.

'She's walking along the path towards the Ewart house, but before she gets there, she sees something she's not supposed to . . .'

'Don't rule out McGill's creepy wanker of a son, Teej. It's possible he—'

Fallan stopped in mid-stream as his phone began to chime. He fished it rapidly from his pocket and flashed it at Catherine, the screen showing a picture of Jasmine Sharp above the line of text identifying her as the caller.

But they both knew she wasn't the caller.

'Put it on speaker,' Catherine said, cutting the engine.

She didn't expect Fallan to comply, so the fact that he did told her how desperate he was, how much he was prepared to lay himself open to her.

'Hello?' Fallan said tentatively, the uncertainty in his tone betraying how fragile he truly was, and no amount of bitterness inside Catherine could deny how human.

'Dead man,' said a male voice, curt and emotionless. 'Collaton Park. Ten on the dot. You come in through the main gate, you come on foot and you come alone. You don't show, she dies. You're late, she dies. Any hint you've got friends, she dies.'

The call clicked off, leaving them listening to the endless drumming of the rain.

Fallan was absolutely still, and yet she got a sense of uncontainable energy from him. It was something that could explode forth at any moment, and she knew she didn't want to be there when it did. All she had to do was imagine for a second that it was Duncan or Fraser being held at the other end of that phone for her to comprehend the magnitude of the forces that could be unleashed.

'You recognise the voice?' she asked.

He nodded. 'It's McGill.'

'Where's Collaton Park?'

'I've never heard of it,' Fallan said, sounding frantic, like this might prove to be a disastrous oversight on his part.

Catherine grabbed her phone and keyed the name into its navigation app. The screen resolved into a map and auto-scrolled from the last place she had used it to a point only minutes from where the car sat in Capletmuir. Her instincts had been on the money.

'It's in Gallowhaugh,' she said, showing him the phone.

Fallan pinched to zoom out, getting his bearings.

'Christ. Collaton Park. I never even knew that was its real name.'

'What's real name?'

'We just called it the Spooky.'

Court Evidence

They found Cal playing a singles match on a blue indoor surface. He appeared to be covering more ground than the ball, zinging back and forth along the baseline, charging the net, chasing back lobs and scurrying after seemingly lost causes to keep every point alive. Anthony estimated that at some stage in every match his opponent must want to kill him.

He spotted them through the window between serves. There was a moment's confusion on his face as the initial recognition gave way to making sense of them in this context. Then he just looked pissed off, once he'd worked it out.

Anthony signalled with two fingers to communicate that they just needed a quick word. Cal responded with an identical digit count to communicate how much he welcomed the interruption, but then held up a palm. He was saying he'd be with them in five, or maybe just telling them to hold on.

'This is the longest I've ever seen him go without eating anything,' Adrienne remarked.

'At least now we know why he stays thin. I'm knackered watching him.'

He served out the game in progress, which turned out to be the last. They watched him shake hands with his opponent, then he picked up his bag and headed off the court, though not before fishing out a banana from somewhere. He was half way through it by the time he emerged into the corridor.

'To what do I owe the considerable ignominy?' he asked. 'I'm not on call.'

'Colin Morrison,' Adrienne stated. 'What do you know about him?'

'The pathologist?'

'Yes.'

'He's retired. Why?'

Cal was prickly as Anthony expected, but he detected an edge to this that was more than mere annoyance at them showing up here.

'We think he might be in trouble,' Anthony said. 'We've been to his flat: somebody's ripped the place apart looking for something, and we think Morrison has fled the country. We're just waiting on Immigration to find out where he's gone.'

'What's the difference between fled and merely left?'

'He had been in telephone contact with none other than Stevie Fullerton quite recently – just a few weeks ago,' Adrienne replied. 'He packed and left in a hurry shortly after Fullerton got shot.'

'Colin Morrison?' Cal asked, his face a picture of incredulous consternation. 'In touch with Stevie Fullerton?'

'Fullerton was in touch with Brenda Sheehan recently too,' Anthony told him. 'She was last seen cooling her heels on your slab. We think Morrison was trying to avoid the same. We're trying to suss what he was into. Did you know him?'

'Of course. Just as colleagues, though. I didn't socialise with him. Or rather, Colin didn't socialise with me. That would never do.'

Cal allowed himself a regretful little smile.

'Why not?' asked Adrienne. Cal was clearly opening the door to something. 'Did he have an issue with your sexuality?'

Jesus, Anthony thought, glad he wasn't the one who had come straight out with that. Adrienne could be pretty direct, right enough. Keeping so many plates in the air, presumably it wore down your tolerance for fannying about.

'Oh, certainly he had issues, very complex ones,' Cal replied. 'Colin is on the team too, you see: he just doesn't wear the colours. I think he had some very unpleasant experiences in less enlightened times.'

Cal said these last few words with arch emphasis. He clearly didn't consider these times particularly enlightened, but this only served to underline the severity of whatever trials Morrison had been forced to endure.

'When did he retire?' Adrienne asked.

'Oh, must be a good five years or so now.'

'So you won't have seen him for a while?'

'Well, that's the thing,' Cal replied, looking a little sheepish. 'I just saw him a few weeks back. He asked me for a favour: wanted me to get the lab to run a DNA sample for him.'

'And did you?'

Cal gave an odd little shrug. They all knew he was hardly going to get hauled over the coals for it. And if he knew how much shit *they* were digging themselves into, he wouldn't be acting coy about doing a former colleague a wee turn.

'Sure. I didn't hear back from him, so it slipped my mind to chase up the results.'

'What was it he wanted analysed?' Anthony asked.

'Skin cells and some traces of blood.'

'What from?'

Cal gave him the finger, which he initially took to mean 'none of your business', but he was merely making the most of an opportunity.

'A ring,' he answered.

The Vengeance of a Patient Man

'I'm a father myself, so I know you'll do anything for your children.'

McGill sounded perversely sincere. Jasmine could make out his words but it was like he was talking to her at a rock concert, his voice almost drowned by sound from a far more powerful source.

She was fighting to make sense of it until she realised that she was only fighting it because it made sense. It made perfect sense, of everything.

'That makes you like a wee remote control for Glen Fallan,' he went on.

His self-congratulatory burbling seemed irrelevant compared to the vastness of what she had just learned, but it wasn't as if he was going to give her time and space to digest the news. Watching her head spin was part of the rush for him.

He was right, though: she was Fallan's remote control, his shock collar. Fallan had understood that from before she was born. That was why he stayed out of her life, out of her mum's life. He knew that the two of them were his greatest vulnerability, that men like McGill could always hurt them in order to get to him. The only way to protect them had been to pretend that he was dead.

It must have been his genuine worst nightmare, therefore, when she turned up looking for him after her uncle Jim went missing. That was why he had initially tried to put her off, and made out he wanted nothing to do with her. But developments had taken such choices out of his hands, which had made it imperative that she didn't learn the truth.

McGill had worked it out, though. It couldn't have been too hard for him to piece together, given that he knew what a female Fallan ought to look like.

All those times Fallan was with her, protecting her, he must have known it was at a greater risk. That was why he had taught her ways to defend herself, taught her to listen to her fear. He knew that one day the time might come when his past would catch up to her, and he wouldn't be there to intervene.

'You should be flattered that he was prepared to go to jail and keep his mouth shut just for you,' McGill told her. 'That was the idea, anyway. But best laid plans and all that . . . So we've had to improvise. It's all a bit more rushed than I had in mind, but the important thing is that I'll make sure he knows you and I had a wee bit of time together, before the end.'

There was something that Jasmine had understood since the moment she was bundled into the van, something that part of her mind had nonetheless been refusing to acknowledge. It was chief among the things that she had sought to rationalise, building up a battery of arguments and explanations that offered reassurance, but only in the same way that anaesthetics offered pain relief. With or without, it would soon be knife to skin.

They weren't wearing masks.

Before the end, he said.

Hers or Fallan's, he didn't specify. He didn't need to. He couldn't kill her and leave Fallan alive. He couldn't frame Fallan and leave her alive.

McGill adjusted his posture, angling his chair away from the table and spreading his legs. His left hand went down to his waist while his right slipped into his jacket and produced her phone. She heard him undo his zip.

'Right, hen. I think we'll send the proud father a wee photo to show him how well we're getting on together. Come on,' he commanded, his voice low and simmering with threat. 'Doon on your knees and get this in your mooth.'

Home and Family

The trees were offering some shelter, but the rain was spilling off the leaves in huge collected drops, splattering Catherine's hair and sometimes running down the back of her neck. She had parked at least quarter of a mile away and followed Fallan along a hidden system of tracks and pathways, behind gardens, between garages, away from roads and pavements. This was *his* Gallowhaugh, he explained: the secret thoroughfares and hiding places he had mapped out growing up here, his status as a particularly detested polisman's son a permanent target on his back.

She was unnerved by how he moved, particularly given his height and build. He was swift and silent, blending into the shadows, going from haste to absolute stillness with no apparent effort of deceleration. He would have been difficult enough to see at the best of times, but on a night as wet and dark as this he could render himself almost invisible. Too bad he had her tagging along, then, but it was his choice.

She had texted Drew before setting off from Capletmuir, told him she'd been called out and would be late. Told him she loved him. He texted back saying he loved her too. He was wrong, though: he loved who he thought she was. They'd both find out his feelings on the true Catherine very soon.

Fallan was right: it was a lonely place to live. And a place where she had to live with protecting Tony McGill from justice was lonelier still. Fallan was good at hiding in the dark. She wasn't. Her whole purpose was to bring matters out into the daylight, where the things that thrived only in darkness shrivelled up and died.

Fallan was doing an advance reconnoitre, getting the lay of the land in the hope that he might be able to identify some kind of advantage before he walked in there, alone. He had led her along these secret paths in order to make an unseen approach to the place identified only on the map as Collaton Park.

As Fallan had explained, 'the Spooky' was the collective local name for this imposing, long-uninhabited mansion house and its extensive grounds; known constituently as the Spooky Hoose and the Spooky Woods. It had been empty as long as anybody could remember, built a couple of centuries back when the surrounding area was still countryside and the south-eastern edges of Glasgow several miles distant. It was boarded up but not derelict, almost as though some immortal owner had taken the huff at what had sprung up around it and would one day come back when Gallowhaugh had been demolished again.

The building itself sat a couple of hundred yards back from the road, unkempt grass meeting broken paving, haphazard hedging and twisted fencing denoting its boundary. It was effectively regarded as parkland by the local youth, a kind of multi-use facility accommodating games of hide-and-seek and soldiers among the younger ones through the day, before transforming by evening into a popular venue for their older peers to partake of cadged fags and sweet cider.

Nobody would be hanging around here tonight, though. The rain would see to that.

'If you know this place so well, why would they choose it?' she asked him.

'I don't know. That part's bothering me too. It's symbolic again, but symbols aren't worth giving ground over. Maybe they figure they're conceding nothing as long they're holding all the cards. The only card that matters, anyway.'

'Symbolic how?'

'I witnessed things here. McGill knows this, because we talked about it once upon a time, when he was trying to play the substitute father figure. This is the place I found out what kind of cop my dad was. Him and his crew used to take a van up here and batter fuck out of people. Nobody gave them any shite because everybody knew that was the payback. It's also where I learned about my dad and McGill. I saw money changing hands as they both sat there in my dad's car.'

384

'Brown envelopes?'

'Poly bags actually. Nothing so middle-class as a brown envelope. Plus it was always fucking raining.'

Fallan froze, holding up a hand to signal Catherine to stop also. Beams of headlights swept briefly across the trees, dispersed and diluted by distance. The arcing motion was caused by a vehicle turning from the main road onto the twisting track that led to the crumbling building. There were two vehicles, in fact, one tucked closely behind the other.

Rather their axles than mine, Catherine thought, given the cratered conditions beneath their wheels, but as they came into sight between the trees she saw that for these vehicles it wasn't going to be a problem. The first was a Toyota Hilux, with high-sprung suspension and a flatbed rear.

The second was a Land Rover Defender.

'I need to get a closer look,' Fallan said. 'Stay here.'

He was gone before she could respond, as if he had teleported. She could see the two four-by-fours continuing their approach, but she spotted no hint of where Fallan might be.

Catherine felt a vibration close to her chest and almost jumped before realising it was her phone. She took it out to see who was calling, thinking there was nobody she would answer for right now. She was wrong, though. It was Drummond.

She looked towards the two vehicles, now nearing the house, wondering how much distance sound would carry on a night like this. Their engines sounded muffled by the rain, but she crouched down and turned to face away nonetheless.

'McLeod,' she said, keeping her voice above a whisper so as to sound as natural as she could.

'Detective Superintendent. I've got some good news. I believe a resolution is imminent in the Fullerton case.'

He still sounded like somebody was working him from the back. There was a hint of relief in his voice though, and Catherine knew she didn't like that.

'What kind of resolution?'

'Neat and final: the kind we like best. I believe Glen Fallan might be ready to confess. I need you standing by ready to take charge. I expect to know more shortly after ten.'

The vehicles had stopped, both facing towards the road, headlights trained on the approach that Fallan had been commanded to take. She glanced at her watch: it was nine forty-five.

She stood there in the darkness, feeling separate from the scene that was playing out in front of her, like she'd felt disconnected at the dinner table.

I've got some good news.

The way he'd spoken, he knew nothing about this was good. But when he said *neat and final*, she could tell he believed that part.

She heard movement near by, and Fallan was at her side again before she could focus on its source.

'There's two of them,' he said. 'Both armed with automatics.'

'Do they have Jasmine?'

'No, and I didn't think they'd be daft enough to bring her. This was never intended to be an exchange. That Defender's got my plates.'

He said this with a grave finality. It took Catherine a moment to catch up.

This was the vehicle that had been driven in the Fullerton hit. It was turning up here so that it looked like Fallan had employed a double bluff, using the near-duplicate Defender in order to give the impression he'd been framed. The face mask, the second gun: it would all add up.

'I got a call from Drummond while you were away,' she said. 'He told me to stand by for an imminent resolution to the Fullerton case.'

'That's why they're doing this here,' Fallan replied. 'It's somewhere that carries personal significance, going right back to my childhood. They're going to suicide me.'

'Jesus.'

Neat and final, right enough. Apart from one thing.

'But what plausible reason would there be for you to kill yourself?'

Fallan swallowed, suddenly having difficulty finding his voice.

'If something happened to Jasmine,' he replied.

And in that broken whisper Catherine saw the true depth of Fallan's despair and the cruel enormity of McGill's vengeance.

He was going to kill her either way, and nothing Fallan could do would make a difference.

She heard a buzz but felt no vibration. It was Fallan's phone.

He glanced at the screen then put it to his ear with a slow dread, the movement automated, soulless.

He managed a low whispered word then listened to the response.

Even in the half light Catherine saw something in him die, then his eyes closed.

Penetration Without Consent

Ever since she'd been led into this bleak little room Jasmine had known deep down that it would come to this: to this vileness that she would be forced to commit. She climbed to her feet, and forgave herself on the grounds that she had no choice.

The short walk around the table was a long march to Golgotha, but on that march Jasmine steeled herself, preparing mind and body to overcome a revulsion a thousand generations older than she was.

McGill had her phone in his hand and his erect penis sticking through the open flies of his trousers.

Fallan hadn't told her why she was doing it, just made her repeat the action over and over: coaching her to refine it, to channel more aggression, to speed it up, to deliver more thrust, to do it again and again and again and again until she could to it without thinking, until it was hardwired to a neural pathway.

Only then did he tell her what she had been learning.

She placed her left hand on the back of Tony McGill's head. With her right she made a fist, stiffening her outstretched thumb. For just a second, his head was a pumpkin. His eye-socket was a pre-cut hole.

Just a second was all it took.

'The quickest way of killing a man with your bare hands is to punch your thumb through his eye and into his brain,' Fallan had explained to her. 'Then rotate it around a hundred and eighty degrees before pulling it out again, taking as much grey matter with it as you can. But as human beings we have such an instinctive disgust of doing such a thing that it would never occur to most of us, even in a life-or-death situation.'

McGill bucked for a moment then fell from the chair with a thump.

Jasmine stood back from the body, feeling a rush that threatened to ping her off the walls. She was thrilling with elation, a dizzying euphoria born simply of relief that this dreaded task was over. It lasted only a few seconds, which was why she was grateful that there was a major hit of adrenaline still surging beneath it, because there was more work yet to be done.

Jasmine turned the table on its side and sat on the uppermost of its legs until the join was weakened enough to break off. It came away with a loud screech of complaint and a resounding snap.

She wasn't sure whether it had sounded suspicious enough downstairs, so she started shouting.

'HEY! HEEEEEY! YOU NEED TO GET UP HERE! I THINK HE'S HAVING A HEART ATTACK!'

She positioned herself against the wall as she heard the heavy, hurried thumps of footsteps charging up the stairs and along the hall.

Teej barrelled through the door and all but slid on his knees in his eagerness to tend the motionless figure on the bare wooden floor. He turned his head in response to the movement behind him, but wasn't fast enough to raise an arm. Jasmine was already swinging the table leg with both hands, smashing it into the base of his skull. He sprawled forward on to his father's corpse, arms flapping for purchase, which left his head wide open for Jasmine to swing at it a second time.

She hit him until he wasn't moving any more. Then she made her way across to the wall where her phone had come to rest after McGill dropped it.

Crime Scene Management

Fallan dropped to a crouch as he carried on the conversation, his voice quiet, calm, moderated, assuring. A father's voice.

Catherine had watched with a hollow dread as all life appeared to drain from his face, but when his eyes closed she recognised that what was really draining was the tension that had rendered him so utterly wired since he showed up at her door. It was hard to get any detail from one whispered side of a phone call, but she could tell the picture had just changed dramatically.

Fallan disconnected, saying he'd call back in a few minutes. He gestured to Catherine to follow him, and began leading her quietly away from the Spooky, back out towards the hidden pathways they had taken to get here.

'Jasmine's okay?' she asked. 'Did she escape?'

'She escaped. Okay is relative.'

'Where is she? What about McGill?'

'Let's just say there's one less person in this world who knows your dark secret.'

'McGill's dead?'

'Yes. Tony Junior too.'

'How?' Catherine asked. 'I mean, who . . .?'

Fallan turned and gave her a look that said she of all people shouldn't have to ask.

'She killed them,' Catherine said.

'What can I say?' he replied grimly. 'She's a chip off the old block.'

Fallan was striding with speed and determination. With the threat to Jasmine no longer hanging over him, Catherine suspected he had plans for the two men standing back there next to the Hilux and the Defender, and she didn't fancy her chances of restraining him.

She was wrong, though. Fallan didn't care about them. They had dropped off his agenda the second he got that phone call.

She looked at her watch. It was coming up for ten.

'What happens if you don't show up like they're expecting?'

'Those guys won't be going anywhere until they get word from their boss. That's not going to happen unless one of those dicks has got a ouija board app for his iPhone. I suggest you get an ARU down here, as well as every other polisman you can spare. They'll find the vehicle and quite possibly the murder weapon used in the hit on Stevie.'

'I'm all over it,' she replied, reaching for her phone.

Fallan placed a hand on her arm, stopping her from making the call.

'Get somebody to deputise for you. We need to get up to Perthshire, right now. Jasmine texted me where she is.'

Catherine was about to tell him she would despatch emergency services to the location right away and have someone drive him wherever he needed to be, until she realised that he wasn't just looking for a lift.

'There's two bodies in a room somewhere between Crieff and Comrie,' he said. 'The girl who walked into that room isn't the same one who walked out. I don't want some other polis making this any harder for her than it already has to be. I want you in charge.'

Catherine nodded. She knew what it felt like to be both of those girls.

To her surprise it belatedly occurred to her that so did Fallan.

In accordance with Fallan's request they were first on the scene, though Catherine had ensured that police and an ambulance would be only minutes behind them.

They found Jasmine sitting in McGill's Jaguar XKR outside the cottage. She hadn't wanted to stay inside the house, but nor had she felt ready to drive anywhere. The engine was running though, just in case. Jasmine wasn't sure whether Tony junior was dead, so she'd have put pedal to metal if she needed to.

She came sprinting from the Jag the second she saw Fallan emerge from Catherine's car. She buried herself in him, her face in his chest, eyes closed. Fallan put one of those huge scarred hands on top of her head and an arm around her shoulders. Neither of them spoke. Jasmine looked beaten and bloody, but as Catherine discovered when she went up the stairs, never was the phrase 'you should see the other guy' more apposite.

Tony Junior was still alive, as it turned out, though his future prospects weren't looking good. And as Fallan later put it, his father's name wasn't going to offer much protection inside, especially once it got around that the infamous Tony McGill, the mighty Gallowhaugh Godfather, had been killed by a seven-stone lassie using one finger.

Laura phoned while the paramedics were strapping Teej and his wobbling bulk on to a stretcher for getting him down the stairs. She was pleased to report that she had each of the two gunmen from the Spooky Hoose safely in custody, and that their astonishment at having half a dozen carbines pointed at them had been a joy to behold. Laura also mentioned that one of them had been carrying a .22 Ruger, precisely the calibre of weapon used at the car wash.

So it turned out Drummond was right: there had indeed been a neat and final resolution to the Fullerton case. As a result Catherine did not, as he had mooted, feel the need to 'consider her position'.

She couldn't say the same for the Deputy Chief Constable.

And the Winner is . . .

Catherine gave Beano a shout when she saw Cal O'Shea coming out of the lift at the end of the corridor, an A4-sized brown envelope in one hand and a clear plastic tub in the other. They converged on her office soon after, along with Adrienne, Cal getting there last because there was a vending machine between his point of entry and his destination.

Cal looked a little tired. There was a detectable slump to his body language as he took a seat, resting the envelope on his lap and the tub of chopped melon and kiwi fruit on the edge of Catherine's desk.

'Cal, how are you?' she asked. 'I gather you've been carrying on like an actual polis.'

'I have indeed,' he replied. 'I've spent a good hour this morning bitching about work and I'm putting in for some stress-related sick leave before I go out and get pissed.'

'Don't forget the overtime,' Beano suggested.

'No, quite. I've earned it,' Cal said, tapping the envelope.

'So what's the script?'

'I tracked down Colin Morrison. I always had his mobile number, obviously, but what I mean is I tracked down somebody whose call he would pick up when he saw the number. He's in Germany: Rostock, to be precise. He's got some friends there, at the university. He's prepared to give evidence in exchange for immunity.'

'I can't guarantee anything until I talk to Dom Wilson.'

'I know. So at this stage everything is off the record. Bottom line is, he was strong-armed by Bob Cairns to finesse the autopsy on Julie Muir.'

'Strong-armed how?' Catherine asked.

'There was an incident with a rent boy. Cairns had the goods on him. Kid was seventeen, so with the age of consent being twenty-one at the time, he could have made it all very nasty. Career-endingly so.'

'What did this finessing entail?' Catherine asked.

'Amendment and suppression. Principally the estimated time of death. Corroborated witness statements had Julie getting off the train at seven forty. Morrison's report had her dying at around eight o'clock. He told me it was more likely to have been at least two hours later.'

'Cairns wanted to conceal where she'd been in the intervening time.'

'That's right. He told Morrison that there was a gangland connection, and that if the truth got out they'd have a bloodbath on their hands. Morrison never bought that, though. Gangland wars were meat and drink to a cop like Cairns. He knew there was something rotten at the heart of it, so he secured himself a little insurance policy.'

'The ring,' Catherine said. 'Mrs Muir said it never came back to them.'

'Correct. Morrison found blood and skin on it, consistent with it having scratched Julie's attacker during a struggle. He sealed it up and kept it safe. He wanted something he could use as leverage against Cairns in the future if he came back asking for him to amend another report. He was also aware of the Ewart factor. He followed the whole case very closely, as you would expect, though he was never quite sure what the real story was.'

'And can you still get DNA off dried blood and skin after twenty-five years?'

'If it's been stored properly, yes, and Morrison knew how to do that.'

'So why did he finally take it out and ask you to analyse it now?'

'He was skint,' Beano interjected. 'His neighbour said his retirement fund took a major bath in the big crash.'

Cal nodded.

'He decided to turn his insurance policy into his pension plan. He sought out Stevie Fullerton because he knew about the

394

Nokturn connection and he thought Fullerton would be considerably more capable than he was when it came to running a blackmail operation. Another reason he launched this now was that Bob Cairns was safely behind bars. He thought that was where the threat would come from. He was wrong.'

'So who was he blackmailing?' Beano asked. 'Gordon Ewart?'

'That was Morrison's plan, but Fullerton spread the net wider. Philippa Ewart is independently wealthy, and so given that she and Campbell Ewart are divorced, Fullerton thought he could dip into two separate pots.'

'He also knew this would give him leverage over Drummond,' Catherine said. 'Whether for money or just clout we don't know, but certainly when you're a drug dealer it doesn't hurt to have a means of putting pressure on the Deputy Chief Constable.'

'What did Fullerton actually blackmail them with?' asked Adrienne.

'He told them he had evidence that would prove Gordon Ewart killed Julie Muir, and that there was an establishment cover-up to frame Teddy Sheehan. He didn't tell them what the evidence was.'

'The fact that they didn't call his bluff speaks volumes,' Adrienne said.

'No kidding,' agreed Catherine. 'If they'd nothing to hide then all he could have threatened them with was what Ewart claimed, regarding his wild years. Instead I got two dead people as testimony to the threat being taken very seriously indeed. But it still begs the question why Tony McGill would be involved.'

Cal held up the brown envelope.

'I suspect the answer lies within,' he said. 'This is the DNA analysis Morrison requested. As yet officially unidentified, obviously.'

'At least it shouldn't be hard to get a comparison sample from Tony McGill,' Catherine mused. 'Just scrape the underside of Jasmine Sharp's thumbnail. Getting a swab from Gordon Ewart might present more of a problem, though.'

Cal skewered a chunk of melon with a plastic fork and held it in front of his face.

'We've already got Gordon Ewart's DNA,' he said. 'He got done for drink driving two years ago, so he's on the database. The sample from the ring isn't his. And though the late Mr McGill *isn't* on the database, I can tell you right now it's not his either.'

'How do you know that without testing?' Catherine asked.

Cal popped the melon into his mouth and crunched it with open relish, milking the moment. This turned out to be a tactical misjudgement, as someone beat him to the punchline.

'Because it's female,' Beano deduced.

Flesh and Blood

Beano leaned over to the cassette recorder and ejected the tapes, popping each of them into an envelope and sealing it across the top. The lawyer let out a troubled sigh but leaned back in his chair, his posture acknowledging that he was relieved the time had come to stand down. Whatever he thought he was here to assist with, he hadn't been ready for this.

Philippa Ewart looked up at Beano, then around at her brief, and then across the table at Catherine.

'Is it finished?' she asked. 'Is that it over? Can I go now?'

Respectively yes, yes and quite definitely no.

'There's an officer here to take you back to your cell,' Catherine said quietly, nodding to the woman PC who had stepped in and was waiting for her cue.

The PC helped Mrs Ewart to her feet and turned her towards the door. She looked confused and disoriented, but there was a fearful dawning in her face.

Catherine had seen this before on many occasions, when a suspect had eluded detection for a long time and then finally been hauled in for questioning. They were so apprehensive about the ordeal of the interview – of finally being confronted with the proof of their crime – that their relief at getting through it temporarily caused them to forget what was coming next.

The longer they had been holding on to their secret, the worse it was, and Philippa Ewart had been holding on to hers for a very long time.

Back in the late eighties, when her serial philanderer husband was regularly playing away and the gin wasn't numbing the pain quite as well as it used to, she decided – working on the 'sauce for the goose' principle – to embark upon an affair of her own with one of her neighbours. The way she described it, it sounded to Catherine like Buffy shagging Spike: a mixture of nihilism, self-loathing and sexual chemistry leading her into an increasingly depraved relationship with the neighbourhood bad guy.

McGill believed it was something more. He was completely besotted, though Philippa thought what he was truly smitten with was the social respectability that she represented. He had daft ideas about the two of them setting up home together, while all she saw in him was an ongoing revenge fuck; albeit it wasn't clear whether it was herself or her husband she was trying the harder to punish. It was a relationship that she simultaneously needed and detested, creating a self-reinforcing cycle of self-disgust.

Unfortunately that self-disgust had a disastrous reflection in her beloved son bringing home some good-time girl who worked in a nightclub.

Her attitude to Gordon's sex life and recreational habits had been 'out of sight, out of mind'. He was young and entitled to mess around. A pity his father hadn't done the same: perhaps that way he'd have got it out of his system. However, the fact that Gordon brought this one to a dinner party at the family home indicated that it was serious, and Philippa was appalled.

She said nothing at first, aware that it was likely to be counter-productive, and hoped that time would take care of the matter. When it didn't, she decided to act before things went too far. She got in touch with Julie and asked her to come up to the house one Saturday night when she knew Gordon wouldn't be around. She was apprehensive about the meeting, and angry too, so she had a few drinks before Julie arrived.

She'd have been fine on gin, she said, but she had started drinking whisky: another self-reinforcing cycle. She only wanted whisky when she was angry, and the more she drank it, the more bitter she tended to become.

She explained how important Gordon was, what a career was ahead of him, and how she couldn't let anything jeopardise that.

To that end she offered Julie money to stay away from him, adding that if she had any real regard for Gordon she'd know it was the right thing to do.

That was when Julie, in her growing outrage, told her she was pregnant.

Philippa claimed she had no recollection of what happened next, but Catherine didn't believe her. She'd heard this story a thousand times.

Drink or no drink, you remember what it is to kill somebody. You remember every last tiny detail, and nothing that ever happens to you afterwards can help you forget.

She strangled Julie with a dog lead. That was why Cairns came up with the theory of Sheehan using a belt: leather and metal, bruising and abrasions.

Somewhere in her mortal struggle Julie scratched Philippa's cheek with her ring, leaving the evidence that would trace back to her a quarter of a century later. Comparison testing had shown that the DNA on the ring was not Gordon Ewart's, but a sufficiently near match as to indicate that it had come from a close relative. A close female relative.

When the rage subsided and Philippa found herself standing over Julie Muir's lifeless body, she called McGill for help.

He made it go away.

He and Cairns moved the corpse, then Cairns handled everything else from there.

Drummond, as far as Catherine could tell, knew nothing of the truth. He probably did think that they had the right man and that Cairns was simply employing means that would be justified by the end.

It was soon after this, Philippa said, that she had her moment of clarity. It was not an immediate response: it came when McGill got lifted down in Liverpool and put inside, out of the picture. Eventually she managed to kick the drink, and thereafter dedicated her time and efforts to alcohol and drugs charities.

'I understand what alcohol can do to people,' she said. 'How it can take away your will and turn you into a completely different person.'

To Catherine's ears, this was another old saw: 'The demon drink made me do it.'

Aye, that plus being an over-privileged bitch who saw the likes of Julie Muir as beneath her and Teddy Sheehan as collateral damage.

When Fullerton started making his threats she contacted McGill again, for the first time since he got out. It wasn't that the flame still burned: she just let him know that if this went public, his part inevitably would too.

McGill was out on licence. A conviction for conspiring to pervert the course of justice would put him away for the rest of his life.

They watched the lawyer make his way out, the door swinging closed on its own weight behind him.

'Some going, Anthony,' Catherine told him. 'Great result.'

'Anthony?'

He was beaming, inordinately pleased that she had called him that.

'Not sure Beano's got much mileage left in it as a handle,' she admitted. 'Can't see you being DC Thompson for much longer. You definitely get bonus points for closing the book on a murder committed when you were still in nappies.'

'I thought she'd put up more of a fight,' he confessed. 'She always comes over in the media as being hard as nails, but I barely had to do anything. She just spewed it all out.'

'All those years keeping a secret like that can take its toll,' Catherine said. 'It becomes a relief to finally be able to talk to somebody about it.'

To anybody, she thought.

A lonely place to live, Fallan had called it, but Catherine didn't live there: she only visited. *You're angry on the road to it and you're unreachable when you get there,* Drew told her. That was because she could only go there alone, and she could bear the loneliness better than she could bear sharing that place with her family.

400

It would be easier in future, though. She would have to go back, inevitably, but there were people she could journey with.

Fellow travellers.

Fellow killers.

The Nature of the Risk

It was a cold morning, but it was well worth the early rise and the extra jumper. He had been awake since five anyway, unable to get back to sleep. That's why he decided to cut his losses. The skies were blue but there was still a wee bit of mist drifting in places. Made you think what this place looked like hundreds of years ago, when it was just moors and woods, long before anybody came up here to blooter a golf ball around.

Doke knew from experience that he'd warm up enough to take a layer off by about the fifth hole, especially if he kept swinging at this rate. His game was literally all over the place, zig-zagging his way up the first two fairways. He wasn't sure where his head was at this morning, but then he'd come here to clear it, hadn't he? Out here alone, that fresh feeling of the morning air and the sense of peace he got when there wasn't another soul in sight.

He'd be grand by the back nine. Sometimes you had to look at it that way: write off the bad start and just concentrate on what was ahead. If you worried about your score being knackered after a few holes, it was pointless. It wasn't like playing on the Xbox: you couldn't reload and start again.

Golf was all in the head: that was why he came here when he needed to think. It was a safe place to think too. You could see folk coming from miles off. He remembered how a guy he knew got ambushed on the municipal course over at Burnbrae about twenty years ago. A team turned up with machetes and hatchets and all sorts: hopped over the wall at the fourteenth, where the fairway ran parallel to the back of the scheme.

That wasn't happening out here. This was the proper countryside. Plus he had a sawn-off shotty in his bag along with the clubs.

When he told people about it he said, 'I've got my woods, my long irons, my nine iron and my shooting iron.'

He told plenty of people about it. The point was that it got around. The point was that folk knew.

He hooked another drive: good length but a horrible pull to the left, taking it over the gorse and very possibly into the burn.

There was just so much on his mind: that's why he hadn't been sleeping. Tony McGill was dead, with Teej heading for the jail whenever he got out of the hospital. The rumour was that it was Glen Fallan. The same Glen Fallan Doke had unsuccessfully tried to have taken out while he was on remand, and who undoubtedly knew this.

Aye, funny he was having trouble sleeping.

Opportunity was knocking, though. The McGill show was well over: not only was the main man pan breid, but two of his top boys had been lifted at the Spooky as well. There was a very large gap in the market. Doke just didn't feel sure he had what it took to fill it.

He was missing Stevie. Stevie would know what to do. He'd have strategies and contingencies and all that shite.

He could see his ball. It was in the ditch but not in the burn itself, just nestling shy of the water. He'd need a pitching wedge to get it up, or else he'd need to drop and take two, but fuck that. Dropping was for shitebags.

He climbed down into the ditch, keeping his eye on his footing. When he looked up again to check where his ball was he saw Glen Fallan standing about five yards in front of it, like Scotty had just beamed him there. That was what had always scared him about Fallan, though: the cunt just appeared from thin air. You never saw him coming.

He'd made a mistake this morning, though. Doke scrambled back up the banking and reached frantically into his golf bag for the shotgun.

It wasn't there.

When he turned around again, he saw that Fallan was holding it down by his side.

Doke felt the cold as a layer of sweat formed spontaneously all over his body. Some instinct told him to run, but he knew that he wouldn't. Something deeper, an inescapable knowledge of his true self dictated that this wasn't something you could run from. The same knowledge dictated that, despite the lies he told himself, he had always known he would one day have to face this moment. And now it was here.

He felt fear, but mostly he felt regret. So, so many regrets, too numerous to contemplate individually, apart from one: he should have listened to Sheila. Not just because of the situation in which he now found himself, but because of all the things that would have been better: all the people who might still be here, and all the ugly things he might never have done.

'A good walk spoiled, eh Doke?' Fallan said. 'Lovely morning for it, anyway.'

'Just get it over with,' he replied. 'Don't kick the arse oot it. You owe me that much, surely.'

Fallan glanced away for a moment and shook his head.

'I'm not here to kill you,' he said evenly. 'If I was, we wouldn't be talking. You wouldn't even see me. That's what I said to Stevie as well, all those years back, when he woke up in the night and found me at the end of his bed holding a gun, despite all the locks he had fitted and his ten-grand security system. I'm not here to kill you. I'm here to tell you what I told him.'

Doke's head felt light with relief, his legs like jelly and his guts turning to water. He was ready to grab any future with both hands, now that he still had one, though it sounded like Fallan wanted to talk about the past.

'Jazz tried to kill Yvonne. He turned up inside her flat in a state of pure rage. She didn't realise he had a key; she'd never given him one, so he must have stolen one of the spares. He'd beaten her up before – you know that – because he thought she was going to cave in to the polis about his alibi, but this time he was there for more. He was already upset about something else that night, and after a few drinks and a few toots and whatever else he was necking he decided on a simple solution to both of his problems.'

None of these things came as a surprise to Doke. Deep down, he knew all of this, or at least could have pieced it together if family loyalty and misplaced anger hadn't kept him in denial. He had been angry at Fallan all these years because it was easier than dealing with the anger he felt towards his brother. Nonetheless, he couldn't help thinking he was missing something in what Fallan was saying. Small wonder, the way his head was spinning right then.

'He had a gun. Fuck knows where he got it, because we both know neither you nor Stevie would ever have allowed Jazz and firearms to come together, even before he got slashed. He was there to kill her, Doke: that's what I need you to understand, same as I needed Stevie to understand.'

Doke managed a nod, but he was still missing something. Hadn't Fallan said *both* problems? Apart from the murder charge, what was the other one? And why would Jazz want a gun to kill a lassie?

Then it dawned on him.

'He was planning to kill you as well,' Doke sussed. 'But why?'

'That was the thing he was already upset about,' Fallan replied, and suddenly it all came into focus.

'You always were a sleekit bastard, Single. I never realised it extended to your sex life.'

'It wasn't like that. And you know Yvonne didn't belong in that world. She was looking for a way out of it. We both were.'

'And this is what you told Stevie? From what happened next, it doesn't sound like he was very understanding.'

'I knew he would be left in a difficult position. That's why I gave him a solution that worked for everybody. What do you think all that carry-on with the envelopes was about?'

'Stevie thought it up to protect us from—'

'It was my idea, Doke. And it was so that none of Stevie's team would ever know that *nobody* got the instruction to kill me. I promised Stevie I would disappear, and I did it in a way that would serve him well. I made him look ruthless, powerful and loyal to his family. I owed him that.'

Doke's brain was running to catch up, rapidly reassembling his picture of the last twenty-odd years to fit the new reality he'd been hit with.

'I know you set up that thing in the jail,' Fallan said. 'And I'm telling you that's the end of it. No comebacks.'

Doke was nodding before he was even aware of doing so. He knew he wasn't a smart guy, but he wasn't fucking stupid either. Fallan was telling him the same thing Sheila had been, and this time he was listening.

'No comebacks,' he confirmed, unable to prevent a long sigh of relief from venting after he spoke.

His fingers were shaking. He needed a pint. He caught sight of a flag fluttering in the middle distance and realised he had forgotten he was in the middle of a round.

'One last thing,' Fallan said, sounding, if it were possible, that wee bit more steely than before.

'Whit?' Doke asked, having stopped himself from saying 'Fire away'.

'Tony McGill used Jasmine to get to me.'

'How come?'

'Because he'd worked out that I'm her father.'

Doke reeled again. At this rate he was going to have to check his own name when he got home.

'But she came to the restaurant and told us she—'

'Think about it, Doke. If Jazz had fathered one wean he'd have fathered twenty. You ever hear of any other wee Jazzlings back in the day?'

He thought about it.

'Jesus.'

'Jasmine's my daughter. It's out there now: people know. So I want you to get the word out in case anybody else is stupid enough to make her a target.'

Doke nodded, eager to convey his assent.

'I hear you, Single: mess with her and they mess with you.'

'No, David. That would be to gravely misunderstand the nature of the risk, in the same way Tony McGill did, before Jasmine killed him with her bare hands then put his bawbag son in the hospital.'

Doke gawped like a fish, but any seeds of disbelief were crushed by the look on Fallan's face telling him this was exactly how it went down.

Something inside him sang. Get the word out? He'd pay for a fucking billboard.

'See, Jasmine and I are making up for lost time,' Fallan explained. 'We want to see more of each other, so we're going into business together. She's bringing me into her detective agency. She inherited it from her uncle: that's the Sharp family business. But I want every bam, rocket and heidthebaw in this town to know that Jasmine's a Fallan as well, and she's been learning *my* family business.'